W9-CAL-428

I STAND BEFORE YOU

S.R. GREY

This is a work of fiction. Names, characters, places, and incidents are products of the author's imagination or are used fictitiously and are not considered to be real. Any resemblance to actual events, locales, organizations, or persons, living or dead, is entirely coincidental.

I Stand Before You (Judge Me Not #1)
Copyright © 2013 by S.R. Grey

All rights reserved. No part of this book may be used or reproduced in any manner whatsoever without written permission, except in the case of brief quotations embodied in critical articles and reviews.

Copy Editing: Gail Cato at CreateSpace

Cover Design: Damonza at Awesome Book Covers

Print and E-book Formatting by Benjamin at Awesome Book Layout

ISBN-10: 0615839878 (print edition only)
ISBN-13: 978-0615839875   (print edition only)

PLAYLIST

Wanksta ~ 50 Cent
Radioactive ~ Imagine Dragons
Dream ~ Priscilla Ahn
Angels on the Moon ~ Thriving Ivory
Halo ~ Beyoncé
A Man I'll Never Be ~ Boston
Sweet Surrender ~ Sarah McLachlan
Tautou ~ Brand New
Breathe Me ~ Sia
Change ~ Deftones
Stay ~ Rihanna (featuring Mikky Ekko)
Hanging By a Moment ~ Lifehouse
Heavenly Day ~ Patty Griffin
Kiss Me ~ Ed Sheeran
Good Enough ~ Evanescence
My Lover's Prayer ~ Otis Redding
Excuse Me ~ Fools For April
Sweetest Thing ~ U2
Found ~ Christel Alsos
Have A Drink On Me ~ AC/DC
Be Here to Love Me ~ Norah Jones
You Make It Real ~ James Morrison

PROLOGUE
CHASE

I lean my head back against the headrest, crank the passenger window down the rest of the way. The June night air rustles through my hair, reminding me I desperately need a trim. I run my fingers through the strands, chasing the path of the breeze.

My grandmother likes to lecture that I shouldn't have hair sticking out at odd angles, strands curling at the nape of my neck.

"You're such a handsome young man, Chase," Grandma Gartner said just this morning, *tsk*ing when I sat down for breakfast. "You look so much like your father did when he was your age. But, you know, *he* always kept *his* hair short and tidy." And then there was a pause, a long, dramatic sigh. She set down a plate of eggs—over easy—in front of me. "My poor Jack. God rest his soul." My grandmother crossed herself.

Her poor Jack, my father with the short and tidy hair— dead and gone.

I thought: *I am not my dad, Gram. He failed us, he gave up on us.* But the words never passed my lips. And they never will. Hearing them would only hurt my grandmother's feelings and she's too good to hear the angry thoughts poisoning my polluted mind. So I keep all that shit locked deep inside.

This morning was no different. I kept things light, said something like, "The girls like my hair like this, Gram. Got to keep the ladies happy, ya know."

Then I ducked and waited for the inevitable swat with the dish towel. But it never came. Instead, the lines in my grandmother's face deepened.

"You don't need to be concerning yourself with keeping ladies happy, young man. You're only twenty. Messing with women at your age will only lead to trouble."

I knew what she meant this morning, and I know it now too. She's worried I'll end up getting some girl pregnant. Then I'll be fucked, well and good. But I'm always careful, take the necessary precautions. Besides, it isn't my womanizing ways that's becoming a problem. If only. No, unfortunately, it's my ever-growing dependency on drugs—something my grandmother would never suspect—that has me worried these days.

These days… Yeah, right. More like these blurry, fucked-up segments of time.

Sighing, I roll the window up just enough to lean my head against the cool glass. *What am I going to do?* I silently ask myself.

What I really need to do is get the hell out of this tiny Ohio farm town I landed back in two years ago. I'm spinning my wheels here in Harmony Creek, hanging with a bad crowd. Problem is I have no plan, no money either. Drugs are my escape and have been for quite a while. My priorities are all fucked up. My life, it's upside down. Every day it seems like getting high—and staying that way—is my only goal. I want to stop—believe me I do—but I don't think I know how to anymore.

A lump forms in my throat at this thought, but I swallow it down. "Hey," I say to Tate, who is driving. "Let's get out of this town."

Tate Cody, my friend…and my partner in crime in everything wild and crazy these days—women, drugs, drinking, fighting—you name it, we do it. And if we're not doing it nowadays, chances are we've done it at least once over the past couple of years. We've yet to slow down; we live on the edge.

I sometimes wonder when we'll fall.

"What do you think we're doing, Chase, my man?"

I take in and process Tate's reply, while he lifts a bottle of cheap gin to his lips and hits the gas. And for this one long, tortuous drawn-out second, I can't make a distinction between what I asked Tate and what I was only thinking. I panic, assuming my partner in crime's response is to let me know it's finally happening, we're really falling.

But then Tate adds, "I'm getting us out of here as fast as I can," and I breathe a little easier. He just means we're leaving Harmony Creek. Not falling, after all. *Shit, I need to ease up on the drugs.*

I glance out the window, and though it's dark I can see we're heading east, nearing the state line. Soon we'll be out of Ohio completely, and in the neighboring state of Pennsylvania. That's where we're supposed to hook up with two girls tonight. They're from New Castle, and we're meeting at a lake across the state line.

I don't really care about all that, though. What I'd really rather do is keep on going. Hop on Interstate 80 and clock the miles to Jersey. Better yet, Tate and I could go farther. We could drive our asses straight into New York-fucking-City. Now that would be sweet.

So while Tate barrels down a back road the police rarely patrol—until you get into Pennsylvania, that is—I pretend we're leaving Harmony Creek for good. No looking back, no regrets, just flying the fuck out of this lame-ass small town.

And speaking of flying, I'm flying a bit now too, feeling fine, baby, fine. I close my eyes so I can savor the s-l-o-w creep of numbness that cocoons me like a warm and fuzzy blanket.

I feel nothing, yet I feel everything.

My skin tingles a little, but when I touch my hand to my face it feels detached, like these parts of my body belong to two different people, neither of them me. That thought makes me happy, escape is exactly what I crave.

Needless to say, I've smoked—a lot—and not just weed. But it's the pills I swallowed a while ago that are starting to wrap me up and spin me the fuck out.

A bottle hits the back of my hand and my eyes fly open. Shit, I forgot I am not alone in this car.

"Drink, fucker," Tate urges.

I take the gin, despite the fact I can barely see straight. *No* isn't part of my vocabulary when I'm like this. And, sadly, more often than not, this is exactly how I am. This is who I am becoming: Chase Gartner, burgeoning drug addict.

As per most nights, Tate and I stopped at Kyle's before embarking on *this* night's little adventure. Kyle Tanner supplies us with more drugs than we could ever hope for. And the quality is always top notch. Kyle takes a certain kind of pride in dealing only primo product. But you'd never guess such a thing if you saw the rundown shithole he lives in.

Our dealer resides on the *other* side of town, over by the closed-down glass factory, in a clapboard house he shares with his meth-addicted dad. Lately, going there has been a contradiction of emotions for me. I love and hate concurrently when Tate and I cross over the railroad tracks that mark the end of the safe neighborhoods of Harmony Creek. Then, I vacillate between love and hate as I watch the Sparkle Mart grocery store appear…then disappear. I lean a little more towards hate when we reach the run-down apartment building where the junkies hang out, where their emaciated bodies lean lazily against the dirty brick exterior.

I sure as fuck don't want to end up there, God, no. But maybe I'm powerless to stop my downward spiral. Lord knows, by the time we start down the long dirt road that leads to Kyle's place, I crave and I want. And love trumps hate by that point. Even the junkies seem less scary. So we go…and we go…and we keep going back.

Tate tells me the road to Kyle's house is the road to salvation. *Salvation, my ass.* I'd be more inclined to say Tate and I are traveling a path to hell. We're in the express lane to damnation, and one step closer to burning every time we travel down that fucking dirt road. I know it, he knows it, but do we ever do anything to stop? Do we try to crawl out of the hole we're wallowing in? No, never.

In fact, Tate wants us to delve in deeper—start selling. He says we'll make, at the minimum, enough money to help pay for the copious amounts of shit we ingest…snort… smoke. Yeah, we do it all, everything short of needles. I somehow know if I ever cross *that* line, there will be no going back.

But I'm considering the selling thing, albeit for a different reason than my friend. Tate hopes to eventually make enough cash to buy his own wheels. He hates borrowing the piece of shit we're currently in—his mom's old, rusted Ford Focus. I just want to make enough money to buy a ticket out of this place. The little bit I earn painting people's houses, picking up construction work here and there—it's not adding up fast enough for my liking.

Hell, I still live at my grandmother's farmhouse out on Cold Springs Lane. Granted, I recently fixed up the little apartment above the detached garage, moved from a bedroom in the main house to an area not too much larger. But that little apartment provides privacy, and that's what I need. I am no longer a teenager, like when I first moved back two years ago. That's why I want, more than anything, to just get the fuck out of here. I'm thinking the money I make selling will make escape a reality, not just some pipe dream. No pun intended.

I raise the bottle of gin to my lips and tip it back. Alcohol heats my throat. "I think I'm going to take Kyle up on his offer," I say after I swallow the burn, the resulting grimace distorting my voice. "I need the money and it's going to take forever to earn it legit."

"You're making the right decision, my friend," Tate replies as he reaches over to take back the bottle.

Whoa… My vision turns wonky. There are three overlapping filmy images of my friend, and then just two.

"It's all about the numbers, man," two filmy Tates tell me.

I tell myself I need to slow down, and then I say to Tate, "That it is." I squeeze my eyes shut to keep from swaying in my seat. "That it is," I repeat.

The irony is that I once had money. Well, my family did, enough that my parents had a trust fund set up for me. Not a big one, mind you, but enough that it would've allowed for me to go to a decent college, get set up in a new city, shit like that.

I have no idea what my future holds nowadays, but I know it's been tainted by my past.

Back when I was around eight my parents moved from this town out to Las Vegas. My dad, who'd been successfully building houses here for a while, started a similar construction business out in Nevada. The timing was right, the stars aligned. We caught magic in the early days of the housing boom. Everything was golden and money poured in. It was happy times. For a while.

During those good times, Mom got pregnant. She gave me a little brother named Will that I still love like crazy and miss every fucking day. We used to talk on the phone all the time, but now I'm lucky if I get a two-word text from my little bro. I suppose when you're eleven years old—and haven't seen your big brother in two years—memories become a little hazy.

That's another thing the extra money from selling drugs will help with: I'll have enough funds to fly out to Vegas to see Will. Or I can just buy him a ticket to come here. As it is my mom, Abby, barely makes enough to get by out there.

But, like I said before, it wasn't always that way. In the early years, my father's construction company grew and thrived, so much so that I once entertained dreams of taking over the business. I used to imagine following in my father's footsteps, as sons are apt to do.

One afternoon, when I was about thirteen, I told my dad I wanted to build homes, same as he did. I showed him some sketches, just some basic designs and floor plans I'd thrown together. My dad was impressed. And not the false kind of fawning parents often try to sell to their kids. No, my drawings truly floored Jack Gartner. I could tell he couldn't believe his eldest son possessed that kind of crazy talent. He told me I should aim high, the sky was the limit. My sketches were incredible, he said, especially for my age. I could be an architect if I wanted, design skyscrapers even.

I had no reason not to believe him.

When you're thirteen you think you can have it all. Life hasn't roughed you up so very much...yet. At least it hadn't for me. So I told my father I'd do both—I would design the skyscrapers, and then I'd build them. My buildings would sell like hotcakes, and I'd be as rich as Donald Trump. No, richer even.

"The sky's the limit," I said, echoing my father's words back to him.

Dad smiled and patted me on the back.

Jack Gartner wasn't patronizing me, he truly believed in my possibility. "You have talent, Chase," he said. "Just don't ever lose yourself. If you can stay true to your dream...to who you are...then you'll do more than fly. Someday you'll soar."

Yeah, right. I sure am soaring at the moment, but I have a feeling this isn't what Dad had in mind.

Tate tries to pass the bottle back to me, but my mood has dampened. The pills, along with the memories, are doing a fucking number on my emotions. I'm sad one minute, reflective the next, mad at everything, contemplative over nothing. I guess I am officially fucked up.

I push the bottle away, harder than necessary, and clear liquid sloshes over the side. "Asshole," Tate mutters.

"Sorry," I say.

Do I really mean it? No, it's just a word, an empty string of letters. Empty, like me.

I tune Tate out. I am high as fuck and lost in my mind. We idle at a swinging red light hanging over an empty, dark stretch of road, and I sit waiting on an imaginary red light in my head, one on memory-fucking-lane.

When I blink, both lights turn green...

My dad started taking me to work the summer I showed him the drawings. I learned how to wire a home, how to put in plumbing, how to lay insulation. And that was just the beginning. I used to watch how my dad talked to the guys. He treated them with respect, and in turn they went the extra mile for him. It was all "Yes sir, Mr. Gartner," "Consider it done, Jack."

When I turned fourteen, my dad bought me a drafting table, a bunch of fancy software too. The kind real architects use, or so he said. I practiced all the time, got pretty damn good. I was building my wings, you see, preparing to fly.

Will was only five, but damn if that kid didn't love to sit around and watch me sketch. For him, I'd draw all kinds of ridiculous structures.

"Dwaw me a house, Chasey," he asked this one day.

I laughed while I tousled his blond hair. I remember the fine strands looked so light in the sunlit room. Hell, they were almost white. "All right, buddy, what kind do you want?"

"A house like a tweeeee," Will sing-song replied, green eyes innocent and wide as he focused on the sketch pad I'd picked up from my desk.

I readied a colored pencil and asked for clarification, "Okay, a tree house, right?"

"No-o-o." Will shook his little head vociferously. "A house that *is* a twee, Chasey."

"Aha, got it," I said.

And I did. I drew Will a tree house shaped exactly like a tree, big, sturdy, loaded down with bushy branches. The leaves I shaded in the color of my brother's eyes. I sketched a door at the base of the trunk, then drew a Will-sized truck and parked it under a low-lying branch. After I finished with some final shading, I held the drawing up for my brother to see.

Will's house looked like one of those tree houses in the commercials with the elves and the cookies, only this one I'd drawn was far better. There was a lot more detail, and I'd drawn the tree in 2-D. In among the branches and the leaves all the rooms were in cross-section, done up in varying shades of blue, Will's favorite color. I also made certain every last blue-shaded 2D-room overflowed with toys.

Will threw his arms around my neck and told me he loved his *twee house*. Then, he leaned back and told me he loved *me* even more.

He gave me a kiss on my cheek. That shit always touched my heart, choked me up a little. "I love you too, buddy," was about all I could say as I held on to a little boy who meant the world to me.

Things are never bad when love is abundant. I thought it would stay that way forever, I did. A home filled with love, a happy family, just a good and easy life.

Man, was I ever wrong.

Shortly after I turned seventeen my world began to crumble. The bottom fell out of the housing market. The wave everyone was riding touched the surf and crashed. My dad's business was one of the first to fail. He had over-extended himself; all our assets were mortgaged. He made ridiculous deals, attempting to keep us afloat, but his efforts proved futile. We sunk faster than a stone.

I sold the fancy architect software on eBay, the drafting table too. I gave the money to my parents, but it was merely a drop in the bucket compared to what we owed. I watched my once-vibrant dad turn into a shadow of the man he once was. My mom, always so young-looking and pretty, developed dark circles under her eyes—from crying, worrying, not being able to sleep. She even tried her hand at the casinos, we were that fucking desperate. But everyone knows gambling is a loser's game. The house always wins in the end.

One night, my mom was at one of those casinos. It wasn't the first time she'd spent hours and hours away, trying to win back what we'd lost. She came out ahead a little here and there, but it was never enough, never enough.

Will had fallen asleep early that night, so my dad and I were more or less alone. He asked me if I was hungry. When I nodded slowly, reluctant to reveal just how ravenous I really was and cause my father any additional undue guilt, he sighed, picked up the phone, and ordered a bunch of Chinese take-out.

I swear I smelled that food before the delivery man even pulled up to the house. Beef Chow Mein, General Tso's chicken, hot and sour soup, and eggrolls, the first real meal I'd eaten in weeks. And even though my dad and I had to sit on the floor—our furniture had been repossessed days earlier—I savored every fucking bite.

Afterward, my dad said he had somewhere to go. There was something he had to do. Would I keep an eye on Will?

"Sure," I told him while shoving white take-out cartons with little metal handles— leftovers I'd saved for Will and Mom—into the fridge.

With my father gone, I had nothing to do. Our TVs were gone, the stereos too. Video games? Forget it. Those were the first things to go. So, I wandered around the house barefoot, padding around on neglected hardwood floors. I trudged from one empty room to the next.

Then I took a minute to look in on Will.

My little brother slept on an air mattress in the middle of his now-barren room. The *twee house* sketch, the only thing left on his four stark walls, had fallen. It lay abandoned on the floor, close to Will's hand, close to where his little arm was dangling off the side of the mattress. To me, it looked as if my brother was subconsciously reaching for the drawing. Three years had passed since I'd drawn Will's tree house— and I'd sketched hundreds of other things for him since that sunny day—but that particular piece of made-with-love art was still my brother's favorite. I think to him it symbolized something more. He'd once said my sketch gave him hope. I guess it reminded him of when things were good.

I stepped into his dark room and picked up Will's hope. I kissed the top of his head and gently placed his *twee house* next to his sleeping form. I made my way back down to the living room, feeling solemn and too fucking worn for seventeen. Tears welled in my eyes, but I refused to let them fall. *Hell with that shit.* The paper bag that had held the Chinese food was still on the floor. Frustrated, I kicked it out of my way. A fortune cookie shot out and landed at my feet. I picked the projectile up, ripped the plastic covering off, and slid a tiny piece of paper from the confines of the cookie.

The fortune stayed in my hand, the cookie ended up in my mouth.

Truthfully, I was still hungry. Crunching away and savoring sugary goodness, I read the words on the little slip of paper I held between my fingers.

As I stand before you, judge me not.

It sounded a little hokey and I almost threw the fortune away. But there was something about those words that made me hesitate, something almost prescient. I ended up folding the little piece of paper in half and tucking it in to my pocket. Maybe I needed some symbol of hope just like my brother. I knew the things happening in my life would eventually define my future, and I guess I hoped no matter what occurred those things wouldn't ultimately define me.

My mom came back later that night, but my dad never did.

Jack Gartner had gotten on route 160, heading west to California. But he never made it out of Nevada. His car was found at the bottom of a ravine, below what the officers who came to our door to break the news termed *a treacherous curve.*

Killed on impact, we were told.

Did he lose control, or drive off the road on purpose?

Maybe his plan all along had been to leave us and start a new life in California. That's what my mom believed at the time. Still does, in fact.

I, however, am not so sure. My father didn't pack a thing. Sixty dollars and a cancelled credit card, that's all he had on him. I think my dad just gave up. He quit on us, and that was the way he chose to end it. My mom can delude herself all she wants, but I know in my heart that I'm the one who's got it right.

Anyway, the bank took the house soon after my father's death. My mom sold off what little was left. For awhile, we became nomads in the desert. We lived in the only big-ticket item that hadn't been repossessed, a white minivan. The Honda Odyssey was home...until Mom won enough money gambling to move us into a cheap apartment. Our new residence was a dump, but at least it had running water. And it was furnished. Kind of.

When we first stepped across the threshold and Mom caught me scowling at the rusty fixtures, the water-stained ceiling, the musty olive-green carpeting, she tried hard to convince me our new place had its good points.

"Like what?" I asked.

"It's close to The Strip. That'll be convenient."

"Convenient for who?" I sniped. "You?"

"Chase," she said pointedly, "it's better than living in a minivan."

She had a point there, so we moved in the next day. Will's first reaction was to run straight to one of the two back bedrooms and hang up his tattered *twee house* sketch. I followed him and watched as he stood on a soiled mattress on the floor—in a shoebox of a room we were going to have to share—and pinned hope on a wall.

After we were settled, time, as it does, marched on. Will and I attended school, while my mom—still fevered and sick with the gambling virus—spent her days in the casinos.

I turned eighteen that April. But no one really noticed. Well, Will did. Not much got by that kid.

He stuck a candle he found in the back of a drawer in the kitchen on a stale snack cake. He made me sit on the only kitchen chair that didn't rock when you shifted, and then he placed the snack cake on a card table we used as a kitchen table.

Will sang me the most beautiful off-key and from-the-heart rendition of "Happy Birthday" that I have ever heard, before or since. When he was done, I leaned forward to blow out the candle. Will stopped me and told me to make a wish first, so I did. And then I blew out the candle. Will clapped and cheered. He asked me what I wished for and I told him it was a secret. I didn't want to tell him I wished for him to be given a better life than what we were, at the time, living. My brother and I split the snack cake in two, dinner for the night, and ate in contemplative silence.

Summer arrived that year and I somehow managed to graduate. But—with my trust fund long gone—college was no longer on the table. With no real guidance, and a lot of pent-up frustration, my downward slide took hold. I was angry all the time, and ended up getting into too many fights to count. The places in Vegas where I'd started hanging were tough. Early on, I got my ass kicked...often.

But then something happened.

I learned how to use my strength, my quickness, *and* my

anger. I started to win. I had a real knack for fighting and rapidly turned into a badass nobody messed with. I earned street cred. All that really meant was guys started showing me respect and girls suddenly wanted to have sex with me. I happily obliged more than a few of the latter.

But all that shit meant nothing, I was empty inside. I had no one to talk to about the mixed-up emotions I didn't know how to deal with. Like, why was I so angry all the time? Why did I like to fight so much? Why did it feel so good to make someone else hurt?

But mostly I wondered why I missed my dad so much.

I missed talking to my father, seeing his face everyday. I had relied on him, I still needed him. But he was gone. He took his own life. Why couldn't I just accept what had happened and forget him?

But I couldn't, and, worse yet, I longed for answers.

Every day, for a while, in my quest for enlightenment, I'd grab the bus outside our apartment and visit my father. Well, I'd visit his grave. At the head of where my father rested eternally, I'd sit under a big stone angel kneeling by his grave—thankful for the little bit of shade she offered under the hot, beating sun of the desert.

Sweaty and lost, I'd ask her if she could tell me why my dad wasn't still alive. Why had God allowed Dad to take himself away? Why did my father choose to leave me? Why would he leave Mom and Will too? Was our love not enough for him? Did he regret his decision when he realized there was no going back?

Of course, the stone angel had no answers, and one day I just quit going. No more sitting in the shadow of the angel, no more hot and beating sun. No more asking questions that could never be answered.

My trips to the cemetery were over, but that didn't mean I wanted to forget that *someone*—even though he'd left—had once believed in me. Despite everything, I still loved my father and part of me yearned to be just like him.

So, July of that year, I had his angel's likeness—the stone one at his grave—inked in profile on the middle of my upper back, between my shoulder blades.

I shift in the passenger seat now.

I can almost feel her back there, watching over me, like my dad's angel watches over him. And like his angel, mine is kneeling. The edges of her heavy robe lie in a puddle of fabric around her. Her wings are folded against her back. Her hair is long, obscuring the side of her face. And her head is bowed. In supplication or in shame, I haven't decided which. But if she's been watching the shit I've been doing these past two years, it's probably in shame.

After the angel tat healed, Mom hit for more money. I successfully talked her into paying for another tattoo, guilted her into it really. In any case, I ended up with big, intricately detailed wings inked up and over my shoulder blades. The top feathers curve onto my shoulders, while the wings dip down the sides of my back, effectively framing the angel.

But the angel and the wings weren't enough. I wanted something more to remember my father, something to remind me always of that final night, when it was just him and me, eating Chinese food on the floor of an empty home, a last supper shared.

I kept coming back to the cookie, the fortune inside, the hope it symbolized.

As I stand before you, judge me not.

Words printed on a piece of paper, but really they were so much more. So I had those words inked—in concise and script letters—around my left bicep.

My tats were but temporal attempts to heal my soul, as my heart remained an open wound. There was no solace to be had at home. In fact, things were getting worse. I started to drink and do drugs to ease the pain and fill the void. I hated what had happened to our family. Seeing Will transformed from an energetic little boy to a sullen nine-year-old left me sad and frustrated. And watching my mother try to heal her fractured heart with gambling—and eventually men—just pissed me the fuck off.

But at least Mom wasn't indulging in one-night stands like I'd been doing. Nope, Abby actually went out on dates. Still, her attempt at dating led to a revolving door of boyfriends. Some lasted a week or two, some a little longer, but the one common denominator they all shared was that not a single one liked me.

Mom told me to try harder, give these guys a chance for her sake. I laughed and told Abby her men could blow me. "Chase, don't be crude," was her response.

By the end of the summer Mom hooked up with what turned out to be steady boyfriend number three. I was no fool; I immediately sensed my days were numbered. I would've had to have been blind not to see the writing on the wall, a wall I didn't realize I was hurtling toward. But it wasn't just Abby's lame new boyfriend disliking me that was a problem. There was something else, something she'd never admit to. There was no escaping it though, not really.

I saw Abby's problem every day when I looked in the mirror.

Standing in a cramped and steam-filled bathroom, hot water running, can of shave cream poised in hand, I couldn't deny the truth in front of me. I'd swipe at the misted mirror with my free hand, leaving it streaky, but mostly clear. And it wasn't me I saw in the reflection, it was my father. That's how much I looked like Jack Gartner, even at eighteen. And *that* was my mother's real problem.

Shit. Even thinking about it now—two years later—fucks with my head.

I glance over at Tate. He's quiet, taking long pulls from the bottle. I shift in my seat and wind up the window the rest of the way. Time to assess my bleary reflection, time to compare it to what it was, time to compare it to the man who made me…I sometimes do this just to fuck with myself.

When I take in my reflection, I laugh. Hell, the resemblance is still uncanny. And just like when I used to stare at the steamed-up mirror in the bathroom, it's my dad's eyes staring back at me now. But these pale blues are all mine. Yeah, *his* whites were never shot with red like mine.

Still, even with the bloodshot eyes, similarities far outweigh differences. Though it's not *short and tidy*—like Grandma Gartner would like it to be—my hair is the exact same shade as her son's once was, light brown. Jack also blessed me with his straight nose, his square jaw, and his defined cheekbones. Everyone used to say my dad was good-looking, I guess I am too. Girls seem to think so, that's for sure. And my mother sure was smitten with my dad.

Abby used to lean across the front seat of the sporty car my dad bought for himself during the good times. Will and I would be in the back, rolling our eyes at each other. My mom would kiss my dad, making him swerve a little as he drove. She'd tell him he was gorgeous, and that she loved him. Dad would laugh and tell Abby he loved her even more. He'd say his love for her burned hotter than the Vegas sun above us. My mom loved that shit. Will and I, however, would groan in disgust and make gagging noises.

Shit, I feel like gagging now. Not because of the memory, but at how closely I still resemble my dead father. I turn away from my reflection. I can't bear to endure this self-inflicted torture any longer. No wonder I was fucking sent away. Too bad I couldn't disappear completely just as easily right now. Guess, in a way, that's why I live my life the way I do, filling it with drugs…sex…violence.

Back then my very presence in my mom's life must have been a constant reminder of all she had lost. When you're striving to move on, you don't need an anchor to the past. She could move forward with Will, he was just a kid. Besides, he looked like her, not like my father. But I was eighteen, an adult, and far too much my father's son for everyone's comfort. I guess it was just too difficult for Mom to look at me—see *him*—and be reminded of all she'd once had.

So the day steady boyfriend number three, a guy named Gary, told her she could move in with him, I kind of fucking knew the invitation wouldn't be extended to me.

Sure enough, on a blistering hot afternoon, my mom sent Will out to ride his bike and told me we had to talk. She sat me down on the ratty couch in our shitty apartment.

I felt like a condemned man waiting to hear his fate, and all the while the noisy air conditioning unit in the window behind me kept blowing gusts of lukewarm air across the back of my neck.

Not that it mattered. I barely noticed. I was mostly numb. In preparation for this "talk," I'd done a couple of lines of coke in my room. Of course, I hadn't brought that shit out until after Will had left. One thing I stuck to was that I never let my little brother see me taking part in any of my newfound vices.

Anyway, that day in the living room, I couldn't sit still. Fidgeting, fidgeting, tapping my foot. Mom took no notice, she was almost as bad. Pacing back and forth in front of me, smoking a cigarette, a new habit she'd just acquired. Gary smoked, so she'd picked up the habit too. *Pathetic*, I remember thinking.

My mother appeared so edgy and wired I almost asked her if she was dabbling in drugs, like me, or if what she had to say was really just that fucking bad. She started speaking before I ever got the chance.

"You're not a kid anymore, Chase," she began, still pacing, ashes peppering the olive-green carpeting.

She took a drag, crinkled her brow, and leaned over to stub her cigarette out in a plastic ashtray on a low table.

"You have to get started on doing something, somewhere, kid," she said as she spun to face me.

She stood right in front of me, and though my head was down I watched her every move. She blew out a breath and I watched her dark blonde bangs lift up off her forehead. A few strands stuck to her skin. Mom was starting to sweat.

"So, Grandma Gartner called the other day," she continued, her words deliberate, pointed, like a knife. "She said she's got lots of room in that old farmhouse back in Ohio. And she sure could use some company."

I looked up at her in disbelief. This woman who'd given me life tried to smile, but she could not. She knew damn well she was spewing pure bullshit. She just wanted rid of me.

"Just spit it out," I ground through clenched teeth, my voice far from even.

"Okay, of course, honey." She looked everywhere but at me. "Uh, so, Gram thinks moving back to Harmony Creek might do you some good, get you out of Vegas, give you a chance to start over, and—"

"Mom, I'm only eighteen. Start over?" I blew out a quick breath. "I haven't even had a chance to get started *here*."

Her expression grew stern. "Chase, don't act like I don't know the things you do behind my back." I tried to protest, but she shushed me. "I know you use drugs. I know you bring girls back when Will's not around. That shit isn't going to fly once we move in with Gary. He won't stand for it, Chase. He has standards—"

I snorted, "The fuck he does—"

"I'm not going to argue with you about it," she said, her voice tired and cracking.

When she reached for her pack of cigarettes, I noticed her hands were shaking. "Honey, I just think Grandma Gartner's is the best place for you right now, okay?"

I picked at a hole in my jeans. "Do I have a choice?" I asked, defeated, and, truthfully, feeling like I'd just been set adrift.

She shook her head no.

I'd known it was coming, but her words still flayed me up the middle and pierced my already damaged heart. I was shocked that my heart could continue beating, since it felt all smashed to hell. But beat it did. In fact, my heart pumped faster and faster, like it was going to burst right out of my fucking chest. Whether my reaction was from cocaine…or despair…I couldn't quite figure.

With my heart pounding like a sped-up death knell, I tried to push some words out of my cotton-dry mouth. "Mom…" I croaked, my voice catching.

I just couldn't finish.

Verbal communication failed me, so I tried to meet her eyes, speak to her soul. Was this really what she wanted? Send her eldest son away? Give up on me? Just like Dad did with all of us.

I searched and searched, but my mother had no answers in her big green eyes, no more than the stone angel had at my father's grave.

Abby took in a stuttered breath and turned away. She swiped at a tear. "It's for the best, Chase," she mumbled.

And then she left me sitting there, all alone, warm air blowing across the back of my neck.

I went back to my room and cut up three more lines.

That was nearly two years ago and here I am. Mom is still in Las Vegas with Will, on steady boyfriend number six, last I heard. She's still chasing the elusive jackpot too, hoping to recapture the life she once knew.

Good luck with that, I think bitterly. *Jackpot, my ass.* If anyone needs to hit a fucking jackpot, it's me.

Suddenly, drug-induced visions of flashing pots of gold

swim lazily into my head, along with some break-dancing leprechauns, and I can't help but chuckle.

Tate looks over. He must think my mood has improved, 'cause he starts talking all excitedly about how much money we're going to make from our new business venture with Kyle. I listen to his voice, not really hearing any words, but then the cell buzzes and I am alert, very alert.

Tate tosses it my way. "That there would be the ladies," he says—all smooth like—as I catch the cell with one hand. Even impaired, my coordination is impeccable.

"Ladies, my ass." I roll my eyes.

Tate laughs, knowing as well as I do that the two girls we're meeting up with tonight are no ladies. They're looking for the same thing we are, but therein lies the beauty.

"What's it say?" he asks, nodding to the cell.

The text is kind of blurry, but, then again, everything is. I blink a few times and my vision clears. When I read it out loud, I mimic a high-pitched girl's voice, just to be an ass. "Crystal and I are almost at the lake. Come prepared. Tammy. Laugh out loud, winking smiley face."

"Dude-e-e." Tate shoots me a knowing sidelong glance. "You know what *come prepared* means, right? You got that covered, yeah?"

As reckless as I am—and that's pretty fucking reckless—I always make sure I wrap my shit up. Better safe than sorry. But as I feel around in the pockets of my jeans I realize I've left the condoms at home. "Fuck," I mutter.

The blue *Welcome to Pennsylvania* sign looms ahead, our headlights flashing off the reflective letters.

Tate asks, "What?"

I rake my fingers through my hair. "I forgot the goddamn things at home."

"Not a problem. We'll just stop at the convenience store across the state line."

"Bad idea," I counter. "Cops are always hanging out in there. You think they won't notice how fucked up we are?"

"How fucked up *you* are," Tate corrects, laughing. "I didn't smoke nearly as much as you."

"You smoked plenty," I mumble under my breath.

But Tate is right, I smoked more. And Tate smoked only weed. Plus, my friend didn't see the pills Kyle slipped me before we left.

Still, I nod to the almost-empty bottle. "You pretty much drank that whole thing, dickhead. You'll never pass a field sobriety test."

"Yeah, but I don't plan on taking one, my friend. And, I hide it better than you." He shrugs. "Trust me, I got it covered. Just wait in the car. It'll only take a sec."

Tate's always confident like this. He can talk anyone into just about anything. I always tell him he's a natural-born salesman. Maybe if we ever get our shit together he can do something legit using his smooth ways. It's cool, it's Tate's thing, and it helps make him popular. He's an okay-looking guy—brown hair, brown eyes, kind of skinny—but it's his smooth talk that gets him in with the girls. They eat that shit up.

We cross the state line, turn into the convenience store. No cop cars. "See, we're good," Tate says, still as confident as ever.

I flip up my black hoodie hood and slouch down in my seat. "Just be quick," I mumble.

Tate hesitates, and I know something is up. "What the fuck are you waiting for?" I ask.

He begins his sentence with "Don't be pissed—" and I cut him off right away, hoping I won't have to kick my good friend's skinny ass. It would be a damn shame really, since Tate wouldn't stand a chance against the likes of me. I am way bigger and far stronger, and the rage within me has no match.

"What?" I spit out, clenching my jaw.

Tate ignores my attitude; he's used to it. "I kind of need you to hold on to something while I go in there. Just in case."

"Just in case of what?"

I am running out of patience. I scrub my hand down my face, wary to hear what Tate the salesman is up to now.

He smirks, and I tell him to knock that shit off, save it for the "ladies."

"Okay, okay." He raises his hands in mock surrender. "I may have kind of asked Kyle to give us a little something to get our entrepreneurial gig started."

"Us?" I say, feeling the anger rise up. "You didn't even know I was going to sell with you until about ten minutes ago."

"What can I say, man." Tate places his hand over his heart. "I had faith."

"Whatever."

I try to stay pissed, because what he did was really out of line, but my anger fades fast. High as I am, these strong emotions are too fucking slippery to hold on to for very long.

Tate hands me a plastic packet filled with little pills, a rainbow of color. "Jesus." I know all too well exactly what this shit is. "X? You're fucking higher than I thought. We're supposed to start small, bitch. Move a little bud, see how it goes."

Tate shrugs. "We'll make more money this way. Like, I know we can sell to the girls tonight. Hell, I bet we can talk them into buying *our* hits."

He's laughing at his own ingenuity, but I ignore him. I'm too busy trying to count the pills in the packet. But being in the condition I am in, it's a bit of a challenge.

"How much is this anyway?" I ask, giving up on figuring it out for myself.

"Twenty hits," he tells me, and then he has the balls to throw another packet in my lap. "Make that forty...maybe a little more."

"You're fucking crazy. If we get caught, Tate, this isn't possession. This is possession with intent to sell."

"That's why I'm leaving the shit here with you."

"Oh, that's real fucking cool." Back to being pissed, even my high can't calm me now. I whip one of the packets back at Tate. "I am so not getting caught with forty hits of Ecstasy, asshole."

"Calm down, man." He gingerly picks up the packet I've just thrown and holds it out for me to take back. "If a cop shows up just hit the road."

"What about you?" I ask as I grudgingly accept the X.

Tate grins. "Don't worry about me. You know I can play it cool. Just swing by after the heat's gone, and we'll be back in business."

"The heat? What is this, the seventies?" I ask, laughing, but Tate's already out the door.

I tuck the two packets of Ecstasy into the back pocket

of my jeans and think nothing more of it. Until a few short minutes later when a state cop pulls into the lot. Then, I panic.

I start climbing over the console to get the fuck out of there, but, suddenly, with every fiber of my being, I know I've just made the dumbest mistake of my life. That, however, doesn't stop me from slipping down into the driver's seat, throwing the car into reverse. I hit the gas, peel out of the parking lot, and leave a cloud of gravel and dust in my wake.

I've got the Focus up to eighty, music playing...loud, loud, fucking blaring. Maybe I can outrun this cocksucker? I'm tapping my hands on the steering wheel along with the beat, flying so fast it's amazing I don't lose control and crash.

But I don't, I stay steady.

I even make it a good five miles down the road before a cop heading my way—backup, I'm sure—screeches to a wide arced stop in front of me. His patrol car blocks the entire road, so I have no choice but to hit the brakes and squeal to a halt.

My car ends up parallel to the cop car, both of us straddling the lanes, engines idling like we're in some fucking action movie. The air reeks of burning rubber, and smoke billows around us. The speakers beat out a song from 50 Cent that is frankly ironic at this point.

When all the smoke clears, the sign for the lake is right smack dab in front of me. I can't help but laugh. The shit situation I'm in, and all I can think of is that Crystal and Tammy are out there, waiting, for two boys who are never going to show.

Two more cops—including the one from the store—pull up behind me. I pitch the door open, tumble from the seat. I hit the warm pavement and try to stand. Someone yells, "Hold it right there, hands on your head."

I hear guns being drawn, cocked. This isn't a movie, I know they're loaded. I squint to try to see what's happening, but all the flashing lights leave me blinded. Before I can think another drug-muddled thought, someone tackles me from behind. My face smacks right into the yellow center line, but I don't feel a fucking thing.

Whoever tackles me yanks down my hood, frisks me, and comes up with my wallet. Oh, and the forty hits of X, of course.

It's all ambient noise from that point on, but I do hear, "Chase Gartner, you're under arrest."

I have no idea that, despite the altered state I'm in, these will be the last coherent words I remember for a very long time.

The time following has no sense of structure. Days, weeks, they all blend together. I'm in jail, facing a long, long list of charges. But it's the X that has me fucked.

Bond is set high. I call my mom, but all she does is cry. Like, these horrible wailing sobs that do nothing but make my head ache more than ever. She keeps apologizing for not having the money and swears she'll help me when she can. I hang up. I won't be holding my breath. The past has taught me not to put too much stock into Abby's flimsy promises. Mirages in the desert are what they are—get too close and they disappear.

My grandmother wants to mortgage the farmhouse, all the property around it. We're talking a good fifty-five acres. It'd be enough to make bail, but I tell her *no way*. She's done enough for me already, and look at how I've repaid her. I don't deserve her money...or her love.

So I'm on my own. And not thinking very clearly. Once all the illegal shit is out of my system, I find myself in a constant state of agitation. I can't sleep, I barely eat. I sweat bullets even when it feels like I'm freezing.

Eventually all that passes, but then all I want to do is fight. Like beat heads in. It's worse than when I was back in Vegas; I feel so much more fucking rage. I sit around clenching my fists, hoping for a chance to kick some poor unsuspecting soul's ass.

Finally, my wish is granted.

They throw a cellmate in with me and my ass is on him like an animal, beating the hell out of this never-saw-me-coming sap. But then two guards see what I'm doing, pull me off the bloodied and broken man, and promptly return the favor.

Another blur of pain.

This one, though, I welcome. The medical staff gives me plenty of drugs, legal ones this time. And still more before I am put before the judge.

Even in the sedated fog I float around in, I quickly learn the law...and some new math.

MDMA, Ecstasy—X, as I like to call it—is a schedule I narcotic, and carries as stiff a penalty as heroin if you're caught dealing, which they naturally assume I was. Casual users don't tote around forty-plus hits of Ecstasy, but dealers do.

I say nothing one way or the other to dispel their myth, I rat no one out. I just stay quiet and accept my fate.

My math lesson continues…

Ten pills are equal to one gram, and I've been caught with over forty pills. Forty pills equal four grams, which is more than enough to be charged with possession with intent to sell. But I already knew that part, right?

My lesson isn't over though. It's only just beginning.

I learn in Pennsylvania, the state in which I've been apprehended, four grams can easily earn you a prison sentence. This is especially true when you don't have enough money to hire a good attorney. Add to that, your public defender isn't getting paid enough to care. Not that you're doing much to help the overworked, underpaid man do his job. And, oh yeah, don't forget that one prior arrest for fighting last fall. It didn't seem like much at the time, but it sure haunts your ass now.

Are you keeping up?

Some final math…

Four grams buys you a six-year sentence at a state correctional institute when you have no resources, and, really, no heart to fight it.

Twenty years of age feels like ninety when your freedom is stripped away.

It takes one hundred and forty-three steps to walk down a long, noisy corridor to reach cell block seventy-two.

And when they turn the key, you hear one life—the only one you've ever known up until now—ending.

"It's all about the numbers, man," as Tate would say.

It sure is, my friend. It sure is.

Four years later…

CHAPTER ONE
CHASE

Seventy-two push-ups on the cold hardwood floor, seventy-two sit-ups. *It's still all about the numbers, Tate, four years later.* But Tate is dead, overdosed at twenty-two. He never went to prison, never spent four years of his life in cell block seventy-two like I did. Yet he threw his life away all the same.

Seventy-two pull-ups at a bar I installed in the doorway of a room long forgotten in a house I don't deserve. *Fuck, no, make that forty-nine.* My ass is tired today, which is why I overslept. Damn Missy Metzger and her glitter-coated lips. Damn my lack of self-control.

Father Maridale would kick my ass all the way back across the state line if he knew what I'd done with the head of the bake committee. *Head.* I can't help but laugh, because that sure does sum it up. Oh, if only the congregation of Holy Trinity Catholic Church knew how Missy spent her Saturday night. In an alley behind the Anchor Inn bar, down on her knees, worshipping my cock.

I shed the gray sweatpants I'm wearing, toss them into an overflowing laundry basket in the bathroom. Laundry, yet another thing I've neglected since getting out of prison. A whole month back in Harmony Creek, and I'm still adjusting to the little things a guy living alone needs to stay on top of.

Speaking of which…11:15…*shit*.

Mass started fifteen minutes ago. Guess I am not going to make it today. A part of me feels shame for my indiscretion with Missy last night, but that part also feels relief. I don't have to face Missy—or her mom—both of whom sit perched every week in the front pew.

I step into the tub and adjust the shower head; turn it on full blast. The pulsing water feels good and cleansing, I just wish it had the power to wash away my latest sin. I didn't go out looking for trouble, I truly didn't. I'd like to think my worst days are behind me. I'm determined to lead a better life, which includes staying clean. Sure, I drink a beer or two some evenings, usually while relaxing out on the porch swing in the back, watching the day fade into night while the frogs sing to each other down at the creek. But drinking is my only vice these days.

Okay, and maybe swearing. No, definitely swearing. But that's it. Just drinking and swearing. And the drinking I keep to a minimum. Drugs? I've given them up completely. And I can't remember the last time I got into a fight.

No, wait, that's a lie. I do remember. It was two years ago in prison. And here's what happened…

This new inmate—some skinhead who thought he was the biggest, baddest motherfucker to step into the joint—started up with me one morning in the exercise yard. He kept shooting his mouth off. That was his first mistake. The second was taking a bullshit swing at me when I laughed at his sorry ass and walked away.

Bad fucking move.

I could go into details, tell you all I did, but let's just say when I was done with him, dickhead was begging for mercy and crying for his mother. No joke. And no real surprise. It's been my experience the biggest talkers fall the hardest and cry the loudest.

After spending a week in the infirmary, the skinhead gave me a wide berth whenever we crossed paths. If he had to address me, it was all "yes, sir," "no, sir," and then he'd get the fuck out of my way. Yeah, he'd been schooled.

I was never the biggest guy in prison—even standing at six two—but I was one of the strongest, one of the toughest. And, sadly, while serving time I learned a dozen ways to really hurt a guy.

But that's all in the past. I'm trying to change my ways, make smarter choices, be a better person. I even have a job working for the church, doing maintenance and fixing shit. I like it, it's good for me. The work keeps me busy. And I need that kind of structure. If idle hands really are the devil's workshop, then I'm safe for now.

I spent most of last week working on—and fixing—an air-conditioning problem in the rectory. And on Friday I sealed more than a dozen leaks plaguing the stained glass windows in the church. Maybe even more impressive— at least to me—is that I've gotten up and dragged my ass to Mass three Sundays in a row. It's a personal best, and Grandma Gartner would be proud if she were here today. Sadly, she's not.

I chuckle, remembering how much she loved Holy Trinity Church, the congregation, especially. She knew everything going on with everybody, and always made it her mission to help when she could. Unfortunately, though I go to church, work for the church, I am sure not social like my grandmother used to be. I keep to myself during Mass, sit in the very back. I'd sit in the vestibule if I could get away with it. But Father Maridale would have my head. Speaking of which, that very same head is usually bowed in prayer—not unlike the ink angel that's tattooed on my back—when I'm at my station in the back. I probably appear to be praying, however, try as I might I find I really don't have much to say to God. At least, not yet.

Now, you'd think a man praying—or at least trying to—would warrant some respect. Apparently this is not the case in the minds of the Holy Trinity parishioners. My faux-praying sure as hell doesn't stop them from turning around and craning their necks, all pretending to be looking at something other than me.

Well, they don't fool me. I hear their whispers, feel their disapproving stares. I always dart for the doors the second Mass ends. I know what they're thinking. They expect me to fuck up again, ruin the second chance Father Maridale—the leader of their flock—is giving me.

Shit, I can't wait to prove every last one of those sanctimonious assholes wrong.

That's why yesterday my simple plan had been to grab a beer and a burger down at the local watering hole, and then head home to catch some zees. But Missy, in her four-inch fuck-me heels, derailed that plan when she spotted me at the bar and started toward me, her purpose all too clear in her walk.

I used to see Missy periodically at parties before I got into trouble. She was never much of a party girl back then, despite her presence at some of the wilder bashes. But people change.

Over the past few weeks—until last night—my only interactions with Missy have been at church, and those usually involve catching her glancing back at me from the front pew. Not disapprovingly like the other parishioners, oh no. Missy always eyes me like I'm a piece of candy she wants to take a bite out of.

I shake my head, chuckle a little as I soap up my body. Missy sure got her wish last night...and then some. Fuck, I have to admit what she did to me felt good, really good, but what a mistake.

Hopefully, Missy will be more successful at keeping her mouth shut than she was last night behind the Anchor Inn. I groan a little at the thought of her making a big deal out of what happened. God, girls and their expectations, reading shit into anything physical that occurs. I hope Missy realizes our little tryst was a one-time deal. Somehow I doubt I'll be so lucky.

I turn so the steaming water hits my back. I have the sneaking suspicion Missy, surely in church at this very moment, is probably looking back and wondering why I am not there. I can picture it perfectly: Missy—who always positions herself between her portly mom and some hot chick I've not yet had the pleasure of meeting—sitting there, not listening to Mass. Instead she's surely thinking about last night and hoping it meant something, like I'm into her or something. *Dream on, sweetheart.*

Now, if the mystery-hot chick who sits next to Missy had been the one to walk into the bar last night, I'd be singing an entirely different tune today. First off, I never would have treated Hot Chick the way I treated Missy, even if she is hot as fuck. Hot Chick just seems too...I don't know... fragile maybe.

She's a slender, tiny little thing. Pretty too, in a classic but understated kind of way. I like her delicate features, her porcelain skin, and the mane of chestnut-colored hair that flows down her back. And I *really* like her heart-shaped ass and the shapely legs she shows off in pretty dresses. Not to mention her perky tits that she tries to hide under pastel cardigan sweaters. Damn, I like those too.

My dick reminds me of just how much I like Hot Chick's assets as I finish showering. I think about lingering a few extra minutes, but there's really no time for *that*, so I push down on my length and turn off the water.

Grabbing a towel from the bar by the sink, I dry off and give myself some time to cool down. I pad back into the bedroom, tamping down any lingering lust-ridden thoughts, and pondering how the fuck I've never run into this hot chick before, seeing as she seems to be around my age.

She must be new to Harmony Creek, I conclude, because I never once saw her back when I was living here. I would definitely recollect if I had met *her*.

If she is new to town I bet she lives south of Market Street—the main thoroughfare running through town. South of Market is where all the important people live—the mayor, members of the town council, prominent business owners, and the like.

I should know; my family once lived there. Back before we moved to Vegas, back when I was a different person, on a different path.

Whatever.

In any case, Hot Chick sure looks like she'd fit in down there south of Market—all prim and proper in her girly-girl dresses and pastel sweaters. I guess what I'm saying is that she's someone who wouldn't be caught dead with the likes of me. Maybe the person I was a long time ago would've had a chance, but the damaged man I've become doesn't deserve someone good and wholesome like that. I'm doomed to make due with the Missy Metzgers of the world.

It's almost noon and Mass should be letting out, which is great. By the time I get over to the church everyone will be gone. I'd rather not go at all, but I have to stop by and pick something up. Now that summer vacation has officially begun, Father Maridale has all these painting projects for me to start on. Most are over in the school next to the church. I'm supposed to get started tomorrow bright and early. But I don't yet have a key, so I need to pick one up. Unfortunately, that entails a visit to the church, and a face-to-face with the priest who saw enough good in me to hire my sorry ass last month.

Standing before the closet in my bedroom, I decide it'd be prudent—especially since I missed Mass—to dress respectably. I flip through the hangers, and stop when I come to the nicest pair of pants I own. I run a finger down the sharp creases of the tailored, black dress slacks my mother bought me to wear before the judge who ended up granting me my freedom.

I sigh and pull the pants off the hanger.

Also thanks to Mom, I now own a nice collection of button-down shirts, in a vast array of colors. I just grab the first one I see—white, crisp, and cotton. Perfect, I'll be in black and white, just like Father Maridale. The sinner and the saint, matched.

While I dress in these so-not-me clothes, I think about how much they must've cost. But it's not like my mother can't afford pricey things these days. Like I said before, people change…and some get lucky.

For Abby, it's the latter that applies. I guess the cost of some fancy duds is a small price to pay when all you want is for your son to look the part of a respectable young man. What a joke. None of this stuff is my style. I am jeans and T-shirts, hoodies and Converse. Comfortable, that's me. But today, like at the courthouse over a month ago, I'll go back to playing a part. All white cotton-tucked, black slacks belted, and leather dress shoes shined to a fault.

After I finish dressing for my role, I comb my fingers through my hair, hair that's grown a lot since getting out of prison. That's right—no more buzz cuts for me. My hair's a little less unruly than usual and, shit, that's good enough.

Downstairs, I grab my keys, then head out to my newest acquisition—a truck I bought following my return to Harmony Creek. She's a beast, not a bitch, a good work truck, a no-frills F-150. Some guy who lives up by the Agway offered it to me for far less than its worth. He needed the money, and I needed something to drive—thanks to the court reinstating my license. Since the deal on the truck was too good to pass up I dipped into some of the money I inherited from my grandmother. The truck is a few years old, and the white paint has a few dings and scratches, but mechanically she's pristine. And that's really all that matters.

I depress the clutch, turn the key. She starts right up. I push the gearshift into reverse and back out of the gravel driveway. There's never much traffic out where I live, so I'm able to back right out onto Cold Springs Lane.

I shift into first and roll up to a stop sign. Still no traffic as I turn left onto the state route that takes you straight into

Harmony Creek central. I live a few miles outside the east boundary of town, where it's all farm-on-farm. Country-styled houses, barns, and, this time of year, endless fields of newly planted corn. Since the church sits directly where country bleeds into town—where the state route becomes Market Street—it's not going to be a long drive. But today I'm in no rush. So I take it slow, shift gears lazily, and focus on savoring this late-spring day.

Being locked up for four years has a way of making you appreciate all the little things you once took for granted. Things like how a slate-gray, rain-promising sky, like the one above me right now, really brings out the emerald green of the low-lying hills in the distance. This is how I imagine a place like Ireland must look every day. It's stunning if you really let yourself see.

I follow the curve of the road and lightning flashes, forking behind a stark red barn in the distance. A light rain begins to fall, and, as I flip on the wipers, two bay mares in a field to my right seek shelter.

This countryside is serene; it takes my breath away. I took all of this for granted for far too long. I didn't know what I had four years ago, what I'd had all along. I used to long to leave, but now I'm just grateful to be back. I missed this place. It's the closest thing to home that I've got.

That's why I'd be crazy to mess things up this early in my return.

So why did I do something so stupid last night?

I don't have an answer to my silent question as I close in on the church. But guilt—the relentless bitch—punches me in the gut and forces me to delve deeper.

Why couldn't I resist temptation? Why was I weak?

But it's like the fucking die was cast the minute Missy leaned over the edge of the bar. An image fills my mind, one of her low-cut red top. It left little to the imagination. So I took a chance. But nobody warned me that the die was loaded. I should have suspected. I should have turned away. Hell, I should have paid my tab, gotten up, and left. But I did none of those things.

Instead, I stayed.

I blame my poor decision a little on being caught off guard. Last night Missy looked vastly different from how she looks in church. Her dishwater blonde hair, usually up in one of those fancy twist things, hung all loose and tumbling down her back. In addition to the cleavage-bearing top that started it all, Missy had on a very short skirt, showing off her tall, thin legs. And she was wearing a *lot* of makeup. Missy is the same age as me—twenty-four—but with all the heavy, dark shit she'd caked around her eyes she looked a lot older. Not that it was bad necessarily. She looked good, I guess, different.

I have to admit her sultry appearance piqued my interest, in a purely lust-filled way. Still, I didn't want to start something up with Missy, and I knew that's what she was looking for. We'd never messed around in the past, even though she was the kind of girl—easy—I often went for back in the day.

But the last thing I need is to get sucked back into *that* lifestyle, which is why sticking around last night turned out to be such a huge mistake.

But it started out innocently enough—

No wait, who am I kidding? It started out dirty and it got downright filthy. Not immediately, though.

After Missy was done flaunting her cleavage in my face, I nodded a curt hello and took a bite of my burger. *Maybe she'll catch the hint and leave me alone*, I remember thinking. Of course, that didn't happen.

Missy sat down on the bar stool beside me, adjusted her skirt, and popped open her purse. She pulled out some makeup thing and proceeded to slowly apply another coat of the glittery shit that was already pretty much plastered on her lips.

"Mmm," she hummed, smacking her sparkling lips together. "I was hoping I'd run into someone interesting tonight. It's good to see you somewhere other than church, Chase. So, how are you adjusting to, uh, life after..." She trailed off, leaving her face in a frown.

"Prison?" I snapped, finishing what she obviously couldn't say. "It's okay to say prison, Missy. I won't get mad and bite."

I guess that was kind of a lie, since I'd done just that. And Missy made sure I knew it.

With an exaggerated sniffle and a pout, she muttered, "Jeez, I was just trying to be polite about it. I was hoping I'd think of a nice word for prison."

I almost choked on my beer. "Don't bother," I shot back. "There's nothing *nice* about prison."

So I was being kind of a dick, but I just wanted Missy to leave. No such luck. The head of the bake committee's indignation was matched only by her blatant attempt to draw my attention back to her huge tits. It pretty much worked too. But the more I saw of those enormous things the more convinced I became they were fake. No way could someone so skinny have tits that big.

Missy crossed her arms across her chest, not to hide, but to emphasize. She leaned forward and feigned a pout. "I think you at least owe me a drink for being so harsh, Chase Gartner."

Harsh? *Oh, please.*

But lest I sound *harsh*, I muttered a soft and tender "sure," while I signaled the bartender to bring another beer for me and one of whatever frothy-shit drink Missy was imbibing.

My T-shirt sleeve rode up when I raised my right arm, thus exposing a tat I had inked in prison—the number 72. Missy's heavily lined eyes zoomed in on my bicep, like a laser beam. She squinted and pursed her lips.

Let her look, I thought.

I was just thankful it wasn't the words that reminded me of the last night with my father that had drawn her attention. Those words are inked around my left bicep, not my right.

The 72, though, sure had captured Missy's attention. She stared and stared. I had a feeling she'd muster up the nerve and ask me what the meaning was behind the number. I wasn't about to tell her the number seventy-two is an homage, of sorts, to the cell block I called home for four long years. I had the seventy-two tattoo done shortly before I left prison. It was like that place had gotten so into me that I needed a permanent reminder. And there was a guy there who did some really nice work. He'd done another piece for me back when I'd first been incarcerated.

That early ink was just a revision of the wings on my back. The wings now rain feathers—just a few—down and around the angel. A couple feathers fall all the way to my lower back. The falling feathers are there to remind me every day that *my* wings are damaged and broken.

Sorry, Dad, I'll never soar.

I don't make it a habit to discuss the meaning behind my tats with anyone. Ever. The number, the words, the angel, the wings, the falling feathers—these are mine, all mine. I hold the meanings behind each piece close to my heart. And I sure as shit don't ever plan on sharing *any* of it with the head of some fucking bake committee.

Missy must have felt my angry gaze boring into her last night, as I thought these same exact things. She wisely diverted her eyes away from my bicep and asked no more questions, choosing instead to focus on the rest of me.

"You have an amazing body, Chase," she cooed, switching up her pick-up strategy. "Look at you." She squeezed my shoulder as her eyes traveled over my back, then returned to my chest. "Don't you look and feel all hard and ripped. Wow, you must work out. Like, a lot."

It was a lame come-on, and I'd heard it before, so I mumbled "whatever," while I turned my head to roll my eyes. Mercifully, the arrival of our drinks brought an end to that line of conversation.

As we drank, Missy switched gears yet again and began to go on and on about the church, singing the praises of Father Maridale. In that assessment, I had no argument. The kindly priest with the shock of white hair who shepherds the flock at Holy Trinity is giving me a chance, something no one else was willing to do.

Father Maridale knew my grandmother for over thirty years, and during the past few, while I was in prison, she must've somehow convinced him I wasn't a completely lost cause. How she did it, I'll never know. But I know Gram never stopped believing in me...even after I let her down... time and time again. If only she had lived long enough to see me walk out of those prison gates, two years earlier than I was supposed to. That would have made her happy, joyous even, especially since it was my mother who made it all happen.

Yeah, that's right. My mother, who'd given up on me six years earlier, finally came through in the end. I know part of it was because Abby had finally hit the jackpot, but I like to think she helped me because she loves me, despite the fact we still butt heads.

Anyway, my mother didn't come into all her newly found wealth at some casino. Nope, not even with all that trying. Remember, the house always wins in the end. But the house had nothing to do with my mother's fortunes. It was steady boyfriend number eight, a man named Greg, who turned out to be Mom's winning ticket. And, in a way, I guess he ended up being mine too.

See, Greg has a ton of cash, and for my mother he was willing to share, especially after they got married. A week to the day after steady boyfriend number eight became husband number two my mother hired a big-shot attorney. She called me up, told me about him, and said he was going to get me out of prison. I thought she was bluffing, a true Vegas gal. But, to my surprise, she was telling the truth.

The attorney she hired was good, and he got right to work. His strategy was to appeal to the governor and convince the court I'd been deprived of due process. Mr. Big Shot Attorney came to see me in prison the day after I talked to Mom. He arrived armed with a stack of legal pads and enough righteous indignation for the both of us.

He asked a shitload of questions…

Was I ever read my rights? *I didn't recall.*

Did the court-appointed psychiatrists overprescribe medications, turning me into a zombie who had no way of comprehending the charges I so willingly pled to? *Yeah, pretty much.*

And that was just the start.

I never would have expected it, but Mr. Big Shot Attorney turned out to be not just a good lawyer, but also a good guy. I slowly grew to trust him. When the time came, he argued my case before the judge, insisting I'd been railroaded. He spread out all the documentation, presented the evidence. He was nothing if not thorough. And when all was said and done, the judge agreed. My six-year sentence was commuted to time served. I couldn't believe it. I was a free man. Finally, I could go home. Unfortunately, I had no home to go to.

I'd already decided—even before I was released—if I got out of prison I wasn't going back to Vegas. There were just too many memories there, most of them bad, some of them sadder than fuck. So no, I had no desire to return to the town that had broken me.

My mother, who had no idea I'd already made up my mind, gently suggested I give Vegas another try on the day she visited with my brother. It was the morning of my court date.

At the courthouse, while we all waited in a holding cell in the courthouse, she said, "We have a big house out there in the desert, Chase. There's plenty of space. I can decorate a room for you any way you'd like."

It was a sweet sentiment, but it was about seven years too late. I had needed a mom who was interested in stuff like decorating and taking care of her wayward son right after Dad died. But what can you do? Mom was more into gambling, not nurturing, back then.

I didn't go into my real reasons for not wanting to go back to Sin City. I just told Mom, "Thanks, but no thanks."

It was ultimately Greg's home she was inviting me into, and her new husband had already done enough for me. Despite all we'd been through over the years, it was still great seeing my mother. She may piss me off, but I'll always love her. She looked so fantastic at the courthouse that day, healthy and together, no more vices. No more gambling, no more smoking. Although I could have sworn I smelled smoke on her clothes. But Greg had definitely gotten her help for her gambling addiction, and she assured me she'd stopped going to the casinos months ago.

I begrudgingly conceded to her that Greg was an okay dude, better than all the rest of the guys who had never cared what my mother did in her spare time. I guess I missed my mom more than I'd realized. I actually got a little misty-eyed when I first saw her that day at the courthouse. Maybe she missed me too. Lord knows she sure held on to me for a small eternity when I gave her a hug.

"I love you, Chase," she told me in a strangled voice as she struggled to hold back tears. "I'm so sorry all this happened to you, baby. I wish we could go back in time. I'd do things so differently."

No, you wouldn't, I thought.

But it didn't matter, and it doesn't now either. And though I couldn't say it back that morning, I think she knows I love her. She is my mother, after all. She's far from perfect, but she's the only parent I have left. And I've lost too much time these past few years to waste any more of it being bitter.

Will, who'd accompanied Mom to the courthouse, stood quietly in the corner of the holding cell that day, eyeing me warily throughout the whole exchange with our mom. I couldn't believe how tall he'd gotten. But he is almost fifteen now. He's a good-looking kid, favors Mom a lot. His hair is dark blond, same shade as hers. His eyes are also the same vivid green. A color that never fails to remind me of freshly unfurled spring leaves.

"Give your brother a hug, Will," my mom said when she was finally done hugging me.

"Do I have to?" he asked, hurt and betrayal evident behind the hard stare he leveled my way.

"Of course not, buddy," I cut in, not wanting to push.

The look of venom I received in return cut to the quick. "I am *not* your buddy," Will hissed, "not anymore. Not ever again."

Fuck, his words hurt like hell, still do. But he has every reason to hate me. I let my baby brother down. I disappointed a kid who once looked up to me like I was some kind of a hero. I am no hero, that's for sure. It seems the only thing I excel in is disappointing the ones I love. Yet another reason why I knew that day that Vegas was most definitely out.

I wasn't sure where I was going to go once I was released. I feared freedom would yoke me in the same way as prison. But then I got word that when my grandmother had died she left me the farmhouse out on Cold Springs Lane, all the property too, and even a little bit of money. Grandma Gartner accomplished in death what she had strived to do in life—she saved my ass. And that in and of itself would have been enough, but she'd also miraculously managed to convince Father Maridale—probably as a dying wish—to have mercy on me.

Father Maridale came to see me the day I was released, once everything was official and I was truly free. He urged me to come home to Harmony Creek and move back into the farmhouse. It didn't take too much convincing, I'd just found out the house now belonged to me.

I guess I could have sold it and moved anywhere. I may have chosen that path in the past. But when I considered it, for a few brief seconds, it just didn't feel right. I hadn't seen the farmhouse in almost four years, but all I could do was sit and wonder if the frame exterior was still the same antique white color I'd painted it one September. Would the shutters still be blue, blue as a country twilight sky? I needed to know, it seemed more than important. Everything in my soul told me it was time to go back.

I did have a home, and it was time to go to it.

Father Maridale must have seen in my eyes that I was going home to Harmony Creek. He immediately offered me a job with the church, painting, fixing things, taking care of some carpentry work. "Can you do that kind of stuff?" he asked.

I nodded.

"The school needs a lot of work too," he continued. "And summer will be here soon. The school is right next to the church, maybe you remember?" I didn't have time to answer; he kept right on going, seemingly thrilled to have someone get started as soon as possible. "Another month and the kids will be on break. You can start over there then. A lot of the rooms need painting, and there's stuff in the gymnasium that needs repairing, too. But until June gets here there's plenty to keep you busy at the church and in the rectory."

My grandmother must have told Father Maridale about my sketches, because he asked to see my work. I was afraid to show him at first, knowing that what my sketchbook contained was a reflection of my life in prison, and the terrible things I'd seen. Needless to say, none of the drawings were virtuous…or particularly clean.

I sketched things like charcoal renderings of bloodied men, beaten inmates, examples of how power is exerted in prison. There's one particularly detailed drawing in my sketchbook of a broken man lying on the floor of his cell, his bones are jutting through his skin. He's in pain and close to dying. His cell mate stands at the bars, smoking a cigarette, indifferent. It's a depiction of something that really happened, something I actually witnessed.

There's another sketch in my book, done in oil pastels. It's of an inmate shooting up. The soft, muted colors contrast so perfectly with the vulgarity of the subject matter. It's more than just a picture of a man jamming a needle into his vein. I saw scenes like that every day, so with this sketch I took artistic liberties.

The cell walls around this chemically blissed-out inmate are peeling back, revealing five beautiful angels with halos and harps. But the angels are naked, their poses pornographic. And the caption, scrolled on a cloud, reads: *simply heaven.*

I fully expected Father Maridale to throw the sketchbook in my face and condemn me to hell. Rescind his job offer, for sure.

But he did none of those things. Instead, he told me I had a gift from God. He said art was subjective, so he'd not offer an opinion on the subject matter. But he did say he'd prefer to see me use my talent to do things like touch up the Holy Trinity fresco in the church, and maybe paint a nice mural over in the school.

"But nothing like that," he joked, nodding to the sketchbook as he handed it back.

"Of course not, Father," I replied, appalled he'd even joke about such a thing.

He asked me again if I wanted the job, and this time I said, "Yes, absolutely. I promise you I'll give it my best shot."

I then thanked him for giving me a chance.

"Don't disappoint me," he warned when he stood to leave.

"I won't."

They say you can't go home again, but here I am. Back where I started. Oh, and the farmhouse, you may ask. It's still antique white. The shutters? Still country twilight blue. When I first walked up the wide porch steps, four years of my life gone forever, it took everything I had to hold it together. *Never again,* I thought. Now that I'm out—devouring every day and feasting on freedom—I can never go back. I would die first. And that's why keeping my life on track is so fucking important.

The rain picks up as I round a bend, the truck swings out. I slow it down a bit. All this reminiscing has me pressing my foot to the gas, harder than necessary.

The stone bell tower and the wooden cross atop the slate steeple of the church come into view. I've almost reached my destination.

As I turn the wipers up a notch, my heart rate increases, in tandem with the blades. *Swish, swish. Beat, beat.* Along with my in-synch heart rate, images from last night start to flip through my head, like grainy cells of film.

Missy's hand migrating to my thigh...*flip*...

Missy slowly turning toward me, smiling like the proverbial fox in a henhouse...*flip*...

And then I see why.

Missy, the devil in disguise, tilts her open purse my way...*flip*...

I see what she wants to me to see. How can I miss it? A little plastic packet nestled in the bottom, half-filled with white powder...*fucking flip*...

"Want some?" Missy asked, nodding to the cocaine in her bag.

That shit still calls to me—and last night was no exception—even though I haven't touched it in years. But if I do it once it will only lead to more. There is nothing to stop me. I don't know if any of my new reasons for being are strong enough to quell the demon that lurks just underneath, waiting. I can't let that monster loose, not ever again.

I scrubbed my hand down my face. *Get it together, Chase,* I said to myself.

To Missy, I said, "It's probably not a good idea."

"Suit yourself," she replied with a shrug, snapping her bag shut and wiping at her nose.

Missy leaned in close. She slid her hand up my thigh, and whispered, "A bad boy like you..." She squeezed and trailed higher. "I thought you'd be more fun."

I chuckled a little and lifted my beer. "Sorry to disappoint," I muttered into the neck of the bottle.

With one hand closing in on my cock, Missy used her other hand to take the straw out of her drink. She licked it suggestively. "The night's not over yet, Chase," she purred, tapping the straw against her lower lip.

Drugs were out, but Missy was clearly offering something I *could* indulge in. It had been a long time since I'd been with a woman. The guards would occasionally sneak prostitutes in, and for the right price you could spend twenty minutes in a locked visitation room with one. The public has no idea of the intricate bartering system that exists in every correctional facility across the land. There's always a black market where you can obtain almost anything you desire, and the prison I was in was no exception. Almost anything can be bought or sold, and everyone has a price. During the time I served I tried to limit my interactions with the women of the night, but a man has needs. So I occasionally paid the going rate for a condom and a blow job. And sometimes, when head just wasn't enough, I bought a condom and a fuck.

The lure of the coke in Missy's bag had left me edgy; I needed some kind of a release. And she was obviously more than willing.

Missy's glass was empty, so I tipped back my beer,

drank down the rest. "You want to get out of here?" I asked, setting the empty bottle back on the bar.

She nodded and her smile widened. I threw a few bills on the bar, then steered Missy through the crowd to the employee exit in the back.

"Should we stop in there?" she asked, jerking her chin in the direction of the restrooms.

I didn't have any protection on me—and apparently neither did she—but I wasn't sure if I really wanted to stick my dick in Missy Metzger anyway. Those glitter-coated lips promised to be more than enough for me, so I shook my head and continued to the door.

But then, when we stepped out into the alley, I almost called the whole thing off. Nasty-smelling drain water dripped by the door, and the alley itself was a noxious mixture of piss and vomit.

Why am I doing this? I wondered.

But then Missy put her hand on my crotch and started rubbing my dick through my jeans. Seedy surroundings were all but forgotten.

Snaking a hand up under my T-shirt, Missy scraped her nails across my abs. "Damn, Chase," she squealed, bouncing up and down on her heels. "You feel *so* good. I can't believe we're doing this."

Believe it, sweetheart. I rolled her top up until the material bunched over her hot pink bra. I skimmed my hands back down her chest, grazing nipples through sheer. Light, so light, I touched her softly, but then I reminded myself Missy wasn't a fragile kind of girl, like Hot Chick seemed to be. So I changed it up—grasping and pinching her flesh, and handling her roughly as I whispered filthy things in her ear.

Missy trembled against me, like she was enjoying what I was doing and loving the things I was saying.

"Yes, Chase, yeah," she moaned, dragging my hand down to panties that were already soaked through. "Please..."

My hand hovered. "Please what, Missy?"

She moaned and quickly shoved the damp material aside. "Touch me," she begged.

But I had other ideas. I told her to touch herself instead and let me watch. She did as I asked, and I eventually joined her. Missy got fucked with four fingers—two of hers and two of mine—until she came.

She collapsed against me after her release, breathing heavily. Once she recovered, she tried to kiss me. I had no desire to comply, but I begrudgingly allowed her lips to pass over mine so I didn't come off as a total prick.

But when I tried to turn my head covertly she caught my lower lip with her teeth and bit down lightly. "Don't move," she whispered, giggling.

I figured the best way to keep her from kissing me was to get her off again. Since my fingers were still in her pussy, I started jacking her off. She'd removed her own fingers so I added more of my own. Missy's breathing quickened as she groaned and grunted, soaking my whole hand. Within minutes, I felt her spasm once more.

I removed my hand from Missy's crotch. Her face was still near mine and she tried to kiss me again. This time, I allowed her, which was probably a mistake, since I immediately tasted something bitter.

Fuck.

I knew right away what that chemical taste was—residue from the cocaine she'd snorted earlier. And sick as it was that bitterness made me crave the coke I knew she had in her bag. I suddenly wanted white powder more than I wanted any part of Missy's body.

A long-dormant voice in my head piped up, *she's already offered to share. I'm sure the offer still stands, especially since you just got her off…twice. Ask her, ask her, go ahead and ask her now.*

But no, just no, I needed to get the fuck away from temptation.

I buried my face in Missy's neck to escape her lips, her coke-tainted mouth. But still, all I could think about was that white powder, and how it used to make me feel—invincible, uncaring, an attitude of fuck the world.

What would one little bump hurt?

Maybe a little more would even be okay. Maybe it'd be enough to stop caring about the past four years and the things I've done. Hell, maybe it'd be enough to stop caring about judgmental people staring back at you; maybe it'd be enough to forget about a brother who hates you so much that he can't remember he used to love you more than life itself.

So, yeah, I opened my mouth, intent on asking for something that could take away the pain. Or at least mute it.

But then I remembered how quickly things can spiral out of control, how one little bump often leads to one big, fat line. More and more, since one is never, ever enough, either.

Everyone has a dark side, but mine has the power to consume me. You hear about not starting down a certain path, and maybe you wonder what exactly that shit means.

I used to myself, wonder, that is, once upon a time. But now I know. I've been there, done that.

And here's exactly how it goes…

The path is dark, black and twisting, the unknown.

But it's also alluring. It beckons your soul.

It calls to you, whispering seductively.

It's good at convincing, so you take one tentative step.

You hold your breath and wait and wait for the world to fall apart.

But nothing happens.

In fact, it feels kind of good to say, "Fuck it. Who cares?"

Scream it, the path whispers. So you do.

And then you push further…you take another step… then another.

Still cool, baby, see? And don't you feel good?

Sure you do. You feel fucking invincible.

So what the hell, what's one more? Make that a few more.

And then…

The fucking bottom falls out.

And, shit, you're tumbling down hills, crashing into boulders, searching for something—anything—to grab on to.

But you're on your own, baby. It was all one big lie.

And you fall.

Down, down low, until you wake up.

And when you do you're battered and bloodied at the bottom, surrounded by rubble from the destruction you wrought.

Your life—that shit's completely ruined.

And there I was last night, about to walk right off the edge…again.

That was me as I felt for the wall behind me, leaned back against the bricks, and closed my eyes. I just wanted to get out of that shitty alley, away from the fucking demon in Missy's purse, away from Missy.

But she misunderstood my sudden reversal. "If you're feeling sick or something, I can just blow you," she stated matter-of-factly.

Jesus.

I had every intention of stopping her, but then she dropped to her knees and popped the button on my jeans. *Zip-p-p.* What can I say? I'd spent the last of my resolve on denying myself the drugs, I didn't have it in me to deny anymore. So I let Missy do her thing.

And, fuck, her thing was pretty damn good, so good in fact that I seriously considered getting back to pleasing her some more. But the selfish, dark part of me had taken over, and I just didn't care enough to bother. Not that Missy seemed to mind. She let me smooth back her hair and fuck her mouth hard and thoroughly.

I told her how much I liked what she was doing, how good it felt. In response, she tried her damnedest to take all of me in, which is never an easy task for most girls. I was impressed with Missy's effort, but I could see it was a struggle for her. I finally took pity on her and gave her a break. I went a little slower, not as deep, just an easy in and out.

"There, that's it," I said softly when she found a rhythm and slowly took in more and more.

Her top was still pushed up above her bra, so I reached down and tugged at hot pink sheer until her breasts spilled over the top. Missy rose slightly so I could more easily grope and caress her soft mounds—real, after all—while she deep-throated me until I was finished.

Shit.

I turn into the church parking lot and shut the memories from last night the fuck down. I park, yank the emergency brake up, rake my fingers through my hair. *Shit, shit, shit.* What the hell was I thinking? I work for this church now, I can't avoid Missy forever. If she blabs that I was with her and she had cocaine, I know what everyone will think. They'll think I've gone right back to my old ways. Hell, they'll probably think I supplied her.

But why would Missy say anything to anyone? I'm sure her drug use is a secret. And I seriously doubt she plans on broadcasting what happened between us in that disgusting alley any more than I do.

So, I take a breath, then another. Yeah, everything might turn out okay. This secret should be safe.

I glance around.

Mass ended a while ago; everyone is gone. The lot is empty, except for one car, a blue Neon with faded paint that looks a little worse for wear. I don't know who it belongs to, but I know it's not Missy's. I was enough of a gentleman last night to walk her to her car. Although I think she was pissed I didn't ask for her number. Oh, well. Like I said before, what happened between us was a one-time deal.

The rain, though lighter than before, continues to fall. Hell, it's as good of an excuse as any to hang out in the lot for a while longer. But I can't kid myself. I just don't want to face Father Maridale quite yet. I know he'll ask why I missed Mass this morning. Guess I'll tell him I forgot to set my alarm. It's no lie. I just won't be relaying the reason why I was too tired to remember.

I slouch down in my seat, flip the radio on. An Imagine Dragons tune comes through the speakers. I like this song, a lot, so I turn up the volume. The music soothes my mind, and I start to feel better, more relaxed.

As if the weather is in synch with my brightening mood, the rain suddenly stops.

Perfect.

The sun comes out and this really good feeling washes over me, like maybe today is some kind of a new start.

Getting out of the truck, I think, *bring it on.* I am more than ready for whatever this new life of mine may have in store.

CHAPTER TWO

KAY

"Number one, you loved the color purple. Number two, you couldn't sleep unless you were holding Peetie." My voice breaks as I hold tight to a stuffed bunny with bent and floppy ears—Peetie.

I'd planned to leave him here—at the grave—but I just can't bring myself to do it. *Her* hands were the last to have touched him, that's why he's missing a nose. And there's this faint hint of red on his tummy, from cherry Kool-Aid-stained-lip kisses.

Her kisses, Sarah's kisses.

What if I leave Peetie here and someone steals him? What if he becomes ruined from the rain, faded beyond recognition from the beating sun? This stuffed bunny is one of the few reminders I have left of my little sister. So, no, I won't take a chance and lose Peetie too.

I gingerly stuff the worn fawn rabbit back into a hobo-style bag that's big enough to hold his plushy body, as well as all the other crap I keep in there.

Clearing my throat, I turn back to the grave, and say, "Number three. I was always Kay-bear, never Kay."

A single tear falls. *God, why does it still hurt so much?*

The dark veil of clouds that have been threatening to let loose since the conclusion of Mass finally do so, and a fine mist of raindrops begins to accumulate on the granite marker before me. I pull the cotton candy pink sleeve of the cardigan I'm wearing down over my hand and blot away the moisture from a name carved in stone—Sarah Stanton.

"Sorry, sweetie," I say. And I am sorry, so very, very sorry.

I should go—before the rain picks up—but I just can't seem to move.

Visiting this grave week after week, recalling and reciting three things about my little sister—lingering when I should leave—these are all parts of my Sunday ritual. One I've done for almost four years now. And today is no different.

I must never forget the things I relay to my baby girl each week, which is why later I'll write in a journal the things I've just said: Sarah loved the color purple, couldn't sleep without Peetie, and never called me Kay.

Using short phrases such as these, I've filled four notebooks in four years' time. Last week I bought a fifth. The new one has a shiny purple cover and a glitter heart etched in the center. Purple, Sarah's favorite color. Never forget, right?

I hate how time has a way of blurring the memories, easing the guilt. I deserve to suffer. My grief anchors me to my guilt. Or maybe it's the other way around. Probably both, a never-ending circle. In any case, I rarely miss a Sunday visit to this little cemetery behind Holy Trinity Church.

And the routine—like a song—remains the same...

Following Mass, I exit through propped-open doors—heavy oak and painted red. A few steps down and I say good-bye to Missy Metzger and her mom, but not before being roped into promising to help out with whatever church fundraiser is coming up. Missy is the head of the bake committee, and her mom runs just about everything else. Seems like there's always talk of cakes and cookies, and changes to be made on the church activities calendar. This week it's sugar and spice and a cancelled picnic. I nod and smile, then slip away to the right and out of sight.

I catch my breath as I meander along the gentle curve of a stone pathway that leads to the back of the church. The cemetery is the first thing you come to. The rectory is back here too, but way off to the right. There's a low gate made of iron marking the entrance to the cemetery. It's deeply embedded in the ground, standing forever crooked and ajar. I always stop here and send up a silent (and selfish) prayer to be left alone, although there's never any need. No one ever bothers me back here.

Most of the parishioners have witnessed enough of my routine at one time or another to know how much it means to me. Consequently, they tend to give me lots of space. I guess they feel bad. Yet another benefit reaped from when others feel sorrow for you.

The irony is that I don't deserve their compassion, not an ounce of their sympathy. What they believe about me isn't true. But only God and two other people (besides me) know the real reason why my little sister was left alone that night, why she ended up in a granite-marked grave behind a crooked and perpetually ajar iron gate.

These are usually my thoughts as I stand at the graveyard entrance. They certainly were today, as I hemmed and hawed and chewed at my lip. But finally—with a heart laden with guilt—I walked down the well-worn path, snaked past the graves, turned left where Jonas O'Neill has been resting in (hopefully) eternal piece for close to a century, and then continued to the very back.

I slowed, as I always do, when I reached the section where the wind chimes, the stuffed bears, and a rabbit that looks just like Peetie all reside. Gifts laid before the feet of children who will never know what their loved ones have brought them. *These* children will never hear the soft tinkling of the wind chimes tied in the trees, never hold the soft and furry animals close to their hearts. Because their little hearts no longer beat with life.

Still, the living persists and stuffed toys are placed and replaced. Most rest against, or on, the small markers. As time passes, the gifts tumble over. Some just go missing completely, which is why I can't leave Peetie. As I look to the sky, I touch my purse and pat the stuffed bunny-shaped lump through the material.

I lower my eyes and stare at the wide trunk of an old oak that's right in front of Sarah's grave. I like to imagine the tall, gnarled tree is a guardian of sorts, watching over all the little children whose lives have been cut short, for reasons known only to God.

I don't know. It's a nice thought and all, but, when it comes right down to it, I know the oak is just an oak, no different from any other tree. I shift in my kneeling position and adjust the hem of the floral dress I'm wearing today. I don't want the fabric to get wedged under my knees and end up soiled. While I strive to keep rose-print-on-linen clean, my bare knees sink another inch into the soggy ground.

I glance up into the branches of the old oak. Even through

the kaleidoscope of leaves, the darkening sky threatens. Things are about to get a lot soggier in a few more minutes.

Okay, maybe sooner…

The rain begins to fall. The bushy canopy of leaves above me provides a modicum of shelter, but cold, fat raindrops still anoint my head.

It's just a passing shower, but judging from the color of the sky it looks as if things will worsen before they get better. Still, I don't want to leave quite yet. I know I should go, I've lingered long enough, but I have nothing really to do, no reason not to stay.

There are no tasks this day to fill my afternoon.

I teach first grade at the parochial school next door, and Sunday afternoons are usually spent preparing for the week ahead. But with the ring of the final bell this past Friday, the start of summer break was signaled. That means, this week, there are no assignments to grade, no lessons to plan, no fun projects to throw together, nothing. And there won't be till fall.

How very unfortunate for me, since my Sunday tasks usually keep me busy, busy. So busy in fact that I've barely had time to pay any heed to the run-down basement apartment I call home. Today, though, with nothing to distract me, I fear my crummy living conditions may very well swallow me up, until I find myself in the belly of despair, faced with no choice but to acknowledge just how pitiful my living arrangements really are.

So, yeah, I am in no hurry to go home.

I shift again and lower my gaze to the ground. The grass all around me is so incredibly lush and so very, very green, thanks to all the rain. In this emerald sea of blades, a clump of wild violets captures my attention. The tiny flowers are within arm's reach. I lean to my right and carefully pluck six—one for each year of my baby sister's too-short life.

I bind the stems together with a skinny blade of grass and place the mini bouquet at the base of the headstone. I whisper once more, "You loved the color purple."

The fine mist turns to a steady drizzle. I need to seek shelter if I plan to stick around and not get soaked. I rise to my feet, smooth out the wrinkles in my dress, and straighten my sweater. A breeze kicks up and I cross my arms. I know there's a small covered bench on the other side of the cemetery. I've sat there a few times when the weather has turned inclement like this.

The rain picks up even more, hurrying me along. I snatch my bag up off the ground, spin around, and take off at a full sprint. Thank goodness for flats. I outrun the worst of the downpour, but by the time I plop down on the bench—thankful to be sheltered from the elements—my cardigan is damp and my ballet flats are soaked.

I kick the squishy shoes off, and bring my legs up until my dress shrouds almost every inch of bare skin. The cemetery is peaceful and quiet, especially with the falling rain. I close my eyes, listen to the pat-pat-patter on the wooden roof above me, and think about my life.

With no class to teach, the next three months threaten to be lonely and long. I have no real friends. Maybe Missy, but it's not like we're particularly close. Apart from church-related things, we don't spend much time together.

It's not Missy's fault, not really. The blame rests with me. I always decline when she asks me to go places with her, places like the Anchor Inn, a local bar in town.

"We'll have so much fun, Kay," she usually says. "Come on-n-n. Maybe you'll meet a cute guy. God, when's the last time you even had a date?" An up-and-down appraisal always accompanies her words, along with a look of pity.

"You're actually kind of pretty, Kay."—*gee, thanks,* I think, but don't say—"You should reconsider. You just never know who you might run into at the Anchor Inn."

Maybe she's right, and maybe one of these days I'll take her up on her offer. Then again, maybe not. I haven't had much luck with men, and I don't foresee any change in the future.

I sigh and toy with my sweater sleeve. It's sad really. Not much gives me joy.

Well, maybe teaching. That I love. I've only been doing it a year, but I enjoy it immensely. Far more than I ever thought I would back when I was taking education classes at college. But the kids are so amazing. They've won me over.

It saddens me to think I won't be seeing the children that brightened my days until fall. Such a long ways away. Sure, I'll probably run into a few kids around Harmony Creek, when they're out with their parents. But I know I'll miss the day-to-day interactions, some of which resulted in little joys I never would have expected. Such as Timmy's silly-happy grin when he hears we're starting a new art project or Hanna's beaming face when she receives a gold star on a particularly tough math worksheet. And then there's Colton's palpable sense of accomplishment when he's able to read an entire paragraph out loud to the class with not one mistake. That warms my heart beyond belief. Just remembering all of these special moments brings a smile to my lips.

I guess it's fairly obvious my whole life is wrapped up in the church and the school. But it's really all I have. That's why I pray the day never comes when Father Maridale pulls me aside and tells me the church can no longer afford to keep me. And it could happen. I'm the newest hire, and enrollment at Holy Trinity is down, more so than last year. There's less and less money coming in. I worry not just for my own job security, but for the future of the school in general. Goodness knows the building itself is in dire need of repairs. The red brick exterior is holding up well, but the inside is a mess—dull linoleum floors, burned-out lighting, peeling and scuffed paint on the classroom walls. It's sad, really.

There's a little bit of money set aside—that's what Father Maridale tells me—but it's not enough to hire workers with the kind of skills required. That's why I was *so* thrilled when Father pulled me aside a few weeks ago and said he'd found someone who could fix up the school at a fair price.

First, I was worried this prospective employee would do a shoddy job, seeing as he was willing to work so cheaply. But then Father told me this guy was more than qualified.

I couldn't believe our good fortune that day. I clapped my hands excitedly and just about gave the leader of our parish a hug. But then Father Maridale told me whom he'd hired, and I froze, wondering if maybe Father was exhibiting early signs of senility.

"You're kidding, right? Chase Gartner? No way."

I was floored. Didn't Father know this guy's past?

"Do you really think it's a good idea to allow him to work alone in the church?" I pressed. "Not to mention in the school."

I know who Chase Gartner is; everybody in this town knows. And just because he shows up in church every week now that he's out of prison doesn't mean he's changed or reformed.

When I said pretty much this exact thing to Father Maridale, he frowned, and told me Chase was a good guy who deserved a second chance. He chastised me and reminded me that it's our duty to help those in need, not to cast judgment.

That last part sort of shut me up. And struck a nerve. I reconsidered. Father Maridale had a point. After all, at least this Gartner guy paid *his* debt to society. And his offense was just some drug-related thing. Not that drug charges aren't serious, don't get me wrong, but they pale in comparison to the secret I harbor.

Yet I walk around a free woman, garnering everyone's pity, when all along it was my negligence that led to my own sister's demise. I hate it, I hate it. *I* should've been the person sent to prison. Perhaps it would've lessened all this guilt weighing me down now.

But that never happened, and it never will. Everyone just calls it what it was—an accident. I, however, know it's one that could have been avoided.

I close my eyes. It bothers me still, and how could it not? Naïve and stupid, that's what I was, but not anymore. Now, I feel older and wiser, and savvy enough to know to keep my mouth shut, not share secrets with anyone.

Back after Sarah died, I hadn't learned this lesson though. Or maybe I just had a burning desire to confess. Was I seeking punishment? Maybe. More likely, I wanted absolution.

Punishment or absolution, I ended up confessing to my mother what had *really* happened the night Sarah died. She was the only one I told, but I soon discovered going to her was a colossal mistake. I received nothing remotely close to absolution from my mother. She did, though, mete out a punishment, thick and heavy as tar, one that still sticks today.

Upon first hearing my confession, my mother stared vacantly at me for what felt like a small eternity, and then she stepped toward me and slapped me hard. Twice, once on each cheek. My face stung and my ears rang, I wore her marks for days.

After a verbal lashing, she disowned me on the spot and kicked me out of the house. "You were supposed to protect her, Kay," she scream-sobbed, pushing me away when I tried to go to her. "It should've been you." I was too stunned to respond to that lovely comment.

"You don't really mean that, Ruth," my father said, rushing into the room, catching only the tail end of our discussion.

To this day, he remains blissfully unaware of what I was really doing the night Sarah died. My mother has never told him, and neither have I.

Ruth *did* mean every word she said that day, just as I knew she had. Sarah had brought my mother a joy I never could—despite repeatedly trying—and my poor judgment led to it being taken away. Someone had to pay, and that someone was me.

When my father realized my mother truly wanted me out of the house he gave me some money and told me to stay at a motel for a few nights until things cooled down.

Only two days had passed since the funeral and my father said it was my mother's grief talking; he said she'd come around.

That was four years ago and my mother still hasn't spoken to me. Not. One. Word. To say her silence hurts would be an understatement. It doesn't hurt, it shatters. But I've accepted, at twenty-three years of age, that I am truly alone in this world.

The rain pounds at the roof of the shelter and I cover my ears. With my present surroundings muted, I continue to remember the past.

Back then, when everything happened, I was nineteen. I was home for summer break, in between my freshman and sophomore years of college. That few days' stay at the motel turned into four weeks, and then I returned to school—lost, broken, and forgotten.

My parents moved back to Columbus, Ohio, where we had once lived, back when I was a child, back before Sarah was born. To his credit, my dad secretly funneled money to me. He continued to pay for tuition and room and board.

But the day I graduated he cut me off. I skipped commencement. There was no one in attendance to watch me walk across the stage and receive my degree, so it seemed a little pointless. Not to mention embarrassing, seeing as all the other students had their families gathered.

That afternoon, hours after commencement ended, Dad drove in from Columbus—alone—to take me out to lunch. That's when he told me I was on my own financially. To me, it felt like a clean break.

I haven't seen my dad since that day last summer, but he calls once in a while. I've noticed, though, his calls have diminished as the months have passed. I think my dad just feels guilty about all that has happened, how the daughter that still lives and breathes remains cast aside. But, like me, he fears my mother and the wrath she can deliver. I'm sure it's just easier for him to pretend I don't exist. My eyes water thinking about it, but it's yet another thing I've come to accept.

All I can say is thank God for Father Maridale; he's been my unexpected savior. He must have heard through the church grapevine that my new degree was in elementary education, as he offered me a job teaching first grade the very week I graduated, two days after the lunch with my father.

I suspect Father Maridale felt bad for me, seeing as I was on my own, with no job, no sister, and—for all intents and purposes—no family. Born of pity or not, I jumped at the opportunity. The only problem at the time was that school didn't start until September. Didn't matter. I found a job waiting tables at a placed called Pizza House within twenty-four hours.

Pizza House is a restaurant in town that everyone loves. It's big, cheery, and bright, located in an old yellow and green frame house that's considered a Harmony Creek landmark.

I loved the place right from the start. All the employees were friendly and welcoming and made me feel like I was a part of something. I even stayed on for a little while after school started in the fall. But juggling two jobs became a bit too much. I was tired all the time and losing focus. The kids deserved a fully functioning teacher, so I gave up Pizza House.

Money grew tight, but it was the right decision. Though I sometimes consider picking up a shift or two, particularly during the holidays when there are no classes. The manager, Nick, told me the day I left that I could come back at any time. In fact, just last week he reiterated that very same offer. I had stopped in to pick up a pizza to take home and Nick rang me up on the register.

But I'll never go back. I know the offer was made—then and more recently—only because Nick likes me, even after our failed attempt at dating.

Nick asked me out last fall, a week after I quit. I had suspected he was attracted to me, even before he acted on it. He was always smiling and trying to find things for us to talk about. Heck, he even helped me bus tables. And the managers at Pizza House never did things like that.

The day I went in to pick up my final paycheck was the day Nick finally asked me out. He wanted to know if I'd like to see a movie with him sometime.

"Sure," I said, "why not."

Unfortunately, despite my agreeing to go out on a date with him, I wasn't all that interested in starting up a relationship with Nick Mercurio.

He's a cute guy; don't get me wrong. Nick is very nice looking, in fact. Lots of girls like him, I witnessed him getting hit on dozens of times when I was waitressing. And no wonder. He has nice, smooth olive-toned skin, wavy black hair, and soft brown eyes. Not to mention he's sweet as can be, at least he always was to me. But I just wasn't feeling it with Nick. I tried and tried to like him, I did. But like many things in life, it just never took.

Nevertheless, Nick and I went out a few times. Dinners

and movies, chaste kisses at the doorstep. The last time he took me out we decided to mix it up—we went to the Anchor Inn to have a few drinks. I got a little buzzed, purposely, hoping alcohol might loosen me up, make me like Nick even. Maybe Nick was hoping for the same thing, he bought me one drink after the other.

The alcohol ended up having the desired effect—to a point. I don't think it made me genuinely like Nick, but it sure made me hang all over him, surely sending the man all sorts of mixed signals. When we left the bar we ended up in the backseat of his car, making out, hidden away in a dark corner of a lot near the bar.

I hadn't been touched—like, really *touched*—in three years at the time and it felt so *good* to feel wanted. My need for human touch heightened my senses and made me feel drunker than I was. The more Nick touched me, the more I lost myself to lust. So when Nick's hands slid over my breasts, I didn't stop him. When he slowly undid the buttons on my dress until the material gaped open, I didn't stop him. I let him trail his hands over my bra and down my stomach, watched even. And when he slid the hem of my dress up my thighs, I gasped and nodded my assent.

Everything felt good, but unfortunately nothing about Nick's hands on me felt right. So when his knuckles brushed back and forth over my panties, waiting for my go-ahead or refusal, I may have pushed into him a little bit, maybe let his fingers linger on damp cotton for a few extra seconds, but then I did what felt right—I made him stop.

My body wanted more, much more, but my heart didn't. And I'd been in that place before—body wanting something the heart stood indifferent to. I couldn't go down that road again. I couldn't continue on with someone I knew I'd never really care all that deeply for. I'd done it once before and, in that case, wrong begat wrong.

Not surprisingly, that night was my last date with Nick Mercurio. Nick drove me home in awkward silence. He knew it was the end, the end of something that never really got started. Even so, he walked me to my door and gave me a hug. He even persevered for a while longer, asking me out a few times more. But I kept making excuses and he finally gave up.

It's just as well. I'm waiting for a man that leaves me breathless, a man who knocks me off my feet right from the beginning. He's out there, I know it. And when the time is right our paths will cross, probably when I least expect it. I've always heard that's how these things go.

In the meantime, I have other things to focus on, like saving enough money this summer to finally get out of the hellhole in which I currently live.

Sadly, the only apartment I can afford is on the other side of town—the bad side—across the railroad tracks, not far from the closed-down glass factory. The building that houses my basement efficiency is a dingy yellow brick box of a structure. I pay rent month to month, shell out a meager amount of cash for a less-than-meager living space. A single rectangular room, a few pieces of furniture—left behind by former tenants—that's what my money buys.

The centerpiece of the room I call home is a sagging sofa. It smells of decades-old sweat and stale smoke. It's disgusting, I know. I've emptied innumerable bottles of fabric refresher in attempts to freshen the faded material, but the smells remain, which sucks, since the sofa doubles as my bed. That's why I cover the flattened cushions with mounds of sheets. Too bad I can't cover every corner, every nook, every crevice, as the rest of the place is just as bad.

On one side of the room there's a sorry excuse for a kitchen, complete with an oven that quit working a month ago, a refrigerator that hums and rattles all night, and a sink that backs up regularly. The oven gave out—with a hiss and a dying gasp—the last time I made something for one of Missy's bake sales. It remains broken, despite my calls to an indifferent property management company. The tiny bath area is a disaster as well. A plunger by the toilet is a must, and it's a fortunate day indeed when the shower actually runs hot.

But all of those things I could live with, I could and I do. I don't require fancy accommodations. I am far from high-maintenance. But what scares me, chills me to the bone actually, is the increasing number of junkies hanging out in the apartment parking lot. It's gone from bad to worse in the past year. There's no getting around it either; the whole area I live in is just plain bad news.

There used to be a Sparkle Mart grocery store, where I'd buy groceries every week, but it closed down last fall. Too many drug-related robberies, the manager told me the day I stopped in to see why they were moving inventory out instead of in.

That was six months ago.

I mark a steady decay every day I drive by. Someone tagged the side of the building in red and black paint, the name of some gang, I think. Weeds pollute the parking lot, growing right up right through broken cement. Directly next to doors that remain locked shut, a lone shopping cart lies broken on its side. Poison ivy tangles up and around the handle. And signs hang crooked in the few windows that remain unsmashed. Sun-faded and peeling: *pumpkin roll, $4.90, we accept food stamps.* Yeah, right. Not anymore.

I need to get out, I know this. Things are getting worse. The number of junkies congregating in the apartment parking lot has reached an all-time high this summer. I figure as long as I keep turning my head when I pass, they'll continue to ignore me. At least, I hope they do. I just need to hold on a little while longer. Then, I'll be up and out. By fall I should have enough money to move. I'm working extra this summer to ensure that I do.

The church secretary, Connie, is going on an extended cruise with her recently retired husband. Just last week Father Maridale asked me if I could cover her position this summer. A blessing, for sure, one I'd not expected. I'll make more money covering for Connie than I ever could waitressing at Pizza House. And I won't have to see Nick every day, since I always feel bad things didn't work out for us.

But the best part is the money. The church offers a steady wage, and though it's not a heck of a lot, it's more reliable than tips, especially in this shaky economy. I start tomorrow, which is perfect. But it's perfect for one huge reason besides the money.

That reason is Chase Gartner.

I mean, hell, the guy has had free run of the property for weeks. It's high time *someone* starts looking into what he's been up to. I snort as I sit thinking about it. I had hoped to keep tabs on Chase right from the beginning, but it was impossible to do while teaching. Kids require constant supervision; there was no free time. But in my new role as church secretary, I expect things will be far different.

First, the church office is located right inside the entrance to the rectory, centrally located and very convenient. Plus, I've noticed Connie always seems to have lots of downtime, I've caught her gabbing on the phone and doing her nails on a number of occasions. I expect it'll be the same for me, but you won't catch me chatting anyone up, nor will I be doing my nails. Nope, I plan to spend *my* downtime keeping an eye on bad-news Gartner, making sure he doesn't do anything stupid. Like screw up...again. Despite Father Maridale's unwavering belief in him, I am not completely sold on the idea of someone fresh out of prison traipsing around all over the church and school grounds. I mean, really!

Chase Gartner. I shake my head and continue to wait out the rain.

His story sure lit up this town four years ago. The news of his arrest, when it happened, spread like wildfire, along with a lot of *other* stories about the man. There were accounts of hard partying, illicit use of drugs and alcohol, fighting, and, of course, sexual escapades with women. Everyone in Harmony Creek ate those stories up; they devoured the tales of a once good guy gone horribly wrong. Chase was like some kind of beautiful fallen angel, but one with a far from holy reputation.

I hate to admit it, but I must be honest. I was equally enthralled by those stories. I guess Chase Gartner has always held my attention, though I've never met him and I certainly don't trust him, especially now that he's done time in prison. But he certainly is good-looking; I've never been blind to the obvious. And I sure remember the stories from four years ago, as clearly today as back when I first heard them.

Another thing I must confess is this: the stories that fascinated me the most were the ones that dealt with Chase's sexual reputation, the tales of his conquests. Of particular interest was that it seemed being "conquered" by Chase was something to remember.

And how did I find this out?

One day I was in the public library in town, hidden in the stacks, when I overheard two girls whispering. Okay, maybe I was eavesdropping, just a little. In any case, when I heard the name Chase Gartner, my ears perked up immediately. Standing very still, so as not to be discovered, I clutched the paperback I'd been reading, held it to my chest tightly, and listened with rapt attention.

Whispers and squeals abounded, making it difficult to decipher much of what was being said, but it became clear at one point that one of the girls had been *conquered* by Chase, and the other was digging for details. To my delight, Conquered was more than willing to share her recently acquired knowledge with her friend. And with me, of course, though she had no clue I was listening in.

"Being with Chase is something to remember," Conquered gushed to her friend as she giggled and blushed. "In fact, he's definitely ruined me for all other men." She sighed. "No one will ever be able to compare."

Really? I thought.

"Oh God, really?" her friend echoed. "Details, honey, give me the dirt. Like, why? How? What makes *him* so good? And just how good is he?"

Yes, Conquered, just how good is he? My fingers dug into

pages penned by Harper Lee as I almost asked the question out loud.

"It's hard to explain," Conquered said slowly. *Try*, I thought.

"Chase is just so intense, so into what he's doing, he makes you feel, like, *everything.*"

Her friend was speechless, as was I.

And then Conquered added wistfully, "Chase's sex is just crazy-good, there's no other way to put it."

And that was when I dropped my book.

Luckily, both girls were too busy giggling and squealing over Chase's crazy-good sex that they took no notice of my bumbling.

I spent another five minutes just standing there, not bothering to pick up my poor forgotten paperback. I was too busy thinking, thinking about how good this *crazy – good* sex with Chase Gartner could possibly be. Because, Lord knows, I sure wasn't getting anything even close to crazy-good from my boyfriend at the time, Doug Wilson. No surprise there. It was a relationship that never should have happened, a relationship bore out of manipulation, nurtured by deceit and lies, and ending in disaster.

And this is how it all went down…

Once upon a time, my family lived south of Market Street—the very best part of town—three doors down from the respected Wilson family, three doors down from their blond-haired, hazel-eyed son, Doug, who happened to have a good-looking physique, one I'd noticed on occasion. I never pursued anything, even though it would have been easy since our parents had been friends for years. I just wasn't all that interested. There was something off-putting about

Doug Wilson. His nice façade held something more sinister, a dark side perhaps. And not the appealing kind, no. I sensed Doug's dark side was more of a flat-out asshole variety. Thus, I had no burning desire to get to know him. But our mothers had other plans.

Our families were close. Our dads played golf together, and our moms...well they were thicker than thieves. Mrs. Wilson and my mom did Pilates together, and hosted neighborhood parties as a kind of overly peppy team. Those things were harmless, but one day, out of the clear blue, they decided to play matchmaker with their kids, meaning Doug and me.

Pushed together by our insistent mothers, we started dating right before the start of college, freshman year. Our mothers were convinced for some reason that we were destined. The hope was that we'd fall madly in love and marry. I think Mom and Mrs. Wilson just wanted to be tied together forever; they were like some kind of disillusioned long-lost sisters. It was ridiculous and silly, but I played along... for a while.

Doug was okay, at first. I thought maybe I'd misjudged him. One thing, he was very clean-cut, the kind of guy my parents wanted me to end up with. That's why I think I said yes when he asked to be my boyfriend, my first boyfriend.

I soon discovered there were a lot of firsts that went along with that title. Doug and I were each other's firsts for a lot of things, most all of them physical. But sadly, as time wore on, those physical things didn't mean all that much to me. I never grew to love Doug the way our mothers hoped for. I stayed with Doug anyway, out of obligation, out of habit, but mostly to please my mother. And she certainly was pleased, sometimes disturbingly so.

This one time, when I was home from school for spring break, my mother discovered my birth control pills. She'd been snooping around in my room. Doug and I always used condoms, but I was so fearful of being tied to him forever by that point that I'd started the pill as extra protection. Instead of being angry, like I fully expected, my mother was thrilled. She said it was great. It meant we were finally getting serious. I rolled my eyes at her utter cluelessness when she turned away. Unfortunately, finding those pills gave my mother and Mrs. Wilson some kind of green light to start planning the wedding. Yes, the wedding,

"Not for a few more years, mind you," my mother assured me with a patronizing pat to my head. "But there's no such thing as planning too early, you know. You're going to have the best wedding, Kay. We'll make sure of it." She didn't mean herself and me—she meant herself and Mrs. Wilson.

Nothing was sacred when it came to my relationship with Doug. It was me and him, and our meddling mothers. I was downright horrified when my mother ran and told Mrs. Wilson all about the birth control. Doug's mother didn't need to know I was having sex with her son. Ugh, where were the boundaries? My mother respected nothing.

My life spun faster and faster, things felt out of control. I was pleasing everyone but myself, and at my own expense. One morning, in the early days of summer break, after close to a year of dating someone I no longer cared to even be around, I woke up and decided to start leading an honest life. I didn't love Doug, and it was time to tell him…and our mothers.

Unfortunately, when I went downstairs to break the news to my mother first, she showed me the guest list she'd been working on for this down-the-road, in-her-head wedding. I froze, suddenly losing my nerve. How could I fess up and tell her I didn't want to be with her best friend's son a minute longer? I'd shatter my mother's dreams. Were hers more important than my own? Maybe so. They certainly loomed larger in my mind.

I was beginning to feel like I wasn't living my own life anymore, I was living one for my mom. But I was afraid if I stopped pleasing her she'd stop loving me. She was hard like that. Always was and still is, now more than ever. And I was right to fear, her love for me was never freely given.

So, that day, I said nothing to Mom, nothing to Doug. I continued to live a lie. I stayed with someone I knew I'd never love. I think Doug sensed it too. I think he'd known for a while. He'd grown bitter, I could tell, but he stayed with me out of spite. Or maybe he stayed with me for the power it gave him. The dark side I'd sensed in him reared its ugly head. Doug began to take things out on me, he made me do things I didn't want to do. He became pushy and mean. But I was weak, and my weakness led to disaster. Not for Doug, not for me, but for Sarah.

I wish now I'd done things differently, knowing how it all turned out, seeing how my family was torn apart. But it's too late, what's done is done. The biggest irony of the sad and tragic situation is that while my mother won't speak to me, she still has contact with Doug. I may be to blame for what happened to Sarah, but Doug Wilson played a part. I guess not a big enough part to be forsaken by the woman who still calls herself my mother, even though she's not been one to me for four long years.

I wish I'd never found out Mom speaks to Doug. It makes the ache in my heart cut deeper. But I did find out, courtesy of my father and one of our short phone conversations. I think he just slipped up, he told me the day he called that the reason he had some time alone on his hands was because my mom was out, having dinner with Mrs. Wilson and her son. She only has one son, so I knew he meant Doug. See, Doug lives in Columbus these days. My father also let out that when Doug's mother goes into town to see her son my mother usually meets them out for dinner.

The three of them sitting around a table, laughing and smiling, while I sit here paying for all of our mistakes. *Unbelievable.* They can all stay in Columbus for all I care. I'm just thankful Doug doesn't live in Harmony Creek anymore. It's bad enough when I know he's in town visiting his family. During those times, I avoid him at all costs. And, so far, we've yet to cross paths.

The rain comes to a sudden stop and breaks me from my disturbing reverie. A sliver of sun peeks out from behind a cloud. I've spent enough time here today, dwelling on the past.

It's time to move on.

I comb my fingers through my dampened hair and stand. Crazy thing, my hair probably looks better all rain-damp wavy. Not that anyone will see. All the parishioners are gone for the day.

My clothes are dry, but the ballet flats are still a soggy mess. However, I am not about to walk barefoot all the way back to the car, so, with a grimace, I squish the shoes back onto my feet.

The clouds disperse as I make my way out of the cemetery. A bright blue sky is revealed, along with the promise of a beautiful day. *Maybe a new beginning*, I tell myself. By the time I reach the stone pathway the sun is beaming, blindingly so. I detour over the grass terrace and start across the church lot to where my car is parked. But I can't see a thing with the sun glaring in my face.

I lower my head and fumble around in my bag, searching for the pair of knock-off designer sunglasses I bought the other day.

"Where are they?" I mumble to myself, nudging Peetie and pushing aside my hardly-ever-used makeup bag.

I spot the edge of a mirrored lens under the stuffed bunny. *There.* Without ever slowing my pace—or lifting my head—I victoriously lift the sunglasses out of my bag. And at that exact second I plow right into someone. "Oomph," I cough out as I make contact with a broad, muscular chest.

I hear a smooth, male voice say, "Shit, sorry."

At the same time, an ominous crunching noise is heard. *Uh-oh, there goes the sunglasses.*

All this happens in just a few seconds, and I sway a little post-impact. Two sure hands find purchase on either side of my waist, steadying me, keeping me right. What a kind stranger. I glance up—curious to see who this tall, kind man is that I've just wrecked into.

Shit.

I realize two things simultaneously: One, I've just collided with Chase Gartner. And two—dear God—the man is absolutely beautiful up close. Gorgeous, stunning, there are not enough adjectives to adequately expound. He's just wow, just...freakin' *w-o-w.*

I've seen Chase in church recently, sure, but it's always from afar.

Picture me throwing a quick glance to the back from the front pews, Missy squealing in my ear, "See, see, he's hot, right? Oh crap, turn around. He's looking this way."

Yeah, that sort of thing.

And sure, Chase always looks damn fine sitting in those back pews, better than in the pictures the newspapers printed of him when he was arrested. But up close, here and now, I can see the guy is physical perfection personified. I am not exaggerating. He's incredibly nice to look at, so look is what I do. Possibly, I stare.

Chase licks his lips a little, in a kind of hot manner that makes me notice right away how highly kissable his lips happen to be—full, slightly moistened, and ready to go. I'm somewhat mesmerized, but I don't want this man to catch me staring at his kissable lips, so I move on up to his eyes. But his eyes, oh my, they do me in more than the lips. I could get lost in their depths, surely I could. In fact, I kind of do just that.

Chase's eyes are this amazing blue—pale and kind of light, but with flecks of gray around the irises. His eyes hold me captive—like they're a weapon he's wielding—so I christen them gunmetal blue.

His eyes, his lips, his hands on my waist, Chase stirs me up and spins me out. A wanton lust courses through me. I like his hands on my body, I like the way his fingers flex when I remember to breathe. And I really do have to remind myself to take in oxygen. *Breathe, Kay, breathe.*

Forget it.

I quickly discover oxygen is secondary when all you can think about is crazy-good sex, and how this gorgeous man is the one who could give it to you.

I make no effort to extricate myself from his grasp, I don't even move. And why would I? I want Chase's hands to stay on my waist. I want him to squeeze a little tighter, maybe slide a little lower. My pulse is flying as I suck in a gasp of air.

My reactions reveal me, though, I see knowing in those gunmetal blues.

The corner of Chase's mouth turns up in a particularly captivating manner, and it tells me two things: One, this man can read women, and two, he's just read me. All in about a minute. *Damn, he's good.*

But, this isn't me, I remind myself. Why am I thinking these lust-filled thoughts? Why am I checking out *Chase-freaking-Gartner*?

Why, indeed? I planned on keeping an eye on the guy, but certainly not like this.

I start to apologize—for crashing into him, ogling him, I don't know which. But he cuts me off with a softly delivered, "Hey, I really am sorry. Are you okay?" His voice isn't just smooth, it seduces.

But what's got me turned around is that under all that seduction Chase sounds sincere, genuine, like he isn't just asking to ask. And damn if that doesn't make him all the more attractive. I step back. Really, I have to, or God knows what I might do. Grab him and kiss him, run my fingers through his kind of messy tawny-shaded hair. Who knows?

His hands slip from my waist, and though a part of me

instantly misses the heady contact, it's actually for the best. I can finally think clearly. Sort of.

"I'm fine," I begin, my voice all breathy and soft.

What the…

I just shake my head, get a grip, and continue, "Really, I'm the one who should be apologizing. I wrecked into you. It's completely my fault. I was distracted, looking in my bag for these—"

I raise the sunglasses up a little and one of the mirrored lenses pops out. I try to hold it in place, but the lens slips and slides and I have to keep adjusting my fingers so it doesn't fall.

"Um, I guess they didn't fare so well in the collision," I glumly conclude.

"Looks bad," Chase concurs, nodding sympathetically. But I see what he really wants to do is laugh.

It is kind of funny. But I guess he feels bad too, 'cause when I go to place the damaged eyewear back in my bag, he says, "Do you mind if I take a look? Maybe I can fix them for you."

"It doesn't matter," I try to tell him, not wanting to waste his time. But he holds out his hand and gives me this sweet, pleading look that no woman could possibly resist. Certainly not this woman, I don't even try, I just hand the man the sunglasses.

Chase smiles and takes the glasses. He starts to mess with the lens, but it slips and slides under his fingers too. It won't stay in place for anyone apparently. He lets out a low growl of frustration, and I have to look away. God, even his growls are sexy. Chase is a sensory delight, sight, sound, touch. I bet he smells and tastes good too. I lean a little closer to see if I can discern the former, but fearing that he'll notice I step back and just enjoy the view.

Chase is lean, but it's obvious he's strong, he emanates physical power. I've heard he never loses a fight, which accounts for the perfect face. What a sexy badass. He doesn't fully fit the part though. Not today. He has the sexy part down completely, yes, but his clothes are too nice to be badass. The shirt, pants, and shoes scream upstanding citizen, nice churchgoing young man. I practically snort;, since we all know *that* isn't true. But his intent is probably to look the part, seeing as he's here at the church. However, even his dressy clothes can't hide his edge of pure bad boy, and the nice fabrics sure can't cover up his amazing body.

His shirt is really nice, a crisp white button-down, with the sleeves rolled up. His exposed forearms display long, corded muscles, muscles that flex and move, especially when he snaps the lens of my sunglasses back into place.

The black pants he's wearing look great too, fitting him to a tee. I find no fault anywhere. Damn, his body is a wonderland, meaning I can't help but wonder what he'd look like unclothed. I've heard he has tats and I'm suddenly dying to see them. Wonder if he'd let me touch them.

I've obviously completely lost my mind.

Chase is just about done—the lens is fixed—so I avert my gaze and try to pretend I'm searching for something in my purse. He assesses the sunglasses for a few more seconds. As do I. From the corner of my eye I see there's a bend in one of the arms, maybe from the collision. Chase straightens it back and says something about the sunglasses being nice. Instead of just offering up a simple thank you, I go into a long-winded explanation.

"Thanks. But they're not really worth anything. They're not real designer glasses. I bought them at one of those dollar stores." Chase glances my way and gives me a little smile. "Not the one in town, the one a little north of here. Do you know where I mean? Up by the Agway on seven…" I trail off. *God, ramble much.*

But Chase doesn't seem all that bothered by my babbling. He hands me the sunglasses, and they look perfect, like brand new.

"Wow, you fixed them," I gush, turning them over in my hands. "Amazing, I think they're actually better than when I bought them. Thank you."

"You're welcome."

He smiles, and oh, what a smile. "I'm Chase, by the way."

We're kind of hitting it off, flirting a little, even. So I don't tell him I already know who he is. Why ruin things?

I just say, "Nice to meet you. I'm Kay, Kay Stanton."

"Kay," he says my name slowly, and I like the sensual way it sounds coming from his mouth. "Like, short for Kaylee or Kayla?"

"Nope, just Kay."

"Hmm, I like it," he says, pressing his lips together and nodding approvingly.

Oh, and I like you.

I think this, but I don't dare say it. I drop my gaze and lick my lips.

I better think of something to say if I want to keep this conversation going. And I do want to keep it going. I don't want him leaving just yet, so I blurt out, "Hey, I didn't see you in church today."

Chase puts his hands in his pockets, turns up the charm. "I'm flattered you noticed."

His tone is pure flirtation, making me fidget and tug at the edge of the left sleeve of my sweater. "Yeah, I did. Notice, that is." A thread pulls loose and I hastily tuck it up under the sleeve, hoping he doesn't notice. "That you weren't there, I mean."

Chase looks down at the pavement, all cute-like, and I can see he's smiling. Hey, he's smiling, not running. I see this as a good sign.

Encouraged, I continue, "S-o-o, you're the guy Father Maridale hired to work on the church and the school, right?"

"I am," he confirms. And then, after a beat, "Father Maridale is a good man. I owe him a lot."

"He is," I agree, nodding. "He truly believes everyone deserves a second chance, no matter what they've done in the past."

I realize what I've just said, and so apparently has Chase. His gunmetal blues pierce, eyeing me like he's just put together that I know exactly who he is. And that I have right from the beginning.

Sure enough, he quietly asks, "You know who I am, don't you?"

And we both know what he means—I know his past.

I wince, sigh. "Yes, I know who you are."

"When did you realize?"

Very quietly—eyes downcast—I admit, "I knew right away, Chase. As soon as I looked up and saw it was you I'd wrecked into."

Neither of us says anything, and I squeeze my eyes shut.

I fully expect him to take off, but instead he says softly, "Hey, it's fine. But can I ask you something, Kay?"

I nod, and dare to open my eyes and glance up. To my surprise, when our gazes meet, I see an emotion I'm all too familiar with—a deep kind of sadness, the kind that reaches into the soul and just kind of burrows there. Chase is lonely, like me. I'm sure of it. And in the recognition that here is someone possibly as sad and alone as I, all sense of pretense on my part crumbles. I've obviously misjudged Chase Gartner.

He scrutinizes my face. Does he see in me what I see in him? If he does, he keeps it to himself. What he does say is this: "I know a lot of people in this town expect me to fuck up again."

I start to shake my head, deny what he's saying. But that would be a lie, and we both know it.

"I see the way they look at me," he continues. "I know what they're thinking, what they say behind my back."

I can't deny what he's experienced, so I just say, "I'm sure it's not easy."

His eyes pin me down, all blue intensity. "So, okay... What about you, Kay? You're part of this congregation." He motions to the church behind me. "Do *you* think I deserve the second chance Father Maridale is giving me? Or do you believe—like everyone else—that he's wasting his time?" He makes a scoffing sound. "'Cause I'll surely just screw up again."

I suddenly feel like crap. Less than an hour ago, I *was* thinking he might screw things up, mess up again. Did I not question Father Maridale's judgment? Did I not think Chase needed watching? I did, but I don't tell him any of these things. What good would it do? And, more importantly, who am I to judge?

I say in a quiet voice, "Trust me, Chase, out of this whole town, I'm the last person you should be asking these questions."

He shakes his head and looks away. "That's not an answer, so I'll take it as yes, you expect me to fuck up again." He doesn't sound angry, just resigned.

I'm so used to shutting people out and evading the tough questions. But if Chase is willing to be this *real* with me, then he deserves a real answer in return.

It takes me a minute to gather my courage, but I finally say, "Okay, it's true, it has crossed my mind that you might screw things up again." He winces, like my admission, said out loud, kind of hurts.

I hurry along. "But now that I've met you, I guess I don't know what to think. I'm sorry I had doubts, Chase, but all those stories…" He rolls his eyes. "It doesn't matter anyway. What I said before is true. I have no right to judge anyone in this town. God, if you only knew…" My mouth snaps shut. I've revealed too much in this effort to be honest.

I know from the way he's watching me that Chase is waiting for elaboration. But I have nothing more to say on the subject. I pray he doesn't push and make things awkward. Thankfully, he doesn't.

Instead, he rubs the back of his neck and says slowly, "So, you've heard things, had doubts. That's fine. But I'm not the same person I was four years ago." His eyes meet mine, and it's evident he's speaking from the heart. This is as real as it gets.

"So," he continues, "fuck the rest of the congregation.

What I want to know, Kay, is if *you* are going to give me a chance?"

I don't hesitate. "Yes, I can. I will, definitely." I mean it too.

He presses his lips together, smiles tightly. "Fair enough."

This has been a heavy turn in a first conversation, but it doesn't feel as uncomfortable as one may expect. Still, for a moment, we both look everywhere but at each other. I want to lighten things back up, get back to flirting and having fun, and I think I know just what to do to make that happen.

I sigh dramatically and say, "Well, fuck, I sure am glad we got that out of the way."

I know the swear word will throw him for a loop—no one ever expects prim and proper me to toss around profanities. If they only knew, I am not so very wholesome. In any case, my tactic works. Chase's eyes widen and meet mine.

"Gotcha," I say.

And then we're both laughing, like *really* laughing. And it's good, like some little bridge between us has just been built.

"So, when do you start work at the school?" I ask when our laughter subsides.

"I'm supposed to start tomorrow," he replies, shifting his tall frame. "Father Maridale wants me to clear out the principal's office, start painting in there."

"Oh, Mr. Kelly's office." I give a quick nod. "That's good, it needs it."

And does it ever, the walls are faded and dull, kind of gray. It's anybody's guess what color they once were. I suddenly have an idea, a way to show Chase I really meant it when I agreed to give him a chance.

"Actually," I begin, "I teach over at the school, so I know every nook and cranny. If you want, I could stop by tomorrow and give you the grand tour. It's kind of a small building, so it won't take long, but at least you'll know your way around after. What do you think?"

The flirtatious smile is back, and it's like we've just passed another hurdle. "I think I'd like that very much," Chase says softly.

I can't help but smile in return; this gorgeous man just has that effect.

Things feel easy, relaxed, enough so that I tell Chase I'll be working for the church this summer. Therefore I'll be seeing him around a lot. Though I no longer plan to keep tabs on him, he's obviously a decent guy.

I give him the story on why I'll be covering for Connie, I tell him about the cruise she's taking with her husband. The discussion then veers back to our tour plans, and Chase informs me he's starting very early in the morning, way before I'm due in. We agree lunchtime will work best for my "tour."

I ask him if he has a key to get in the school, because I could lend him mine and he could give it back to me when I see him. He thanks me for the offer, but says Father Maridale is giving him a key today.

"That's why I'm here." He glances to the rectory behind the church. "I should probably get going so I can catch him before he heads out."

I redirect him to the church itself and tell him he's more likely to find Father Maridale in the sacristy. Father likes to get to work on next week's homilies right after Mass on Sundays. He can almost always be found seated at the desk next to the closet for the vestments. I tell him all this, and Chase thanks me for steering him in the right direction. We say our farewells, and he goes one way and I, another.

By the time I reach my car, I notice there's something different in the way I feel. There's a little more hop in my step perhaps. A squishy hop, as my flats are still wet, but a hop nonetheless.

I like Chase Gartner. I say it in my head, try it on for size. It feels right, so I say it again, this time out loud, as I get in my car. "I like Chase Gartner."

Yeah, I do.

And, sure, he's insanely attractive—and I kind of hope his hands end up on me again—but it's more than just that. Chase may very well be one of the most real people I've met in a long time. I want to get to know him better, see if my impression of him, now that I've officially met him, holds true. And I want to give Chase a chance, like I promised. Heck, maybe it's time I take a chance of my own, live a little.

Lord knows—literally—that I hide myself in this church. I wrap myself up in the role of the poor girl who lost her little sister in a tragic accident, the young woman whose parents cast her aside like a ragdoll. I keep myself from living in the present by clinging to the past, holding fast to guilt and grief. I'm good at it; it's what I know. It's been my life for four years now, but frankly it's getting old. Maybe it's time to stop and reassess.

I glance in the rearview mirror; the iron gate at the cemetery is barely visible now that everything is filling in green. Sarah would want me to live; I know this in my heart. I think of Chase. He clearly wants nothing more than to move on from his past. So why can't I let mine go?

Maybe I can learn something from this man I misjudged. Maybe it's time to reconsider this life I am living, let this old life go and start anew. Father Maridale counsels me all the time to make peace with the past, he tells me again and again that there's nothing wrong with moving forward. He says I have a right to live my life, a duty, in fact.

I long to embrace his words—so much so that it sometimes hurts—but, honestly, I am terrified. What if I can't move on? What if I try and fail? What if I get close to someone—say, someone like Chase—and everything blows up in my face? What if he gets to know me, maybe even grows to care, and then finds out the truth of what happened the night Sarah died? After my mother, I don't think I can handle another person turning away.

But life is about taking chances, I remind myself.

I turn the key in the ignition and the Neon comes to life. One thing for certain, Chase has made me feel a lot of things today, things I thought I'd never feel again—excitement, giddiness, lust, possibility. But the most important one— the one I want to cling to like a girl who's been stumbling around for too long in the dark and has just spotted a sliver of light—is hope.

CHAPTER THREE
CHASE

I find Father Maridale in the sacristy, just where Kay said he'd be. But he's not working on a homily, no. Maybe he was—there is an open Bible on his desk—but, at the moment, the priest who has given me a shot at redemption is leaned back in a swivel chair, talking on a cell.

I hesitate at the open door, fully prepared to turn around, come back later if need be. However, Father Maridale spots me and motions for me to come in. He gestures to a chair situated next to the desk. I don't want to sit right where I can hear his whole conversation, so I point back toward the nave, and silently mouth, "I'll wait out there."

Father nods and I leave him to his call. Once I'm back in the nave, I sit down on one of the pews in the front and stretch out my long legs. The view up here is vastly different from the one I'm accustomed to in the back. Up here, everything seems bigger, more in your face. The altar, the richly colored Holy Trinity fresco—they're all larger than life.

As I soak it all in, my artistic side takes note of the texture and detail in the fresco, while layered decades of incense and melted candle wax fill my nose. I breathe in deeply, glance around, I think I like it up here. Maybe this is where I should sit next Sunday at Mass. Closer to God, closer to Kay.

Just as I'm seriously considering making the move—like maybe the front is where I've belonged all along—a statue of to my left, some saint, catches my eye. I have no clue who the plaster sculpture is supposed to represent, but shit, whoever painted the features did a damn good job. The eyes are remarkably lifelike, disturbingly so, especially since they're directly trained on me. I know it just looks that way from this angle, but I nevertheless find myself scrubbing a hand down my face, and mumbling, "Not you too."

I then turn my back on the saint.

Hell, I've had enough of real people judging me in this supposedly sacred place; I sure as fuck don't need statues doing it too. I know it's my own guilty conscience causing all this grief. My succumbing to carnal weakness last night has apparently made me paranoid.

I remind myself that, at least, I stayed away from the drugs. I just wish I'd stayed away from Missy as well. Not that I feel especially bad about all that occurred. I just wish the person the acts were committed with didn't attend this church. Does that make me a hypocrite? Yeah, probably.

Suddenly I have a far more disturbing thought. Jesus, I hope to God Missy doesn't share what happened outside the Anchor Inn with Kay. Surely she wouldn't mention that she was toting around coke, or that she offered to share, but the messing around part...

Girls and their gossip, I know how that can go. There are more than enough tales still floating around about me and my past, and Kay's heard too much already. Our discussion today shed light on that unfortunate fact.

Kay Stanton.

I lean back against the hard wooden pew, think about the pretty girl who always sits right about here. I finally know Hot Chick's name. And I like it, I like *her*. Kay seems, I don't know, sweet. Something I sometimes forget women can be.

Shit, I have to chuckle a little when I think of how she ran right into me. Talk about serendipity. Sweet girl stumbled a bit and seemed kind of dazed, but thankfully she wasn't hurt. That had been my first concern. But once I realized she was all right, in the time it took her to recover, I just let myself thoroughly enjoy the view.

Kay is actually much prettier up close, more delicate than I originally thought. Her skin is translucent, creamy and smooth, like its begging to be touched. And from what I saw in those caramel-brown eyes, maybe, just maybe, she'd like to be touched by me.

Speaking of touching… That body, oh, that body. I shift a little and the pew creaks. *Fuck.* The way she felt beneath my hands, tiny and soft, like I could break her in two. And break her I would. There's not enough good in me for such a gentle soul. Not to mention, it was more than apparent, as our conversation progressed, that Kay's not ripe for break-ing. She's already been shattered by something.

Sweet girl sure isn't good at lying, that's for certain. Well, maybe at first, when I mistakenly thought she didn't know who I was. That was my error. I should've known bet-ter. Kay does lives in *this* town, after all. Anyway, when she blurted out that Father Maridale believes in second chances, no matter what a person has done in the past, I knew then and there she'd known all along exactly who she crashed into.

I expected the judging to start. I was ready. That's why I just cut through the bullshit and put sweet girl on the spot. But then I saw an emotion in those caramel browns that I never would have expected—sadness. And maybe understanding. Did Kay see the same in me? Is she broken and damaged too? Maybe so, based on all her talk of "not judging" and "if only I knew." What the hell was that supposed to mean? If only I knew *what*?

Not that I expected an answer, and she sure wasn't volunteering. Kay shut me out. Had sweet girl said too much? The look on her face indicated she had indeed. I say that with certainty since I know that look all too well. I've worn it often. It's a look that says butt the fuck out. So I did just that. I let the whole thing drop.

It doesn't matter anyway. No secret of Kay's could ever be as horrific as *any* of the shit I've done, most of which is unfortunately public knowledge. That's why it meant a lot when she actually agreed to give me a chance.

That's all I'm really asking for from the people in this town. See me as who I am—who I am striving to be—not as who I once was. And if it turns out Kay is the only one willing to do so—besides Father Maridale, of course—then so be it. Acceptance from two people—who, from what I've observed, are kind and caring—is good enough for me.

As I sit waiting for Father Maridale to emerge from the back, I come to a conclusion. I *really* like Kay Stanton. And because of this feeling I have for her I care about what she thinks. Additionally, I kind of can't wait to see her again, which is a weird one for me. I usually don't give a shit about stuff like that. But damn if lunchtime tomorrow can't get here soon enough.

But before I have a chance to think about why I feel so strongly for a girl I've only just met, Father Maridale emerges from the back.

"I'm sorry, Chase," he begins, his light brown eyes apologetic as he takes a seat near me on the pew. "I didn't mean to keep you waiting for so long."

I tell him it's all good, the extra time allowed me time to reflect. He nods approvingly, probably thinking I meant I was praying. Not quite.

Father asks me how I've been doing lately and if everything is okay. His expression tells me that what he's really asking is why I wasn't in church this morning. Like, is something going on. *Not anything I care to share*, I think in my head. Outwardly, I take a deep breath, apologize, and simply say I overslept.

I don't think he buys my explanation completely, but he lets it pass. He gives me the key to the school, and we shift gears. We talk a bit about the work he'd like for me to get done during the upcoming week. It's mostly all painting projects over at the school, but a few repairs too.

Father Maridale tells me he's already purchased all the paint I'll need. "The cans are in the hall next to Mr. Kelly's office," he explains. "And there are drop cloths and ladders in the storage room a few doors down from there. You can't miss it, there's a sign on the door." He pauses, appears to think for a minute. "Oh, and I also bought some new brushes and rollers. I think that should be everything you need to get started, but if not, let me know."

It sounds like he has everything covered and whatever

he didn't buy I'm sure I have at home. I assume we're finished talking, so I stand.

Father Maridale starts to get up too, and as he does, he asks me if I need someone to show me around the school. "I have a few extra minutes," he says. "I can take you over there now."

"No," I reply. "I mean, thanks, but I'm good. Kay Stanton is giving me a tour tomorrow."

Father relaxes back into the pew. "Oh, you know Kay?" He arches an eyebrow.

"Well, no, not really," I admit, raking my fingers through my hair. "I mean, I've seen her here at church, but I only just now met her." Father is listening intently, waiting for more I suppose, so I add, "We ran into each other in the parking lot"—I don't mention that we literally did just that—"and just got started talking."

Now, Father Maridale looks as if something has been made clear. "Of course, of course," he muses, staring at the statue that was eyeing me earlier. "The parking lot, yes, Kay would have been coming from the cemetery."

"Cemetery?" I ask, perplexed.

I haven't given much thought as to where Kay may have been before she ran into me. I'm aware there's a small graveyard behind the church—I've already cut the grass back there twice—but I can't imagine why Kay would have been out there in the rain. It was pouring earlier, not an optimum time to be paying one's respects. Come to think of it, though, her hair did look a little damp. Fantastic and sexy, all wavy and long, but definitely damp.

Father Maridale is giving me a contemplative look, like maybe he's deciding if I'm worthy to hear whatever story he's thinking about telling me. And I know there's a story, because around here there always is. Father motions that I should sit back down. Yeah, just like I thought—a story to be told.

I sit back down on the pew and Father Maridale begins his tale. "You probably don't know this since you were away, but Kay once had a little sister named Sarah, her only sibling." He exhales audibly. "Unfortunately, Sarah died…a few years ago." *Shit.*

"Such a tragic accident, the child was only six years old." I guess I look appropriately aghast—and I am. Father nods his head in shared understanding. "I know, I know, such a terrible loss, one that Kay has had great trouble bearing. She visits her sister's grave every Sunday after church. I used to hope those visits would help her heal, but now I just don't know…"

As Father trails off, shaking his head, I think about how I used to visit the grave of someone I lost unexpectedly as well—my father. I went every day for a while, hoping to find solace, maybe some answers. Losing my father was devastating, and I know a part of me will never really heal, but I can't begin to imagine what it would have been like to lose my baby brother. Sure, Will's almost fifteen now, hardly a baby—and barely on speaking terms with me at the moment—but that doesn't mean my heart doesn't clench at the thought of him, well, dying. God, poor Kay. I had no idea.

Father Maridale starts to speak once more, "The loss of Sarah was God's will. There's nothing we can do but accept these things when they happen. I've told Kay this many times, but she continues to blame herself."

What?

Before I can think to curb my curiosity—or my language—I blurt out, "Why in the hell would she do that?"

Father gives me an admonishing look for cursing in church, and I mumble a heartfelt apology. Then, I get an explanation.

"Kay was watching her sister one night, babysitting while her parents were out. Kay fell asleep and young Sarah snuck out into the backyard. That little girl loved the water. And, well, there was a swimming pool behind their house." I shake my head, trying to wrap my head around where this story is obviously heading. "Tragically, Sarah had not yet learned to swim. Kay woke up when she heard her sister's cries for help, but by the time she got out to the pool..." Father bows his head, appropriately stricken. "Well, it was just too late to save her."

I don't even know what to say. Clearly, this is the root from which Kay's sadness stems. But she shouldn't blame herself. It was a tragic accident, just like Father Maridale has just said. Sometimes things happen that you have no control over. It's a sad fact of life I accepted years ago.

Father is watching me carefully and I have a feeling I know what's coming next. After all, he's aware of my reputation.

Sure enough, right on cue, Father says, "Chase, you should know that Kay is fragile. Not only has she lost her sister, but her family has abandoned her as well. And—"

"What? You're kidding." Again, I can't believe what I've just heard. Abandoned by her family? I know it's rude to interrupt like this, but could this story get any worse?

Father frowns at my interruption, but continues, "Sadly, I'm not kidding. Kay's mother blames Kay for the accident, even after all this time that has passed. I believe this is the main reason why Kay has had such a hard time forgiving herself." He takes a breath. "Now, I'm not saying to stay away from her." A hand is waved in the direction of the school. "Take your tour. You two have something in common, both of you share a troubled past. Perhaps a friendship would be beneficial to the both of you. Kay could certainly use a friend; even I can see that. She spends far too much time alone. But, Chase…" He trails off, and I know what's coming next—the "don't take advantage" spiel.

Father Maridale is nothing if not realistic, and he probably believes everything he's heard. Unfortunately, most of the stories *are* true. I've done some fucked-up shit, no doubt. I'm more sinner than saint, as last night so clearly illuminated. But I have no intention of hurting Kay in that way, or in any way, really.

I tell Father as much, and I *think* he believes me, although he appears a little wary. He should believe me. I mean, Kay is giving me a chance. Why would I do something stupid, like make a dickhead move on her and fuck everything up?

Curious as to when this tragedy happened, I ask Father, "How long ago did Kay lose her sister?"

"Four years ago this summer, the same summer you lost your way."

Lost my way? Well, that's a nice way of putting it. It's interesting, though, that Kay and I have something else in common. Both of us were dealing with tragedies around the same time, though mine was purely of my own making.

There's not much else to say, and I sense Father Maridale is readying to go. But I have one more thing to ask, something I've been thinking about since coming back. I tell him I would like to rent out the apartment I lived in before I went to prison, the one above the detached garage on the property that I'm still getting used to saying is mine. I could use the extra money, and some company out there in the country might be nice.

I figure if I put flyers up in the church, there's a better likelihood I'll end up with a steady, reliable tenant. The apartment is such a great little space and I'd like to get someone in there who appreciates it, not someone who might fuck it up all to hell. I've heard horror stories of nightmare tenants and I certainly don't want to take a chance by posting flyers just anywhere. I worked too hard to make the place nice, I intend for it to stay that way.

In the month or so I lived there, back when I was twenty, I made a lot of improvements. I updated the kitchenette by installing all new appliances. Though, to be honest, those improvements were at my grandmother's insistence. Kitchens were very important to her. Me? Not so much. But once I got started on fixing things up, I decided I might as well make the whole place nice. So I constructed and put in wood beams all along the sloped ceiling, in between skylights my dad installed years ago. I painted the place too, laid all new carpeting, and fixed a bunch of small things.

The work kept me busy. At the time, I was hoping it would also keep me away from the drugs that were starting to consume my life. No such luck there. I still recall being high as fuck the day Tate helped me carry a couch over from the main house. We were already lit, but we smoked another bowl once the couch was in place and we were setting up the TV. Another night, I went to a party at Kyle's and ended up snorting a shitload of coke. When I finally got home, sometime the next day, I was so restless and wired that I spent hours and hours refinishing an antique iron bed that I found down in the unused garage portion of the building.

I shake my head thinking of how out of control I used to be, how my burgeoning addiction ruled my life back then. Thank God I didn't fall back into that trap and succumb to cocaine's siren call last night.

Father's brow is crinkled as he watches me. "Is everything all right, Chase?" he asks.

"Yeah, yeah," I say quickly, too quickly. "I was just thinking about the apartment." *Oh, and all the drugs I used to do.*

"Well," Father says, standing up, "I don't mind if you put up flyers. You can even ask Kay to run off some copies for you, if you want. I'm sure she won't mind. Did she tell you she'll be working at the church office all summer?"

"Yeah, she did." I nod as I answer, and then we basically wrap things up.

When I go back out to the parking lot, I open the door to my truck, but I don't get in right away. Instead, my eyes wander to the area behind the church, to the cemetery, where the iron gate that marks the entrance is barely visible now that all the summer growth has filled in.

I still can't get over the story Father Maridale just told me, Kay losing her sister in such a tragic manner. And her sister was so young. I can't even imagine walking in Kay's shoes, handling a tragedy of that magnitude. I think back to when my own sibling was six. Will was the sweetest kid back then, always trying to be a big boy, always wanting to be like me.

It's hard to believe, but once upon a time I was a really good role model, courteous and kind, a nice kid. I got excellent grades, drew crazy-cool pictures that everyone loved, and excelled in an array of sports. No surprise Will wanted to do everything I did back then. Sadly, it didn't always work out so well for him, at least not at first, and definitely never in athletics.

My brother was persistent and determined, though. With a lot of studying and hard work, he started to pull down some decent grades. The drawing thing he always had in spades, so he was okay there. My brother has natural ability, just like me. But his art has always been different than mine. Whereas I can recreate anything in real life— people, objects, places—my brother's talent lies in graphics. Like comic book-type drawings, cartoons, caricatures. So, with art he was cool, but when I think of that kid and sports I have to chuckle.

I was good at everything athletic, but Will, not so much. Though he's slowly coming into his own now, in those early days, my kid brother was a gangly, uncoordinated mess. There's a nine-year age difference between us, so that may have played a part. Still, it didn't stop Will from wanting to do everything I did, including sports.

Against my better judgment, I usually gave in. I'd lob baseballs to him in the backyard, baseballs that he'd swing at and miss. I'd shoot basketballs with him in the driveway where Dad installed a hoop. But Will would miss the basket by a mile all the time. And the kid always begged to join in when he'd see me and my friends playing football in the empty sand lot next to our house. Of course, I could never say no.

So I'd prep everyone to go easy on him ahead of time. Then, Will would come out in his little pads, and big helmet my mom always insisted he wear, and hell if he wouldn't try his damnedest to keep up. There we'd be in the field, one of us throwing Will the football, all gentle and light. But my brother would invariably forget to put his hands up in time to catch the ball. Sometimes he'd not turn around at all, and the ball would bounce right off his back. I knew some of those hits had to hurt, but I never saw him cry. Will just remained the same kid as always, determined. He never gave up.

Stubborn and tough, that's Will. Maybe he's more stubborn than tough, now that I think about it. Hell, I'm still waiting for him to return even one of my calls, or reply to any of several texts I've recently sent him. I know I'll probably be waiting a while longer before he finally comes around.

Until then, I'll be content with reminding myself of the times Will liked being around me, how he loved hanging out with me and my friends. How it didn't matter we were so much older, or that everyone knew my brother was a klutz. He still always managed to fit in.

Right from the start, my friends knew to be cool with him. Otherwise, they'd have to answer to me. But I never had to follow through with any threats; my friends accepted Will of their own volition. Little bro was funny and cool in his own unique way, and he won everyone over just by being Will. At one time or another every friend I had told me they wished they had a little brother like mine, and not a day went by that I didn't count myself lucky that Will was in my life.

I smile at the memories, choosing to forget that I fucked things up by turning into a criminal. I want to remember the kid who adored me, the Will who trusted me not to fail him. But, like my dad, I did. Just in a different way.

But I'm still here, I remind myself, *I can fix things.* My dad, he's gone forever. There will be no fixing from him.

I take my phone out. What the hell, it's worth a try. I dial Will's cell. It goes straight to voicemail, like it always does these days. Will doesn't want to talk to me, clearly. That thought squeezes my heart so fucking hard it hurts.

Well, fine, I can be as stubborn as that little shit. I'll keep trying. I'll bug him forever, if I have to. I will never give up on that kid. He'll come around. I know he loves me somewhere deep inside. At least, I hope he does.

I shoot a final glance to the cemetery, then get in my truck. Life can change in an instant; mine sure did four years ago. Kay's did too, as I now know. I make myself a promise before I pull away: I am not going to spend any more time beating myself up over what happened last night. It's over and done. But I sure as fuck won't be making the same mistake again.

In some ways it was a wake-up call, reminding me of the temptations I need to avoid—getting blown in disgusting alleys behind bars; women like Missy who are all-too-willing to do the blowing; and, for sure, blow itself.

I need to spend my time concentrating on things that are important—being a better person, mending my relationship with my brother, and doing a good job for the church.

Maybe, just maybe, if I start accomplishing these things, people like Father Maridale and Kay Stanton won't ever regret giving me a chance.

Later that evening I'm searching the house for my old digital camera.

It has to be here somewhere, I tell myself.

I need to find it so I can take a picture of the apartment above the garage. I want to add a photo to the flyer I've just done up. Sadly, my cheap cell is talk and text only, so finding the digital is a must.

I rummage through the cabinet drawers in the kitchen, scour the buffet in the dining room, and proceed upstairs. I go through all the drawers in the dressers in the bedrooms, the closets too. *Nothing, nada.* I have no luck. Time to hit the final frontier, the attic, where it's hot and stuffy and everything smells like mothballs and dust.

Once I'm up in the stuffy space, ducking so my head doesn't hit the low ceiling, I peel off the T-shirt I changed into after returning from church and toss it to the floor. Shit, I need a fan up here. But there's none in sight, so I resign myself to just grin and bear the heat.

I start my search by going through some boxes marked *my old stuff*. In the first one, there are clothes of mine that no longer fit, some old sports equipment, and a few so-so sketches I drew one summer. But there's definitely no camera. I sit back and watch dust motes dance in a stream of dying light coming in through the window and think: *What next?*

Some of my grandmother's recently boxed-up belongings are on the other side of the attic, but I have my doubts the camera will be found in any of those. Still, you never know. I rub the back of my neck, wet with sweat already, and say, "Fuck it."

I crawl on over to where the boxes are stacked.

The first box I flip open is filled with old photo albums, yellow and worn. I have no desire to peel back the past and travel down memory lane—happy memories from a time long ago, no-fucking-thanks—so I hastily seal that box back up and push it aside roughly.

The next carton I come to contains a bunch of VHS tapes, and some record albums at the bottom. The vinyl is mostly stuff from the seventies, mixed in with a few of Gram's old albums. The tapes are movies, all from the eighties.

Ah, my father's stuff.

I thumb through the records, perusing titles of songs my dad once played for me on my grandmother's old record player. That old thing still sits down in the living room, dusty and unused.

I set the records aside and start to go through the movies. These are movies we used to watch together, sometimes as a family, sometimes just me and Dad.

It suddenly hits me—hard and fast, like a punch to the gut—that my father is gone forever. His ears will never hear this music, never again. He'll never again watch these movies. There's no coming back from where my father has gone. He'll never again walk through this house that, by all rights, should be his. Not mine. And it's sad to think now how this house once knew his laughter, his good times, and his bad. Hell, this house watched my father grow, from a boy to a man. I think of how much his mother, my grandmother, loved this house. But she's gone too. Sadly, now, this house knows only me.

I wrap my arms around myself, to keep my guts from falling out. Because, fuck, it feels like they just might. Times like these, stumbling upon reminders of all I once had, it comes back to me—how very much I miss my family, all of them. But especially the one I'll never see again, my dad.

My eyes sting, but I blame it on sweat dripping from my brow. To distract myself, I set aside some of the vinyl to take downstairs—Led Zeppelin, vintage Aerosmith, Boston, a few more. Then, I go through the movies one by one.

Before we moved to Vegas we used to come over here to Gram's house—Dad and I, sometimes Mom—and we'd watch this shit. When I pick up the box for *Terminator*, a flash of a seven-year-old me begging my dad to let me watch it runs through my mind. We still lived in Ohio at the time, I remember that. I also recall Mom wasn't around that day, and Grandma Gartner was busy in the kitchen, making homemade pizza for her son and grandson. After some convincing and pleading, my dad finally said, *oh, what the hell.*

So we watched the movie together on the couch, with Grandma Gartner shaking her head when she brought in the pizza. And I loved it, the pizza, the movie, spending time with my dad.

Mom joined us for our next movie night. When she wanted to pick the movie, though, Dad and I shared a look.

"Oh, Jack," she said as she flipped through the video-cassette boxes, "let's all watch *Pretty in Pink*. It's so cute." She held a box up, one with Molly Ringwald and friends on the cover.

I rolled my eyes. "Mom, please…God, no." That cover, the girl in pink. *Kill me now,* I thought.

Thankfully, Dad came to the rescue. He could always be counted on to be the voice of reason.

"How 'bout we compromise, Abby? *The Breakfast Club* is good too. And I think Chase will like that one much better."

Dad paused and Mom seemed to consider. "What do you say, honey? You okay with that one instead?"

Mom gave in fairly quickly—she always did with Dad—and we ended up watching *The Breakfast Club*, as a family, all snug and cozy on the couch. What a fucking picture we must have been. Dad slipping Mom kisses when he thought I wasn't looking, and Mom covering my ears every time Bender swore. Her efforts, though, were only halfhearted—she was well aware I'd heard her and Dad say much worse.

I've been up here for a while and sweat is running down my bare back. It doesn't look like I'll be finding the camera anytime soon. I'm hot and I'm thirsty and I've had enough of memory lane, so I give up the search. I tug my T-shirt back over my head and go downstairs, taking Dad's old record albums with me.

Since I can't find the camera I decide to go with plan number two: I'll just sketch the apartment right on the flyer. Fuck the camera. I can probably draw the details a whole lot better than what low mega pixels will end up showing anyway.

My newest sketchbook is on the buffet in the dining room, where I've been keeping it lately. Under it, in the top drawer, there are an assortment of colored pencils, charcoal sticks, and oil pastels. I grab a bunch of the colored pencils and set everything out on the dining room table, including the flyer I made up earlier.

Before I get started, I turn the ceiling fan on low and grab a lemon-lime soda out of the fridge. When I settle back down at the table, I wait a few minutes for my drink and the cool rotations of the fan to cool me off. Then, I get to work on sketching a few practice drafts in the book. After I know how I want to present the apartment I go right to the flyer. In no time at all, I've created a fucking damn good depiction of the space I plan to rent.

Over in the apartment there's a half wall separating the living room from the bedroom in the back, but I draw the wall as transparent. That way, prospective renters can see both rooms are furnished. There's not a lot of stuff, but there's enough, and it's nice. Using a dark blue pencil, I shade in the coloring of the small couch Tate and I dragged up when we were both high, and then I sketch the TV and the little wooden table it sits on. For the bedroom, I draw the lines of the iron headboard, the one I refinished when I was all coked up. I add in an old trunk that sits at the foot of the bed and the small dresser up against the wall on the left. I mark two side-by-side doors on the farthest walls as *closet* and *bath*.

Once I finish with all the shading and coloring, I have a fairly kick-ass flyer. Hell, I'd rent the apartment if I didn't already own the house. I've had a rental rate in mind for a while now, but since the place looks so good I up it a bit. What the hell—it's still a sweet deal.

Once I'm finished with the flyer, the need to sketch keeps the colored pencils going. It's like that sometimes, like I have to get whatever image is haunting my head out onto a piece of paper. Like I need to give the image life, give it some substance, make it real. And the image currently in my head—searing my brain, in fact—is of Kay. And how she looked this afternoon when she wrecked into me in that parking lot.

She probably has no idea what I saw in her eyes—want, lust, need. A need I definitely could fill. I had every intention of following through. 'Cause let's be honest, I'm incredibly attracted to Miss Kay Stanton. But after hearing her story from Father Maridale—and seeing the pain in her eyes when our own conversation got real—there's no way I'll be pursuing that course of action.

Kay is a sandcastle on the beach, and I'm a fucking hurricane. I'd not only wash her away, I'd fucking destroy her. Even Father Maridale sees that, which is why I received the warning, in not so many words, to not corrupt her. But that doesn't mean I can't draw her as I see her in my head, the image of this afternoon from my perspective.

I pick the sketchbook up and flip to the back. Then, I start to draw Kay, hair a little mussed, bottom lip slightly pouted. I draw her eyes and the sex I saw in them, sex... for me. I sketch every detail, down to the veins in the petals of the roses that were printed on her dress. I shade in the soft texture of her cardigan, the little pink thread that came loose that she didn't think I'd see. But I missed nothing this afternoon, and I miss nothing now. Kay's immortalized on paper in minutes.

I take a look at the finished sketch, holding the book up to the light.

Sweet girl is, appropriately, a lot of pink. Pink roses, pink sweater, pink cheeks. And pink places I can only imagine. Now *that* kind of pretty in pink I could get into, literally. But I won't and I can't, but, fuck, does my body want to. *Shit.*

I rip the page from the book. No one can ever see what I've drawn since it's blatantly obvious I don't see my subject as just a friend. But I can't bring myself to throw this sketch away, even though it'd be prudent. It's just too, I don't know, special maybe. Kay may appear wanton and sexual in my sketch, but I've also drawn her as the incredibly beautiful, stunning woman she is. And I can't bring myself to destroy the image I've created.

Against my better judgment, but following my heart, I fold the drawing in half and tuck it in the back of the sketch-book, wondering the whole time if Kay sees herself this way. Does she know how truly beautiful she is? Someone should make sure she knows if she doesn't. Too bad that someone can't be me.

Resigned that I will, sadly, never touch Kay Stanton, I put the sketchbook back on the hutch, turn everything off, and go upstairs. But when I lie down to sleep, I can't stop thinking of sweet girl's beauty, her fragility—pink and deli-cate. Not unlike the roses on the dress she wore today.

Thinking of those roses remind me of a time when I was very little, three or four. I see my father giving my mother a single flower. It may have been a rose, I was too little to know, but I recall trying to touch the pretty bloom. But my dad wouldn't let me. He said it was a special, fragile flower and I had to leave it alone. Just like Father Maridale said to leave Kay alone. She's fragile, don't touch her.

I toss and I turn, thinking about that damn flower, and what eventually happened.

Naturally, being a curious and stubborn toddler, I didn't listen to my dad. First chance I got I crawled up on a stool and put my little fingers all over that pretty pink blossom.

Big mistake… Let's just say I quickly learned what frag-ile meant.

When my mom came in and caught me touching the flower, I yanked my hand back.

And that's when all the petals fell off.

That night I dream of my father. We're standing behind the church, next to the iron gated entrance. "Am I dying?" I ask my dad. "Or am I already dead?"

Why else would I be at a cemetery with my dead father?

My dad laughs, but it sounds far away, like an echo in a valley. "No, son, you're very much alive. You're just getting started, in fact. You have a lot more living to do."

I take a step into the cemetery and my dad tries to follow, but he's stopped in his tracks.

"What's wrong?" I ask as I turn back.

"The ground is consecrated, I can't go in." His filmy hand points to his milky, opaque form. "Suicide, you know."

The sun is shining brightly and I have to shield my eyes. "Why'd you do it?" I ask my father.

He shrugs a shoulder, much like I often do. No answer. My dad is as silent as the stone angel at his grave used to be.

There's a noise from inside the cemetery and we both turn to see. It's Will, he's running around the markers, smiling and laughing. He's little and happy, like he was before my father passed. Dad and I smile identical smiles, but then Will trips and falls and we're both brought to action by his cries.

Dad and I move to help Will, but only I can cross over. Dad puts his hand out like he's touching an invisible barrier that's been erected between us. I hesitate, but Will cries out once more.

"Son, go help your brother."

"But-but…what about you?" I implore.

Dad starts to fade away. "You can't help me, Chase, but

your brother still needs you. He always will. You're there, I am not. Don't make the same mistakes I did, son."

Will is crying, Dad is fading, and I am somewhere in between. My hands reach out to both, but before I can choose which way to go, I wake up.

CHAPTER FOUR

KAY

Monday arrives in sunny, warm glory. I slip a simple dress over my head and adjust the crisscross of smooth fabric in the back. I feel light and free, pretty in mint green cotton and sandals with oh-so-skinny straps.

When I leave my apartment the junkies lingering in the parking lot rake me over with their empty eyes. Hard stares delivered without apology as I walk to my car. But not even their lascivious looks—or the one long, drawn-out wolf whistle—can bring me down today.

Remember all that hope I was feeling yesterday? Well it's officially blossomed. I am finally ready to give this "living a full life-thing" a real shot.

I owe this in part to Chase Gartner. If you had told me twenty-four hours ago I'd be singing this tune I never would have believed it. But it's true. Chase's passion to move forward has inspired me to do the same. Good looks *and* an inspiration? That guy really is amazing.

I smile to myself. No wonder I can't wait to see him today.

A little while later, after I'm safe and settled at Connie's desk in the church office—well, *my* desk for the summer—time becomes a countdown of hours, a race with the clock. I take a few calls, type up a memo for Father Maridale, and make some last-minute changes to June's online church calendar. But other than those minor tasks things are slow and the morning hours seem to drag on. Needless to say, the second noon arrives I jump out of my seat and race over to the school to find Chase.

The man I seek is standing outside the principal's office, amid drop-cloth-covered furniture he's dragged out to the hall. Chase is turned so his back faces me. The first thing I notice is his tawny hair. It's far messier than it was yesterday, but in a very sexed-up, delicious kind of way.

Chase is busy doing something with his cell and doesn't notice me right away. *Fine with me.* I stay put and check him out. I love the way the worn and faded denim of the jeans he's wearing seems to hug his ass. Everything looks so firm and taut. And I can't help but notice how his black T-shirt pulls tantalizingly at his wide shoulders, especially when he sets his phone down and moves a couple of paint cans from the table in front of him to the floor. The sleeves of his tee ride up slightly as he moves and the edges of two tattoos become slightly visible. There appears to be one tattoo on either arm. I lean forward and squint, quietly. I don't yet want to be discovered.

The ink on Chase's right bicep appears to be a number, but I can't be sure. However, when he wedges a screwdriver under one of the paint can lids and pops it loose, his arm muscles flex and the sleeve of his shirt inches up, revealing more of the tattoo. It's definitely a number, a seventy-two, I think.

Over on Chase's left bicep, the tat is much harder to see. It's a scroll of words, that much is clear. But the letters are small and inked in a dark script, making it too hard to read from where I'm standing. And I can't move or he'll hear me. So I just watch for a few seconds, enjoy the view, and then take a tentative step forward.

Chase hears the tap-tap of my sandal heels and turns around.

"Hey," we both say simultaneously.

For every one step I take, Chase takes two. I count three of my own and then I am face-to-face with this stunning man. Even though he's obviously been painting all morning he looks great. Neither of us says anything at first, but then Chase smiles and asks me how my day has been.

"Good, it's been good," I reply.

Chase is so close and his eyes—more blue than gray in the hall lighting—make a pass over my body. Quickly though, so quickly I almost miss it. But I sure don't miss the heat in his blues when they catch and hold my gaze.

Chase takes me in and stirs me up. He makes me feel special, just with the look he's giving me, like I may be one of the most beautiful women he's ever seen. I know I am not, but I like how he has the power to affect me like this. And I like the fact that—though it may be fairly demure, in length and style—the thin straps at the shoulders of my sundress and the cross of fabric in the back have me displaying far more skin than yesterday. I don't quite know why but I want to bare even more for Chase Gartner. My body, maybe my soul—

"You're looking pretty today," Chase says softly, breaking me away from my errant thoughts.

His voice is seductive, unintentionally I'm sure. Still, his words warm my cheeks.

I thank him, and hope against hope that I am *not* blushing beet red. But I suspect I am.

And then I'm certain of it when Chase dips down and bumps my shoulder playfully with his own shoulder. "Come on, shy girl," he says, a smile playing at his lips. "Let's get this party started."

Oh yeah, the tour. Party, indeed. I laugh a little. "If only," I mumble under my breath.

Sadly, my tour hardly qualifies as fun. But nevertheless, Chase gives me his full attention from the moment we get started. He's already been through the administrative offices, he informs me, the storage areas too. So I skip those rooms and lead him around the corner to the classrooms that are scattered along the long hall to our right. It takes all of about five minutes to walk past and peer into twelve square rooms filled with empty desks and empty chairs.

"Which one is your classroom?" he asks when we reach the end of the hall.

"Oh," I breathe out, surprised, but pleased that this gorgeous man is interested enough to make such an inquiry.

I point to where the tour started, at the other end of the hall. "It's down there. It's the first one we passed."

We start back down the hall side-by-side, our bodies parting the gray sea of lockers once more. When we reach the first classroom on the right, I say, "This is it."

Chase nods and we step inside. This is the first day of break, but nostalgia washes over me. I glance over at my desk wistfully, and then to all the little, empty desks. Chase, meanwhile, walks around the front of the small classroom, examining and touching everything. He taps the chalkboard with his knuckles, picks up and checks out a dried-up potted plant on the ledge beneath the windows, and then flips an eraser sitting on a desk over. Chase appears to be very hands-on.

When my hands-on companion reaches my desk, he picks up a big, shiny red ceramic apple that is sitting next to a pencil sharpener. There's a goofy, lopsided smiley face on one side of the apple. Chase turns to me and quirks an eyebrow.

"From one of the kids," I explain. "Well, actually one of their mothers."

With care, Chase places the smiling apple back down on the desk and continues his perusal. He walks down the middle row of desks, lifting up a couple of the tops on his way to the back.

"They're all empty," I tell him as I lean against the frame of the door.

Chase shrugs one shoulder, continues to the back of the room, and then returns to the front of the class. Not just the children's desks are empty. The whole room is mostly devoid of supplies and décor, with the exception of a few drawings pinned up on the corkboard trim around the sides of the chalkboard.

The drawings have garnered Chase's attention, so I explain, "Some of the kids chose to leave their artwork here for next year's class."

One particular sketch seems to have captured Chase's attention. It's a drawing of a teacher pointing to a chalkboard in front of a full class. The teacher is just a stick figure lady with *burnt sienna* crayon-colored hair. An A of lime—a dress—cloaks her stick body. The drawing is basic; a depiction created by first-grade hands. But out of all the little pictures this one is clearly the best. It stands out, a gem among mediocrity. Despite its simplicity, there's a lot of detail— windows with a springtime view, crooked white letters on a black chalkboard, the red apple on my desk that Chase was handling just minutes ago.

"That's supposed to be you, right?" Chase asks, glancing over his shoulder at me as he points to the stick figure lady.

"Yes." I laugh.

He turns back to the drawing and taps the construction paper. "This is actually very good." I nod, even though he's still focused on the drawing and can't see me. "For having been drawn by someone so young," he qualifies, still turned away.

"It is really good," I agree. "One of my students, Timmy Froehlich, drew it. I think it shows great potential. He's got talent, that's for sure."

Chase nods slowly in agreement, and since I'm curious as to why badass Chase Gartner is taking such an interest in the cutesy drawings of my students, I take a chance and ask, "Are you interested in art? Do you draw?"

Gorgeous cheeks redden ever so slightly. "A little," he says quietly, before starting back to the door, head down.

"Wait," I say as he hurriedly walks past me. I follow him out into the hall. "Are you any good?"

Now, badass Gartner is definitely blushing, avoiding my stare.

"You are, aren't you?" I press, laughing a little at how cute his sudden shyness is.

He stops, turns to me, and shrugs his shoulders. "I don't

know, maybe. I guess I'm okay. I'll show you some sketches sometime and you can judge for yourself."

His eyes meet mine, and the way he looks at me—really looks at me, like he's trying to see *in* me, or figure me out—makes me blush, for the second time this day.

Wondering if I'll ever get used to this man's unexpected moments of intensity, I softly mutter, "Come on," and then I lead the way to the stairwell across from my classroom.

We finish off the tour with the gymnasium downstairs and then return to the hall outside Mr. Kelly's office.

"That's it," I proclaim with a dramatic flourish of my arm. I frown. "Sadly, we've reached the end of the tour."

Chase leans back against the wall and crosses his well-muscled arms. "Well, that took all of about…what? Ten minutes?"

I pull my cell from my purse. "Fourteen minutes, actually." I toss my cell back in and look up at Chase. "I told you there wasn't much to see."

"But there was," Chase responds softly, a smile playing at his lips. "I got to see your classroom."

"Yeah, you did."

I'm not sure where we should go from here. Like, should we part ways, or hang out in the school a while longer? I've no idea, but luckily Chase has a great suggestion.

"It looks like we still have about forty-five minutes for lunch. Would you want to grab a bite to eat?"

Spending forty-five more minutes with Chase is something I am not about to decline. I don't tell him *that* exactly, but I do accept. And after a short deliberation, we decide on a diner on Market that's only a short walk away.

The old-fashioned restaurant—known to everyone in

town as simply *the diner*—has been a Harmony Creek staple for years, situated on the same busy corner since the fifties. I haven't walked into the place in ages, but I've eaten meals there with my parents in the past, a lifetime ago.

When Chase and I walk in, I glance around. Nothing has changed; everything's the same as I remember. Black-and-white checkered linoleum floor, an old-fashioned soda fountain along the back wall, Formica counters, and dozens of black-and-white framed photos on the walls. Grainy images of how things once were in this small town. Booths, covered in maroon vinyl, line the row of windows in the front and stretch around to a closed-in section on the side.

Chase and I ask to be seated at one of the booths with a view to the outside world.

"It smells so good in here," I say to Chase as the hostess leads us to our booth.

"You're not kidding," he replies.

After we're seated, we peruse the laminated menus and order. Chase chooses today's special: the double-decker burger and fries. I stick with a salad.

"Hungry?" I ask when the food arrives and my good-looking lunch companion digs right in.

"Starving," he says, looking up at me briefly before returning to his big, manly bites.

I imagine Chase probably doesn't cook much for himself, seeing as he lives all alone out in that old farmhouse. But I don't ask anything, I just let him eat in peace.

By the time Chase is finished, I'm still picking at my salad. It's not that I am not hungry—I am, quite a bit in fact—but I feel self-conscious. It's silly, I know, but I am just not used to eating with another person, especially not someone as undeniably gorgeous as the man across from me.

When the waitress brings our check, I reach in my purse for some money. "I got this," Chase says.

I know he's not making a whole lot more than me working for the church, so I throw up the hand not digging around in the purse and wave it back and forth. "No, no. I have money—"

"Seriously, Kay," he interrupts, putting his hand over the check like it's already decided.

I huff, and he adds, "Think of it as my way of saying thank you for the tour."

I have to laugh at that one. "My tour was barely worth the cost of our iced teas, Chase."

My comment is not entirely in jest. I truly believe I should pay my share, and the "tour" just doesn't cover it.

Chase picks up the check. "I have a proposal, then." Suddenly, I am all ears. "You let me get this," he continues, waving the check a little, "and, in return, I'm going to ask you for a favor. There's something I need help with."

"Okay," I agree, before I even know what I'm agreeing to.

Heck, I could be agreeing to birth his firstborn. Not likely, but it's sure fun to imagine, especially the part pertaining to exactly *what* we'd have to do for me to uphold my end of the bargain. It would definitely require engaging in some of that crazy-good sex Chase supposedly knows how to make happen.

While I am lost in inappropriate thoughts Chase would probably be shocked to learn, he pulls out a piece of paper from the back pocket of his jeans. He unfolds and places it on the table.

"I have an apartment I'd like to rent. I drew up this flyer last night." Chase taps the piece of paper. "The place I want to rent is on my property, but separate from the main house. It's above a garage that's not been used in years." He runs his fingers through his hair, making a few strands stick out at funny angles. I suppress a smile. "So, if you could make some copies of this flyer for me, I'd really appreciate it. That's worth the price of lunch, right? What do you say, sound like a fair deal?"

Even if I paid my own bill, I'd still make the copies for Chase. But since he seems so determined, I accept his proposal. In doing so, I am a little saddened that no crazy-good sex is in my future. But I'm also really curious to see this apartment. Anything has to be better than mine. Maybe I can afford what Chase is asking and he won't have to even bother with flyers.

"May I?" I ask, my fingers grazing the edge of the paper.

"Sure."

I slide the flyer out from under Chase's hand. All the apartment specifics are listed, as well as a price, and a very sharp, colorful picture.

But, wait…I take a closer look.

The picture isn't a copy of a photo, not one taped to the flyer either. Nope, it's an actual drawing, an incredibly good drawing. It's very detailed, better than a photo. It is art; real, true art.

"You drew this?" I ask on an exhale of air. I am beyond impressed.

Chase just presses his lips together and gives a quick nod.

This guy across from me isn't just an artist; he's an insanely talented one. He just draws a little? Yeah, right. Obviously he played this talent down back at the school. Not only is the rendering of the place he wants to rent amazing, but the apartment itself is incredible. It puts my basement atrocity to shame.

My apartment is dark and stuffy, whereas this one appears bright and welcoming. Skylights line the low, sloped ceiling, showing off a rather nice living space. It's not huge, but it'd be more than adequate for a person living alone, a person like me. On one side of the space, there's a living room area, complete with a sofa, coffee table, and even a TV. On the opposite side, separated by a breakfast bar, there's an adorable little kitchen. If Chase's drawing is accurate—and I feel sure it is—then all of the appliances must be new, they look immaculate.

A working oven! What a dream. I hold the flyer close to my face. Like when Chase was checking out Timmy's drawing in my classroom, it's now my turn to evaluate and assess.

There's a kind of half-wall drawn between the living room and bedroom, but Chase has made it transparent so the details of the sleeping area are on full view. The bedroom is as nice as the living room, kind of a retro shabby chic. There's a double bed with an iron headboard, a trunk at the base, and a nightstand with an old-fashioned lamp.

"This is amazing," I exclaim. "It's really a great place, Chase. I'm sure you'll find a tenant in no time."

"That's what I'm hoping," he replies.

I glance at the price, wishing that the future tenant could

be me. But what he's asking is out of my price range, at least until I have more money saved.

Maybe Chase sees how I bite my lip in contemplation, or how my eyes fill with disappointment. In any case, he ventures, "Are you looking for a place?"

I start to shake my head, and he quickly adds, "We can always negotiate on price, Kay. My first rate was lower. I'd be more than happy with that."

I see Chase is sincere, but I can't ask him to take less than what he will surely get for such a fantastic space. Even the higher price is a deal...for someone who can afford it.

Chase must misunderstand my reticence, for he tries to convince me. "This place is completely private, Kay, if that's what you're worried about. The garage sits away from the main house, with a whole separate parking area branching away from the driveway. So, it's not like you'd be stuck seeing me around all the time, if that's what you're thinking."

"It's not that," I slowly answer, since it's not, not at all. "It's just..." I trail off.

Chase waits for me to continue, one eyebrow lifted, like he's saying, *Yeah, so what's the problem?*

I try to explain, without bringing up the money part. "I may be looking for a place in the future. Like, this fall. But right now I'm stuck with what I have." I sigh. "But I have to admit"—my eyes settle longingly on the flyer—"this place is much, much nicer."

I realize then that Chase has no idea where I live; it's not yet come up. It's kind of common knowledge where the Gartner property is, out on Cold Springs Lane. But my place...ugh. It's not like I run around announcing from the rooftops, "Hey, everyone, guess what? I live in a dump down in the scariest part of town."

However, there's no avoiding the subject now. "Wait. Where do you live?" Chase asks.

With a lot of dread and hesitation, I tell him. And—big surprise—his expression morphs from mere curiosity to out-and-out disturbed.

"You're kidding," he mutters in a low voice. "Kay, that's no place for a woman to live, especially by herself."

"Sexist, much?" I scoff and level him with a no-nonsense stare.

He scrubs his hand over his face and leans back in the booth. "I didn't mean it like that."

He sounds sincere and I know he didn't intend any offense, but I just wish he'd drop the subject. I can't meet his blues; I stare down at the table instead.

"It's just that it's not safe down there for anyone, really." Softly, he adds, "I know exactly where your building is. I used to, uh... I guess you could say I used to hang out down there a lot. That was a long time ago, sure, but the whole area was bad even back then."

I glance up and something flashes in Chase's eyes. That something tells me he knows all too well the kind of people who hang out on my side of town—junkies, people searching desperately for their next high. Maybe Chase once sought to score there too? Why else would he be so familiar with the area? I know his past, I know why he went to prison—convicted for dealing Ecstasy. But beyond what's common knowledge there's too much knowing in the gunmetal blues of the man sitting across from me.

There's a well-known dealer that lives just down the

street from me, not far from the closed-down glass factory. It's probably not a far-fetched guess to assume Chase
has spent time at that dealer's house. It's a popular party
spot, and has been for years. I've personally never ventured
down the dirt road that beckons the drug-needy, but many,
many people have, looking for the false salvation the dealer's selling. Was Chase once among that crowd? I can't help
but think yes, most likely.

The waitress arrives to take the check and I smoothly
change the subject. Things lighten up from there. On the
way back to the church, Chase and I exchange phone numbers. We start joking around again, flirting like we were doing earlier.

At one point, I ask Chase why there's no paint on him.
After all, he's supposedly been working all morning. With a
smirk he says he's just *that* damn good and knows what he's
doing. *Yikes.* That comment—and the suggestive way it's
delivered—elicits my third blush of the day. And I am quite
sure—from the smug look on my flirtatious new friend's
perfect face—that it's the exact reaction he intended.

I may be blushing, this is true, but I decide that I like
this playful version of Chase Gartner the absolute very best.

And so it continues…

Tuesday I get a text, a little before noon: *Hey, sweet girl.*

The cute endearment makes me grin, but it also thumps
my heart.

Hey, artist boy. How goes the painting today?

It's going, he texts back. *Are you hungry? Want to see
what's up at our diner?*

Now, my heart actually skips a beat. I like this "our"
stuff.

Before the first text arrived, I'd taken a tuna salad on wheat out from a brown paper bag. Now, I hastily stuff it back in.

With an uncontained smile, I text back: *Absolutely. Meet you out front in a few.*

Five minutes later Chase and I are walking down to the diner, "our" diner. I'm kind of quiet, deep in thought, thinking of how I really like spending time with this guy at my side. A bee buzzes a circle around my head and Chase waves it away, all protective-like. I smile in gratitude.

Chase gives my shoulder a bump with his arm. "Ah, now I've got your attention. Not much to say today, huh, quiet girl?" He raises an eyebrow. "Everything's okay, right?"

Walking next to Chase, things are so far beyond *okay* I can barely contain myself.

I return the bump, with my hip to the top of his leg. "Maybe I'm just saving all my talking for when we get to the diner," I shoot back. "Just wait, soon enough you'll be missing the quiet me."

"Any you you're giving, Kay, is fine with me," is his quiet retort. His words make my heart skip two beats this time.

Despite his ability to say these things that make my heart thump and skip, I am actually growing more comfortable around Chase. This complicated guy may have moments of intensity that catch me off guard, but there's this current of ease—of rightness—I feel in just being around him. You know how once in a while you meet someone you just connect with, right from the start. Well, it's like that, but...more. I feel connected to Chase, but pulled to him as well. Something is developing here, something intoxicating. Whatever it is it makes me positively giddy. I don't want this feeling to pass, but I sure hope Chase feels something similar.

At the diner, back in the same booth as yesterday, we order food and talk about our mornings. We also eye each other knowingly a while later when our waitress, who has turned into a bitch since shortly after we sat down, ignores us for the umpteenth time. I've already told Chase I suspect our disgruntled server's change in attitude—from overly friendly at the start to progressively dismissive—is a direct result of him not flirting back when we first sat down and ordered. The waitress, a different one from yesterday, worked her game pretty hard initially, giggling and trying to catch Chase's eye as she took our orders and brought us waters. She gave up though when she realized the beautiful man seated across from me wasn't going to play with her, a fact that pleased me far more than it probably should have. But it did, especially since our waitress is very pretty.

We finished our meals a while ago, but Miss Disgruntled has yet to clear our plates. I also asked for more water about ten minutes ago, but that's apparently been forgotten as well.

While we wait, I steal a few leftover fries from Chase's plate, and we check out the old photographs lining the dividers between the big windows. The photo closest to Chase depicts a part of town that was once all farmland.

"The first house my dad ever built is in the plan that's there now," Chase says, unmistakable pride in his voice as his eyes remain on the faded photograph.

Everyone in town knows Chase's father passed away several years ago out in Vegas. Suicide is the rumor. But even though it was a long time ago, there's no telling how raw the wounds remaining still may be. If there's one thing I've learned, firsthand, it's that time doesn't always heal every wound, especially those on the psyche. Therefore, I tread carefully.

"That's pretty impressive," I begin. "I've driven by that plan a lot, and those homes are *very* nice. Really well-built, too, I've heard."

Chase's eyes stay on the photo. "Yeah, I guess they are." His voice is so low I can barely hear him.

"So, you're family has always lived here? Like, your grandparents, are they from Harmony Creek too?"

I'm trying to not talk specifically about his father—those wounds obviously still run deep, as I suspected—but I don't want to change the subject completely. I'd like to learn more about Chase's background.

"Yeah," he replies, looking away from the picture and back in my direction. "My grandparents were born here and they lived here all their lives. The house I live in now has been in our family for decades."

"That's out on Cold Springs Lane, right?"

I know the answer, but I want to keep the conversation flowing. Chase nods, and then, to my delight, he shares a little bit of detail from his early childhood.

His parents lived with his grandmother in the Cold Springs Lane house right after they were first married. They were young, he tells me, just turned twenty. Chase was born soon after. He says some of his earliest memories are of living in the farmhouse. He recalls his father once putting him up on his shoulders, walking around the property, and telling him it would one day all belong to him.

"Never thought it would be this soon though," Chase

says sadly as he glances back at the picture of the land where his dad built his first house.

Chase seems to become a little lost in his memories as he continues talking, telling me how his mom used to read him bedtime stories when he was really little. She'd tuck him in his covers, kiss his forehead, and promise him their family would always be together.

"We're strong, honey," he tells me she'd say. "I love you and your father more than life itself. Nothing will ever tear us apart."

That's what she'd tell the little boy who grew into the stunningly handsome man now sitting across from me. But even I know how that turned out.

Chase suddenly looks like maybe he's divulged too much, and he quickly moves his story forward, detailing instead how his father's construction business started to do really well. His parents moved out of the farmhouse, stayed here in Harmony Creek for a few more years, and then moved out to Nevada. His little brother, Will, was born out there, back when Chase was nine.

"Las Vegas, wow, can't get much different than here," I say. "So, what was it like?"

I mean the climate, the city, but Chase thinks I mean something else, something more personal. He looks away, out the window, to where there's a family walking by—a dad, a mom, a little boy.

"It was good...for a while. And then, not so much."

Chase doesn't elaborate, and I don't press. It's obviously a touchy subject. It's tense for a few beats, but then Chase asks me if I was also born here in Harmony Creek.

The tension lifts, I pilfer a few more fries, and breathe a

sigh of relief. "No, I was born in Columbus. We lived there for a while, and then we moved out here."

"How old were you when your family moved here?" Chase asks, sliding his plate closer so I no longer have to reach.

I grab another fry, dip it in ketchup. "We moved here when I was ten," I reply between bites.

"That explains why I never met you when I was a kid," he says, like this is something he's been thinking about, considering. "We moved out to Vegas when I was eight. How old are you?"

"Twenty-three."

Chase picks up one of his fries. "That's what I thought. You're a year younger." He takes a bite. "You would've still been in Columbus when we left Ohio."

"Where in town did you live right before you moved out west?" I ask. "Out near your grandmother's house?"

There are only two fries left and Chase indicates I should eat them. I swirl one through the ketchup. Chase watches my movement for a few seconds, then answers. "No, we lived south of Market."

"No way!" I exclaim, pointing my fry at him before biting into it. "That's where we lived too," I add.

The roads we once lived on—we soon discover—were only a block apart. How differently my life may have turned out if Chase had never left Harmony Creek back when he was a boy. Perhaps my first boyfriend would have been him instead of Doug Wilson. How great would that have been? The whole course of history could have been altered, and maybe Sarah would still be alive today. Yeah, maybe... If only and what if, they don't count for much in retrospect.

Chase notices that I've gotten quiet, and I must look as distraught as I feel, because he asks in a very worried tone, "Hey, what's wrong?"

I quickly compose myself. If there's one thing I'm a pro at, it's pulling my shit together and deflecting other people's concerns.

With an ease I don't feel inside, I try to make a joke. "No, it's nothing. Just, I mean, south of Market...to where I live now." I gesture to the window, in the direction of the west side of town. "Pretty pathetic, huh? It's quite a drastic change, even I have to admit."

The waitress comes to the table—at long last—and finally refills our waters. Chase continues to ignore her. She huffs, loudly, as she leaves. I take a drink. Chase's blues never leave me. "What?" I say, setting down my glass.

He sighs and runs his fingers through his hair. "Kay, it's none of my business, I know. But I thought about it a lot last night, and I still can't wrap my mind around the idea of you living down there. I don't want to make you angry, but I have to say—one more time—I think you should seriously consider moving."

He's right, but I try to play it down. "I'll be fine, Chase. I've lived there for a year now, and I've never had a single problem."

I don't share that I fear the junkies and their leering stares; I don't tell him the area has gotten so downtrodden that the only grocery store closed its doors. No, I say none of those things. Even so, I'm sure Chase is well aware.

He taps his long fingers on the table. "Still, I don't like it." He sighs. "Are you sure there's no way I can talk you into renting the place above my garage?"

"Chase..." I begin, "I would, it's a great place and I'd love to live there. But, I...just...can't."

He shrugs one shoulder, like he's done trying. For now. He probably thinks I'm worried about how it will look if I move onto his property, but it has nothing to do with that. I just don't want Chase taking less money for my sake, it's just not right. And I would never ask him to wait until the fall to rent his place. He probably needs the money now. I just have to forget about his amazing apartment and stick with my original plan. I'll save money this summer and find a new apartment in the fall. If his place happens to be—by some miracle—still available, well, then maybe.

We drop the apartment conversation and talk returns to family. Chase asks me some questions, and I tell him some things about my early life.

He asks what it was like growing up in Columbus. "Not much different than living here in Harmony Creek, just a little bigger," I reply.

I don't say much about my parents. And I definitely don't touch on the shell of a relationship we currently have—nonexistent with my mother, not much better with my dad. I also only say a few words about Sarah. Like, I mention that I once had a little sister, but she passed away.

I don't need to say more. When her name passes my lips I see right away—from his expression of sadness and pity—that Chase already knows the story, at least the story everyone assumes to be true. I can't say I'm surprised. Gossip is like a pastime here in Harmony Creek. That's how I know so many things about Chase, things he'd never dream I knew. Or maybe he would. He knows this town as well as me.

Chase must sense that I'm uncomfortable, he smoothly steers the conversation back to his own early years. He becomes more open, to a point. It sounds like he once had a great life in Nevada, until his father died. He doesn't say much about his dad dying—just that he did—but it becomes clear that was the point where many of Chase's troubles began.

A few of those he shares.

But he paints in broad strokes, giving just an overall picture, leaving out details, like how he really felt about everything that was happening.

Chase mentions that he, his mom, and his brother lived on the road for a while, after his dad died and their house was repossessed. At some point his mom won some money and the three of them finally moved into an apartment.

That's it, that's what he says. All nonchalant, like it was no big deal he lived in a minivan with two other people for a while. Or that it was acceptable his mother spent much of her time in casinos, leaving Will in Chase's care, and giving her eldest far too many opportunities to get into trouble. Some of which I know all about, like his drug use.

That's what he talks about now, albeit briefly.

Chase touches on the fact that he once used, and though it's only a mention, I appreciate his honesty on the subject. Despite his downplayed version of events, it's very apparent drugs once played a huge role in his life. I also sense Chase is uncomfortable talking about drugs and the role they once played. After his first few remarks, he quickly changes the subject. So quickly in fact that it tells me a part of this man still battles to stay clean.

We're both quiet for a few minutes, and I assume Chase

is done talking, but then he mentions his brother. His whole face lights up when he talks of this Will-kid. But when he mentions how he had to leave Vegas, leave Will, back when he was eighteen, Chase's expression saddens.

He tells me when he returned to Harmony Creek the hardest part was leaving his brother back in Vegas with their mom. Chase didn't want to come back, his mother made him. He doesn't say it outright, but I can tell Chase still misses his brother very much, even after all these years.

I ask Chase to tell me more, hoping for a happy story. In a weird way hearing about his little brother makes me feel better about Sarah. Even though I will never again be someone's older sister, Chase sharing his older-sibling perspective comforts me. And the obvious depth of his love for his brother reminds me of how very much I once loved Sarah. I still do, but that love is static, unchanging. Chase's relationship with his brother is the opposite, it's ever-changing. Mine with Sarah will forever stay stuck in place. Their relationship is dynamic, full of *life*.

My heart needs life. I've been immersed in death for far too long, and I yearn to soak up any stories Chase has that celebrates living. So that's exactly what I do when he shares this happy tale…

"Will," Chase laughs, reminiscing. "That kid was so uncoordinated when he was younger. Shit. And funny as hell." He pauses, smiles this really genuine smile that makes me grin right along with him. I don't care if I'm living vicariously; at least I'm *living* again.

Chase continues, "But Will was always too stubborn for his own damn good. Still is, in fact."

A flash of pain crosses Chase's face when he utters that

last sentence. It tells me there's a rift between him and his brother. It doesn't take a genius to figure out it probably has a lot to do with Chase going to prison. I don't pry though. I just let Chase talk. And soon he's wrapped up in telling me about a time he and his little brother were catching lizards in the backyard of their house in Vegas, the one that got repossessed.

"God, Kay, it was so funny." Chase chuckles. "Will was probably around five, I don't know, maybe he was six. Anyway, there were always these lizards in our backyard, tons of them, little guys, all brown and skinny. Kind of cute, though, you'd like them. They run like crazy when you get too close. But they're harmless. They don't bite or anything and you can catch them if you're fast enough."

"I bet you were fast," I muse, biting my lip. Just looking at Chase—all lean and streamlined—you just know he'd be quick.

Chase smiles at me, like he knows what I'm thinking. He probably does, he seems intuitive like that.

"I guess I was fast." He shrugs. "But my brother sure wasn't."

Chase sits back in the booth and presses his lips together, like he's suppressing another laugh. "That poor kid couldn't catch a single lizard that day. I'd already caught, like, a couple dozen in less than an hour, and I was hardly trying. Will, though…" Chase shakes his head. "He couldn't catch a single one."

"Why not?" I ask. "Was it because he was so much younger?"

"Nah," Chase says, "that wasn't it. His friends always caught plenty when they were over. Will was just too impatient, and he couldn't judge distance for shit. Every time he spotted one—like, after bunches ran past without his even noticing—he'd jump at the poor sucker like some kind of a maniac. Then, in all that haste, he'd trip right over his own two feet and fall on his ass."

I try to imagine this cute little kid running around a backyard in Vegas, stumbling around, while trying so hard to keep up with his much more coordinated older brother.

"So, what happened? I bet you felt bad and caught one for him."

"No, no way." Chase pauses. "I mean, yeah, I felt bad, but Will would never have gone for me catching one for him. He had to do it himself. Otherwise, it was like it didn't count. He was like that with everything." Chase takes a breath and the smile in his blues warms me. "So, I sat there and waited, slowly let go of all my lizards as the day came to an end. I thought maybe Will would catch one of those. But no, that kid didn't even notice them running off. He just chased other random lizards around the yard until it finally got dark."

"Did he ever catch one?" I ask. I'm invested in this story now and hoping for a happy conclusion.

"He did," Chase confirms, flicking the base of his water glass with his finger.

"Yay," I cheer, making Chase look up at me from under these long, long lashes. He smiles, I smile wider. "See," I continue, "Will's persistence paid off. I bet he was ecstatic."

"Beyond." Chase nods. "In fact, he was so damn pumped he almost squeezed the poor thing to death."

My eyes widen, imagining one squished and lifeless lizard. "Oh, no," I gasp.

"Don't worry," Chase says in a hurried voice, probably due to my horrified expression. "I saved the little fellow from Will's death grip." He chuckles again. "Kay, you should have seen that lizard run. I mean, they're all fast, but this one was so relieved to have made it that he looked like he was nothing but air. Like something out of a cartoon or some shit."

I sigh. It's official. I love the way Chase tells stories, especially this one, reliving a once happy time with his brother. I settle in the booth, all set to hear more. But when Chase glances up at the big clock on the wall, I know it's time for us to get back to work.

"Tomorrow?" he asks as we rise to leave.

"Yes," I say enthusiastically, "absolutely."

And just like that the diner becomes part of our daily routine. I quit bringing brown bag lunches. Sometimes one of us texts prior, but mostly our lunch dates are a given.

Wednesday, I go over to the school to meet Chase. Thursday and Friday, he comes to get me. We sit at the same booth every day, share more and more stories. We are slowly becoming friends, real friends.

I learn more about Chase, and he learns more about me—little things, big things, lots and lots of stuff. Like, I discover Chase was born in April, he learns my birthday falls in February. His middle name is Michael; I tell him mine is Marie. I love pickles, but Chase hates them with a passion. He gives them to me, with a grimace, whenever they're on his plate at lunch.

I also discover Chase loves lemon-lime soda, like to a bizarre extent. He even brings a small cooler of the stuff to work. Not the name-brand variety, mind you, just the store brand in the no-frills green metal can, big yellow letters spelling out *lemon-lime* on the side.

One afternoon in the hallway of the school, I tease him as he finishes off a can. "All that sugar, Chase." I shake my head in mock disapproval. "You better watch. You could end up fat. It creeps up on you slowly, I hear. You might not even realize it until it's too late."

We both know this is so far from reality that it's laughable, but that's kind of the point.

Chase pitches the can into a recycle bin and plays along.

"You think?" he asks as he lifts up the hem of his T-shirt and displays probably the finest washboard abs I've ever seen.

It's not easy, but I resist the urge to reach out and touch the cut abs *and* the trail of fine hair leading down into his low-slung jeans. I swallow, hard.

Chase smirks as I mumble, "Nope, I was wrong. You're good for now."

And is he ever. Damn, like I needed a reminder of how hot Chase is. When we get to the diner that day I ask for extra ice in my water.

I think about the other things I've learned about the hottest guy in town, a guy who I can now call my friend. One of my many discoveries is that Chase has quite the appetite, he orders huge lunches. I noted this the first day we ate together, but it continues throughout the week. And like our first lunch, I still order salads…or a small sandwich.

It's not like I'm trying to eat like a bird, not anymore, and it's not that I'm too nervous to eat around Chase, like day one. It's just that the smaller stuff is all I can afford.

Needless to say, I'm secretly pleased when I find out Chase likes to share.

Besides the pickles from his plate, he orders extra fries every day and gives me half. He knows I won't let him pay—apart from that first day—so I suspect it's his way of surreptitiously buying me food.

Another thing I learn—and this is definitely my favorite—is that Chase likes to tease and play. I think, maybe, he's just that way with me. And that makes his teasing and playing so, *so* much better, like it's our thing, something between only us.

But today, Friday, the teasing and playing are on the back burner for now. We're just having a regular discussion. Chase has just returned from the restroom, and I've packed away my thoughts. He picks up on the story he was telling before he got up from the table, reiterating again how he thought he was really going to die from embarrassment when Father Maridale asked to see his sketchbook the day he was offered the job. He tells me about the artwork inside, says it's all prison-related stuff. And though he gives me some light details, I have a feeling he's abbreviating the content.

"Can I see it sometime?" I dare to ask.

Chase seems to ponder my request. His jaw flexes, and he appears somewhat conflicted. At last, he gives me a "Maybe."

That's good enough for me. Possibility, that's what Chase and I are all about.

I take a sip of iced tea. "What was it like?" I softly ask, toying with my straw.

Chase looks up. "What?"

"Prison," I whisper.

Based on his grimace I know I shouldn't have asked. Chase pushes away his plate of half-eaten grilled cheese, and it's not because he's saved some for me. No, he looks upset. He leans back in the booth and scrubs his hand down his face. "What do you want to know exactly?" His tone is flat.

I shrug. "I don't know. I guess…just what it was like in general."

When he doesn't answer right away, I hastily amend, "Look, we don't have to talk about it." I push my own plate away and almost knock over my glass. I stop it from falling and keep my eyes glued to the table. "I'm sorry, Chase, I shouldn't have brought it up."

"Hey, hey…" He places his hand on mine. It's rough and calloused in places, but also smooth in others, and definitely warm and strong all over.

"I don't mind you asking." He squeezes my hand gently. "But there's nothing really to tell. Whatever you imagine prison is like, Kay, however horrible. Multiply it by a hundred times, maybe a thousand, and you still won't even be close."

"Chase…" I glance up and we hold one another's gaze.

A dozen emotions pass. The resulting connection gives me the confidence to flip the hand that's under his over. Our palms touch—rough against soft—and it feels so very *right* for some reason. Before I even know what I'm doing I wrap my fingers around Chase's hand and squeeze lightly. And for about thirty seconds, there is no one in the diner but me and my wayward boy. Or so it seems.

His eyes hold mine, his mouth opens. I fear what he

might say. Reject me, or not reject me. Both are equally scary at this point.

Fear overrides everything else and I yank my hand away. "Sorry," I mumble, my gaze skittering away.

Chase says nothing, but I feel him watching me. At the same time, the lingering warmth from his hand having been on mine has my whole arm tingling. When our hands were touching, and our eyes meeting, something happened, some stronger bonding. I mentally chastise myself for chickening out and not letting the moment play out.

Under the table, out of sight, I hold the hand touched by my complicated and beautiful friend. I cling to the possibility that something—something that gives me butterflies in my stomach and skipped beats in my heart—may be starting here.

Without looking up, I whisper, "We should get back."

As we head back to the church, nothing further is discussed regarding the whole sort-of-but-not-really-hand-holding exchange. We amble back, side-by-side, in somewhat awkward silence, until Chase notices me trying to readjust the tie holding my ponytail in place.

"Here, let me," he offers.

Suddenly, there's mischief in his blues. I grin in relief. This is Chase getting us back to where we need to be. So it's an easy decision to accept his assistance, even though I know some sort of tomfoolery is afoot. Truthfully, I have no idea what he's up to, but I can't wait to find out.

I turn so my back is facing Chase, but instead of adjusting the hair tie, like he's supposed to, he slides the band all the way down my hair in one smooth move. Then, he promptly takes off.

"Hey," I call out after him.

Stopping several yards away, Chase turns back to me and dangles the hair tie from his fingers. "Come and get it, sweet girl," he purrs.

He's talking about the hair tie, I remind myself, momentarily wishing he meant something else entirely.

"No fair, Chase. I have a dress on here." For emphasis, I flip up the hem of my eyelet lace dress. "How am I supposed to catch you when I'm wearing this?"

Chase cocks his head to the side, his hungry eyes on my bare legs. "I don't know, lacy girl. Why don't you hike that pretty dress up a little higher and try to catch me."

Oh. My. God.

I want to hike my dress up for Chase, and, damn, do I long to catch him. Hearing him *say* these things though, in that sex-promising voice, makes me have to remind myself to breathe.

"I dare you," he taunts. And that's all it takes.

For Chase, I accept dares, I'm learning to take chances. He makes me feel unafraid. I'm willing to let go and live when I am with this man. So, with no further hesitation, I lift white lace up with abandon, and take off after my favorite Chase—playful Chase.

Thankfully, I have on flats and I miraculously manage to catch him. Well, okay, he lets me catch him. But it still feels good. I play-punch him in the arm with one hand, while making sure my dress hem is back down and in place with the other.

"Ouch." He pretends like my play-punch really hurts, which makes us both laugh, because, really, who is he kidding?

"Okay, tough girl, turn around," he says, spinning me so my back is facing him and he can put the tie he stole back in my hair.

I stand perfectly still while Chase works my hair back into the tie. His fingers work adeptly, but also gently and carefully, never pulling or tugging. It amazes me that hands that punish and perpetrate violence against men—I've heard of how brutal some of his fights have been—can touch me like this, tenderly, so sweetly. But I already know Chase is complex and his actions are sometimes contradictory. After all, the same hands that break bones also create beautiful art. Yet another contradiction of this complicated man. This complicated man that I am *really* starting to like.

Chase's fingers graze the back of my neck lightly as he secures the tie and the hair around it. I shiver a little, my body instinctively leaning back into him.

Maybe Chase feels the pull too, because he places his hands on my shoulders, his lips at my ear. "All done, sweet girl," he murmurs, his warm breath caressing my neck and giving me goose bumps.

Our bodies are so close, touching, but not. Heat radiates from his chest to my back. His proximity, his lips at my ear, I am left all aflutter. But then Chase breaks the spell when he gives my newly secured ponytail a little flip and steps away.

When we start to walk once more, I *cannot* stop smiling. I glance over at Chase, and though he stares straight ahead, I see a grin on his lips too.

I decide this day with Chase Gartner—my friend, my maybe-possibility—is the best one yet.

The weekend is weird with no Chase, no lunches with him at the diner. I do see my sharply dressed boy on Sunday, at Mass. He's sitting in his usual spot in the back, and I'm sitting with Missy and her mom.

I find it odd that Missy doesn't glance back even once to where Chase is seated, nor does she urge me to do so. Nonetheless, I steal a peek on my own and when Chase looks up I give him a quick wave. He smiles and waves back, and then he bows his head.

When I turn back to Missy she's glaring at me. "Why are you waving to *him*?" she hisses.

I shrug my shoulders. "I don't know, Why not? You're the one who's always going on and on about how hot he is. What's with the change in attitude anyway?"

She snorts. "He may be hot, Kay, but he's also a real prick." She says this low, so her mom doesn't hear.

The organ music begins to play so I don't have a chance to ask anything more. But I have to wonder: Did Chase do something to piss Missy off? I didn't think they really knew each other all that well, but maybe I'm mistaken. Or, maybe her crush has just run its course. Who knows? Who cares? I let the thought slip away as I open my hymnal.

The minute Mass ends, Chase is out the door, which is just as well. I have my weekly visit to attend to. But this week when I kneel at Sarah's grave I don't just tell her three more things I'll never forget about her. I also tell her all about my new friend, Chase Gartner.

"I think you'd like him," I say while clearing grass clippings from her marker. "He has a younger sibling too. A brother named Will. He's turning fifteen soon."

I pick up the tiny bouquet of wild violets from last

week. It's wilted and dried. I sigh and put it back. "Chase doesn't say it outright, Sarah, but I can tell he misses his little brother. It's kind of sad. He told me Will won't talk to him anymore. And the look on his face…I just don't know."

I exhale loudly and think about how Chase quietly told me on one of our walks back to the church that his brother hates him for going to prison. I'd suspected as much. Anyway, Will refuses to respond to any of Chase's calls or texts. I told him I feel confident his little brother's cold shoulder won't last forever. That made him smile.

What I didn't say is that Will is alive, not gone like Sarah. And where there's life, forgiveness always has the chance to prevail.

The next two weeks are more of the same. Lunches with Chase go on, and we continue to learn more and more about one another. There are smiles and laughter, playing and flirting, and more confiding.

Something I keep to myself, however, are my feelings for this man. They've deepened considerably and Chase is becoming more than just a very good friend. He represents life and friendship, two things that were seriously lacking in my pre-Chase existence. But it's more than just the hope and possibility Chase shows me that draws me to him. There's definitely something else, something strong, something burning. I don't know, though, if I'm ready to label all these foreign emotions I'm feeling. Maybe that's because I have a secret I don't know if I'll ever be able to share. And that bothers me, because we're starting to share just about everything.

Chase and I share a lot, we've become much more open, but I still can't bring myself to divulge the biggest secret I hold—the facts surrounding what really happened the night Sarah died. I worry if I confess to Chase what role I played—or the things I should have done, but didn't—he'll see me as a different person. What if that happens and he turns away? Losing him would hurt badly. Just the thought alone leaves my stomach heavy and knotted. I don't know if I can take that kind of a chance. So, for now, I keep this secret hidden.

I push these thoughts away as I work through another Monday morning, the start of the last week of June. This Monday is the same as most. I am sitting at my desk, counting down the hours till lunchtime with my guy.

At five to twelve, I am out the door, and, within minutes, halfway down the steps to the gymnasium, where Chase is working on repairing one of the backboards.

I catch sight of him and stop in my tracks.

He's up on a ladder, and since today is a scorcher, especially in the non-air-conditioned school, my gorgeous friend isn't wearing a shirt. Chase's entire upper body is bare, all toned and hard and tight. He even has a little bit of a tan from the work he does outside. His jeans hang low on his hips, revealing two indentations on either side of his lower back, right above the band of his black boxer briefs.

I fan myself a little and catch my breath. His lower body is nothing short of amazing—strong legs, great ass— but my eyes return to his bare back, to where ink I had no idea existed is on full and vivid display. I can't help but stare. I'm frankly mesmerized by the intricacy and beauty of the tattoos Chase has on his back and shoulders.

There's an angel inked between his shoulder blades, in profile with her head bowed. The angel is beautiful, but in a sad and tragic way. Framing her are large wings, inked above and on either side. The tips trail down the sides of Chase's back, while a few feathers cascade down around the angel. One or two even reach to just above those sexy indentations.

Still unaware that I'm on the steps, Chase reaches to tighten something on the backboard. His two other tats that, up until now, I've seen only bits and pieces of are finally fully visible. The number—72, just as I thought—inked on his right bicep is clear as day, the ink heavy and dark. The mysterious scroll of words trailing around his left bicep is also fully visible, but the words still elude me. I can't make them out from this distance.

Chase turns and catches sight of me. He smiles. "Hey, you snuck up on me," he says as he begins climbing down from the ladder.

His T-shirt is draped over one of the bleachers. He picks it up and fluffs it out, unknowingly making his upper body muscles tense and flex. I know Chase's body is incredible, but I've never seen it like this, half of it bare. Nor was I aware my badass boy was this heavily tattooed. *Damn.* Chase is so lean and ripped, and such a real-life bad boy. There's something very alluring about all that.

Today I have on an above-the-knee skirt and cotton blouse, but I suddenly wish I'd worn something more revealing. I fumble with the button at the top of my shirt, debating whether I should undo one more. After all, I have a valid excuse—it's stifling hot in here.

But before I muster up the nerve to pop open a button,

I notice Chase eyeing me curiously, gunmetal blues focused on my fingers that are caressing a button. I quickly lower my hand. Chase looks away and pulls his shirt over his head.

"Am I early?" I ask, pretending as if I am not aware that I'm exactly on time.

It's kind of hard to come up with witty banter when you're almost drooling.

Chase gives me another funny look, and all I can envision is him walking over to me and hiking my skirt up, much like I hiked it up myself the day I ran after him to retrieve my hair tie. That day, I hiked just a smidge, but today I want Chase to hike higher, much higher. I want to feel his hands, his gentle fingers, on my legs, all over my body. I loved the way his fingers grazed my neck when he slipped the tie back on my hair. What could those adept fingers do to other places on my body?

God, I want Chase Gartner, more than ever before. My body burns to feel his touch, anywhere and everywhere, and I long to touch him too. I want to run my fingers over the lines of his tattoos, trace them with my tongue. But this isn't all about lust. I long to touch Chase in these ways because I've grown to care for him—as a person, as a man, as my friend. Touching him, letting him touch me, it feels like a natural progression. We share so much emotionally that sharing ourselves physically seems inevitable. How much longer can we deny this attraction?

"You're not early," Chase is saying. *Focus, focus.* "I lost track of time."

I nod absently and work on pulling myself together.

By the time we reach the diner—our diner—we're thankfully back on track. Or, at least, I am. Chase seems mostly unaffected by my earlier ogling, even though it had to have been obvious to him.

Suddenly, I realize something, something terrible—maybe Chase isn't all that attracted to me. Sure, he flirts, but that doesn't mean anything.

Insecurity rears its ugly head, making me doubt. Chase is an incredibly beautiful man. He could have anyone he wants. Why would he want me? I'm probably far below his usual standards. I mean, I know he likes me as a friend. But is there a possibility of something more? Maybe I've just been fooling myself.

An all-consuming need to know washes over me. I absolutely have to find out if I'm the only one feeling this attraction, this pull. With renewed purpose, I set my iced tea down on the table. "What are you doing tonight?" I ask.

Chase is swallowing a bite of a club sandwich and he coughs. Once he's recovered, he says, "I don't know. Nothing much, I guess. Why?"

I have to be brave, keep taking chances. No need to stop now, this could be the deciding factor as to where this relationship is heading.

Although this is harder than I thought.

I inhale, exhale, and say in a hurried jumble of words, "Wanttogotoamovietonight?"

For a long moment, Chase says nothing, and I feel like a fool. "Just forget it," I mumble.

"No, wait. I'd love to see a movie with you. I was just thinking though. You do know they're renovating the theater here in town, right?" I nod slowly. Oops, I'd forgotten about that. "Well, that means we'd have to go to the cinemas up north, which is maybe an hour away." Chase runs his fingers through his hair, like maybe he's a little nervous now too. "So, uh, why don't you just come over to my house after work? We can watch something there. I have on-demand, so we'll have lots of choices."

Chase waits for my reply, eyebrow raised. Of course, I agree. His idea is even better than my suggestion. This way I'll get to see Chase at home, in his own environment. That thought gives me an extra little thrill.

I know where Chase lives, but he insists on giving me directions just to be sure. He informs me he's finishing up early today, so he'll already be home by the time I make it out to his house. I tell him that's fine with me.

"It's a date, then," Chase says as he offers me a rather stunning smile.

I wonder if he's serious. Is this really a date? Maybe. I hope so.

I don't know what I'm looking for exactly, but I hope to find it tonight. Just a sign, something tangible, I suppose would be nice. Something to let me know this thing between me and Chase has potential, and that it's definitely not one-sided.

I'm nervous, in an excited kind of way, the rest of the afternoon. Whatever the outcome, this is a step forward in our friendship. Our interactions so far have been limited to the church grounds and the few surrounding blocks. Tonight, though, in Chase's home, I may finally get an answer to the question that's burning me up inside: Does Chase Gartner like me the way I like him...romantically?

CHAPTER FIVE

CHASE

Maybe I am deluding myself, but it seems this friendship thing is really working. I've successfully kept feelings that confuse me—feelings that have me all twisted up inside—under wraps. Consequently, I can proudly state that Kay Stanton is the first female friend I've ever had. In fact, surprisingly, she's turning out to be the best friend I've ever had as well.

I like how free and easy it is to talk to her. My girl is incredible like that. Sometimes I feel so comfortable I even find myself telling her way more than I originally intended, I get *that* lost in the sharing of my stories. It's never been that way before with anyone else, only with Kay. Maybe it's because sweet girl is such a good listener?

Nah, I think it's something more.

I have to admit my feelings for Kay are like nothing I've ever felt before.

Nothing, ever.

I want her, of course. What man wouldn't? Kay is sexy and beautiful, very desirable, very fuckable. But it's more than just some physical thing. I want to be around her all the time. And I actually care about what she thinks, about me, about life, about this crazy fucking world we live in. I guess I just want to know what she thinks about everything.

In addition, I like to see Kay happy. In fact, nothing

pleases me more. That's why I tease and play so much when I'm around her, that shit never fails to make my girl smile wide and true. And when Kay smiles at me—in that way only she can do—I know…I just fucking know…she likes me more than just a friend.

Actually, I'm pretty certain Kay is looking for a sign that I feel the same way. I do, obviously, but I can't tell her. Maybe Kay doesn't realize she's too good for the likes of me. She sees only the best parts of me, and if I could be that way all the time, then maybe. But I don't know if such a thing is possible. I'm sure I'll fuck things up somewhere along the line. I almost always do with the people I care about.

These are my thoughts as I nervously get ready for our "date" tonight. Shit, I don't know what this is we're even doing this evening. I called it a date earlier, but I was just fucking around. I think.

Whatever.

I glance around my bedroom. There are some clothes strewn on the floor, so I gather those jeans and tees up now. After I set aside a pile of laundry, I turn to check out the clock on the bedside table.

Fuck, it's after five, Kay will be here soon.

I hurriedly shower and go back to my room. I tug on a clean pair of jeans and one of those nice button-down shirts from my mother. I glance in the mirror above the dresser while I roll dark blue sleeves up to my elbows. I guess I look okay. All I know is that I want to look nice for Kay. *Not that this movie night is a date or anything,* I remind myself.

After I'm ready, I get to work on cleaning and straightening up around the house. It's not that I'm exceptionally messy, but I am a guy and sometimes it takes me a while to get around to picking things up, especially clothes. Leave it where it falls is my standard motto. But I get things in order now. I throw a load of laundry into the washer, vacuum the area rugs in the dining room and living room, dust the stand the TV is on, and straighten three forest-green throw pillows that reside on a snow-white couch. I shake my head. Gram and her love of light colors. Thank God I've never spilled anything when watching TV in here. I wouldn't want Kay to think I'm a complete slob.

The record albums I brought down from the attic a few weeks ago are still scattered across the coffee table. I was listening to one in particular a day or so ago. It's still on the turntable of Gram's old record player, so I go over and retrieve it. When I place the vinyl back into the colorful seventies-era cover with the big spaceship, I have to laugh. There's one song on this record that perfectly captures my situation with Kay.

Yeah, if only I could find that man, sweet girl.

With a resigned sigh, I stack the albums together and slide them onto the shelf beneath the coffee table. Then, I take a look around. All in all, the place looks damn fucking good. I run my fingers through my hair. What next? The house is clean and I'm dressed and ready. I look down. My feet are bare, but I don't think Kay will mind.

Kay...

My feelings for her are so screwed up, but I can't get her out of my head. If she were any other girl, I'd just bang her and get her out of my system. Then, I'd probably move on. But she's not any other girl, she's Kay, she's my Kay. And though I'd love to bang my Kay—sweet and slow, hard and fast, any way she'd want it—I sure as hell don't have any desire to move on afterward. Far from it, in fact.

Fuck. Could it be any more obvious this woman is seeping into my pores?

You'd think I'd be running for the hills, before my girl splits my heart in two. But do I want to get away? Hell, no. I actually want to get closer to Kay, lay my heart out before her, and let her do with it what she will. If only I had the balls to take a chance, I think she'd handle my heart carefully. She's sweet like that.

Sweet Kay. I can't help but smile. But she's more than just sweet. She is so, so many things, and every single one of them I find cute as hell.

My girl is attentive when I talk, sitting and listening to all my stupid stories with rapt attention. Who else would do that? Only her. But she's also more, so much more. Kay is shy-girl blushes and smiles, pretty in pink, and sexy as fuck in summer dresses. Sweet girl is vulnerable at times, but brave at others. Such a girly-girl most of the time, but sometimes she's a wannabe-tough girl who delivers weak-ass punches with enthusiasm, like she did the day I stole the tie-thing from her hair.

I sit down on the couch, laugh as I recall. I was such an ass to take her hair tie, but the payoff was well worth it—I got to touch beautiful girl's hair. And fuck, was it ever soft and silky, wavy at the ends. I couldn't stop myself that day from imagining her chestnut mane fanned out on a pillow, me above her, moving in her, feeling her, inside and out. My voice was a little husky when I whispered in her ear. I knew that was why she was blushing when she turned around. But that was okay. I like that my words have the power to pink her cheeks. She's easy like that, and at times I can't resist. But apart from all this fun we have, there's something more.

It touches me somewhere in my hardened heart that attentive girl gets so into my stories, especially the ones that include my brother. Maybe my heart's not so hardened after all. 'Cause the day I saw Kay getting so emotionally invested in the outcome of my story about Will and the lizards, I wanted nothing more than to reach across the booth and kiss her. She's never even met my brother, but there she was, rooting for him to catch a lizard. Her heart is pure and good like that, just another thing I like about my girl.

Except Kay's not really my girl, now is she? Not in the way I wish she could be; that's for sure. And I need to remember why this is so. How could I miss the curious look Father Maridale gave us the other day when we were leaving the church office to go to lunch? Trust me, I didn't. Father was coming in as we were going out, and when he caught my eye he shot me a look of warning. I gave him a little bit of an eye-roll back, one I hope said: *yeah, yeah, I'm following your rules, just being her friend, even though it's fucking killing me.*

Father Maridale nodded like he'd heard my thoughts and patted me on the shoulder, then continued on his way. Thankfully, Kay was talking about something and seemed completely oblivious to the whole exchange.

Speaking of Kay, the doorbell rings. She's here. *Shit.* I am so fucking nervous about tonight. I hope this is a good idea.

When I open the front door, Kay smiles and the feeling that everything is right when we're together helps to calm my nervous ass. And, wow, now that I look—like, really look—I'm kind of floored. Kay looks amazing. She's wearing the same lacy dress she had on earlier at work, but she's lost the cardigan, so I can clearly see how her body fills out the dress in all the right places.

This lacy number is similar to the dress she was wearing the day I stole her hair tie, except this version is blue instead of white. And it's a whole lot shorter. So much so it takes me an extra few seconds to pull my gaze away from her smooth-looking legs. But I do, I look up. And that's when I notice Kay's hair appears extra soft and shiny. More so than usual, like maybe she just brushed it out before she got here. I think she has on a little makeup too. Her lips are dewy, and her eyes, kind of smoky. Whatever she's done, she is stunning.

And I think to myself that, true, Kay may not be my girl in all the ways I'd prefer, but she's most definitely my girl when it comes to this friendship we've developed. In that, we belong to each other.

"Hi," Kay says all shy-like, as if she's suddenly not sure if she should be here. To me, she looks like she's belonged here all along.

I say hi and invite her in, but she doesn't move.

"Kay, are you coming in?" I ask when she shifts slightly, looking a little nervous.

"Oh, yes, of course."

Aw, sweet girl makes me smile. Guess she just had to get her bearings.

Kay steps into the hall and, trying to be subtle, she glances up the stairs, and then leans forward slightly so she can see into the rooms off to the left and the right. She's obviously curious about this house I live in, so I offer to show her around. I don't know why, but she gets pretty excited about a tour.

The house is of moderate size, not overly big, but not exactly small. It's a typical farmhouse, I guess. The rooms are a bit old-fashioned, and there's definitely a country-living vibe, thanks to Gram's decorating. But I'm changing things bit by bit, slowly making this place my own, starting with fixing things that were broken and moving into the twenty-first century.

I've fixed up a lot in the past few weeks—polished the hardwood floors, got all the ceiling fans working, cleaned out the upstairs bedrooms no longer in use, and even ordered Wi-Fi for the computer Gram bought the year I got arrested. It was still sitting on the open rolltop desk in the living room, dusty and unused just like the record player.

Kay and I start down the hall. I point out the living room to the right and the dining room on the left. There's a powder room and an empty room farther down the hall, but there's not much to see in either so I lead the way through the dining room, past the hutch, and into the kitchen.

As we step in, Kay gushes, "Oh, I love these old farmhouse sinks."

She walks over and runs her hand along the porcelain surface of the sink that's been there for years. She glances up at the copper pots hanging above the center island, takes in the small table and chairs over by the oven, and allows her gaze to travel to the window above the sink.

The view is of the land behind the house, and since there's a lot of it I'm hardly surprised when Kay's eyes widen. "Wow, Chase, all this property is yours?" she asks.

"Yeah, it's all mine, all the way down to the creek." It feels weird saying that, like it's not yet set in these many acres now belong to me.

"Did your family used to farm?" she asks as she continues to gaze out the window. "That's lot of land for just a big yard."

I chuckle. A big yard is exactly what it is nowadays. But that wasn't always the case. "Yeah, my grandparents farmed, a long time ago, back when my grandfather was still alive. That was before I was born." I gesture to the window, to the gentle slope of land on the other side of the glass. "My grandmother gave up farming after my grandfather died. I think she hoped my dad would someday take over, but he never had any interest. His heart was always in building houses."

"Well, it's really pretty back here," Kay muses, still seemingly enthralled by the sea of green.

I decide we've seen enough of the downstairs and lead Kay upstairs. I start to show her the bedrooms along the long hall, opening doors along the way.

The room that was my grandmother's is just about cleared out. I went through and boxed up most of her things after I first moved back. I put away her keepsakes, and gave a bunch of her stuff to the church for the next rummage sale. That's what she always said she wanted whoever was left to do with her stuff when she passed, so that's what I did. But there are still a few pieces of furniture in her room.

Kay glances around and gives me a couple of "oh, very nice" responses, but otherwise doesn't say much.

Things are the same—mostly cleared out—in the next bedroom we come to, the one that belonged to my father when he was growing up. It's also the bedroom my parents used when we lived back here when I was a little kid. Cleaning out that room was tough. There were things in there from when my parents were first married. One of the keepsakes I found was a small wedding album, the cover all lacy and white. In the photos, Mom is showing. She must have been about five months along, pregnant with me. I always knew I was unplanned. But, damn, my parents still looked happy. Guess I was a surprise, but never unwanted.

I also found ticket stubs from a bunch of movies my parents went to, and mushy cards they'd given to one another. I just boxed that stuff up and put it up in the attic next to my Gram's keepsakes.

I give Kay a peek into my father's room of fucking memories, then close that door real fast.

"Which one is your bedroom?" Kay asks when we're left standing in the hall.

"Oh, it's down there." I gesture to the other end of the hall.

I lead the way past the bathroom and my grandmother's old sewing room. My bedroom is simple and basic, not much to see. I got used to living spartanly in prison. There's nothing on the light-colored walls, no paintings or art, not even my own, though my sketchbooks, filled with my art, rest over on the dresser. There's a double bed with a pine headboard up against one wall, a bedside table with a clock, and a closet.

That's about it.

The only bright colors in the room are the blues and greens on the quilt, made for me years ago by Gram, and now folded at the foot of my bed. There's color in my sketches, lots and lots, but those books are closed.

I watch as Kay takes it all in, the plain wood floor, the bare walls, the complete lack of décor.

"Well," she says at last, brow crinkled, "you kind of have a minimalist vibe going here, but everything is very tidy."

I chuckle. "Yeah, you should have seen it before. I cleaned before you got here."

"So, you're secretly messy?" There's a twinkle in her caramels as she asks.

I shrug one shoulder. "Maybe a little—not too bad though."

Kay continues to glance about, her gaze eventually falling to the sketchbooks on the dresser.

"Are those your drawings?" she asks, all cute-like, her voice excited. "Can I see them?"

I wince. The sketchbooks she's asking to see contain my sketches from prison, and, unfortunately, I don't feel quite ready to share them with her just yet. Bad enough Father Maridale flipped through one of them that day at the courthouse.

"Maybe not those books…" My voice trails off.

My girl's expression gives away her disappointment, so I backtrack. "I mean…you can see them, just not right now." I run my fingers through my hair. *How do I put this?* "The sketches in those books are a little harsh, Kay. I'll let you see them, I promise, just some other day. If you really want to see some of the things I've drawn, there's a better sketchbook in the dining room. There's a bunch of stuff in there, all recent, and much…nicer."

Kay nods, but still appears a little crestfallen. I want to

put the smile from earlier back in place, and I think I know just how to do it.

"Hey, there is something I'd like to show you. It's pretty cool and I think you'll like it."

Kay perks back up. "Really, what is it?"

I go over to the window that's opened a crack, open it all the way, and take out the screen.

"What are you doing?" she asks, tucking a strand of hair behind her ear as she walks over to see what I'm up to.

"Just trust me on this one." I hoist one leg over the sill, to where the roof is even and flat. I straddle the open window and offer her my hand. "Come on, I want to show you where I go to sketch, and, sometimes, just to think. The view from up here is amazing, better than the one from the kitchen window even."

I kind of can't believe I'm sharing this private piece of myself, but I know Kay will get it. She gets me, she'll get this. She kicks off her low heels, game again for one of my suggestions. Trusting, my sweet girl is so damn trusting when it comes to me. I need to be careful with that.

Trusting girl puts her hand in mine and we smile at one another. I swing my other leg out onto the roof and help her over the sill. It takes some care since she's in a dress, and it is kind of a short one. I try not to look when it rides up, but I do catch a glimpse of white, silky panties. I try not to groan as I think how much I wish I could touch her there, right fucking *there*.

Kay hurriedly straightens herself out once we're out on the roof, and I turn so I'm not staring.

There's a long ledge next to the window and I sit down on it. I stretch out my legs and pat the spot next to me. Kay comes over and sits down. A light, warm breeze kicks up while the sun sets off in the distance, streaking the sky in hues of red, orange, and pink.

"This is the kind of shit I draw when I'm up here." I motion to the sunset.

Kay and I are sitting so close that when I bring my knees up to sit more like she is our bare feet almost touch.

"It's peaceful up here," Kay says, curling her pink-painted toes next to my foot, "and very scenic. I can see why you like it." In a softer voice she adds, "Thank you for sharing this with me, Chase."

Kay gets it, just like I knew she would. I smile at her, and then we just sit quietly and watch the sun sizzle into the horizon. I am decidedly happy I shared something so important to me with someone who always seems to see what I see.

I shift slightly and the sides of our feet touch. Neither of us makes any move to change positions. So, with bare feet pressing close, her warm skin against mine, I point to off in the distance, to where the tree line begins. "Part of the creek Harmony Creek is named for runs through there. You can't see it from here with all the trees filled in, but it's just over the hill."

"Do you own the land down by the creek too?" Kay flexes her foot and I nudge back with my own. She stares straight ahead, but I catch her shy-girl smile.

"Yeah," I answer after a beat, trying to suppress my own lips from curving up into a silly grin. "I go down there to fish sometimes."

"Oh, that sounds like fun."

Wait, what? I shoot her a sidelong glance. "Really?" My voice betrays my skepticism.

"What?"

One more flex, another nudge, and two surreptitious smiles, one from each of us.

"I just can't see you fishing," I say.

The breeze blows Kay's hair and she tries to smooth it back into place. "Oh, really? Why is that?"

I nod to her dress, raise an eyebrow. "Oh, I don't know, girly-girl. Just don't see too many lacy dress-wearing people down at the creek."

I chuckle and she huffs, "Like I'd wear this dress to go fishing, Chase."

She rolls her eyes dramatically, but I can tell she's not really offended; she's just playing like we do.

"I'd probably catch more than you," she continues, all sure and cocky as she turns her head away and raises her chin a little.

"Ooh, a challenge." I nudge her foot. "Wanna bet on it?"

She looks down at our feet, which are closer than ever. "Sure. What are we betting?" she whispers.

"I get to pick the terms?" I ask, astonished she'd allowed such a thing.

Her caramel eyes meet mine, and damn, my girl looks determined. "Well, you pick whatever I have to do if you win. And I'll pick what you have to do if I win."

I think about it for a minute. I'm pretty fucking sure I *will* win, so I want to make my prize worthwhile. What's the one thing my girl has been holding out on, something that's been driving me crazy?

I say it now, "If I win, you move into my apartment."

Her eyes narrow. "Chase—"

"Oh no, baby girl." I can't help but smirk, she walked right into this one. "You agreed. You said I get to choose whatever I want if I win. And that's what I'm picking."

"Fine, fine," she mutters. "But if *I* win then *you* have to sit up in the front of the church for, let's say"—she ponders—"an entire month. *And* you have to sit between me and Missy."

Fuck, I better win, is all I can think as I quickly look away. Sitting in the front would be bad enough, but sitting between Missy—who's had my dick in her mouth—and sweet girl Kay? Uh-h-h, no fucking way, talk about uncomfortable.

Nonetheless, I agree to her terms, a deal is a deal. Besides, I am so going to win this bet, there's really no doubt about it. We shake on it to make it official, and since it's getting late I suggest we go back inside to get started with a movie.

Once we're back down in the living room, I turn the TV on and hand Kay the holy grail—also known as the remote. But first I show her how to work it.

"Go ahead and pick something," I suggest when she pulls up the on-demand menu. "I'm game for anything. I'll go grab us something to drink, okay?"

Kay mock-rolls her eyes. "Sure, as long as it's nothing lemon-lime flavored."

She may sound all disgusted, but there's a teasing twinkle in her eyes.

I put my hand on my chest and back up a few steps, pretending to be wounded. "Hating on the lemon-lime? That's just plain wrong, Kay, blasphemous even." I point at her.

"Admit it, you tried one last week and loved it. You know that shit is awesome."

"Okay, okay, it was good," she admits, letting out a laugh. "I don't know about awesome though..." She trails off and I frown. "Oh, quit looking at me like that. Fine, lemon-lime it is."

I tell her I'm just kidding and if she really wants something different I also have iced tea and beer, but she insists on the lemon-lime. Maybe Kay wants to help me get the sodas, or maybe she wants to keep talking, but, in any case, she puts the remote down and follows me to the kitchen.

She doesn't come in all the way. She just kind of lingers in the doorway between the kitchen and the dining room while I get the drinks. I can see her over the door of the refrigerator and it's apparent something in the dining room has caught her attention. She takes a step back, grabs whatever it is, and holds it up. It's my sketchbook.

She arches an eyebrow at me. "You said I could see this when we were upstairs, remember? Do you mind?"

I close the refrigerator door and give her a one-shoulder shrug. What the hell, I did say she could see it. I try to think of everything that's in there. Since the book is new, the sketches are recent, which means it contains just shit I've sketched around here. Various views from the back porch, sunsets from the roof—like the one we were just viewing. I think and I think, recalling all that I've drawn as of late.

There are sketches of fields and farmland, a detailed tree branch with apple blossoms I did in oil pastels, and a charcoal of the empty barn at the back of my property. *Yeah, it should be fine*, I finally conclude, *there's nothing in that book that could potentially embarrass me. Except...*

143

Fuck, too late. Kay is already looking down at a loose page, one torn from the book, one with a fold in the center. I know exactly what she's found—the sketch I did of her the day we met. The one I folded and tucked in the back, the one I couldn't bear to throw away.

Well, that decision just bit me in the ass.

"Ah, Kay," I mumble, cringing.

"You drew me," she says softly as she gazes down at the sketch. She doesn't sound angry or offended, like I fully expect her to. Nope. Instead, she sounds kind of awed and... pleased.

I run my fingers through my hair, press my lips together. I decide to just be honest, more or less.

"The night I drew the flyer for the apartment, uh, after I was finished...I kept picturing you in my head. It was the same day we'd met in the parking lot. So, I sketched you the way I remembered..." I nod to the drawing, still in her hands "...the sweater, the dress, it's what you were wearing that Sunday."

"I remember perfectly," she whispers. She looks at me, then at the sketch, then at me again. "And is this how you saw me that day? How you see me in general?"

I take a breath. Hmm, this could go either way. True, she looks very, very pretty in the drawing, but she also looks very fucking sexual. But I drew it, I need to own it.

I say, "Yeah, it's how I see you, Kay."

I wait for the fallout, but it never comes.

Sure, her cheeks pink. That makes me smile, though, knowing I caused it. This reaction doesn't seem bad, no, not at all. Kay seems happy.

"But," she begins, astonishment in her tone. "I look so... sexy, maybe...and kind of *beautiful*."

She says the last word like she can't believe I'd see her like that.

Shit, what should I do?

This is where I *should* take a step toward her, but I can't. If I do I *will* kiss her, I'll shower her with words, tell her how sexy and beautiful she is, and how I want her so badly that it fucking hurts.

If I do even one of those things, I know it will lead to more, much more. And I've made a promise—to myself, to Father Maridale. *Fuck.* All the stuff I thought I had so under control, I apparently so do not.

So, like an idiot, I try to blow it off. I flippantly say, "Of course you look good, Kay. You're pretty." It's a cop-out, a scaled-back response.

I don't go to her, like I should, like my heart tells me to. I don't take her in my arms, don't cover her in kisses. Nope, I just stand there near the doorway, two lemon-lime sodas in my hands, saying lame-ass shit that doesn't even come close to expressing the depth of my feelings for this beautiful, sexy woman. *What an ass I am.*

Surprisingly, Kay doesn't seem too upset. In fact, my girl is fucking beaming, staring down at the sketch, like something she's been curious about has just been answered, and in the way she was hoping.

In a very-pleased tone, she says, "Thank you, Chase." Her words are soft and quiet, accepting, happy.

She folds the drawing and slips it back in the book. And I know that she knows, she fucking knows. I see it in her eyes, the smile she's trying to hide. She knows I see her as much more than "pretty." To me, she's fucking beautiful.

I hand her one of the cans of soda and suggest we get started on picking out a movie. Once we're back in the living room, we debate, all in fun, over what to see. I tell her to make the final choice. I assume she'll choose one of the chick flicks she was pushing for, but she picks an action film. I'm quite certain she chooses that one because she thinks I'll like it, which is sweet, but I don't really care. I'll watch anything with my girl.

Besides, I can barely pay attention. I'm entirely too preoccupied, trying to figure out what's really going on with us, 'cause there most definitely is something happening here. And whatever it's been up to this point, it just grew more powerful this evening.

I can no longer deny this "something" that's been building between us for weeks, and it feels bigger than the both of us. It's like I'm caught up in a current, a current of destiny. And, frankly, I'm losing my will to swim against it.

That little realization tells me what I've known—but resisted—all along: friendship will never be enough. Not for either of us.

We start out on opposite sides of the couch when we sit down to watch the movie, but it's like we're subconsciously drawn to one another as the show progresses. There's some space between us at the moment, but not a lot. Kay is sitting kind of sideways, leaning toward me with her legs tucked up under her. I am leaning to my left, in her direction. I didn't move closer to her on purpose, nor do I think she did to me. We just seem to gravitate to one another.

See, destiny, my heart tells my stubborn brain. My brain

shoots my heart the finger. But my heart just laughs, smug, confident it will win in the end. And I kind of want my heart to win, but there are so many reasons why I shouldn't.

First of which, Kay has only ever seen one side of me, the good side, the side that is laid back most of the time, the side that is flirty and fun, generally nice. But there's darkness in me too, I am still fucked up. Her sweet soul couldn't begin to fathom the many demons I still battle—my night with Missy, case in point. Kay would surely be disgusted if she learned of the things I did with the head of the bake committee, her sort-of friend that she wants me to sit beside if I lose our stupid bet. *Fuck.* And what would sweet girl think if she knew just how much I craved the coke Missy had in her purse that night? Kay has no idea what those cravings are like, how they all come back to you when temptation is near, sometimes like they never even left. My girl has never craved oblivion and destruction the way I have; she's too good for those kinds of fucked-in-the-head thoughts.

It was a fight that night not to use—it *is* a fight. Not every day, but it is there, lurking under my skin, waiting for something big enough to push my resistance all the way down to giving in. Really, I don't know if the battle to never use drugs again will ever be completely won. And it's not fair to drag Kay onto that battlefield. I don't want her to end up battered and bruised, caught up in a fight that's not even her own.

I abruptly straighten, suddenly feeling shameful and undeserving. I lean away from Kay, put my elbow up on the armrest. She glances my way and gives me a lazy smile, like I'm someone special. Too bad I am nothing even close to special.

Kay untucks her legs and stretches them out in front of her. "Yeah, I have to readjust, too," she says, completely misinterpreting my move away from her. "I think my right foot fell asleep, like, twenty minutes ago."

She smiles again and I try to smile back.

What am I going to do? I may be in control tonight, but my resolve is clearly crumbling. This back-and-forth shit is tearing me to pieces. My feelings for Kay are turned, twisted, and jacked. Fuck, my girl deserves so much more than me, but me is what I long to give her. How do I stop whatever is developing between us when I really don't want to anymore? How do I fight fucking destiny? Do I keep resisting?

My heart tells me the answer is simple: *Quit resisting.*

But will I ever be what Kay deserves? I ask back.

My heart tells me it doesn't matter, Kay gets me, she already accepts the man I am, imperfections included.

I relax a little. I decide to go with the flow, for now, and pray my heart can keep us both from getting hurt.

CHAPTER SIX

KAY

Tuesday is everything I love about summer: baby-blue skies, high clouds, and warm morning sun. An anemic ray struggles to stream through my basement apartment window. It almost reaches the spot where I stand. I step closer and closer, until warmth finds my upturned face. I stop, I bask.

My heated cheeks remind me of someone who has this same effect on me, someone who's fast becoming my own personal ray of sun. And that man—my badass-artist boy, my contradiction, Chase Gartner—is occupying my thoughts more and more.

Last night was fun, watching the movie with my complicated friend. He puzzles me though. Sometimes it's impossible to discern what he's thinking. Does he like me more than a friend? Does he think I'm pretty? I like him, so these things carry importance. However, last night I think I may have finally received an answer in the sketch he drew of me.

Seeing the way Chase captured me the Sunday we met gave me a pretty darn good idea of what he's thinking, and one question was perhaps answered. I think my artist boy sees me as something I could only ever hope to be—beautiful. Though when he realized I saw the truth in what he'd drawn it seemed he felt put on the spot.

He backtracked a bit, used the word "pretty," not "beautiful, but it was too late. I've learned enough of that man over the past few weeks that I saw right through his no-big-deal façade. The sketch created by his hand told me everything I've been dying to know—Chase Gartner is as attracted to me as I am to him.

And thinking of this newfound knowledge as I stand beneath the thin strand of light created by the summer sun, my heart soars high, way up into the outside blue, up into the high summer clouds.

I gather my things and leave my apartment. I feel better than fine, my heart up high even as I walk across the parking lot. I am ten feet tall and feeling grand. Unfortunately, these high spirits land me in hot water when I let my guard down. I feel it before I see it, but there's no mistaking I've been noticed.

There are three junkies hanging out over by an alley that skirts around the side of the building. My car is in a space nearby, leaving me no choice but to pass right by the junkies. As I near the three miscreants, I mistakenly make eye contact with one, a short, stubby guy with unwashed hair. He's leaned up against the building, his beefy arms crossed over his chest. He's built like a fireplug, not as skinny as his blank-stare, soul-lost pals. Naming him Fireplug in my head, I determine he must be fairly new to this kind of life. Even so, as I pass, his dark, empty eyes rake me over, like it's his right. My stomach turns. I suspect this junkie wants more of me than what his eyes can give him.

Isn't it enough that he's already taking something? I think with a shudder.

I frown and his expression challenges, his eyes dare. *Go ahead and say something,* they tell me. *See what happens.*

Of course, I remain silent.

I'm all too aware of how helpless I am in this situation. Suddenly, the flimsy sundress I slipped over my head this morning feels like nothing. The thin material, the short hemline, the scooped neckline, these stylish details make me feel nothing now but vulnerable and exposed.

The blue cotton fabric matches today's sky perfectly, but I, unfortunately, don't blend in. Fireplug with the greasy hair stares and stares, his lips curling up into a feral grin, one that reveals a missing tooth.

I avert my eyes and just run the rest of the way to my car, wedge heels on my feet be damned. The danger of living here has just been ratcheted up a notch. I've been noticed, and by someone who probably won't forget, something I've successfully avoided for a whole year. *Damn.*

What I should do is quit being stubborn and ask Chase about his apartment. I know for a fact it's still for rent. He told me just the other day that the only person who's gone out to view the place, a male college student, decided not to take it. The kid supposedly liked the apartment, but Chase said the guy ultimately decided he'd rather remain in town.

I fumble with my keys and keep my thoughts busy, trying (in vain) to ignore the stares burning into my back. I've saved a little extra these past few weeks and could possibly swing the rental rate Chase is asking. I guess the only thing still holding me back now is a sense of pride. It's stupid, I know, but I feel like maybe I should just find a place on my own.

Yeah, right. Who am I kidding?

My real concern is that if I live in such close proximity to Chase I'll just fall for him even more. I already feel like I'm moving faster than him, so I certainly don't need to make things harder for myself.

These thoughts distract me from the junkies, but my heart still races when I jump into my car and speed away. Even though Fireplug and his lecherous stares are left behind me in the lot, I remain uneasy.

I spend the rest of the drive to work coaxing my heart back to a regular rhythm. "I am calm, I am calm," I whisper out loud, hands gripping the steering wheel harder than necessary. "Everything is fine now. There's no more danger."

My attempts to relax come to fruition, and by the time I reach the church it's like the early morning scare never even occurred. Or so I think.

The morning flies by, and a little before noon Chase calls instead of texting. He asks me to meet him in front of the church in roughly ten more minutes. Apparently Father Maridale is having him take a look at the Holy Trinity fresco, the larger-than-life colorful painting behind the altar. The shades and tones are still bright, but there are a few areas that could use some touching up. There's a certain way to do this, Chase tells me, to preserve the integrity of the original painting, and that's what he and Father Maridale are discussing.

Ten minutes later, as Chase requested, I'm at the base of the church steps, waiting for him to emerge. And, unbeknownst to me, I am about to find out the effects from this morning are still with me.

I begin to make a call on my cell, a call to Missy I've yet to return. But just as I find her in my contacts, I feel someone come up behind me. Startled, I spin around and drop the cell. Chase catches it.

"Whoa, sweet girl, someone's a little jumpy today." His blues fill with question. "Hey, did something upset you this morning?"—*if only you knew*—"Is everything okay?"

No. "Yeah, everything's fine."

My gaze locks on the phone as Chase hands it back. I don't wish to share the details of my morning run-in. Why worry him? And why confirm his belief that I should move as soon as possible?

So, with a smile, I just say, "You startled me, that's all."

I guess Chase assumes my skittishness has something to do with the call I was making. His brow furrows, and he glances at the phone. "Who were you calling?" he asks.

"Oh…I was calling Missy. There's a big bake sale coming up in conjunction with the Fourth of July carnival." Chase appears impassive as I pause. "You do know Missy is the head of the bake committee, right?"

Chase nods curtly and some emotion I can't peg darkens his expression. But as quickly as I pick up on it, a second later, it's gone. *Strange.* What is up with those two? Just this past Sunday when I waved to Chase and turned back in my seat, Missy was shaking her head. "What?" I asked her.

"You're playing with fire, Kay," was all she would say, shaking her head like she knew something I didn't.

Again, I wanted to question her cryptic comment, but the organ music started up right then.

I shake off the memory and finish my explanation to Chase. "Missy called and left a message last night, asking if I could bake cookies for the sale. I always help out." I sigh.

"But I won't be able to this time. My stupid oven broke last month."

I half-expect Chase to tell me he'll take a look at it, or maybe even offer up the use of his own oven—he's usually helpful like that—but instead he just changes the subject.

"Hey, do you want to mix it up a little today?" he asks, rubbing the back of his neck and squinting into the sun. "Maybe we could eat lunch down at Pizza House?"

Crap, I think, *anywhere but there*. With my luck Nick will be working. Chase isn't my boyfriend or anything, but Nick got to know me well enough that he'd probably pick up on my attraction to Chase. Why rub it in Nick's face? Not to mention, I certainly don't want my intuitive friend to catch on that I have a sort-of history with the manager at Pizza House. There's too much of a chance our entire lunch could turn completely awkward.

I tell Chase I'd rather just stick with the diner. "Besides, it's like they know us there. They might miss us if we don't make our usual lunchtime appearance."

The crap I'm spouting is just that—crap. I highly doubt the employees at the diner care whether Chase and I show up every day. Chase looks like he's thinking exactly the same thing, but he humors me and we end up sticking with the diner, potential trip to Awkward-Ville averted.

I don't know how it happens, but the next day I find myself divulging to Chase that I haven't had a relationship with anyone since college, not since Doug Wilson. I don't count last autumn with Nick. It was something, sure, but not the kind of relationship Chase and I are currently discussing.

This discussion is about serious relationships, meaning ones that involved sex.

Chase confesses his longest relationship, one he had with some girl back in Vegas, lasted only a couple of months. Then, his dad died, and his life—as well as that relationship—fell to pieces.

That sure doesn't mean Chase hasn't had sex since then. Quite the contrary. He knows I'm well aware of this, so he spares me any further details of his past beyond his two-month girlfriend.

I tell him about Doug Wilson, my only real boyfriend and the only guy I've ever had sex with. Chase watches me with interest. Unlike him, my lack of a boyfriend for the past four years means I've also gone without sex for just as long. I hint at that, but don't come right out and say it. I give Chase a minute to figure that one out for himself as I line up my shot and prepare to putt a bright pink golf ball.

Chase and I are playing miniature golf at a course behind an ice-cream parlor/putt-putt golf course that just opened across the street from the church. It was Chase's idea to come here this evening. We both finished work at the same time and ran into each other out in the parking lot. Not literally, like our first meeting, but as I was opening my car door Chase was walking up to his truck. We smiled at each other and laughed about a stupid joke the waitress had told us earlier during our lunch at the diner. Chase then said he didn't feel like going straight home, it was too nice an evening. The sun was still high in the sky and the breezes blew warm as they whipped around us. I asked what my restless boy felt like doing.

"How 'bout a game of mini-golf?" Chase asked as he

gestured to the newly opened place across the street. "I heard the ice cream is good and their putt-putt course is fun." He raised an eyebrow. "What do you think? Golf first, ice cream after, and winner buys the cones. You game, baby girl?"

And that's how we ended up here under sodium lighting, hitting golf balls through rotating windmill blades and, just last hole, a blue whale's mouth. All the while talking about relationships and sex. *Oh, boy.*

My club makes contact and the pink ball flies through a metal loop-the-loop on the green before coming out on the other side. The ball does a little hop and I get my first hole in one. I don't mutter "fuck, yeah" like Chase did when he got a hole in one at the last hole.

But I do execute a little spin, making my flouncy skirt flare out as I yell, "Yay!"

Chase gives me a high five and starts to write my score down on our scorecard. I notice he seems distracted. I figure he must still be thinking about what I told him right before I putted—that I haven't been involved with a man for four years. I discover I am absolutely correct in three-two-one...

"So-o-o," Chase says slowly, looking up from where his golf pencil is no longer moving, "does that mean it's been four whole years since you last..." He trails off and coughs, but I swear I hear him say "fucked" under his breath.

Not only is it all kinds of hot to hear Chase say the word "fucked" in reference to me, but what he's asking is pretty clear. Even if his words weren't enough—and, trust me, they were—his quirked eyebrow and questioning gunmetal stare put to rest any doubts.

"Oh my God," I sputter. "I can't believe you just asked

me...*that.*" My cheeks are surely red. Not pink, red. Good Lord, is the beautiful Chase Gartner really asking me to confirm that I haven't gotten laid in four years?

Chase shrugs and gets back to writing on the scorecard. "Just keeping it real, blushing girl. We talk about everything else, right?"

"True," I say, because he's right.

We share a lot, more and more each day, and far more than I've ever shared with any other person. I think the same is true for him. In fact, I'm sure of it. The things we tell one another we'd never share with anyone else.

For instance, just last week, I ended up telling Chase about my fractured relationship with my parents. Right after he shared with me that he still loves his mom, even after all that's passed between them. But he wishes every day that things had turned out differently. I told him I knew how he felt; I often wish the same for myself.

We were coming back from lunch at the time, and when Chase noticed my eyes misting, he stopped and pulled me to him. He gave me a hug of epic proportions. It was a sweet and simple gesture, full of warmth and caring. And I hugged him back just as big, thinking maybe he needed holding as much as I did. As we held tightly to one another, like two lost ships on a sea of confusion, I breathed in the guy I've grown to care for so very much. Chase smelled clean—a hint of paint, soap and shave cream...and just pure, delicious male.

A day later, Chase and I were discussing music over lunch. He mentioned he's been listening to some old albums he found up in his attic weeks ago, classic rock that once belonged to his father. Chase said listening to those old songs—songs his dad had once loved so much—makes him feel closer to the man who left his life too soon.

"Way too soon, Kay," Chase said that day at lunch, his blues melancholy.

I knew right there and then the hole in my boy's heart gapes as wide as my own. I wanted to share something important, as well, it seemed only fair. So I told Chase about my journals for Sarah. I even shared the details of my weekly ritual. I told this man who always gets me how every week I visit my sister's grave and recite three things I remember about the little girl I lost. I confessed that even with my soothing ritual, my heart still aches. I told Chase how I always write those memories down in a journal, for safekeeping, so time can never sneak in and steal them away.

Someday I'll show Chase the things I've written. I never thought I'd show another soul, but Chase's soul is becoming entwined with mine. I also know I'll eventually tell him my secret—what really happened the night Sarah died. But I am not quite ready yet. Unloading that secret requires more courage than what I'm currently holding on to.

So what Chase just said is true, we do talk about everything; "keeping things real" is how we roll.

Even today at lunch, Chase, to my surprise, opened up about prison. He said not every day was horrible, most were just boring. Or "boring as fuck," as my dirty-mouthed boy put it. Chase said he found things to fill his time—he read *a lot*, lifted weights, and sketched for hours. "If you don't find outlets, the never-ending boredom will drive you insane," he told me.

Chase also shared that prison is more than just boredom. It's learning to live with no freedom and no privacy. You discover these things quickly, he said, like as soon as you go through central intake, right at the beginning. There you are strip-searched and whisked through medical assessment. Part of the process involves being tested for everything under the sun. In fact, you're tested periodically. When Chase mentioned testing he eyed me pointedly. I guess it was his way of telling me he's clean and healthy, he has no diseases. I quickly told him I'd been tested as well, at my last gynecological exam. That's about as personal as it gets, no doubt. And it's, for sure, "keeping it real."

I scoop my pink ball out of a little plastic cup on the green. "Yep, Chase," I say as I'm about to keep it real. "Sad but true, but I haven't done *it*"—I mime little air quotes with my fingers—"for four long years."

He's quiet so I continue. Only now I ramble, like I do when embarrassment floods over me. "Hey, there's always the convent. I figure I already have an 'in,' seeing as I'm involved with the church." I sigh dramatically so Chase will know I'm trying to make a joke, cover this embarrassment. "*And*, I hear if you successfully make it to the five-year mark with no sex you revert back to virgin status by default. One more year, woo-hoo, I've so got this covered."

A smile plays at my ever-perceptive boy's beautiful lips. He knows this conversation needs this levity. And he knows just how to play along, what to say next.

We step up to the next hole, and he shoots me this utterly sexy sidelong glance. "Virgin status, huh? Is that so?"

"Yep, it's true."

"You know," he says, his voice low and suddenly inviting, "we could save you from a life spent at the convent. It'd be a shame, really." His blues travel up and down my body in a way that makes my breath hitch.

He leans in close, until his lips are next to my ear. "If we leave now, Kay, we could go back to my place and, if you'd like, I could end that drought for you."

Oh, could you ever.

Time freezes, I am suddenly back in the library, four years ago, listening to two girls talk about how good Chase's sex is—*crazy-good*, that's what one of them said. And now, he's offering his crazy-good sex to me, right here, this evening.

I seriously consider, but unfortunately Chase is just kidding. His soft laugh and bump to my shoulder before he steps away tell me as much. I kind of wish he wasn't kidding though. No, I definitely wish he wasn't, because I want this man. In any way I can have him.

I don't let him know this, God no. I just push crazy-good sex away playfully, and say, "Shut up."

But my hormones are a-humming. I check out Chase's ass when he lines up his next putt. For the love of all that's holy, he wears his jeans so well. I never tire of seeing faded denim on his finely sculpted ass. I admire his wide shoulders, his tapered waist. And I know the T-shirt he's wearing hides all those sexy tats.

God, I bet this man is better than ever in the sack. Suddenly an image of him pounding into me enters my mind. *Dear Lord.* I fan myself with my hand. When Chase glances back at me, I pretend like it's the summer heat—not him—that's getting to me.

A few holes later, our miniature golf game ends. Chase wins, so I buy the ice cream. But I eat my cone is a rush.

When I'm done I say, "Sorry, but I have to go. I have an errand to run."

On the way home, in the hopes the next time my gorgeous friend offers to have sex with me he just may not be joking, I stop by the clinic with the extended hours and get the shot for birth control.

A day later I show up early over at the school. Chase is up on a ladder, painting the ceiling in one of the classrooms. Unfortunately, unlike the day in the gym, he's wearing a shirt. It's a tee, dark gray and kind of on the snug side. It shows off his strong back, wide shoulders, trim waist where his jeans hang low. His hair is tousled, particularly in the back. The overhead lighting from above has a way of making all the gold and bronze highlights stand out, more so than usual. There's a depth to Chase's hair, just like there's a depth to the man himself. It's hard to tear my gaze away, but I do, taking in the rest of the area.

There are paint cans haphazardly placed along the covered floor, and a bunch of wet paintbrushes off to the side. A cooler sits perched atop an overturned plastic bucket. I know exactly what's in there, Chase's stash of lemon-lime soda. My boy brings out my mischievous and playful, and suddenly an idea comes to me.

Quietly, and with stealth, I flip open the cooler top and grab what appears to be the last can of soda. *Perfect.* As the lid drops back into place it attracts Chase's attention. He turns on the ladder and calls out, "Hey."

But my butt is already out the door.

I scamper and turn down the hall, start down the tunnel

of lockers. I have on pants today, not a dress, and thankfully flats too, so I get a good head start. When I hear Chase approaching the turn to the hall, I toss the can of soda into a random locker and slam it shut.

I'm rather amazed Chase isn't on me yet, but when he rounds the corner I see what caused the delay. Not only did he have to come down the ladder, but clever boy has also taken the time to choose a weapon to use against me—a skinny paintbrush covered in bright white paint, surely one of the wet ones I noticed on the floor. *Uh-oh.*

Pale blue eyes dance deviously as Chase asks, "Where'd you hide it, naughty girl?" He gives me a sultry look that would make any other woman cave.

But not me, I remain steadfast as I start to back away. "Oh, I don't know," I sing-song. "It could be anywhere. I'd suggest starting with the lockers."

The hall is lined with lockers. Chase looks around and frowns. I laugh. He takes a step forward, lifts and brandishes the paintbrush. "I have ways to make you talk, you know."

Holy crap, his voice is filled with the promise of sex. *Crazy-good sex,* I remind myself.

"Is that what you want, Kay-baby? Does my girl want to play?"

Oh, do I ever.

I egg him on. Pointing at the paintbrush, I say, "You wouldn't dare."

My boy smiles another wicked smile and chuckles. "Oh, but I would."

He's not kidding, that paintbrush has my name written all over it. So I promptly take off.

Of course, I only make it a few feet before Chase catches me. With a strong but gentle arm around my middle, he spins me around and slowly backs me up against the lockers. I am breathless, but not from running. What I like, what turns me on, is that I've just been pursued. Pursued and caught, by this gorgeous, sexy guy who I may tease and call my boy, but there's never been any doubt in my mind that he is most definitely all man. It's particularly clear now as his body engulfs and surrounds me.

I close my eyes and breathe…him…in. Pressed up against me like this, he's all soap and paint, clean, and goodness. There's something special that's just *him*. I forget we're playing and just stand there, breathing in all that is Chase Gartner.

But then he touches my nose with the paintbrush—so very gently I barely feel it—and that simple motion snaps me back to reality.

"Oh. My. God." I touch my nose with disbelief, feeling for wet paint. "I can't believe you really just did that."

Chase is holding back a laugh, and I give him my best scowl in return. He laughs harder, and I think it must be because he's just turned me into a white-nosed, scowling clown. But then I look down at my hand, the one I raised to my face. There's nothing on my finger, no white paint, nothing.

"Gotcha," Chase says quietly, dropping the paintbrush. It clatters to the floor.

He has gotten me, he's gotten me good. The paint on the brush is dried, there's not a single smudge on me.

"Oh, I see how you play, tricky boy," I say while Chase stands before me and smirks victoriously.

"Have fun finding your soda," I snipe, trying to sound mad, but I can't muster up any ill will since, really, I'm having a blast. We're always at our best when we're playing.

I try to slip past Chase, leave him to his search, but he traps me by placing his hands against the lockers at either side of my head. "Not so fast," he says softly.

Suddenly, this isn't about sodas, paintbrushes, or games any longer.

My breath catches and our eyes meet—blue on brown. Does he see how much I want him to kiss me right now? Maybe, because his hands move from the lockers to wrap around my waist, so much like the first day we met. Only this time I put my arms around him too, placing my hands on his lower back.

Without thinking, I slip my fingers under the hem at the back of his tee. With warm, warm skin under my fingers, I trace little circles around those sexy indentations above the band of his boxer briefs.

"Kay," he whispers, his pale blues conflicted and pained. "Don't."

My eyes stay with his, and though I think he might, he doesn't stop me, not even when my fingers inch upward. Chase's back is so strong. His muscles flex and move as I touch and press. When I find an area where the texture of his skin differs, I trace with my fingertips what feels like the edge of a falling feather. Chase's breathing picks up. I know I'm turning him on—heat radiates between us—but I have no desire to stop exploring.

I find another falling feather, then another. Chase sucks in a breath as I continue to trace and touch. He's not the only one feeling this palpable excitement, my fingers tremble as they move across his back.

"Why are the feathers falling?" I whisper-ask, my heart racing as I press my palms to the wings.

With breaths uneven and eyes lust-hooded, Chase answers, "Because my wings are broken, baby, because *I* am broken."

"You're not broken." I touch the angel between the wings on his back for emphasis. "You're putting your life back together. Building isn't breaking, Chase."

He chuckles a little and kind of shivers under my touch. "You're too sweet to me, baby girl. You give me entirely too much credit." He brushes my cheek with his thumb, but his eyes are on my lips. "I just wish..."

"You wish what?" I ask when he falters. "What aren't you saying? Don't hold back with me, Chase, please—"

He touches my lips with his finger, cutting me off. "I'm afraid," he whispers.

My hand covers his. "Why?" I murmur against his finger.

How could Chase be afraid? He's strong, in so many ways. He's fearless, as far as I can see. But maybe he doesn't see himself the way I do. Why else would there be resistance in his gunmetal blues, like he's battling something?

"I'm no good for you," he says, pained, as if uttering the words hurts him. "You could do *so* much better than me, baby."

"That's not true. You're good for me, Chase. You help me in ways I can't even begin to explain. You make me want to live, to embrace life even. I was barely surviving before I met you."

I've laid it on the line, and his resistance is crumbling, I see it in every part of him—his eyes, the expression on his beautiful face, even the way he holds my body, one hand moving to the small of my back, arching me toward him ever so slightly.

I lean my head back against the locker and he nuzzles my neck. "What if I end up being bad for you?" he asks against my skin. "What if I hurt you?"

"You won't."

He lifts his head and searches my eyes. "How can you say that, sweet girl? Being with me will never be easy. I meant it when I said I'm broken. You make me feel more whole than I ever have in the past, but there will always be something missing. I'll always be trouble, Kay."

My hands are still on his back, still under his tee, and I touch everywhere—the angel, the wings, the falling feathers. "Then be my trouble," I whisper as I touch and touch and stare into blue depths.

Chase leans in close, close enough that his warm breaths caress me. I breathe in the life in his breaths, *his* life. "Be my trouble," I whisper again.

My trouble-boy's lips—so soft—just barely touch mine. We both still, lips touching, breaths shared. This is what we are, two broken people who when connected are made whole, made right. I feel this everywhere, my body, my heart, my soul. Does Chase feel it too?

He must, he asks, "Do you feel it, Kay?"

I nod and my lips brush his. Chase angles his head slightly and catches my upper lip with his mouth. My boy kisses me softly, just once.

Time stops.

He moves to my bottom lip and nips gently. I let out a stuttered breath. Chase nudges my lips open with his mouth and our tongues touch. My boy groans and pulls me to him. He kisses my mouth open farther as he cradles the back of my head.

This kiss—*this* kiss—has been building for weeks, and now that it's actually happening, it torches and ignites. We become all lips and tongues, little nips, scorching heat, and unleashed passion. I arch into Chase. I need to feel how much he wants me. And, damn, he wants me *bad*.

I want him just as much. I push my hips against him suggestively, letting him know how I feel.

He stills my grinding and just holds me to him. I feel him grow even harder for me. "Chase," I breathe out against his lips.

He kisses me hard, tells me between frenzied kisses, "You feel so good, beautiful, beautiful, sweet girl. Feel how much I want you." He circles his hips against mine. "I want you like this all the fucking time."

I moan and clutch at his body. I am weak with lust and want. My boy's hand wraps around my hair and urges my head back. I yield to him. He kisses down my neck, over the thin material of my blouse and the sheer bra underneath. I want him to unbutton and unclasp, but he does neither. Instead he finds my right peak with his mouth and sucks my nipple through the barely there fabrics. It's tortuous and teasing, wet, warm, and erotic. Chase moves to my left breast and does the same. The material keeping him from my skin becomes so wet that it feels like he has my nipple right in his mouth. When he uses his teeth, I gasp. "So good," I murmur.

I start to slide down the lockers, but my boy is careful with me, keeping me right, handling me like I might break. And maybe he thinks I might, since he's making promises, promises to never hurt me, and saying things like, "I want this so badly, Kay. I want *you*. But we'll move at whatever pace you want. You control this, baby. Just…" His lips return to my neck. "…just let me be good to you."

There's nodding on my part, and tears. Because this is what I've longed to hear, and this is the only man from which I've ever desired to be told these things.

Chase kisses away all my runaway tears, right down and along my cheeks. He kisses below my ear…tilts my head back…kisses across my chin…and returns to my lips. The way he moves me to suit him, carefully and gently, it gives me an idea of what it will be like to have sex with him. And I can't wait. It's going to be everything I imagined, but so much more. My body wants Chase, yes, but more importantly, my heart does too.

But right now I want to feel him let go a little bit, I need to show him he needn't be so careful with me. I kiss him hard, then harder still. He responds. His lips devour mine, and his hold gets a little rougher. He grinds his erection into me and our kisses become frenzied—lips, tongues, and hot, hot breaths. My hands trail up and down his back, my fingers spreading. I want to feel as much of Chase as I can. I want him skin to skin, but not here, not in a hallway where anyone could walk in and find us. I guess he's thinking the same thing. He seems to gather himself enough to slow things down.

When we finally break apart, chests heaving, our eyes meet. "Hey," he whispers huskily. He kisses the tip of my nose. When he leans back, he smiles. "Guess we got a little carried away."

"Guess so." I laugh.

He chuckles, but his eyes are serious. "Do you really want to do this, Kay?" He nods to where our bodies still press to one another. "Us. You and me. Do you want to see what we can be together?"

I place my hands on his cheeks. "Yes, Chase, I do. I want this so much."

And I do, my heart tells me we could be good together—great and epic—like the stuff of everlasting romances.

Chase leans his forehead against mine. "My sweet, sweet girl, let's try it, then. I want this too. And I can promise you one thing." I look into his eyes. "Baby, if you allow me, I am going to be so fucking good to you."

I don't doubt a word he says.

It feels like we've created a bubble for ourselves, and neither of us cares to disturb it, so it's a pretty easy decision when we opt to stay in for lunch. There are vending machines in the teachers' lounge, where we buy pretzels and chips and a Diet Coke for me. I show Chase the locker that holds his last can of lemon-lime, and then we head down to the gym.

Our junk food lunch is eaten on the bleachers as we sit side-by-side. We're silly and giddy, with lust, and maybe with the fact that we are officially entering into a relationship with each other, something beyond friendship.

I feed Chase a pretzel, since we're long past all pretenses and I can do things like that now. He does the same, nudging my lips open with a chip. I crunch, bite, and swallow.

"If we could go anywhere in the world, right now," he asks out of the blue, "just the two of us, where would you have us go?"

I don't even have to think. "Paris," I answer.

I feed Chase another pretzel and tell him to pretend it's a piece of baguette. After he swallows he asks, "What's a baguette?"

"A baguette is like a French version of a loaf of bread. It's long and skinny, crusty outside, but soft in the middle."

Another chip is nudged at my lips, and this time Chase tells me to pretend it's a piece of this baguette-thing, but covered in brie. I still his hand. "Hey, how can you not know what a baguette is, but you know brie?"

He shrugs. "My mom once bought a cheese called brie and I remember really liking it. She told me it was from France."

"Hmm..." I mumble before I eat the offered chip, pretending what Chase suggested, that my boyfriend is feeding me brie-covered baguette.

"So, why Paris?" he asks.

"It's romantic, Chase. We could eat brie on pieces of baguette for real. We could sit at a café up on Montmartre. There are artists there, selling their wares along the sidewalks. You could sell your art there too. You're certainly good enough."

Suddenly shy boy blushes. It's not often I can make Chase blush, so I enjoy it for a few seconds, and then I tell him more about Paris, all the things I've read. When I finish he touches my cheek. "I wish I could take you there, Kay."

I nudge his shoulder with my own. "I'm pretty happy right where I am."

The next thing on my lips isn't another chip, it's Chase. Lunch is forgotten as we kiss and kiss and kiss. When our lips are so swollen we have to take a break—at least for a few minutes—we talk.

"Think they're missing us at the diner?" Chase asks, sitting back and taking a drink of his lemon-lime soda.

"Nah," I reply.

He brushes my hair back and covers my neck in a few cool, lemon-lime kisses. "You thought they would the other day," he murmurs against my skin.

I stiffen and Chase leans back. "What's wrong?"

"It's nothing really," I say slowly. I need to tell Chase what I should have fessed up to the other day.

I take a deep breath, and then do just that. "I just didn't want to go to Pizza House because there's someone that works there that I used to kind of date."

Chase's expression darkens. "Not that Doug guy, right?"

I've told him most of the stuff about my past with Doug Wilson, how the relationship started with our mothers' influence, and how it degraded over time. It burned Chase to hear Doug didn't treat me right, particularly as time wore on. If Chase only knew the real truth of how horribly that story ended.

I dispel those thoughts. I'll tell Chase everything, but not today. Today is too special to ruin it with sadness.

"No, not Doug," I answer, "He's in Columbus, remember?"

"Right," Chase mutters, "lucky for him."

It thrills me to no end to know Chase longs to defend me, but we've gotten off track.

"Anyway," I say, getting back to the subject at hand. "I

went on a couple of dates with the manager at Pizza House last fall, after I quit waitressing there. His name is Nick. He was nice and all, but it just didn't work out. I guess I was worried it might get awkward if he saw us together."

Chase looks a little confused, and I'm certain he's thinking about our conversation yesterday when we were playing putt-putt golf, our discussion about relationships and sex.

I hastily add, "It never got serious, Chase. We never had sex."

He nods, looking a little relieved. "Well, we can stick with the diner if that's what you're more comfortable with."

And that's that, we discuss it no more.

When we're finished eating, Chase guides me to him as I drink the last of my diet soda. I giggle and laugh, his hold on my waist is so light it tickles. "Stop tickling," I mock-complain, scooting away.

Chase takes the can from my hand and pulls me on top of his body in one swift move. He lays us back on the bleacher, me on top of him. "Okay, no more tickling," he says quietly.

True to his word, there is no more tickling, but there is a lot more kissing, and more touching too, but still all over the clothes. When Chase's hands curve down over my ass, I push my center into him. Even though I have on pants, they're just thin linen, and I feel Chase hardened length beneath me. He groans when I circle my hips.

My hands explore his arms, his chest. Damn, his whole body is so hard and strong. "You're so strong," I tell him.

He thrusts up into me a couple of times, showing me how he could use his strength on me in some very good ways. We grind and move against each other awhile longer, but when things get too heated, Chase stills and says, "We better slow things down, baby."

I nod against his mouth.

"Hey, make me a promise," he says, his lips brushing mine.

I lean back so I can see his face. His blues are hooded, filled with lust, but also somewhat troubled. "Sure. Anything, Chase," I worriedly reply.

His fingers trail down my cheek. "Don't let me hurt you, baby. I couldn't live with myself if I ever did anything bad to you."

I know he doesn't mean anything physical, that's not even a consideration. Chase doesn't want to hurt me emotionally, but I don't see that happening either. He's already so careful with me. It just doesn't seem possible he could ever hurt me. I think he just thinks I'm more fragile than I am. But I promise him, nonetheless, so he'll feel more comfortable.

While I'm still lying on top of him, I play with the sleeves of his tee. I kiss the 72 on his bicep. Chase told me the day we talked about prison that he had the number done in memory of his cell block number.

I move to his other bicep, kiss the scroll of words I've never been close enough to read. I do so now, reading them out loud in a reverent whisper, "As I stand before you, judge me not."

It strikes me as interesting that *I* could have these same words written on my body, it would certainly be fitting. "What does it mean?" I ask.

I can see from Chase's face that talking about this tattoo

is going to be hard for him, more so than any of the others. I think about telling him he can share this one with me another time, but I hold off. I sense he needs to get this out. In fact, I'm certain of it. That's how well we've learned one another.

Chase takes a deep breath and I go to move, but he holds me in place. My boy wants me on him, so I stay as I am, sprawled on him as he tells me about the last night with his father. He talks of how they ordered Chinese food and ate on the floor of their empty, about-to-be-repossessed home. He tells me how his little brother slept through dinner, and how afterward his father asked him to stay with Will while he took care of "something."

Chase's lips press together when he gets to this part of the story. I place my head on his shoulder and wrap my arms around him as best as I can. While I hold tight to my heartbroken boy, he rubs his hands up and down my back in a motion that's meant to soothe us both.

"He never came back," Chase whispers. "He drove off that road on purpose, I know it, Kay. He didn't care enough to stay."

Chase has told me enough good things about his father that I feel honest in saying, "He still loved you, Chase. He did."

"Not enough, apparently" he says sadly as his arms tighten around me.

I hold on to Chase, wishing I could take away his hurt. His pain resonates in my own heart, it wraps around my soul, mingling with my own deeply rooted pain. Chase has become an incredibly important person in my life, his happiness is as important to me as my own, maybe even more important, at times like these.

It's at that exact second I realize—in a rush, like a wave crashing all around me—I have fallen in love. I am head over heels in love with Chase Gartner.

CHAPTER SEVEN

CHASE

It amazes me that one day can be so perfect, and then the next can turn to shit in an instant. That's exactly what happens as Friday dawns. Not at first though.

The day starts out great, I wake up buzzed. Not on drugs, not on alcohol. I am buzzed on life, buzzed on Kay, buzzed on the afternoon we spent together in the school yesterday during lunch. Kissing Kay—finally giving in—felt right. And good. Damn, real good.

No, good doesn't even begin to fucking describe what I felt. Finally kissing my girl was something better than good. It was the best. No, more than that too. It was fucking indescribable, okay? Giving in to all I've kept buried inside awakened in me something deeper, some feeling yet not experienced. Well, until now. I didn't say a thing, but I realized what this feeling was—*is*—when I was holding my girl next to the lockers, when my mouth was on hers.

I fucking *love* Kay Stanton. I do. I love my girl, with all my good and all my trouble.

The resistance I was fighting? Yeah, that shit has not only crumbled, it's fucking annihilated. I am done for; sweet girl owns my ass. Maybe the more appropriate thing to say is that she owns my heart. Since, after all, it's my heart that swells with all the many things I love about my girl…

I love that I can make her laugh. I love that I pink her cheeks. I love that she's sweet and tastes like honey. But there's more. I particularly love the sexy little moans she makes when we're kissing. Those sounds go straight to my cock. Speaking of which, I want to make my girl come—make her fucking explode—using not only my dick, but my fingers and my tongue. But this is more than just something sexual with Kay. I want to make this woman happy. And not just the fleeting kind of happiness I can give her with a few good orgasms. No, my girl deserves to feel that rare, deep-in-your-heart brand of happiness, like the kind I feel for her.

I guess what it comes down to is this: I just want my sweet girl to let me love her.

That's why I said so many things I previously kept inside. My girl—and it really feels like she *is* my girl now—deserves to know what's in my heart. I'll be good to her, I will, or I'll die trying. I won't allow myself to hurt her, and because I made her promise, I feel confident she won't ever let me.

Maybe she's not as fragile as I first suspected, but she's still never been with someone quite like me. I am nothing like that asshole she dated years ago, Doug-fucking-Wilson. He was just some wannabe-bad guy, a manipulative dick who took advantage of Kay being such a good person. I'd never do anything intentionally bad, like that, but I still worry, because let's be honest, there's a part of me that will always be bad.

There's blackness on my soul, ugly smut that's rubbed in there for good. I can't erase my past, or change the things I've done. And I've done some bad, bad things—to myself and to others. I am capable of destruction, in so many fucking ways. The battle with my dark side ebbs and flows, true, but it's never completely absent. Lately, it's been ebbing, which is great. But the black, the darkness, it's always lurking, just waiting to be unbridled.

These worries, though, can't minimize the perfection of yesterday. And that's what kissing my girl was—fucking perfection. I hated when Kay and I had to part and get back to work. If I'd had my way, I would've hung out with her all day in that gym, just kissing, talking, and loving her, slow and easy.

And what I told her was true. I'd give her Paris if I could. I can't take her there, unfortunately, but I do have a few ideas. I'll see what I can do.

Anyway, the few hours following our time in the gym went quickly, thank God. After work, we went to dinner. Not at the diner, no way. Yesterday was special and called for celebration, so I took my girl to one of the nicer restaurants in town. There, we ate by candlelight, even indulged in a bottle of wine. Who knew I had it in me to be such a fucking romantic? But when I'm around Kay, I become someone different, someone better, someone I wish I could be all the time—that guy is good.

Maybe Kay sees this in my soul. It sure seems like she sees someone special. Maybe I can be the man I thought I could be a long time ago. I am finally starting to believe I have it in me.

I don't know. But I'd count myself a success if I could live up to all the potential my girl sees.

However, right now, I don't feel so great. I sure as shit don't feel as if I'm bursting with potential. At the moment, I am pissed as hell and ready to throw my fucking cell against the bedroom wall. In fact, it takes everything I have in me not to do just that.

See, I texted my brother ten minutes ago to wish him a "happy birthday"—Will turns fifteen today—and the little prick finally responded. I felt cautiously joyful when I heard the alert, like the perfection of yesterday might be continuing right into today.

But I guess not.

My brother's response put an end to that foolish thinking. Will's text read: *Fuck off.*

I feel like texting back: *You little fucker, you finally answer me and that's the best you come up with?*

But I don't do any such thing. Instead, I run my fingers through my hair and gently set the phone back down on the dresser. If that little shit was here in front of me he'd never have the balls to "say" something like that to my face. But he's not here; he's thousands of miles away. Despite the distance, despite the "fuck off" text, I can't help but still feel love for the brat. I guess that's why his texted flip-off hurts so much.

I go into the bathroom and get into the shower. I turn the water on, and lean my forehead against the cool tiles.

Fuck.

The emotions I've been through these past twenty-four hours—all extreme highs and lows—I'd say something is bound to give. Sooner or later, it will happen. Something is about to push me too far. I just don't know when, or how, or what will set me off. But I'm teetering at the breaking point. Of that, there is no doubt.

By the time I'm back in my bedroom, drying off and getting dressed, I am wound up tighter than ever. I feel knotted and bound, pulled taut at the center. So when I get to the church a little while later, I head straight into the school and start working. Best if no one sees me like this, especially not Kay.

A gallon of white paint later, the classroom I started on yesterday starts to come together. And I feel better, calmer, more relaxed. But then my cell rings and I see it's my mother. *Fuck, what now?*

When I answer I get an earful, which is amusing since I haven't heard anything from Abby in over a month.

"Chase, you have to talk to Will," my mother tells me in a hurried jumble of words.

This is her greeting.

"Hello, to you too," I throw back, my comment dripping sarcasm.

Yeah, I am aggravated. However, Mom ignores my smartass tone and moves right along.

"It's getting ridiculous with that kid. No one here can get through to him. Do you know what time he got in last night?"

She's venting so I just grunt out a, "Nope."

"Well, he didn't, Chase, your brother stayed out all night." Mom pauses so I can let that sink in. "Will finally stumbled in about two hours ago."

This is all a little concerning, so I ask, "He was okay, right?"

Mom sighs, and sounds resigned when she says, "I think he was drunk, he just went to his room." Another pause, and then in a pleading voice she adds, "Chase, honey, can you talk some sense into your brother? I really think if anyone can get through to him, it might be you—"

"Yeah, I doubt that," I interrupt.

"What? Why would you say that? Will looks up to you, he always has. He'll listen."

I lean my ass against a piece of furniture I covered earlier and scrub my free hand down my face. "Mom, Will doesn't look up to me anymore. Maybe he did a long time ago, but he sure as hell doesn't now. Hell, the kid won't even talk to me."

I leave out that dear little brother sent me a lovely "fuck off" text this morning, Mom's dealing with enough.

I hear the sound of a match striking and Mom sounds like she's lighting a cigarette. She supposedly quit, but I had a feeling she still smoked. I smelled it on her that day at the courthouse. Well, at least she's not out gambling to relieve her stress.

"I don't know, sweetie," she says on an exhale. "I know I shouldn't dump this on you, but I didn't know who else to talk to. Greg's getting sick of Will's behavior." I roll my eyes. *Greg*...of course. "Your brother just doesn't listen anymore. And ever since school let out he's been running wild. This isn't the first night he's stayed out until morning."

Mom takes a draw from her cigarette. "We told him there'll be repercussions if he continues this way, but it doesn't seem to matter to him. He does what he wants, Chase." She pauses and adds quietly, "I know he's been drinking for a while now too. Bottles have been missing from Greg's liquor cabinet, and the other day I found a few in the back of Will's closet. They were all empty."

I still don't know what exactly my mother expects me to do. But I do offer this: "I'd talk to him, Mom, I would, but he seriously wants nothing to do with me. You saw how he acted at the courthouse the day you guys were out here. The kid hates my guts."

"Your brother doesn't hate you," my mother insists. "He just hates all the stuff that's happened to you in the past. He's angry, yes, but I know for a fact Will loves you, honey. Very, very much."

I hope she's right even as I mutter, "I don't know about that."

"Listen...Chase..." Mom's voice fades in and out, like some faraway radio station. She must be reaching for an ashtray or something. "If I can get Will to call you, would you talk to him, then?"

"Of course," I say.

Mom sighs in apparent relief. "That would really mean a lot, sweetie. Oh...and..." She trails off and I know she's holding something back.

"What?" I ask to prompt her.

I hear the sound of another cigarette being lit, and then, "If Will starts talking to you again...and you can get through to him...what would you think about me sending him out to Ohio to stay with you for the rest of the summer?"

Fuck. My limits are straining. She's not going to send Will away like she did me.

"Mom..." I close my eyes for a second to keep calm. "The answer to every fucking problem that arises with your kids isn't to send them away."

It's kind of a shitty thing to say, but it's true, and Abby needs to finally hear it.

Mom must feel guilty for sending me away six years ago, because she starts talking real fast, like she does when she knows she did wrong. "That's not fair, Chase. You were out of control when you left Vegas."

"Sending me away didn't help, it just made things worse. You thought Gram, of all people, could control me? She was an old lady." I'm finally letting out what I've kept bottled up for years. "You pawned your *problem*—me—off on someone else and look what happened. I ended up in prison. Yeah, great decision, Mom."

Mom chokes back a sob. "I told you I was sorry for all that, Chase. I'm sorry, I'm sorry, I'm sorry, okay? How many times do I have to say it for you to finally believe me?"

Mom starts crying hard now, and I feel like a real dick. I should've kept my stupid mouth shut. She didn't say she wanted Will here forever, just for the summer. I wouldn't mind my brother staying here for a couple of months, but only if he wanted. I'd never force him to leave Vegas, like what Mom did to me.

Her crying lessens, but I have to fix what I've messed up. "Mom, mom, shh, everything's all right." Her breathing hitches. "Look, I shouldn't have said those things. You're right. I was out of control back then. I have no one to blame for what happened but myself and—"

"I still gave up on you, baby," she interrupts. "And I regret it every day. That's why I helped you as soon as I could." This is true—my mom did hire the sharp lawyer who ultimately got me out of prison. "I am not giving up on Will, okay? Just forget I mentioned sending him out to Ohio."

"Mom," I sigh. "I'll talk to him, all right? Just get him to call me."

"All right, I'll try," she sniffles.

"Don't worry, I'll straighten him out." I sound more confident than I feel, because what I really feel is sad.

I feel sad for Will, a mixed-up kid. And I feel sad for Mom losing the love of her life, my dad. She got stuck raising two headstrong boys by herself, when, really, she was never emotionally equipped to handle that sort of burden.

I feel like I should have some magic solution to make everything right. It's unreasonable, I know, but I can't shake my emotion.

The white walls I painted before Mom called suddenly feel like they're closing in on me. What I really want is to go to Kay, but she doesn't need to be dragged into my fucked-up family situation. I've burdened her with enough already, like all my troubled-past baggage.

Mom calms and we hang up, but I feel shittier than ever. I can't stay in this school a minute longer; I have to get out of here for a while.

I stop by the church office to let Kay know I'm heading home early. She asks me if I'm all right, and I tell her I will be. When she waits for me to elaborate—because sharing our bad, as well as our good, is what we do—I tell her I'll explain everything later.

My always-understanding girl doesn't press, she just accepts. What I should do is ask her if she wants to hang out later. Tonight is the start of the weekend, after all. But I really just need some downtime, time alone to put my shit back together. I figure I should be good by tomorrow, so I ask Kay if she wants to do something in the afternoon. Maybe drive up north to the cinemas and see a matinee movie.

This puts a smile back on my girl's face. I need to hold her, be close, so I wrap my arms around her. I hurriedly check to make sure we're alone, and then I kiss her like I did yesterday, my lips a little everywhere.

"I want to see you happy, baby," I tell her as I nuzzle along her jaw. "But I'm just no good today. Tomorrow…" I kiss up to her honey-flavored lips. "Tomorrow, I'll make it up to you, okay?"

Kay nods and kisses me in return. I love the feel of her soft lips pressed to mine. And I love that she's as into this as me. Things start to get a little heated, but I try to maintain some control. After all, we are in the rectory office, and Father Maridale could walk in on us at any time.

Oh, fuck it.

My tongue wraps up with my girl's tongue as her hands move down to my ass. Our bodies kind of smash together, and our kisses escalate from simmering to boiling over. When we finally break for air, I take a step back. We give each other these big, goofy grins. We're so fucking ridiculous, but who cares? This is what love feels like.

A part of me considers telling Kay right there and then that I love her, but I hold off. Those words are way too precious to give away in the church office. I want the moment I give my heart to my girl to be better than this.

I take her hand in mine, and we just speak with our eyes for a minute. Kay gives me a look, like maybe she has something she wants to tell me too. But she remains silent.

After a beat, we sneak in a few more stolen kisses, and then I leave.

As I walk to my truck, I feel better than I did prior to seeing Kay. I flip the keys in my hand and ponder some things. Like, I wonder what Kay wanted to tell me. It seemed like it might be something good, based on the smile in her eyes.

Shit, maybe Kay loves me, like I love her. Could it be possible for sweet girl to feel more for me than some kind of a friendship-lust thing? I sure hope so.

I think about this—and more—as I pull away from the church. But my inner reflection grinds to a screeching halt when my cell phone rings.

I glance down, and, shock-upon-shock, it's my brother.

When I answer his first words are, "Mom made me call."

I have a few choice words of my own in mind for a retort, but I hold my tongue. I know this kid has been hurt, by me, by fucking life. So I need to move slowly and rebuild his shattered trust.

I opt to stick with a nice, benign, "Hey, Will. How've you been?"

"Okay, I guess." Awkward silence, and then, "Oh, thanks for the happy birthday text."

I laugh. "Does that mean I should delete your earlier reply?"

"Yeah, delete it." Will chuckles a little, and I know he's softening, the ice is finally breaking. "Sorry about that. Mom was on my ass when I typed *fuck off*. I think I was probably saying it more to her than to you."

"That's okay, kid," I reply. "But you should show Mom more respect. She's trying, you know."

Will doesn't respond to my commentary on Mom. Instead, he snorts, "Kid? Shit, I'm not that much younger than you, bro. Besides, I'll be eighteen soon, and then I'll be a grown-ass adult. I'll finally be able to do whatever the fuck I want."

I laugh. "Shit, you have three more years before you have the right to call yourself a grown-ass adult, *kid*." We both crack up, but then I quietly add, "And, Will, you know you have six more years till you're legal to drink."

My brother sighs. "Guess Mom filled you in, huh?"

"Guess she did."

"I only took Greg's booze once, okay?" My brother pleads his case. "My friends wanted to start celebrating my birthday early, that's all. We drank a little last week in my room. Mom needs to fucking relax."

"She's just worried about you, bro. She's doing her best, you know."

That last gets a very sarcastic, "Yeah, right."

He's not completely off-base, but I have to be the adult here. "Will, you *are* only fifteen. I heard about you staying out all night. You need to slow down. Underage drinking… what else do you do? You better not be getting fucking hi—"

"Like *you* never partied," he interrupts.

He's got me there, but that doesn't mean I want him to make the same fucked-up choices I made. I tell my brother as much, and he listens. I mean, I think he does. He remains quiet and doesn't fight me at least.

I don't mention anything about Mom's proposed plan to send him to Ohio for the rest of the summer, but I do tell Will he's welcome to visit anytime he wants. My brother thanks me, and when he does I hear just how young he really is. But I also hear how tired he sounds, and not in an up-all-night kind of way. No, Will's tired tone is the sad, this-life-is-wearing-me-out variety.

My heart pulls and stutters. This kid should get to enjoy being what he is, a kid. But I guess that's a luxury that was taken away from both of us a long time ago. I can't lie to myself—Will's just as damaged as I am from the shitty past we share.

So, I make it my mission to cheer him up. I spend the remainder of the call just trying to get my baby brother to laugh. I try so hard to make him feel like the kid he actually is, especially since it's his birthday. I tell him crude jokes—filthy ones, really—until he's laughing so hard he's practically crying. And slowly, slowly, he starts to open up. Just a little at first. And then more and more, like a dam breaking.

He tells me about last night, the eve of his birthday. He and his friends got really drunk. No surprise there. Will doesn't say if they did anything else, and I don't ask. I just listen without comment.

My brother talks as I drive the rest of the way to my house, and when I pull in the driveway, he's telling me about his art. He's still drawing, comic book stuff. His dream is to someday have his own series of comic books.

I am just relieved this kid still has a dream. I ask him to send me some samples of his work. He promises to e-mail me some stuff he just recently finished. Shit, I can't wait to see my brother's art. It was good before, but now that he's older I have a feeling Will's art is going to amaze me.

Our call comes to a close as we run out of words, but I sense Will wants to ask something more. He's stalling, just like Mom does when she's trying to get up the nerve to ask something she knows I won't like.

"What's up?" I ask.

Will starts to speak, but then hesitates. I wait him out, and finally, he gets to the point—my brother wants me to transfer some money into his banking account.

"Mom's being a bitch after last night," he says. "And

there are a bunch of art supplies I was hoping to buy later today. Can you do it? I'll pay you back."

He won't, but that's not really the issue. The problem is that I know—I fucking know I should refuse him. If Will is asking now, and not waiting for our mother to come around, then it's probably because the money is for something he's not supposed to have.

Art supplies, my ass.

Fuck, I just hope the money's not for something illegal. I should tell Will no, but with the connection I've just made with him, I can't bring myself to deny him.

So, I get all his bank information. And then we hang up.

I sit in the truck for a while. Shit, I should feel good. My brother is talking to me again. And things are beyond fantastic with Kay. But damn if I can't shake this sense of dread washing over me, this feeling of foreboding.

I give myself a few more minutes, trying to get a grip. I'm so knotted up and bound, I can't relax. And the longer I sit, the more it feels as if those imaginary ropes are being pulled tighter. But the worst part is that I feel like some force I have no control over is about to pitch me out to sea, bound and helpless. And in that condition, there will be no chance.

I will surely sink quickly.

CHAPTER EIGHT

KAY

Something is up with Chase, but I can't imagine what it could possibly be. Yesterday was wonderful, perfect really, and I was hoping to spend more time with him today. Guess that won't be happening.

Alas…

If my complicated boy needs time to himself, then who am I to deny him? He did say he'd tell me what's bothering him later. And that's good enough. Besides, the kisses he so enthusiastically bestowed made me forget everything, at least for a while.

But after all that delicious affection, now that Chase is gone, I feel a little empty. Worse yet, I have a feeling the off-kilter vibe to this day is only just beginning.

Ominously, the next person to step into the rectory office is Missy Metzger. And she looks like she's on a mission.

I sigh and slump into my chair at the desk.

I mean, I've already told Missy I can't make cookies—or anything else, for that matter—for the upcoming bake sale that's part of the big Fourth of July carnival next week. It's not as if my oven has miraculously started working. I try to circumvent a labored discussion by telling Missy exactly these facts as she approaches. However, I soon discover the bake sale isn't even on my sort-of friend's radar today.

She waves her hand dismissively. "Oh, don't worry about making anything, we have it all covered. Maybe by the August rummage sale your oven will be working." She gives me a questioning look and I shrug. "Well, if so, you can get in on that one."

I don't tell her it's not likely I'll have a working oven by August, but Missy doesn't seem too worried about it anyway. She hops up onto the edge of my desk and crosses her legs, making her miniskirt rise even higher. I've noticed the head of the bake committee has been dressing in skimpier clothes lately. Wonder what's up with that?

"So-o-o," Missy drawls as she picks up a freshly sharpened pencil, "Chase Gartner, huh?" She blows shavings from around the lead tip and shoots me a sidelong glance.

I reply nonchalantly, "Oh, you saw him leaving?"

"I saw more than that, sweetie." Missy winks and points the pencil at me. "So, you and Chase making out in the rectory, you're lucky Father Maridale didn't walk in."

She's right, so I say, "No kidding."

Well," she continues as she toys with the pencil, "this is all very interesting, Kay. What's going on with you and the town's resident bad boy?"

There's no sense pretending, so I just spit it out and admit we're officially dating.

Her eyebrows go up and the pencil goes down. "Really? Like, he's your boyfriend?"

I nod and Missy purses her lips, seemingly losing herself in thought.

I've wondered for a while why there's this odd vibe between Missy and Chase, so I ask, "What's your problem with him anyway? You used to think he was hot, but now you act like you can barely stand him."

"Oh, I still think he's hot, honey. Some things are indisputable. But, I told you before, the guy is a prick. He's a player, Kay. You should watch your step."

I know my boy's past reputation, but there's something in Missy's tone that makes me think she may have firsthand knowledge of something. But that can't be right. Chase would've surely mentioned if anything had ever happened between them. I mean, I think he'd tell me.

My stomach sours at the thought of Missy and Chase having done, really, anything. Maybe this is part of what Chase is referring to when he says he's trouble? But my guy and the head of the bake committee? Ugh. I can't even.

I force myself to ask Missy, "Why do you say he's a player?"

She flips her blonde hair back. She used to always wear it up, but that's another change I've noticed. Her hair is down almost all the time now.

"I've just heard things, that's all," Missy replies, picking up the pencil she set down earlier, and studying it intently. "I'm sure it's all the same stuff you've heard. He does have a reputation, you know?"

I nod, but I also breathe a sigh of relief. I know Chase has a past. A past filled with many...conquests. Thank goodness Missy isn't among them. That would just be weird.

"Hey, I actually came in to ask you a question," Missy points the pencil at me once more as she, thankfully, changes the subject.

"Okay."

"What are you doing tonight? Do you have any plans?"

I thought I had plans, but Chase made it clear I'd not be seeing him until tomorrow. Do I really feel like sitting home all night? Not particularly. My life has changed a lot in the past few weeks. I'm more apt to take chances, live a little, so to speak. So far, I've done this chance-taking, this life-living thing, with Chase only. Makes sense, since he's the one who got the whole thing started for me. But I feel ready to expand my horizons. I'm ready to make others a part of my life too.

With my new attitude and renewed enthusiasm, I look up at Missy from my seated position at the desk, and ask, "Why? What did you have in mind?"

A smile creeps along her lips as she drums the pencil excitedly on the desk. "You're really up for doing something?" I nod and Missy actually squeals. "Oh my God, this is great. We are going to have so much fun, you'll see."

Missy's reaction makes me realize this is the first time I've ever agreed to do anything with her outside of church obligations.

"So, where should we go?" I ask.

She hops down from the desk and straightens her skirt. "Ooh, I know. Let's go to the Anchor Inn."

I groan a little inwardly because that place is such a pick-up joint, but it's also one of the only bars in town where you can dance.

Oh, what the hell, I think. To Missy, I say, "Okay, that works for me."

We finalize our plans—I'll meet her at the entrance to the Anchor Inn at eight o'clock so we can go in together and find a booth. After Missy leaves, I debate whether I should call Chase and tell him my plans. I decide against it. He wanted some time to himself and calling will make it seem like I'm trying to find excuses to contact him. So, I let things be.

After work ends, I speed back to my apartment so I can get ready. I shower and pick out a cute outfit I've never worn. I bought it last fall when I was sort of dating Nick, but we quit seeing each other before I ever got around to wearing it.

I get the scissors out and cut off the tags. The jeans are this nice deep, dark indigo color. The cut is skinny, but the denim is stretchy. I tug indigo up my legs and over my hips. I zip up. The jeans are snug, but for the most part, comfy. The blouse, I find I love. It looks fantastic once it's on my body. The fabric is light and summery, a pale yellow crinkled chiffon. Floral embroidery stitching runs all along the neckline and up over the shoulders. I pair the whole ensemble with a pair of flat-soled metallic sandals.

When all is said and done I take a spin in front of the mirror in the bathroom. I have to say I look good, maybe a little sexy, even. Too bad my night is about to be spent with Missy and not with someone I *know* would fully appreciate my appearance this evening.

Oh, well.

Three hours later Missy and I are seated at a booth near the bar, drinking margaritas out of salt-rimmed glasses. The music blares around us, and the place is filling up rapidly.

"Are you having a good time?" Missy yells over the music.

She's wearing a low-cut top and a pair of tight jeans. The blue fabric *v* of her top is so low and revealing I have to resist the urge to tell Missy she's about to have a nip-slip any minute. Somehow, I don't think she cares.

I take a sip of my margarita, and answer her question, "Yeah, it seems fun here, so far."

I am exaggerated a little, I'm mostly just bored. But soon the alcohol from the margarita begins coursing through my system, and I begin to think there may be the potential for good times ahead.

I bounce a little in my seat to the bass beat of the tune that's playing, and say, "We should dance."

"Sure." Missy holds up her margarita "After we finish our drinks, yeah?"

I nod and start sipping.

Just as we finish off our margaritas, and are about to hit the dance floor, I spot Nick Mercurio, manager at Pizza House and one-time date of mine. He's with a friend, some guy I've never seen before. But the guy bears a striking resemblance to Nick. The two of them just got here, but, even from this vantage point, it's apparent they're both a little drunk. I try to hurry Missy along so we can get out to the dance floor and lose ourselves in the crowd. I don't care to deal with Nick and any alcohol-fueled advances tonight.

Unfortunately, Missy is fumbling around in her purse, searching for who-knows what, and taking forever. "Come on," I prod, standing up.

"Okay, okay."

Missy starts to slip out of the booth, but it's too late. Nick has spotted me. He waves enthusiastically, and heads to our table, his friend following.

"Hey, isn't that your manager from when you worked at Pizza House?" Missy asks as she settles back into the booth.

Before I can answer she adds, "Ooh, he's cute. And who's his friend?" She licks her lips. "Mmm, I want to meet them both."

I roll my eyes. Not to be crude, but Missy is like a bitch in heat sometimes. Nick and his friend close in on our table; there'll be no escaping now.

Damn, I'll have to talk to him.

His friend-that-I-don't-know is, in fact, cute, just as Missy has observed. This guy actually looks *a lot* like Nick, same dark hair, olive-toned skin, similar dark eyes. He's most definitely tall, dark, and handsome, like Nick.

The guys reach us and an awkward greeting is exchanged. Nick introduces his friend as his cousin, Tony. *No wonder they look so similar.*

As Missy begins to flirt shamelessly with Tony, Nick kind of chuckles and turns to me. "Do you want to dance?" he asks.

"Uh, I…"

I look to Missy for help, but she chimes in with, "Actually, we were on our way out to the dance floor to do just that." She loops her arm around Tony's.

Oh, great, this is so not what I wanted.

The four of us make our way to the dance floor, Tony and Missy lead the way and Nick guides me forward with a lightly placed hand on my back. We fight through the crowd and stop somewhere in the middle. And then we carve out a little space of our own in between packed bodies and start to dance.

I'm just relieved the song is a fast one, since there's no way I am pressing my body up to Nick's for any slow songs. Not only would Chase surely not like if I did something like that, but leading Nick on is the last thing I care to do tonight.

While I dance facing Nick, I also make sure to keep a respectable distance away. The up-tempo makes it easy enough, but it sure doesn't deter Missy. She dirty dances with Tony like there's no tomorrow, grinding her ass right up into Nick's cousin's groin. Not that Tony seems to mind. He appears to love it.

Nick laughs and looks pointedly at me. *Is he kidding?* I just shake my head.

The song changes to something a little slower and Nick tries to wrap his arms around me so he can pull me closer. I slip under his grasp and tell him I have to use the ladies' room. Really, I'm just done dancing for the night.

"I think I may leave soon," I yell over the music to Nick.

He just shrugs and says dismissively, "Whatever, Kay."

He steps away and turns to where his cousin and Missy are really ramping up the grinding. When Missy sees Nick alone, she puts her arms around him, effectively sandwiching herself between the two cousins.

I turn and make my way through the crowd. When I reach the edge of the dance floor, I glance back. Through the crowd, I catch a glimpse of Nick, Tony, and Missy. The two men have their hands all over Missy, right there in the middle of the dance floor. They're basically feeling her up. No one seems to care though. The whole scene starts to become very dirty and wanton, and there's no doubt the three of them will move and escalate elsewhere sooner rather than later.

The margarita I drank earlier churns in my stomach. Why am I even in this place? I wish I were somewhere with

Chase right now, anywhere but here. There's nothing at the Anchor Inn for me.

I go to the ladies' room and splash cool water on my face. Whatever alcohol I consumed has long since left my system. I just want to leave. A night I thought had the potential to be fun is shaping up to be something far different.

I go back out to the bar and look for Missy, so I can tell her I'm definitely going home. However, she's nowhere to be found. I go over to our table and pick up the tab our waitress has left us. When the waitress comes back around, I hand her the money for our drinks, plus a generous tip.

"Hey, thanks," she says, tucking the money into her apron. She adjusts her high-on-her-head ponytail, and starts to clear off our table.

"Did you happen to see where my friend went?" I ask. "I wanted to let her know I'm leaving."

The waitress points to the area from which I just came. "I think she went back there."

"By herself?"

The waitress shakes her head. "No, there were two guys with her." *Nick and Tony, no doubt.*

Now, I'm torn. Do I leave, or do I first check on Missy? She seemed pretty much into what Nick and Tony were doing to her, but I want to be sure. Missy isn't some close friend, but I do like her, and I'd never forgive myself if I left and later found out she had needed rescuing.

I take a deep breath and head back to the hallway leading to the restrooms. Beyond the men's room, there's a heavy-looking door marked as an exit. Another closed door in between the restrooms is marked *stairs*. I place my hand on the handle of the door marked *stairs*, but hesitate when I hear muffled grunts and groans coming from the other side. I try the doorknob, but it's locked.

"Missy?" I pound on the door. "Are you in there? Are you okay?"

I hear skin-slapping sounds and Missy moan-answers, "Go away, Kay. I'm—Oh, God—fine."

A man's voice—not Nick's, so I guess it's Tony's—calls out, "Hey, come on in and join us."

Missy giggles, and then groans in what sounds like pleasure. She's obviously fine.

I don't answer. I just turn away and run out of the heavy door marked *exit*. I trip a little, right myself, and spill out into a smelly alley. I'm in the back of the Anchor Inn, and everything reeks of urine and God-knows-what else. I hold my nose until I'm around the corner and at my parked car.

I hurriedly jump in and turn the key in the ignition. Before I pull away I think about all that has happened. I'm surprised and disturbed by what I've learned about Missy tonight. Again, it worries me that she and Chase behave so uncomfortably around one another. Every time I bring one's name up to the other there's always this weird tension. Despite Missy's denial earlier, I resolve, once I get up enough nerve, to flat-out ask Chase if they're hiding something.

But right now all I want to do is go home. Nothing has gone right today, and I am more than ready to just go to sleep and start fresh tomorrow.

Unfortunately, a short while later, when I pull into the apartment lot and park, I sense things are about to get a whole lot worse. Fireplug and his friends from the other morning are blocking the entrance to the building. They're standing around in a loose circle smoking something out of a pipe.

When I get out of the car, a chemical-like odor—like burning plastic, maybe—wafts in my direction. The junkies are not smoking weed, that's for sure. *Meth or crack, then*, I think. *Shit, the tweaked addicts are the worst.*

I try to hurry past their huddled bodies, clutching my big hobo bag to my body like a protective shield, but Fireplug stops me by stepping into my path. "Whatcha got in the bag?" he asks, his eyes dark and his words slurred.

Unlike the other day, he's not leering. He just appears desperate and strung out. I try to shoulder past.

"Where're you going in such a hurry?" Fireplug grabs for my bag and his two friends chuckle. "Don't you know you gotta pay a toll first? It's a new rule, just started to-night."

One of the other junkies, skinny and gaunt, adds, "Yeah, we be the trolls under the bridge from your bedtime stories, little girl."

"More like my nightmares," I mumble under my breath.

It's a mistake to engage them, but my comment slips out before I can stop myself.

Fireplug immediately gets in my face, his breath fetid as it washes over me. "You think you're better than us? Is that why you're giving us attitude, bitch?"

I just want to get into the building, so I mumble, "No."

His grip on my bag tightens, but I hold on to it with everything I've got. I'm tired of being frightened. "Get out of my way," I grind out.

I try again to slip past the junkies, but Fireplug won't let go of my bag. I yank harder. He stumbles a little, and that's when he reacts. He raises his arm and hits me in the face. He uses an open palm, but it's still a hard slap. I gasp as my cheek stings and my eyes water. I'm reminded of the time my own mother hit me. Tears well up, like some sort of automatic reaction. Fireplug laughs sinisterly and plucks my bag out of my now-lax hands. I offer no resistance, but he pushes me so hard that I fall on my ass. He calls me a filthy word and spits in my direction. His saliva misses me, but barely.

I've made so many mistakes today. I should have pressed Chase to talk to me, I should have declined the offer to go out. And I should have left the bar without searching for Missy. Then, I wouldn't have heard a guy I used to date—and his cousin—getting it on with my sort-of friend in some gross stairwell. But most of all, I wouldn't be here now, sitting on my ass, at the mercy of three men who are drugged out of their minds.

The enormity of it all prevents me from moving. I sit and watch as Fireplug goes through my purse. He laughs as he throws my life all over the ground. His pals watch and cackle; they do nothing to stop him. And neither do I—I am powerless, like I've been so, so many times before.

"What the fuck is this shit?" Fireplug laughs as Peetie, Sarah's stuffed bunny, flies past my head. I close my eyes and something that feels like my makeup bag hits me in the shoulder.

When I dare to open my eyes, the sunglasses Chase fixed the day we met are falling to the ground. Fireplug lifts his foot to step on them. I glance up and his dilated eyes dare me to try to stop him. I look away and hear sickly crunching as Fireplug stomps on the sunglasses with his heavy, black boot. They are beyond repair now, even Chase's talented hands can't fix this shit.

Finally, my empty bag hits my lap.

But Fireplug hasn't thrown everything out; he holds my wallet and my keys in his grasp. He takes money out of my wallet and drops everything else. Holding up two twenties, he growls, "This all you got?"

I nod lifelessly and he kicks my thigh, hard. I cry out. "Well, that's not going to be enough, I'm afraid," he tells me.

I don't know what he has planned, but the other two junkies quickly take off. My thigh aches and my cheek feels tender, but I decide I am not going down without a fight. Not tonight. Maybe there's rage in me like there is in Chase, because I suddenly wish I had my badass boy's strength to beat the shit out of this asshole.

Fireplug leans down like he's going to try to scare me some more, and I snap. From somewhere deep inside me I find the courage to lift my sandaled foot and kick this loser right in his chin. He doesn't cry out, but he's stunned enough that he steps back. I have time to right myself. Unfortunately, I am not fast enough.

I am on my knees, reaching for my keys, when I feel Fireplug grab hold of my ankles. I fall forward as he starts to drag me away. My new blouse's chiffon fabric snags and tears from the gravel in the lot. I scream and struggle but no one comes to my aid.

I'm too frightened to even consider what may happen next, but suddenly Fireplug lets go of me. He takes off just as a police cruiser flies by. A second one follows. But the cops aren't even stopping here—they continue westward. I guess the lights and sirens were just enough to scare off my assailant. Thank God for small favors.

I crawl back to where my stuff lies on the ground. Tears blur my vision as I gather what I can find in the dimly lit lot. I jam everything in my bag—pray that I haven't missed anything—and then using the keys I retrieved, hands shaking, I let myself in the building.

I can't stop trembling. I keep telling myself I'll be okay once I'm safely locked in my apartment. But all that happens when I step through the door to my home are more panic attacks. I double over and breathe through my mouth, taking in big gasps of air. I eventually calm enough to realize I can't stay here any longer. In fact, once I leave tonight, I know I'll never step through that door ever again.

I begin to toss everything I own—which, sadly, isn't a hell of a lot—into one old suitcase and a beat-up, old oversized duffel bag. I think about where I should go. A hotel, no. The church, I think not.

There's really only one place in this world where I know I'll truly be safe, only one man whose arms have the ability to hold me and make everything better.

So once I finish packing, I haul my bags out to the car and drive straight to Chase's house.

I stand on the porch of the old farmhouse on Cold Springs Lane. I know how I must look. My jeans are dirty, and there's a muddy boot print on one leg. My blouse is snagged and torn, my hair is knotted, and my cheek is red and swollen. I touch it lightly and wince. It's obvious I've been struck; Chase will surely see this when he opens the door.

I know he won't stand for this—the junkie *will* pay. A part of me is counting on it, to be honest. My guy will do what I could not. With that thought in mind, I sit my bags down and ring the doorbell.

A few minutes pass, and then I hear heavy footsteps coming down the stairs inside. Chase opens the door. His eyes are bleary, like he just woke up from a dead sleep. I'm sure he was sleeping; it's after midnight now.

My boy has on nothing but a pair of basketball shorts riding low at his waist. Usually I'd be gawking, but, instead, I keep my eyes on his bare feet. "Hi," I whisper.

I glance up and Chase sucks in a sharp breath. His fists clench. "Fuck, Kay...Who fucking touched you?" His voice is low and calm, but his gunmetal blues are shooting bullets.

"I'll tell you everything in a minute, but first"—I gesture to my bags—"is that apartment still available?"

CHAPTER NINE
CHASE

One thing is clear: someone is going to pay for putting their hands on my girl. While I get Kay and her shit into my house, she gives me a recap of what happened an hour ago in the apartment lot of her building.

"I am going to lay that motherfucker out," I say when she tells me what the junkie did to her.

She asks me not to exact revenge—tells me I shouldn't— but her eyes say something completely different. Kay doesn't fool me. She wants fucking vengeance as much as I do. I never would have thought it before, but, as time goes on, I see more of me in my girl. She's not all sweet and shy, not all the time. Maybe we aren't so very different after all. There's good and bad in both of us, and that's what binds us together, for better or worse.

Kay waits in the hall when I go into the kitchen to grab an ice pack from the freezer. I wrap the frozen bag up in an extra-soft tea towel, and hold it to my injured girl's cheek as I guide her up the stairs. I'll be able to see her injuries, the damage done to her, more clearly under the bright lighting in the bathroom.

But as Kay gently takes the ice pack from my hand and moves to walk in front of me at the top of the steps, I get a preview—a good glimpse of her clothes. Her jeans and shirt are absolutely ruined.

No doubt, these articles of clothing were once very nice, tight little jeans and a billowy yellow shirt with embroidered flowers. But now the fragile-looking fabric of the shirt is snagged and torn to hell, and the jeans, streaked with dirt, are in equally terrible condition. I spot what looks like a boot print on the thigh area of the dark denim and almost lose my shit. *Fucking cocksucker junkie.* I strive to keep my rage in check, though, since I don't want to get too fired up and scare Kay.

She obviously dressed in this nice outfit for some reason, so, out of curiosity, I ask, "Where were you before all this happened? Did you go out somewhere?"

"Yeah," she mumbles tiredly as we start down the hall. "I went to the Anchor Inn."

Shit, that place. I'm glad the lights are dim so Kay can't see my *what-the-fuck* expression.

"You didn't go alone, did you?" I ask, holding my breath and praying she did no such thing.

She stops and turns to me in the hallway. "No, of course not, Chase. I went with Missy"—*Christ*—"but I, uh, left early."

Hmm, something happened, causing Kay to leave early, and she certainly looks all evasive at the moment. Wonder what went down? I'm curious as hell, but I ask nothing more. I'll worry about digging out those details later.

We go into the bathroom, and Kay leans back against the vanity counter. I need her more at eye level to better assess the damage to her cheek, so I lift her up so she can just sit on top of the damn thing. Sweet girl scoots back a little and I step between her knees. As she lowers the ice bag, I take it from her and set it on the counter.

The fluorescent lighting in the small space shows me everything I need to see.

"Motherfucker," I swear under my breath.

There's an angry red mark on Kay's cheek and her flesh is slightly swollen. She winces when I touch her there.

"Who did this to you?" I ask. "Who do I have to fuck up? Give me a name."

When she shrugs and says she doesn't know the guy's name, I say, "Then, give me a description."

I lift the ice pack and place it back against her cheek—as gently as possible—and she tells me what I need to know.

A junkie, built like a fireplug—short and stocky, not as skinny as the others. He's wearing black pants and heavy boots, also black. He has on an orange plaid shirt, but it's faded and soiled. "Got it," I say when she's done.

She touches the hand that holds the ice. "What are you going to do, Chase? Don't get into trouble. Please. And don't get hurt."

At this last, I scoff. I tell her not to worry, this isn't my first rodeo. I've taken out far tougher and crazier motherfuckers than this asshole. And I still remember how to lay low and stay under the radar. I won't get caught.

When I finish speaking, she gasps. "God, Chase, don't kill him or anything. He's not worth that."

I laugh and push hair back from her face. I kiss the cheek that's not hurting. "I'm not going to kill anyone, baby. But this loser has to pay for what he's done to you. No one—and I mean *no one*—raises a hand to my girl and gets away with it."

She makes me put down the ice and urges me to come closer. I am there in an instant, parting her sweet lips with my own. My tongue touches hers and I taste my girl, all sugar and honey. I position my body between her legs, and she scoots forward. Sweet girl pressing up against me, denim and the light material of my basketball shorts the only barriers separating us. I get hard in an instant, I can't help it. Adrenaline and lust fuel my libido. I suspect Kay feels similar emotions. After what happened to her, she's surely pumped on adrenaline—and now, lust—as well.

So I am not the least bit surprised when she moans into my mouth and wraps her legs around me. I try to hold her in place, but she moves nonetheless, roughly, desperately. She grinds her hot little center against my cock as our mouths move together. I groan and try to behave, but I can't help but push farther into her, feeling her heat since the fabrics separating us are so damn thin.

Our hips keep moving together, even when our mouths break apart. My amped-up girl leans back on one arm and watches my eyes. I see something primal in hers. The hand not holding her upright is in my hair. She licks her lips, and tugs and pulls with her fingers, making my head jerk back a little. It hurts like fuck and I wince in pain, but also in pleasure. I let baby girl take this aggression out on me. She needs to feel back in control. And, hell, it's not like I don't like it. Frankly, it's turning me on even more. But when her hand leaves my hair and travels down my chest, and she reaches into the waistband of my shorts, I stop her.

"Why not?" she asks, her quickened breaths making her voice waver.

Kay's been through a traumatic experience and what

she's feeling is tension turned into something sexual; her body is seeking release. Under any other circumstances I'd roll with it, but not when all we've ever done up to this point is make out. Besides, I have an asshole to take care of. Later, I'll take care of Kay.

She keeps pushing, grinding, and all-out pleading with her eyes. "You really want our first time to be on the counter?" I ask, raising an eyebrow. She slows her movements, smiles, and shakes her head.

I kiss her some more, just nice and gently. Her hips rock a little with mine, but far less frantically. We move in slow and gentle motions, just savoring the reactions we're able to elicit from each other.

This is what Kay really needs right now, soft touching and caring. When we're together, I want to love her just like this.

Soon everything slows, and then stops completely. Kay asks me to just hold her. I do, and we stay wrapped up in each other's arms for several minutes. I console and try to help my girl find all the fortitude she needs to start to heal.

"I'll always be here for you," I whisper in her ear. And it's true—I don't plan on ever leaving this woman's side.

She pulls back slightly, caramel-browns searching mine. "Really?" she asks, doubt and hope and about a hundred other fucking emotions I can't begin to figure out in her gaze.

My slaughtered and abused heart beats harder and stronger. Kay heals me. I marvel at how hard I've fucking fallen for this girl. "Yes, really," I say back.

"Why?"

"Do you really need to ask?" My voice is soft and choked on emotion.

"Tell me, Chase. Tell me what I think I already know. Tell me what you're feeling. I feel it too, I do."

My slaughtered heart stitches back together, more solid than ever.

"I love you," I whisper. "I love you so fucking much, baby girl."

Kay kisses me lightly on the lips, and when I tighten my arms around her she gives me her heart too.

"I love you, Chase Gartner," she whispers. "I love your trouble, I love your kindness. I love all your good, and all your bad...I just love *you.*"

Kay takes a shower and I wait for her in my bedroom. I'm seated on the edge of my just-slept-in, still-unmade bed. When she comes to the doorway—dressed in barely there shorts and a baggy T-shirt she must have gotten out of her suitcase or bag—she has her purse in her hand. And she looks panicked.

I am up in a heartbeat. "What is it, baby?" I take her face in my hands, carefully since her cheek is still red, though less swollen thanks to the ice. My eyes search hers.

"It's Peetie, Chase." She pulls away and stares at the floor dejectedly. "I left him. He was in my purse, and I thought I picked everything up that that asshole threw on the ground, but I must have somehow missed him." Her voice grows more panicked, all while I am wondering: who the fuck is Peetie? "I can't lose him, Chase. I just can't lose him too. He belonged to Sarah."

Ah, now I understand. Kay showed me one day after lunch the stuffed rabbit she's been carrying around in her purse, she explained it had once belonged to her sister. Now that I think about it, I remember her calling it Peetie. She also told me she'd intended on leaving the stuffed rabbit at Sarah's grave, but just couldn't do it. So she put Peetie back in her bag, and that's where he's stayed since then. Close to my girl every day since.

"I'll get him back," I promise, hoping none of those punk-ass junkies picked him up or kicked him somewhere where I won't be able to find him.

I get Kay calmed and situated in my bed. I ask her if she wants fresh sheets but she tells me the ones on the mattress smell like me and that makes her feel better. It kind of wows me that I have that effect. But, shit, I can go with that. I kiss sweet girl's forehead and promise to be back soon. She tells me again to be careful. I promise to watch my step and to be discreet in what I'm about to do, but she really needn't worry. Who I become when I fight is no one Kay would even recognize.

Five minutes later, I slowly become that unrecognizable man.

I am now fully dressed—jeans, work boots, a tight shirt that can't be easily grabbed—and in the bathroom, staring at the mirror, looking at someone else and seeing a version of me I don't often unleash. This is the darkest side of me, beyond selfish. This is me guided by rage, by base instinct. I want only to dominate and inflict pain. And, tonight, I want justice.

I think about what happened to Kay—every detail she told me before I left the bedroom. However, I know there's more to her story of the time spent with Missy at the fucking Anchor Inn. She said that guy she went out on a few dates with last fall, Nick-whoever, showed up with his cousin, and the two of them seemed to hit it off with Missy.

I bet.

I can only imagine what sort of spectacle ensued, obviously something that upset my girl enough to make her leave the bar early.

But I can't worry about that stupid shit now, it's irrelevant. None of those people hurt my girl. Maybe they upset her a little, but nothing like what the junkie in the parking lot did. That piece of shit laid hands where they didn't belong. We'll see how much he enjoys *my* hands on *him*.

I crack my knuckles, make a fist. Yeah, I have more for him than some lame-ass smack across the cheek. Fuck, do I ever.

I've been kind and gentle with my girl, but in front of the mirror I am a different man. My eyes are hard, my muscles flex. Shit, I know I am strong, but rage makes me swell bigger. And soon I'll be using all this strength at something I'm good at—fucking motherfuckers up. My adrenaline pumps. The dark craving to beat the fuck out of someone rises in my veins. My blood runs hot, my temper hotter. I look down at my hands. I *want* these fists to spill blood, to break fucking bones. This is part of who I am; this is the trouble I warned Kay of.

When I see the ice pack on the counter, reminding me of what happened and where I'm going, it takes everything I have not to punch the fucking mirror right before my eyes. But I'll hold it together for as long as I'm in this house, this house with Kay down the hall. She's had enough scares for one night. She doesn't need to see me like this, nor does she need to hear my destruction. Hell, I'm so amped at the moment that if she walked in here and came on to me right now, like she did earlier, I'd not be able to stop. I'd fuck my girl hard and fast. Our first time would, in fact, be on the counter. And it would not be gentle. No, not at all.

Fuck. I clearly need to get out of here.

By the time I'm outside and getting into my truck, my lust has tapered. All my testosterone has only one focus—hunting down the fucker who hurt Kay...and making him pay dearly.

I pull away from the house, leaving the woman who gives me reason to believe salvation is possible lying in my bed. I speed past the church, turning away from the cross on the top. Tomorrow I'll think about repentance, for where I'm going, for what I'm about to do.

It's late and there's no traffic so I close in on my destination in no time—this dirty part of town where I once bathed in sin, immersed myself in it really. And where, tonight, I will sin again. Because vengeance belongs only to God, but tonight it motherfucking belongs to me.

I find Peetie first, lying on the ground near the apartment entrance. Next to him are the sunglasses I fixed for Kay the day we first met. Only now her fake-designers are annihilated, crushed beyond repair. I step over them and pick up Peetie. He's a little dusty, but basically unscathed. I brush the stuffed rabbit off and throw him in the truck. I turn back and assess the area.

Most of the building is dark, the tenants either fast asleep or out. But that doesn't mean there's no activity. Orange lighter flames flicker from an alley snaking back the side of the structure. I walk closer, not to partake as I once might have considered, no. I have only one mission tonight—find the junkie who messed with my girl. And that mission is about to be accomplished.

Finding the guy isn't difficult. Apart from the description Kay gave me, he's the only one whose face freezes in terror when he sees me coming his way. With the look I have on my face, he knows exactly why I'm here. The other junkies aren't stupid either. They see my expression and disperse with haste.

Now, it's just me and him.

Fireplug—Kay's term, not mine—backs away. His hands are up as he retreats. "Hey, was that your girl, man? Things got a little out of hand. I didn't mean to hurt her or anything."

I say nothing, I am not here to fucking talk it out. Besides, I'm too busy estimating the number of steps to my target, counting them down in my head.

Ten, nine…

"I'm sorry, man." *Useless babbling.* "I let her go, that should count for something, huh?"

Eight, seven, six…

"Please," he cries, "I just needed the money." I laugh.

Five, four…

He changes tactics, the real him emerges. "Fuck you, dude. You know what, I'm glad I hit the fucking cunt. I would've done more too."

And that is the wrong fucking thing to say.

Three, two, one…

At the last second, this dick pulls out a knife and tries to stick me. But I am *so* much faster. My fist flies out and connects with his face. The knife falls and skitters away. The junkie drops. Blood pours from his mouth and his nose, but I'm just getting started. I see red, I feel black rage.

"Get up," I growl, standing above him. "You get off on hurting women, you sick fuck? Get up and try me, pussy."

This dude is dazed and whimpering, holding his bleeding face. With the hit he just took from me, he should be out like a light. But whatever drugs he's taken keep him conscious. Good, I want him to feel my wrath unleashed. I'm not done yet. .

Fireplug rolls, gets up on one knee, wavers, and finally straightens. When he's upright he takes a swing that I easily step out of. I notice the left side of his jaw is askew. Fuck askew. I flex my fist, clench tight, and promptly shatter that shit all to hell. Now when the junkie falls, he stays fucking put.

I am wired on pure adrenaline, testosterone pumping. A primal, base instinct deep in the darkest recesses of my mind urges me to finish him off, to exert my full dominance and leave his whole body just as shattered as his jaw.

I am powerless to stop my actions when I draw my leg back; poised to deliver what will surely be a death blow to this scumbag's skull.

Suddenly, someone jerks me off balance. I straighten my leg to keep myself upright and bloodlust is momentarily forgotten. It's enough time to spare the junkie, but that doesn't mean I am not still infuriated.

I round on whoever is fucking dumb enough to insert

their ass into this volatile situation. "What the fuck?" I growl.

My fists are up, ready to lay another motherfucker out. But when my brain registers who just stopped me from killing a man, I falter. "Jesus, Kyle?"

My one-time dealer steps back away from me. "Gartner? Shit, man, fuck." He looks as shocked to see me as I am to see him.

This man I used to party with—and buy fuckloads of drugs from—stands before me. Only four years have passed, but he looks at least a dozen years older. His brown eyes are black tonight, pupils dilated. He's obviously high on something. His hair looks darker than I remember, but I think that's only because his skin is so much paler. His clothes hang on his body. Kyle Tanner is skinny and reeks of body odor.

My one-time dealer chuckles and glances dispassionately to the junkie on the ground. "Chase Gartner, out of prison and down here fucking up my customers. Should I even be surprised?" He laughs. "Shit, I heard you were back, but I didn't expect to see you so soon." His dark eyes meet mine. "Now that you're here, though..."

He doesn't care about the broken man on the ground as anything more than someone who buys. And now he's asking me if I want to buy too.

I shake my head. "No, I'm good. In fact, I'm leaving."

I start to walk away, but Kyle puts his arm out. Like his emaciated ass could stop me.

"Brave," I say, chuckling and staring him down.

He very wisely drops his arm. "Hey, that's cool. Glad

you're good for tonight. But, if you ever change your mind, just know my door is always open, my friend."

Kyle isn't any kind of a friend; he sees nothing more than dollar signs when he looks at me. I was once a consistent paying customer, one who bought *a lot* of fucking drugs. But that's all in the past. My girl is back at my house, waiting, and the desire to get back to her is so much stronger than any urge to use.

"I'm finished here," I say, pushing past.

The junkie whose ass I just kicked moans, and Kyle calls out, "Wait."

I reluctantly turn around. Kyle's leaning over the junkie. I can see the guy is a mess. He's bloodied and battered, and can't talk to save his life. He'll probably need medical treatment, but he'll live.

Kyle's dark eyes bore into me. "Something set you off, Gartner. You're not so very different than you once were. You just keep telling yourself that you are, keep feeding yourself the lies." I turn back around and start to walk away. I don't need fucking Kyle Tanner getting in my head.

Still in earshot, I hear Kyle laughing as he yells, "I won't mention your name when they want to know who did this. I owed you one, man. And now we're even. You never told them where you got the X, did you?" I don't answer, I just keep on walking.

Kyle is undeterred, he keeps talking. "I appreciate that, my friend. Come see me at the house. Anything you want, Chase. Blow, weed, pills, I got all your old favorites. First buy, it's on me."

I clench my fists and shut Kyle out. When I reach my truck, I jump in. I can't get away fast enough. When I glance in the rearview mirror I watch the old life I revisited tonight fade back into the past. But, still, I don't feel right, I am edgy and irritated.

To settle my nerves, I tell still air, "I have changed. That's not me anymore. I *am* different."

It sounds convincing to my ears, it really does. But if what I proclaim so easily is true, then why did I almost kill a man tonight? Why did I enjoy spilling his blood? I can't lie—I thoroughly enjoyed breaking that junkie's face.

But the bigger question, the one nagging at me the most is this: If I am so different, then why the fuck are my hands shaking when I think about Kyle's offer?

CHAPTER TEN

KAY

I hear Chase return. The sound of the shower turning on down the hall rouses me from my half-asleep state. As exhausted as I am, it's a surprise full sleep has eluded me thus far. But worry has kept me semi-alert.

I roll over and hold tight to the pillow that's comforted me while waiting for Chase to come home. The smooth, cotton covering smells of my retribution-seeking man—soap, male, and also trouble. But it's that propensity for trouble that has made him my hero this night.

Before long, the water stops and the bedroom door creaks open. I roll over. Moonlight casts the room in monochromatic tones and my eyes meet Chase's in the silvery glow.

"Did everything go okay?" I ask. "Are you all right?"

Chase nods once and remains standing in the doorway. He has his basketball shorts back on, and, like earlier, the rest of him is bare. Dampness darkens his hair, and water he's not completely toweled away beads on his wide shoulders. From what I can see, though, there's not a single mark on him, no injury marring his beautiful, strong body. Everything must have gone my badass boy's way down at the apartment lot.

I think about asking for specifics, but then Chase jerks

his head in the direction of the stairs. "I'm going to sleep down on the couch. I just wanted to check in on you first. Do you need anything? Water? Another blanket?"

The night has turned kind of chilly, but I closed the window a little while ago, so I'm not in the least bit cold. Nor am I thirsty.

I sit up and lean back on my elbows. I shake my head. "No, I'm fine." And I am, but that's primarily because my guy is back, unharmed.

Chase turns to leave, but I stop him. "Stay?"

My words turn him around.

There's no reason why he shouldn't sleep in his own bed. I tell him this, and add, "Besides, I don't want to be alone. Not tonight. You shouldn't be by yourself either, Chase."

It's true, we should be together tonight. I pull back the covers and pat the side of the bed next to where I'm lying.

Chase doesn't hesitate. He crawls into bed and lies down on his side, so that we're facing one another. For the longest time nothing is said, we speak only with our eyes, blue on brown, conveying friendship, trust, love, and having each other's backs.

When Chase lifts his hand to brush my hair over my shoulder I place mine over his. His knuckles are slightly swollen and I feel abrasions under my fingers. My badass boy has sustained injuries, albeit small ones.

Chase winces and I loosen my grip. "Sorry," I mumble.

"It's okay," he whispers back, his voice low and rough.

"Was it bad?" I ask.

Chase knows what I'm asking. Not so much about the fight itself—it's obvious he fared well—but, rather, I'm asking how difficult it was for him to return to that side of town, to be around drugs and users, to be back where he himself once used.

"I didn't think about it much until I saw my old dealer," he quietly says. "The guy I told you about…Kyle."

The evening we were at the miniature golf course, across from the church, Chase opened up about the days and weeks before he was arrested. As I'd suspected, my boy made the pilgrimage down that well-traveled dirt road to Kyle Tanner's house a number of times. He also told me that—though he was caught with forty-plus hits of X—he never actually dealt any drugs. He admitted he would have, he'd planned to that night, but he was arrested before a single deal was ever made.

Just because Chase never had the chance to deal drugs doesn't mean he wasn't in deep. My boy was fully immersed in his chemicals of choice at the time. He's told me this and more. He said it's still no picnic trying to stay clean, those chemicals still tempt him. Drugs call to him on occasion. That's why I know seeing Kyle must have made an already bad situation—being in that part of town, fighting like he used to do—worse.

I tentatively touch the light stubble along his jaw, and ask softly, "Are you okay?"

He presses his lips together. "I think so."

He sounds uncertain, and I venture, "What did Kyle say to you?"

"He offered me drugs, baby. That's what dealers do." Chase flips onto his back. He starts to run his fingers through his hair, but grasps hard instead. "He said I could have whatever I wanted. First buy, no cost."

My hand is partway to touching his shoulder and I freeze. "You said no, right?"

He moves my hand and sits up, then scrubs his hands down his face. "Of course I said no, Kay."

I sit up behind him and wrap my arms and legs around him. I lean the uninjured side of my face to the angel on his back. I press until I feel the texture of her against my cheek.

"I'm sorry for asking, Chase. I know going back down there had to be tough. And seeing Kyle, I just…" I sigh against his back and listen to his steady breaths. Inhaling and exhaling life. "I just wish there was more I could do to help you."

I feel him relax slightly, and Chase whispers, "You do help me, sweet girl. Every day, all the time, you make me stronger. You give me the strength to be better. You're a big part of why I said no to Kyle."

"I wish you wouldn't have even seen him," I lament to the angel on his back.

Chase turns and faces me. He takes my hands in his. "He actually did something good, Kay. He stopped me from going too far with the junkie."

His eyes meet mine. He's not kidding. *Shit.* Chase might have killed someone tonight had it not been for Kyle Tanner.

I swallow hard. "You would have stopped, Chase, even without Kyle's intervention."

My boy stares at our linked hands. "Yeah, I guess," he says, not convincingly at all.

Chase almost killed for me tonight. This knowledge is both heady and terrifying. I let go of his hands, and run my fingers along his shoulder, down his arm. Fingertips brush over the *As I stand before you, judge me not* tattoo.

I don't judge this man I love. His actions were in defense of me. And he didn't kill anyone, he stopped. Whether that was because of Kyle, or if he would have anyway, it doesn't matter. What matters is that nobody in my life has ever loved me enough to defend me with that kind of passion. I've never been the reason for anyone to unleash rage like that on someone who's done me wrong. But Chase did those things for me tonight. *I* hold the power to unleash his passion. And what I want to do now, in this very instant, is unleash my badass boy's passion for something positive, something that will heal us both.

I lean forward and press my lips to his. Chase sighs and lays me back with care. He settles his weight on me, slowly and tortuously covering my body. I wrap my legs around him, and he showers my face with kisses. As he grazes his teeth down my neck, I feel his arousal when he starts to gently thrust against me.

Tension builds as our kisses deepen. I know part of this is raw sexual buildup—from earlier tonight, from the other day in the school—but there's something more. Chase is wired from fighting—hyped up from all that transpired down in the lot—and the resulting flood of emotions. And I am just as tightly wound.

Chase, breathing hard and rising to his knees, lifts the hem of my tee. His blues question before he continues. I nod my head, lift up slightly, and raise my arms. Chase peels my T-shirt up and off, then lays me back.

My boy, still on his knees, takes in my now-bare upper body as I lay before him. I part my legs, inviting him to come closer. He positions himself between them. With one hand under my bent knee, Chase urges me to open more for him. As I do, he presses his very hard to my very soft.

With his arousal pushing at my core, and even through the fabrics of our shorts, I gasp and pull Chase down to me, finding the warmth and wetness of his mouth. He kisses me hard, our chests touching—bare skin to skin. I can't help but moan out his name. His shorts and mine have become nothing more than frustrating barriers, so I wiggle and squirm until my shorts and panties slide together partway down my thighs.

With that accomplished, I get to work on pushing Chase's basketball shorts down. When my fingers hook under his waistband, I realize he has nothing on underneath. *Oh, God.*

I rock beneath him, pushing my bare pussy up against his still-covered cock. "Take them off," I plead.

"Baby, baby," he whispers in my ear. Chase stills my hands at the waistband of his shorts. "Tonight doesn't have to be about me, baby girl. Just let me love you."

I assume Chase is hesitant because we don't have any protection, so I tell him about the clinic and the birth control shot. "And we already know we're both healthy," I add.

"That's not it," he insists. "I want to be with you, but I want our first time together to be perfect for you. You deserve perfect, Kay."

I would prefer "perfect"—whatever that may be—but I don't want to not do anything tonight. I need more than kissing. I tell Chase this, and he laughs.

"Oh, baby girl, I plan on doing plenty to you tonight." He raises himself to his elbows and pushes his arousal into me. We both moan.

"Fuck," Chase groans and sits up.

My shorts and panties get tugged the rest of the way down until they gather at one ankle. I spread for my boy and he watches. I kick the fabric at my foot away, until I am finally nude before Chase Gartner.

Chase makes short work of his basketball shorts, then kneels between my legs. My eyes travel over his body as his travel over mine. I think we're both in awe. At least, I am. Chase with no clothes on is something to behold. He's hard and lean, all pure muscle.

And his cock…well…

The part of Chase that makes him all-male—*very* male—is glorious. He's long and thick, and I just want to just touch him, worship him, and feel him inside of me. I reach down and grasp his length, stroking velvety skin over steel-hard male.

Chase pumps into my hand and places a hand on my knee. "Let me see you, baby," he asks as he spreads my legs wider.

He stays on his knees as I continue to stroke his length. His fingers gently touch my folds, opening me with his movements as he glides back and forth, spreading my slick wetness everywhere.

"Beautiful," he murmurs as he watches what he's doing to me. "You're beautiful opened up like this, Kay."

His oh-so-talented fingers swirl at my entrance. He draws lazy circles around my clit that set me aflame. What's already slick and wet gets slicker, wetter. His fingers make another pass at my slit and dip inside. I've mostly just been breathing hard, but now a moan escapes me.

"Is this okay?" he asks, pumping slowly, fucking me gently with his long fingers.

"Uh-huh," I groan.

It is good, so good, amazing. It's been so long, and even before it's never been quite like this. Chase certainly knows what he's doing. When his slow pace becomes too tortuous, though, I urge him with my hips to move faster. He complies, finger-fucking me hard, until I cry out and buck up against him awkwardly.

"Easy, sweet girl, easy," he murmurs.

Chase continues to work me as he settles on one elbow beside my head. His dick is still in my hand, but I'm slacking. It's just too hard to concentrate with what he's doing to me.

"I'm sorry," I say, my breaths ragged and shaky.

I feel like I'm so out of practice that I'm disappointing the man I love and wish nothing more than to please.

"Trust me, what you're doing feels great," he whispers, kissing the shell of my ear. "Just let me take care of you first. Let me make you feel good, baby."

I tell him he's already making me feel pretty amazing. He chuckles and moves my hand away from his dick. Then, he kisses me. With our mouths moving together, his fingers do incredible things that leave me moaning and panting.

Everything I heard that day in the library is true—Chase Gartner gives crazy-good sex. He makes me feel like I've never felt before. It's like my pleasure is his sole focus in the world. Maybe it is. It sure seems so as my head spins and my body succumbs to waves of Chase-induced ecstasy.

I have no time to recover. Chase sits up and his fingers leave my body. He gets back in the position he was in earlier, kneeling between my legs. Kissing down my chest, he takes one nipple in his mouth. He sucks and licks, covering my peak in hot wetness. He moves to the other side and does the same. My nipples are wet with his saliva, and my hips rock of their own volition, wanting more.

I rock and rock, but Chase stills my movements with his hands. He smiles one of his heart-stopping smiles, then kisses down my body, over my stomach, and over one hip. He stops and nips at the bone, then moves lower still.

I think I know what's coming, so I grasp at the sheets. When I feel his mouth where my need lies deep and ready for more, I look down so I can watch this beautiful man give me pleasure.

I smile as our eyes meet. Chase runs his tongue along my inner thigh mischievously.

"Sweet girl, let's see how sweet you really are." His words heat my cheeks. "Are you going to watch me make you come again?"

Rubbing the light stubble on his cheek gently against my leg, he glances up. I do want to watch, so I nod my head.

His wide shoulders shift and his muscles bunch as he cups my ass and lifts me up to his mouth. When his tongue touches me, my head falls back. So much for watching, I can barely think now. Chase licks and sucks and does things with his tongue that send me over the edge in no time. I scream out his name, but he gives me no reprieve. He continues his dizzying assault with his mouth until another climax builds and builds. But before he allows it to crescendo, he rises back to his knees and places his cock right at my entrance.

I push, too caught up in the moment to care about "perfect" any longer. The tip goes in a little, but Chase pulls back. He strokes himself and whispers for me to watch. "Want to get off together, baby?" he asks in a sex-raspy voice.

I'm so worked up I almost come again just hearing his words. I nod vigorously, up for whatever he has planned.

Chase rounds the tip of his cock at my entrance, teasing and taunting, stretching me open with his girth. I move with my crazy-good sex man until he almost slips in. He leans back and handles his length, stroking up and down a few times while I watch. His hand passes over the engorged head, and then he places the underside up against me. Chase holds himself there—still, unmoving—his eyes never leaving mine. "Don't move, baby. Don't move yet, okay?"

I nod and stay perfectly still, my sex throbbing beneath Chase's heavy length. Slowly, he begins to move, soaking his cock with my wetness. Using slow and steady upward thrusts that allow the head of his penis, then his length, to stimulate my clit over and over, my boy brings me to orgasm. I arch and moan out, "Oh, Chase, god, yes."

What he's doing is hot and erotic, and so close to full-on sex that Chase comes right after me. He lifts up and hot liquid spurts onto my lower stomach. Neither of us moves, and what he's just given me drips slowly down to where he just was. "Should we get a towel?" I whisper.

Chase kisses my lips. "Not yet, baby." He touches my most sensitive area once more, his fingers mixing my juices with his own until I am slick with both of us. "I want you to come one more time for me. Okay?"

Before I have a chance to answer, which would definitely be in the affirmative, my solely focused man pushes into me as many fingers as I can handle, while his thumb gently circles my tender and swollen nub. I arch and move with him, and, soon enough, Chase Gartner gets exactly what he wanted.

We lie sleepy and drifting. I am nestled against Chase's warm body, and he is telling me the specifics of what happened with the junkie. I know it shouldn't, but it turns me on that he exacted revenge for me. He fought for me, did what I would have liked to have done to my assailant myself, but couldn't. Does it make me a bad person to feel this way? Maybe. But mostly it feels like justice was served.

I am also thrilled when I learn Chase found Peetie. The fact that my ass-kicking, secretly soft-hearted guy not only remembered what I'd requested, but followed through, makes me love him all the more.

When Chase is done talking I tell him the details I left out earlier regarding my night out with Missy. My head is on Chase's chest, and I feel him tense slightly when Missy's name is mentioned.

This is my chance. I finally ask, "What is it with you two anyway?"

When he hesitates to answer I look up at him. "You never, uh, did anything with her, did you?" I cringe as the words spill out of my mouth.

Chase has to feel my heart rate quicken, seeing as my chest is pressed to his. He runs his hand down my back in a soothing manner. "You mean, like, fuck her?" he qualifies.

I wish I could see into his eyes, but the moon has moved to another part of the sky and the room has darkened.

"Yeah," I confirm quietly. "That's what I'm asking."

"No," he responds quickly. "I never fucked Missy Metzger."

I breathe a sigh of relief, though something still feels off. I start to rephrase my question, but I'm interrupted by my own yawn. I am mind-muddled sleepy and physically worn out, so I ask nothing more.

Chase rolls to his side, taking me with him, and we snuggle. His strength and his power make me feel safer than I have in ages. "I love you," I whisper as I drift off.

I hear Chase say it back, and then he murmurs something about "tomorrow" and "perfect." I am insanely curious to learn what he has planned, but before I can ask for details, sleep consumes me.

CHAPTER ELEVEN
CHASE

The next morning I wake up long before Kay. I stretch, and then watch her sleep for a little while before getting out of bed. My girl is so fucking beautiful. Her face is nothing less than serene when she's sleeping. I hope she's resting easy, knowing she never has to go back to that shitty apartment. Her home is here now. Well, next door at the apartment, but still, on my property, where her safety will never be jeopardized. I'll make the fuck sure of that.

I flip the sheet back and get out of bed. The covers on her side slip down just enough to expose one of Kay's breasts. I feel a stirring in my groin, making me think of a thousand hot-as-fuck ways to wake her up, but I leave her be. Kay needs the extra rest.

Sweet girl has had a rough night, at least early on she did. Hopefully, what we did before we went to sleep relieved some of that stress. I know it sure as hell helped me. I was so wired after everything that happened in the apartment parking lot that I needed a release. Kay needed a release as well, I am sure, and she got, well, several.

When it comes to sex, I think in some ways I may be opening a whole new world for my girl. I know her dickhead-south-of-Market prissy boy never did shit to her like I did last night. And I have to say I was pleasantly surprised to discover sweet girl has a little bit of a dirty side. Who knew? But she sure liked when I stretched her wide with my fingers, she liked me seeing her opened up like that. I was worried that I may have pushed it a little when I used my cock to make her come, but she fucking loved that too. Hell, she was so soaking wet, I almost couldn't stop when I started to slip in. God, I can't wait to actually fuck my girl. I am going to rock her world, that's for sure.

I have a shit-eating grin and a hard fucking cock when I step into the shower, but then I remember Kay asking me about Missy Metzger. My erection subsides immediately. My girl suspects something, that's obvious. I wasn't lying outright when I told her I never fucked Missy, but it is kind of a lie of omission. After all, Missy and I did engage in sex acts—my fingers were in her pussy, and her mouth was on my cock. We made each other come, for fuck's sake. I think Kay would probably want to know these things happened, even if they did occur before my girl and I met.

By the time I am out of the shower and dressed, I have myself convinced I'll tell Kay everything, but not until she's all settled in next door. One thing at a time, I remind myself.

Yeah, right, who am I kidding? I'm just stalling. But I'll tell her, I will…later.

I run over to the apartment above the garage to make sure it's all sparkling and clean, and then I head back over to my kitchen to make some breakfast. Well, I toast some bread and pour some orange juice. A cook, I am not.

Just as the toast pops up, I hear the shower start to run. I smile, realizing I like the idea of someone in the house with me. It's been way too lonely around here. But, no, that's not exactly right. What I like is that it's Kay who's in my space. With her, I like sharing. In fact, I like it so much a big part of me wishes she would stay over here in the main house with me and share my bed every night. But I know, for now, the right thing to do is let her have the apartment, and keep my mouth shut about moving in together. I remind myself we've only just established ourselves in an official relationship. I need to slow the fuck down. But I can't help it if I'm in a hurry to keep moving forward, I feel like I've known Kay for years. We've become that tightly woven.

I finish my toast and take my juice with me into the living room. I settle at the rolltop desk and turn on the computer. When I check e-mail I'm pleasantly surprised to discover my brother has actually done what he promised—he's sent me some samples of his art, along with a picture of him and my mom.

In the body of the e-mail, he tells me the photo was taken last night, after Mom insisted he have a piece of the oversized birthday cake she bought him.

I enlarge the attached photo.

In it, Mom and Will are standing behind a table, a huge, heavily decorated cake in front of them. Will's dark blond hair is longer than when I saw him a couple of months ago, and he looks like he's really filling out, finally getting some muscles on his lean frame. He's taller too. He's got an easy half foot on Mom, which means he's almost as tall as me.

I take a closer look at my mother; her smile is strained in the image. Guess Will had her stressing yesterday evening, same as yesterday morning. I have a feeling this trouble with my brother is only just beginning. I shake my head and move on to the next attachment, Will's art.

There are two pages, pages from the comic book he's supposedly putting together. From the illustrations in the panels, and the speech and thought balloons, I quickly gather Will's story is an end-of-times tale. The action takes place in a war-devastated Las Vegas. The first couple of images depict several ragged, war-weary civilians wandering aimlessly along The Strip. Heavily armed, grim-faced soldiers stand posted in front of what's left of the once magnificent and opulent resorts and casinos. The Luxor's glass panels have been shattered and the turrets of the Excalibur are flattened. Fires rage everywhere. Cars sit abandoned on the road, vandalized, and stripped to the frames in some cases.

In the next several panels, Will introduces the reader to the hero of his tale, a man named Champion. Some soldier is barking for him to "move along." These words are enclosed in a speech bubble, the font bold and jagged.

I take a closer look at the hero of the story. Champion is a tall man with defined muscles and a light-brown crew-cut. His primary mission appears to be rescuing scantily clad women in distress. In one panel, Champion saves a buxom blonde in a string bikini from the raised baton of a crazed-looking soldier who is about to punish her for breaking one of this new society's rules. In the next panel, another woman, this one a redhead, and—I take note—even bigger tits, is trapped in a burning building. The hero rescues her as well. She hangs on to him, pressing her body to his with gratitude.

I chuckle at the subject matter, typical, testosterone-fueled teenage-boy fare. But I have to say, the art itself is fantastic. Will has developed into an impressive artist. The colors he chooses are bold and hold the eye, his lines are sharp and sure. My brother draws with a confidence I've never seen in him before. Maybe this is his calling.

While I am studying Will's art, I hear Kay's light foot-steps in the background. I turn in my chair and give her a smile, then I ask her if she's hungry. She says she's not. My well-rested, satiated girl pads over to me. She wearing a cute, casual outfit—jean shorts and two tank tops, one black one over a white one.

When she reaches the desk, her eyes go to the computer. "Wow, did you draw that, Chase?" She leans in closer. "It's really good."

"It is good," I agree, putting my arm around my girl's waist, and positioning one leg so she can sit down on it. "But I didn't draw any of it. This is all Will's stuff. He sent it to me last night, but I opened it right before you came down."

Her face turns to me, eyes wide. "He's talking to you?" she asks.

I give her a quick nod and her arms are around me before I know it. "Oh my goodness," she says into my neck. "Chase, this is so great. I knew he'd come around. I'm so happy for you both."

She leans back so she can give me a kiss, a kiss that makes Will having been mad at me all worth it. After a pro-longed return kiss from me, I fill my girl in on the events of yesterday. I explain why I was in such a bad mood dur-ing the early part of the day. I tell her all about Will's "fuck off" text when I sent him a happy birthday message. I admit my mom's call asking for help with my brother's bad be-havior—when I'm thousands of miles away—brought me down further. Finally, I wrap up with Will's call, explaining how things were a little tense at first, but then we just start-ed talking. I tell her I think he and I may be making some real progress. Kay seems happy for me, but a little wary. My girl is worried for my heart, I know, which is why I feel compelled to share with her that Will asked me for money.

Kay frowns. "Did you send him any?" Her voice is soft, her brow creased with worry.

I sit back and run my fingers through my hair. "Yeah, I did." I admit, sighing. "I transferred a small amount into his account. Not much though." I shrug. "It should be all right."

"Oh, okay." Kay shifts on my leg.

She begins to study Will's comic pages, examining every panel intently. She's quiet, too quiet, but I know it's because she doesn't want to say too much and put a damper on the excitement I'm feeling over rebuilding all the shit I ruined with my brother. I realize my girl doesn't want Will manipulated me, or taking advantage of my wanting so badly to repair the relationship with him. I don't want that, either, but he and I have to start somewhere.

Kay, still studying Will's art, suddenly says, "Did you notice the hero—this Champion guy—looks kind of like you?"

She points to one of the panels, and I lean in to take a closer look. "Huh, I guess he does resemble me a little."

"He definitely does, Chase." She laughs. "His hair is just shorter, but other than that…" My girl takes my chin in her hand and smiles knowingly before she lets go.

Shit, maybe she's right. And maybe that means there's still a part of Will that looks up to me.

Kay turns back to the computer and clicks the jpeg file. The photo of Will and my mom expands, filling the screen. "Your mom and Will?" she asks.

"Yep."

"They sure look a lot alike," she muses.

"They do."

My girl turns to me, then back to the picture on the computer screen. "You look a little like your mom, Chase, but not a whole lot. I guess you take more after your Dad?"

Ha, understatement of the year.

I don't say a word. I just locate a folder of old photos my gram scanned and saved onto this computer. When I find the right one, I double-click it. Scanning the thumbnails, I search for a picture of my dad from when he was about my age. When I find what I want, I open it. The picture enlarges, replacing the one of Will and Mom.

Kay's jaw drops. Her eyes slowly move from the picture on the screen to me, then back to the photo. The picture is of my dad out on the front porch of this very house. Jack Gartner is holding up what would end up being one of the first of many award plaques he received over the years. This one was for quality home-building. If you didn't know any better, you would think the photo was of me. That's how much he and I look alike in this image.

Kay stares at the photo, and then her eyes dart back to me again. She reaches out and trails a finger down the smooth skin of my recently shaved cheek. "My God, you look exactly like your father, Chase."

"I know, baby, I know." My hand covers hers and I bring her palm to my lips.

She thanks me for showing her the photo. She also gives me a sad smile; my girl knows how hard it is for me to be reminded of my father.

I close the picture. Kay's still eyeing me and biting her

lower lip. I know that's her contemplative look. "What are you up to?" I ask.

"Hold on," she says suddenly, twirling out and away from my hold. "I have something I want to share with you too."

She's out of the room in a snap, but gone for only a few minutes. When she returns, there's a small photo album in her hand. It's the kind you slip the photos into, the type with clear sleeves on either side. But when she stands next to me and flips through the album, I notice it's mostly empty.

"My mom has all our best pictures," she hurriedly explains when she sees me staring sadly at all the empty sleeves.

I open my mouth to tell her she doesn't have to explain anything to me, ever, but she just shakes her head, so I stay quiet.

Kay reaches a page with pictures and puts her thumb there to hold her place. She whispers, "Even though I don't have many, I still have a few…a few of the very best."

I can't see the photos since the album is mostly closed, but I put my hand on her hip and give her a reassuring squeeze. Sweet girl smiles at me and slowly hands me the album.

There are four photos—two per page—of a cute little girl who is smiling big in every shot. She beams like my girl does when she's really happy, this little girl definitely has Kay's smile, and her hair is the same chestnut-brown shade as Kay's hair. But the little girl in the photos has green eyes, not the caramel browns I've come to know so well.

"That was Sarah," Kay says, voice cracking. "She was five in those pictures."

As hard as it was for me to pull up my dad's picture, this is obviously fucking ten times harder for Kay. I put my leg out and she sits down on my lap, she rests her head on my shoulder. I hold the book where we both can see. I trace the edge of one of the sleeves holding a picture of Kay's little sister. "She's adorable," I say quietly.

"She was," my sad-voiced girl says back.

All of the photos are of Sarah in an apple orchard. From the fiery colors of the leaves on the trees, it looks to have been around harvest time. In the first two shots, Sarah is picking ripened apples from a low-hanging branch. In the next one, she's sitting on the ground, placing her just-picked apples in a bushel basket that's almost as big as her. In the final shot, Kay's little sister is grinning wide at the camera, looking up with love at the person taking the picture. Kay doesn't have to tell me she was the one behind the lens.

"We went apple picking that day with my dad." Kay's voice is soft and bereft. "That was Sarah's last autumn."

My girl shakes her head once, and I see she's trying not to cry.

"Hey, it's okay to be sad." I rub her shoulder.

Kay fans her face and takes a deep breath. Only one tear escapes and she swipes it away quickly. She apologizes for getting emotional, and I tell her, "You never have to apologize to me for what you're feeling." It's the truth.

Kay turns the page and there's one more photo of Sarah. In this one, Kay's little sister is sleeping, holding the stuffed rabbit I rescued last night. "She couldn't sleep without Peetie," Kay whispers, and then she sits up abruptly and her tear-filled eyes search mine.

"What?" I ask. "What's wrong, baby?"

She shakes her head slightly. "I was just thinking, re-member how I told you I was planning to leave Peetie at Sarah's grave...but I couldn't?" I nod. "Do you think I'm wrong to keep him, Chase? Do you think he should be with Sarah?" Her face is panicked, but I sense this isn't really about Peetie. "What if I'm making wrong decisions and don't even know it? Maybe I'm just selfish, keeping things for myself—no, keeping things *to* myself." Her caramel-browns implore. "What if you found out something about me, and then realized I am not the person you think I am, Chase?"

I place the album on the desk. "Come here."

I give her the biggest hug possible, which is pretty huge since my arms encompass her.

"I know you, right?" I whisper into her ear. She nods. "Well, I love that person, the person I *know* you are, Kay. Don't ever doubt that, baby. Now, what's this really all about anyway?"

Kay holds on to me like she fears she'll lose me if she lets go. *Never going to happen.*

"I have to tell you something, Chase," she begins. "Something about the night Sarah died. The story you heard isn't the truth, and I need to tell you what really happened. I made a horrible mistake that night and it cost Sarah her life. You deserve to know what it was, but I...I...I'm terrified to tell you." She finally breaks her hold and leans back.

She can tell me anything, there's nothing to fear. I brush her hair back and say all this and more, but every time my girl attempts to divulge this secret, it's like she *physically* can't get the words out, like she's been traumatized or something.

"Why are you so afraid?" I ask, since I know it can't be me that's intimidating her. I'd never judge her, and she knows it.

She takes a deep breath. "I told someone once, and…it didn't go so well."

"Your mother," I guess.

"Yes," she answers listlessly.

Fuck, her mother really does blame her for Sarah dying. Father Maridale was right. I sigh and shake my head. "And this secret is why this woman won't speak to you?"

I'd like to get "this woman" alone in a room for a few minutes to shake some sense into her. Hurting my girl like this—wounding her, really—talk about a bitch move of epic proportions.

Kay nods, and I bring her to me once again. I tell her she doesn't have to *ever* share this secret if she doesn't want to. I'll love her no matter what she decides to do—tell, or not tell. But if she feels she must disclose whatever it is, I think she should hold off for a while. Hell, she's just getting over what happened at her apartment building last night. And, sure, her cheek may only be a little red and swollen today, but I can see there's still a bruise on her leg, and surely there's a bruise that's not visible, but still there, on her psyche. She's wounded. Waiting is best for now. After I say all of this, Kay whispers, "Thank you, Chase," against my chest.

We sit quietly for a few more minutes, but then Kay slides off my lap and takes the photo album back upstairs. Even though she swore she wasn't hungry when she first came down earlier, I figure a piece of toast and some juice might do her some good.

I go into the kitchen and place two slices of bread in the toaster, and pour some juice for each of us. Kay comes into the room just as I'm buttering. With emotions now settled, we sit at the kitchen table, eat buttered toast, and talk about getting my girl moved into the apartment above the garage.

"I can't wait to finally see the apartment in person," she tells me between bites. "It looks so awesome in the flyers."

"You're going to love it," I tell her.

A short while later we head next door to Kay's new living space, her "awesome" new apartment. I carry her suitcase in one hand, and, in the other, a duffel bag that looks like it's been beaten to hell and back. Kay follows me across the driveway and up the wooden steps trailing along the far side of the detached garage. When we reach the top and step inside the apartment, my girl's eyes grow wide.

"Oh my God, Chase, this place *is* incredible," she gushes as she spins around, taking everything in.

There's a lot of light coming in through the skylights, so there's no need to turn on any of the lamps. I point out some things I think she may like in the little kitchenette, and when I open the door to the still-brand-new oven, she peeks in. "You never cooked when you lived here?" she asks, disbelief on her face.

I shrug. "Uh, I wasn't too into cooking when I lived over here. But, does toast count?"

"No, silly boy, Toast absolutely does not count." Kay reaches up and tries to mess up my probably already-crazy hair, but I dodge her hand. She swats my ass instead. "Ohh," I drawl. "Into the kinky stuff, I see. Hmm, wish I'd known that last night."

I am totally teasing, but sweet girl's cheeks pink all the way to red.

"Chase, you're bad," she says in this trying-to-be-but-unsuccessful chastising voice.

I know she loves the "bad" side of me, very much, based on her reactions in bed last night. I tell her exactly that, using very graphic words. She can't disagree, but she sure blushes crimson red. Damn, she's adorable.

I'm still smirking, smug, as we step into the living room area. There's a ton of sexual tension in the air now, so I keep my distance. Otherwise, there's a good chance we'll end up on the couch, doing what I'd like to be doing right now. But I meant what I said last night—I want everything to be perfect for Kay when we consummate this relationship.

From a safe distance, I watch as Kay makes her way slowly around the living room. She pats the dark blue cushions on the couch. She sits down, stands up. Too-cute girl steps over to where the TV sits on a stand. She runs her index finger along the top. Smiling, she gives me a sidelong glance. "Did you dust recently?"

I admit I stopped over before she was up so I could make sure everything was spotless for her arrival. This earns me a kiss on the cheek. "So sweet," she murmurs.

We wrap up the tour with the bedroom and a peek into the bath in the back. Kay turns back to the full-sized bed and plops down on the plushy cover. She tells me she loves the refinished antique iron headboard, and then adds while glancing about, "In fact, I love the whole place."

"I'm glad you like it," I say. "I kind of figured you would."

"There's only one thing."

"Oh, what's that?"

"There's nothing on the walls, Chase, nothing. They're way too bare."

I shrug, but she's absolutely correct. There is nothing on the walls, not in this room or any of the others. I just never got around to hanging anything up when I lived here. But what Kay doesn't know is that I have a plan to remedy these empty walls, I just can't tell her yet. It's part of my surprise for her, part of making everything "perfect" for my girl. And if it's going to be ready for this evening, which I hope, then I really need to get started on it soon.

I lift Kay's suitcase up onto the bed, and she starts taking out her clothes. It doesn't appear as if this task is something she needs my help with, so I tell her I have a few errands to run and ask if she'll be okay if she's alone for a while. She rolls her eyes and laughs at me.

"Just checking," I say.

We'd originally planned on a going to a movie this afternoon, but I'd rather have my girl alone later this evening. I ask her if she still wants to hang out, but maybe more toward dusk. "And do you mind if we just stay in tonight?" I ask.

"That's fine," she says, pushing my shoulder playfully.

"Just checking on that too," I tease back.

I give her a good-bye kiss, and then leave Kay to her unpacking. I head back over to the house to start researching the surprise I'm planning for Kay. I haven't forgotten how she said on the day we first kissed that if we could go anywhere she'd have us go to Paris. Well, I don't have the means to take her there, but I may have a way to bring Paris to my girl.

Once I'm back in the living room, I sit down at the computer and start researching all the famous Parisian sights. I print out a few of the most well-known; I know I'll need them for reference. Next, I look up grocery stores in the area. There's one north of here that sells gourmet items. I print out the address. The grocery store is near the dollar store where Kay bought the sunglasses the junkie destroyed last night. I decide I'll stop there, as well, so I can buy my girl a new pair.

Fuck, this girl owns my ass. But do I care? Nope, I fucking love that she has this kind of hold on me. Simply because I love her right the fuck back. And I'm going to show my girl I can make her happy if it's the last thing I do.

Tonight, I will give Kay Stanton her "perfect" evening.

CHAPTER TWELVE

KAY

After Chase leaves, I get to work on unpacking and settling into the space above his garage, my new apartment, the one I secretly hoped to end up in someday. I think back to the first day we went to lunch at the diner, when Chase first showed me the flyer. I thought his apartment looked amazing then, but here, now, in person, it's so much better.

What I said to my boy is true: I love my new home already.

Streams of sunlight pour through the skylights above me as I glance around, soaking it all in once more. Everything is as it appeared in Chase's sketch—bright, warm, and welcoming. This space has the makings of a happy space, the antithesis of the basement apartment in which I lived for a full year. I stayed there too long. I should've left sooner, money issues or not. Well, one thing for sure—I will never again step foot in that place. I plan to compose a letter to notify the property group that, as of last night, I have vacated the premises. The key, I'll return with the letter.

I take a break from unpacking and step back into the living room. When I sit down on the sofa, I run my hand along the soft, smooth fabric. I lean back, turn my head, and breathe in deeply. No stale odors here. This sofa smells terrific, fresh and clean, with maybe a hint of the guy I love.

I straighten. I just can't believe this place is all mine now. I spend a few minutes just letting all the newness sink in, then I get up and return to the bedroom so I can get back to unpacking my things.

It doesn't take long to put away my stuff, there's really not all that much to organize. I utilize the small closet and wooden dresser, folding and hanging various articles of clothing and placing them in appropriate spots. When I'm done, I flip the lid up on the trunk at the base of the bed, half-expecting to find some of Chase's stuff—and hoping a little that I do—but it's completely empty.

Not for long, I decide. It's there that I carefully place my Sarah journals, as well as the small photo album I shared with Chase this morning.

Once my bags are empty and everything is in place, I consider myself officially moved in. Acknowledging this brings a smile to my face. I know in my bones I am going to love living here, especially since I'll be in such close proximity to my blue-eyed boy.

My mood lifts even higher as this thought sinks in, maybe it even soars a little. Heck, such a good mood washes over me that I plop down on the edge of the bed and decide to text Missy. I don't mention last night at all, nor do I bring up what happened with her, Nick, and his cousin. And I most definitely do not utter a word regarding my encounter with the junkie. It's none of her business. What I do text is that I once again have access to a working oven and can bake cookies, if need be, for the upcoming Fourth of July carnival bake sale.

It takes only a few seconds for Missy to reply with, *Great, can you do snickerdoodle cookies?*

After I breathe a sigh of relief that, like me, Missy has made no mention of the events last evening at the Anchor Inn, I answer back, *sure can*. I even include a smiley face for good measure.

Missy sends a return smile, and our texting concludes.

I hold the phone contemplatively. The head of the bake committee wants snickerdoodle cookies, so snickerdoodle cookies it shall be. I am completely fine with her request. Lord knows I've made enough cookies over the years that I have the recipe for snickerdoodles memorized. Baking them will be a snap.

I type a quick note in my cell as a reminder to pick up the necessary ingredients Monday after work. The fourth isn't till Thursday, but the carnival begins Tuesday evening. Missy will want the cookies Tuesday morning—that's how we always work things like this—which means I'll most likely be baking well into Monday night. This could work to my advantage though. Every good baker needs a taste tester, right? And luckily I know just who to ask.

Chase is perfect for the task. Not to mention, he's sure to love every minute. Based on his penchant for sugary lemon-on-lime soda—and the more than occasional ice-cream cone from the place across from the church—I am well aware my guy loves his sugar.

Speaking of Chase, I hear his truck backing out of the driveway. Guess he's leaving to go out and run his errands. I have to wonder what he's really up to though. I have a sneaking suspicion he's putting together something for me—for us—for tonight. Probably working on that "perfect" something he has promised. If that's the case, then I know I better rest up while I have the chance.

I lie back on my new bed and burrow under the fluffy down comforter covering the top. I am already relaxed, but wrapping up in clean-smelling, fresh linens ensures sleep finds me rather quickly.

I sleep soundly, and don't wake until hours later.

There's a soft, waning glow edging through the skylight directly above me when I open my eyes, bathing me in what I estimate to be early evening light. Stretching and yawning, I check my cell. I am right—it's almost seven o'clock in the evening.

I rub sleep from my eyes and check the cell more thoroughly—there's one missed text, from Chase, sent just a few minutes ago. It reads: *My house, eight o'clock, sound good?*

I text back: *perfect.*

Not yet, bb, but it will be, is my boy's cryptic reply, leaving me simultaneously thrilled, nervous, and infinitely excited.

Five minutes later, I am in the shower, taking an extra-long time, savoring the steady, hot stream of water. It's been so long since I've experienced anything more than ten minutes of tepid flow. This, in contrast, is heaven. Utilizing my recently unpacked toiletries, I shave everything that needs shaving and deep condition my hair. Once I'm done and out of the shower, I dry off and go back into the bedroom. There, I slip a cute linen sundress over my head—the shade is pale pink, a color I know Chase enjoys seeing me in.

I debate on how much makeup to wear. I never wear a lot, but tonight is a special evening. Plus, I'd prefer not to show up at Chase's doorstep sporting the mark left by the junkie. But when I pull a tube of concealer out of my make-up bag, and prepare to dab a glob on my cheek, I notice the swelling has subsided completely, and the mark itself is almost completely faded. Since there's no need for cover-up, I wipe my fingers on a tissue and toss the tube back into the bag.

In the end, I just go with a tiny bit of liner, a sweep of mascara to each set of lashes, and a touch of clear gloss to my lips. With my minimal makeup complete, I slip on a pair of flat sandals.

It's almost eight by the time I'm ready, so I leave in a hurry and head across the gravel driveway to where I suspect "perfect" awaits.

When I reach the porch, I notice the front door is wide open and the screen door is unlocked. I think about just going in, but decide to ring the doorbell, lest I catch my guy off guard. The last thing I want is to ruin any surprise he's planning.

After a beat, Chase yells down from the top of the stairs that he'll be right down in a minute.

I duck down slightly and peer through the screen. I catch a quick flash of Chase walking by in nothing but a towel, looking all lean and muscular. The temperature, though not exceptionally hot this evening, suddenly seems to rise. A quick minute or two passes and, while I'm still fanning myself with my hand, Chase starts down the stairs.

My beautiful boy is as breathtaking as ever—freshly showered, hair slightly damp and tousled, and face clean-shaven. He's dressed casually this evening, which always suits him best. Faded, worn jeans hang low on his hips and he has on a nice dress shirt.

On his way down the stairs, he lifts up the hem of the button-down he's wearing, seemingly debating whether to tuck in or not. In that flash of seconds his taut abs are left exposed. *Oh my.* Sadly, my peek is too brief, as Chase lets the hem drop back into place, opting to leave his shirt untucked. As he reaches the last step, Chase rolls his sleeves up to his elbows. The shade of this particular dress shirt is a light bluish-gray, a perfect match to his gunmetal blues. Just as I think that, Chase turns those stunning eyes on me, holding me captive as his gaze so often does. I smile, he smiles, yet we don't say a thing. Sometimes words are just not necessary.

Chase opens the screen door and steadies it with his hip. In order to step past him and into the hall, I have to brush up against his body. He's solid and firm and smells deliciously fresh and clean. I hesitate. We are chest to chest, but only half so since he's so much taller.

"Hey," I murmur, glancing up.

"Hey back at you," he quietly responds, catching my eye.

He grins at me. Well, he actually kind of smirks, all knowing-like. I sense my boy is confident his surprise—whatever it is—will impress me, which only serves to ratchet up my curiosity.

I step the rest of the way in and, in doing so, purposely bump his leg with my hip. He closes the screen door and I playfully ask, "So, what are you up to, sneaky boy?"

He laughs. "Dying to know, eh?"

Why play coy? "You know I am, so tell me. What do you have planned for our evening?"

"I'm not giving it up yet, curious girl. It's a surprise." Chase's blues sparkle playfully. "But you'll find out soon enough."

"Must be something *really* good," I reply, basing my comment on the smug look he's shooting my way.

"Oh, it *really* is. Only the best for my girl, you know." He delivers a feather-light kiss to my cheek, and then his fingers pass lightly over the faded red mark. "This looks much better."

"It does," I agree, then I step back and lift my dress a little to show him how well the bruise on my thigh is also healing. "See, this one's really fading too."

Chase's expression darkens briefly. "You shouldn't be marked up at all, baby." His lips press together, and I know he's thinking about the junkie and all that transpired last night.

I don't want the upbeat mood we have going to dampen, so I quickly suggest, "Hey, let's not talk about any of that, okay?"

Chase nods slowly, and I nudge him, trying to get him to smile again. It works. Thankfully he morphs rather swiftly back to carefree.

"Okay, surprise time," Chase announces, sending a dazzling smile that could melt hearts my way. It certainly melts mine.

Chase covers my eyes with one hand, and, with his other hand at my waist, he steers me toward the base of the staircase. Walking behind me, he guides me up the stairs, down the hall, and into what I assume is his bedroom. My eyes are still covered, but I know from the warm breeze coming in that we're standing in front of a window.

My boy lowers his hand from my eyes and tells me I can open them. I do.

The window we climbed out the other night is in front

of me, we are indeed in Chase's bedroom. But before I can turn around to where I feel my boy's warm body behind mine, he puts his hands on my shoulders and makes me promise to remain where I am.

"Part of your surprise is on the dresser," he explains. "If you turn around now you'll see it, and I'm saving that part for later. Okay?"

I am insanely curious to see what Chase has put together, but I murmur an assent and do as he asks. I keep my eyes averted. He steps beside me and takes out the screen, then climbs out onto the roof. With one long leg in and one out, my boy helps me over the sill, just like he did the other night.

When we're standing out on the flat rooftop, I notice a big, plaid blanket stretched out close to the little ledge up against the house, where we sat the other night and watched the sunset. There are four votive candles on the blanket, one at each corner, keeping the checkered material in place. The flames flicker in the breeze against the backdrop of a setting sun that is streaking this particular evening sky in indigos and violets.

"Is it always this beautiful up here?" I ask, marveling at the second amazing rooftop sunset I've been lucky enough to see.

Chase leads me over to the blanket. When a warm gust of air blows a strand of my hair across my face, my attentive boy brushes it back. "It's usually pretty nice up here, but you make it positively stunning."

"Chase..." From any other man, Chase's words might sound cheesy, but his voice holds such sincerity there's no doubt these words, these consonants and vowels, come only from his heart. And that leaves me speechless, my own consonants and vowels trailing off into air around us.

Chase kneels down on the blanket and reaches for my hand. I place my fingers in his palm and lower myself down next to him. I tuck my legs to one side so I don't give Chase a show. Well, not yet anyway.

"Are you hungry?" he asks, a smirk playing at his lips.

That smug expression tells me that, despite my attempt to be discreet when I sat down, my boy still caught a peek of the cute pink lace panties I chose for tonight.

"A little," I reply, getting back to his question.

Chase reaches to under the ledge. There's a shopping bag tucked underneath and I can't imagine why. But when my full-of-surprises guy pulls a baguette out of the bag— then a round of brie—my eyes widen.

"Wow," I say as he places both items on the blanket. "This *is* a surprise!"

He catches my eye and smiles. "There's more."

I am already beyond impressed, but Chase isn't done yet. He pulls two wine glasses out of the bag and places them on the blanket, next to the baguette and brie. With the setting sun as a background, Chase pours white wine into each of the glasses. The candles flicker, making the gold-toned liquid shimmer. My boy begins to add something from a bottle labeled *crème de cassis*, and I raise an eyebrow.

"It's a liqueur," he explains. "You add just a small amount to the wine."

When he sees I'm a little baffled, he elaborates, "I found the recipe on the Internet earlier today. The liqueur added to the wine creates a drink called Kir. The article next to the recipe said it's popular in France. You can buy it at almost any restaurant or café. And it's supposedly very good." He finishes pouring and proffers me a glass. "Guess we'll find out."

As the sun drips and melts into the horizon, and the beautiful man sitting next to me picks up his own glass filled with this supposedly popular French drink, I feel a little overwhelmed, a little choked up, but in the best way possible. Whether it's his intention or not, Chase is giving me more than a romantic, French-themed rooftop picnic, he's giving me a memory, one I can hold on to, when things inevitably get tough. I see now what my sweet, sweet boy has done. This surprise *is* perfection. It's tangible, yet not. Truly, it's boundless.

"What do you think?" Chase asks.

I take a sip of the blush-tinged Kir...and wow! "Mmm, this is delicious," I gush.

Chase tears a small piece from the baguette and spreads a little brie on top. He places the bread at my lips, and I take a bite. "Better than chips and pretzels?" he asks, referring to our impromptu lunch in the gymnasium.

I laugh and nod. And then I admire.

Chase Gartner is so unaware of how gorgeous he really, truly is. He's always handsome, but he looks especially so right now. He's all tousled tawny hair, pale blue eyes, and perfect features, the waning daylight muting everything to soft focus. My boy also has a touch of a tan from the days he works outside in the sun, so his skin is slightly darker than usual. He's sun-kissed and stunning before me.

Chase asks me if I like the brie-on-baguette, and I nod enthusiastically, partially because I do, but mostly because the guy feeding it to me looks so damn amazing. "It's fantastic, Chase. I love it."

As the sun sets, we eat and drink. We savor our rooftop Parisian picnic. When we're just about done, Chase reaches into the shopping bag once more and presents dessert.

"Do you like chocolate mousse?" he asks as he spoons a portion and feeds me a creamy bite.

"Yes, absolutely," I say before I swallow the fluffy bit of heaven.

My boy takes a bite of his own, and I ask, "So, Chase, all of this is so decadent and romantic." I gesture around. "I love everything, very much, but I'm curious as to how you came up with this idea."

My boy smiles and looks down as he swirls the spoon in his chocolate mousse. "You gave me the idea, sweet girl, that day in the gym, our pretending with the chips and pretzels." He shrugs. "I don't know. That day was so good, and you seemed so happy. I thought maybe if I gave you the real thing I might make you even happier."

I touch his arm. "I am happy, Chase. I was then, and I am now. This is wonderful. You always make me happy."

"You said you wished we could go to Paris, remember?" Gunmetal blues hold my gaze and I nod once. "I wish I could take you there, Kay, I do. I would in a heartbeat, I promise. But since I can't, I decided I'd try to bring Paris to you."

My heart skips a beat. "This is better than Paris, Chase. Really, it is."

And it is. Nothing could top where I am right now, up here on this rooftop, drinking Kir, and being fed bits of brie-covered baguette and chocolate mousse by a beautiful, complex, thoughtful man. A man I've fallen head over heels for, a man I fall for a little more each day.

I lean forward and kiss his cheek. "I love you," I whisper.

"I love you too," he says back, his hand reaching out, his thumb grazing my bottom lip. He finds a smidge of mousse and swipes it away.

As the sky darkens, we lie back on the blanket. For the longest while, we talk and cuddle, all while millions of stars twinkle above our prone bodies.

"Those are the same stars we'd see if we were in Paris, baby," Chase tells me at one point.

"I know, but I like these stars better," I reply.

Chase sits up and blows out the candles. The countless pins of light blanketing the velvet-black sky glow even more brightly.

"There always seems to be so many more stars out here in the country," I say as I sit up and settle back into Chase's chest. He wraps his strong arms around me.

My boy looks down at me and smiles. "Those stars are always there, baby. We just see them more clearly out here is all."

Maybe there's deeper meaning in what Chase is saying. Maybe everything is clearer out here. I know my mind feels free and unburdened at the moment. As if to illuminate that fact, I immediately come to the conclusion that, for once in my life, I have not a care in the world. It's just me and my guy. And everything is perfect, just as Chase promised it would be. This man has brought me Paris. And in doing so, in doing something so thoughtful and caring, he's taken away all my worry, all my fear. In a way, it's like we're not even in Harmony Creek right now. Sure, we're physically here, but Chase has ensured that tonight we exist in a world of love and friendship, one we've built together for the past several weeks. But this love feels like something much bigger. I know in my heart destiny and fate rule our love; they have from the moment I crashed into his arms that Sunday in the church parking lot. I smile to myself, I wanted a man to sweep me off my feet, and that sure has happened.

The air eventually grows cooler, and I shiver in response. Chase, taking notice, suggests we go back inside. "I still have to show you the rest of your surprise anyway," he reminds me in a voice as whisper-soft as the velvety black night.

Chase takes my hand and helps me up. What could possibly top a romantic sunset picnic on the roof? What could be better than lying beneath the stars, feeling so very much in love?

I'm about to find out...

It's dark when we step back over the window sill and into Chase's bedroom. I can't see much until he switches the lamp on by his bed.

Then, my breath catches in my throat.

I step closer to the dresser, my hand reaching out. I am speechless. My artist boy really has brought Paris to me. First, out on the roof, through taste, touch, and smell. But now, in his lamp-lit bedroom, it's through sight.

A set of sketches, done in richly hued oil pastels, rest propped up on the dresser. A café in Montmartre, a tree-lined view of the Champs Élysées, the Arc de Triomphe in a base-to-top angle. And that is just the start.

I stand before the sketches—these pieces of art—brought

to life by Chase's unbelievably talented hands. A bakery that reads *boulangerie* on the awning, where baguettes—like the one we just ate—are displayed in a basket in the window, next to chocolate éclairs and croissants, steam rising from their golden tops.

I touch the edges of each drawing, one-by-one, tentatively. Every sketch is as beautiful as the next. The colors are stunning, rich and dark, the detail is pristine. Chase's ability to recreate these lifelike scenes blows me away. So much so that words temporarily elude me.

Two of the pieces at the edge of the dresser my boy has framed. They rest all set to display. The first framed sketch is of Notre Dame Cathedral, and the other framed piece depicts arguably the most recognizable landmark in Paris— the Eiffel Tower. Both are springtime scenes, pink-blossoming trees pepper the landscape, along with daffodils and tulips that are in full bloom.

I turn to my insanely talented artist boy, who never ceases to amaze me, and who is currently leaned up against the frame of the door, as nonchalant as ever, savoring my reactions.

I find my words, at last, and, in a reverent voice, say, "My God, Chase, these are incredible." I shake my head. "No, that's not good enough. I don't think there's even a word to describe how beautiful these sketches are." I glance back at the sketches, then to the artist himself. "You should draw professionally, Chase, you're certainly good enough."

My boy blushes as he peers down at the floor. *So shy sometimes*, I think. "I don't know about that," he replies quietly.

"It's true," I insist. "You're a real artist."

Chase, still leaning against the doorframe, crosses his arms. Blue-gray cotton pulls taut at his biceps and wide shoulders. "I'm glad you like the sketches, baby girl," he begins, smiling and catching my gaze, "'Cause they're all yours now. I drew them for you. It's the rest of your surprise. I finished the one of the bakery just before you got here. On the first try I fucked up the word 'boulangerie.'" He chuckles. "So I had to start that one over."

I turn back to the art, still in awe. "So you're saying you drew all of these today?"

"Yeah, I got started after I got back from the store. I only had time to frame two of them though. I'll fix the others for you tomorrow and we can hang them up in your apartment." He shoots me a knowing glance. "That should take care of that blank-wall problem, yeah?"

"No more blank walls," I muse.

That's why Chase looked so smug when I said something about the walls this morning. He was already planning this surprise then.

"No more blank walls," he echoes back.

I am so thrilled and excited with this part of my surprise that I start to tell Chase all the places I plan to place his artwork—the boulangerie will go in the kitchen, Notre Dame and the Arc de Triomphe I plan to place side-by-side on the wall above the dark blue sofa, and the Montmartre café and Champs Élysées pieces just feel like they belong in the bedroom.

"What about the Eiffel Tower?" Chase asks.

"Hmm…" I consider.

The Eiffel Tower sketch is one of the best. It's stunning enough to brighten any room all by itself.

I suddenly have an idea. "Wait."

I pick the framed Eiffel Tower sketch up, and turn so I'm facing Chase. I give him a look that hopefully conveys: *you are going to love this.*

"What?" he asks as he watches curiously.

"Just a minute," I huff as I turn back around, kick off my sandals, and start to climb up onto his bed. I steady myself using the pine headboard, then straighten. "You shouldn't have blank walls, either, artist boy."

I glance back and Chase shakes his head, but in a way that says he likes where I'm going with this.

I hold the Eiffel Tower up so it's centered above his bed. There's a nail in the wall and I position the frame on it. "I think this one belongs right here." I secure and straighten Chase's artwork. "What do you think?"

I step down from the bed, and my boy comes up from behind me. He toys with one of the thin straps of my dress. It slips down and he kisses my exposed shoulder. "I love your idea. I think it looks great up there. Every time we're in this room we can pretend like we're right in the shadow of the Eiffel Tower."

"Why did you do all this, Chase?" I whisper, leaning back into his powerful chest.

Strong arms surround me, and I suddenly want this man around me even more. I want him on me, in me, all over me. I want his strength, his talent, his love.

My boy trails his nose up my neck and whispers in my ear, "I did this because you deserve perfect, Kay. I meant it when I said that last night."

"This *is* perfect," I say quietly, though I mean so much more. "It's better than perfect actually."

Chase knows what I'm saying, I am telling him the time is right, there will never be a more perfect moment than right now for what we're about to do. With gentle hands, he turns me so I'm facing him. His blues are heavy-lidded, hungry with lust...and love.

"I love you, baby girl," he tells me. "Let me show you how much."

Before I can respond, my boy is on his knees before me, sliding his hands up my bare legs, lifting my dress, and hooking his fingers into the edges of the lace panties I tried earlier to keep from his view. Not now—they're fully on display. Chase holds my dress aloft and kisses the little pink bow he discovers at one hip. He moves to the other pink bow at the other hip and does the same. Then, he's slipping all the bows and all the lace down my legs. I'm weak-kneed and breathless, trembling with love. But love holds me up with all his strength. I place my hands on his shoulders and lift one leg, then the other, and pink lace is discarded to the floor.

Chase delivers soft, wet kisses—to my hips, to my thighs—then he lifts me easily and lays me back on the bed. He drags me down to the edge slowly, my hair fanning out on the covers behind me. Chase, kneeling between my shaky, weak legs, showers the insides of my thighs with more scorching little kisses that burn straight up to my center.

I hike my dress up higher on my own, making my boy chuckle. At my haste, I suppose. But then he hisses in a breath of air. "You're beautiful," he tells me when I fully expose myself to him.

Chase stands and starts to unbutton his shirt. He undoes a few, then says, "Fuck it," and just pulls the material over his head, revealing all his flexing muscles and beautiful tattoos. Blue-gray drops to the floor while I admire and ogle the body it was just covering. Chase takes no notice of my wandering eyes, my boy's too busy leaning over me, putting his knees on the bed, pushing me up farther as he gets to work on undoing all the tiny buttons at the front of my dress. It doesn't take long before loosened and gaping fabric is slid over my breasts and pushed down until it gathers at my waist. Chase unhooks my bra, and pink lace is pushed aside and discarded as his hot mouth descends to my breasts.

He uses one hand to cup a breast, plumping it into his mouth, while his other hand raises the lower part of my dress up over my hips, allowing the fabric to join the rest of my dress gathered at my waist. Chase leaves me barely clothed like this as he parts my folds with his long, adept fingers. When he finds me wet and wanting, he groans around my nipple. His fingers make a pass at my entrance, spreading my wetness and circling my clitoris. I suck in a ragged breath and bury my own fingers in his hair.

My boy releases the breast he's been concentrating on and moves over to the other, licking, sucking, and driving me wild as he works my body with his mouth and his hands. I feel so close to release, but Chase releases my breast with an audible *pop* and removes his fingers from my sex. He scoots me back a little more and hovers over me. His knees are on either side of me, still clad in faded denim, but the top button of his jeans is undone. His arms straighten, caging me in as he holds his body up above me, feral and dominating. I am small beneath him, and I like it…a lot.

His eyes move over me hungrily. The only thing keeping me from being completely naked is the gathered fabric of my dress still at my waist. This, Chase now seems to notice. "Lift," he demands.

I do as he asks and he slips my dress over my head in one smooth motion. "Lay back, baby, let me see you naked before me."

The small lamp by the bed is still on and when I acquiesce to Chase's request I know he can see all of me. I am laid bare and open. He blazes a path with one hand down my stomach. When he reaches a hip, he grips tightly, and rocks me a little on the mattress, like he's testing out for when he fucks me. I can't help but moan out his name.

"Baby..." He leans down and parts my lips with his own. Our tongues touch.

I could kiss this man forever. But he begins to kiss lower, down my chin, down my neck. I arch up and he places a hand under me, at the small of my back. He moves my body into his kisses as his mouth travels between my breasts and down over my abdomen, then lower still, to where I need and want him so very badly.

His breaths caress my sex, promising and hot. I cry out his name, tell him how very much I want what he's about to do.

"I know, baby," he replies, and then he kisses my clit, very softly.

He uses only his lips at first, but then his tongue darts out and he licks where he's just kissed, over and over and over. "Oh, Chase," I rasp. "Yes-s-s."

Chase's hands move my hips in unison with the rhythm of what he's doing to me. When he senses I'm close—and

I am—he keeps one hand on my hip, while the other trails down to below where his mouth is nudging me closer and closer to release. Chase slides a finger into me while he sucks on to and pulls my clit into his mouth, all while gripping my hip tightly, hard enough to leave a mark. It's too much amazing sensation, I cry out in pleasure and tumble over the edge. Chase licks and kisses my sex as the last shudders of orgasm wrack through me. Slowly, he moves up my body until he reaches my mouth and kisses me deeply.

When we break for air, I am smiling, smiling and saying over and over in my head, "I love you, I love you, I love you."

And maybe I say it out loud, since Chase is saying it too.

And while he tells me "I love you back, baby girl," he's parting my legs to accommodate his body as he settles on top of me.

My all-encompassing boy is above me and on me, elbows at either side of my head, keeping his weight from crushing me. Somewhere in all my bliss I notice he's ridded himself of his jeans. We're skin to skin, completely bare, with my boy's hard and throbbing pressing into my soft and wet.

I raise my head, allowing our lips to meet. Chase kisses my mouth open. I taste me on his tongue, but I also taste Kir and a hint of chocolate. While my tongue explores Chase's mouth, he pushes his cock to my core. Our bodies are so close, pressed together, but it feels nowhere close enough.

I twine my fingers in his hair, then trail fingertips up and down his back. When I settle my palms on his inked wings I try to press Chase closer. But his body is on mine as close as he can be. There's no space between us, but it's *still* not enough. I shift and the tip of him pushes into my entrance. I sigh. *That's better.*

"You feel so good, sweet girl, I can't wait to be inside you," Chase whispers into my ear.

"Then don't wait," I say back in a sex-husky voice I've never before heard coming from my mouth.

Chase holds where he is, partially inside me, pressing and throbbing with the promise of more. He leans back so our eyes meet. He watches my reaction as he pushes into me another inch. I gasp. He's big, and he stretches me wide with his girth. But I want to be opened up like this for Chase; I want him to stretch me to my limits. My body belongs to him, it's his for the taking, and the sooner he takes me the sooner he can mold me to fit him.

I nod quickly, and Chase pushes into me more, stretching and filling me with his love for me, making us one. He's almost in completely, but I know there's still more to go. I close my eyes and feel, just feel. Because *this* is how love should feel. It's like nothing I've ever known before. It moves me, it consumes me. It's so overwhelming in fact that, for a second, I choke up.

Chase stills. "Are you all right?" he asks. He cups my chin and his thumb brushes over my kiss-swollen lips.

I arch up. "I'm good." He shifts and I moan. "It's just…I want all of you, Chase. Give me everything." I gasp. "Don't hold anything back."

My boy knows what I mean. I want more than just his body.

"I'm already yours, Kay. I have been for a while now, long before I let you know. Maybe I've been yours from the day we first met, who knows? It sure feels like maybe I have."

I feel Chase's words as they fill my heart, mending the broken pieces. And then I feel *him* when, with one powerful and love-fueled thrust, he fills me all the way, like I've never been filled before, stretched and pulsing, coming apart once more. Coming still when Chase starts to move, *really* move.

My love gives me everything he's got, using all his hard and all his muscle, using his love and his trouble, his good and his bad. My boy fucks with intensity, and I finally become enlightened as to what crazy-good sex really is. But I know I'm getting more from Chase than anyone has ever gotten from him in the past. He also gives me more than I've ever received from anyone in my past. This man gives me friendship, he gives me hope, and he makes possibility real. Frankly, in many ways, Chase has given me back my life. Maybe I've given him his life back too.

I look into my boy's blues and hold his gaze as he moves inside my body, more slowly now, more deliberately. He mouths, "I love you."

I say it back.

And with Chase loving me slow and easy we both come—together as one—in the shadow of the Eiffel Tower.

CHAPTER THIRTEEN
CHASE

I dream my girl has me in her mouth, and it feels so fucking good that I don't want it to stop. I wake up kind of groaning and quickly realize this is not a dream. *Praise Jesus.*

Shit, Kay's lips wrapped around my cock may be the best thing I've ever felt. No, check that, this is second best. Nothing could top being inside her last night.

But…fuck.

My girl does some swirling motion with her tongue, and I know I am not going to last much longer. *Christ.* I try to warn her, give her some time to move, but she stays right where she's at, rocking right along with my increasingly erratic thrusts. When I explode, she takes everything I give her.

After I recover, I brush back her hair, since she's still leaning over my cock. "You didn't have to do that, you know," I say.

She sits back, touches her mouth, and smiles shyly. *Did she like it?* Shit, I think so.

"I wanted to," she replies with a shrug. "Although I've never before…uh…"

Sweet girl has just sucked my dick with abandon, but discussing it makes her blush. Could she be any cuter?

I chuckle and pull her back to my body. "Never what, baby?" I want to hear the word she's reluctant to say come out of that warm, sweet mouth.

She presses her cheek to my chest and whispers, "Swallowed."

It's probably selfish and possessive as hell, but I'm secretly thrilled to hear she's never done that for any other guy. Hopefully, I'll remain her only. Guess that makes me territorial too, but it's just how I feel. Besides, it's not all one-sided here. I shared a first with Kay last night too, and I tell her now.

"Last night was the first time I ever did the deed without a condom."

She glances up at me, a kind of surprised expression spreading over her features. "Really?" she asks.

I smile down at her while caressing her back. "Yes, really, and let me tell you, Kay, you felt amazing. Incredible."

She places her chin on my chest. "Well, until last night, I'd never done it without a condom either."

My territorial, thrilled-to-hear-this meter goes up another notch. And all of this is nice to know—important, of course—but not nearly as monumental as our most important shared first: neither of us has ever been in love before.

We talk about this now.

I guess it shouldn't, but it surprises me to discover all these feelings are just as intense for Kay as they are for me. This love, so powerful and consuming, is so much bigger than the both of us. On this, we agree.

"You're in my soul, Kay," I confess.

My girl covers me with her naked body. She straddles

my hips and leans down to place her hands on my cheeks. "God, I love you," she tells me as she cups my face.

And then I spend the next few minutes reveling in the kisses she showers on my lips, along my jaw, and down my neck. My hands travel down to her ass as I lift my hips off the mattress and press my growing arousal against her sweet spot. I want Kay to feel all my need, all my want, all this crazy fucking love I have for her. My girl presses back, slick and ready against me, letting me feel, in return, all her need, all her want, all the crazy fucking love she has for me.

"Fuck, sweet girl." I push up into her all the way, sheathing my cock. "Does this feel as good to you as it does to me?"

She nods against my neck. Even though I am deep, deep inside her, I remain perfectly still. "Say it, baby, tell me it feels good. I need to hear it. Make it real."

"It is real," she pants out. "It feels amazing, Chase. *You* feel amazing."

She tries to grind down on my dick to create some friction, but I hold her as we are, just letting her feel me in her, as I feel her all around me. *Fuck.*

When I can't take it any longer—this not moving shit—I flip us over, never leaving her. I begin to move slowly as I settle on top. I just want to love Kay easy right now; she's probably a little sore from last night.

"You own me, sweet girl," I whisper as I s-l-o-w-l-y pull out almost all the way.

She gasps and arches up to me, so I ease back in a little. "You own *this*," I tell her.

And since she so fucking does, when she keeps her hips raised, and slides herself down my length so that my cock impales her inch-by-agonizing-inch, I just savor the feel and let her do whatever the fuck she wants. She circles her hips and fucks me till she's gasping and crying out my name. But when I see she's about to tumble—she looks so damn close—I know I can't let her fall until I tell her one more thing.

I place her hand over my heart and catch her gaze. While I am pushing inside her as fully as possible, I tell this woman I love so fucking much what is more important than even our joined bodies. "Baby, you own my heart, and it's yours forever."

The morning is pretty well shot by the time Kay and I finally leave my bed. Both of us were so wrapped up in each other we forgot today is Sunday. And that means we forgot about Mass.

"How pissed do you think Father Maridale will be once he realizes we both skipped Mass?" I ask Kay after we're showered and dressed and just hanging out, rocking lazily on the swing out on the back porch. "I think he's going to figure we're together."

She shrugs her shoulders, pulls her legs up to her chest, and adjusts her jeans shorts. "It's our business what we do, Chase."

"I don't know about that," I retort with a chuckle.

I then tell her how Father Maridale warned me not to hurt her. "I'm sure that meant I wasn't supposed to get involved with you," I add.

My girl does not appear happy to hear this. "I can make my own decisions," she snaps.

Her lips set, and she stares out over the land, which is vibrant green and kind of sparkly under today's exceptionally blue and sunny sky.

My girl bites her lip. Quietly, she asks, "Is that why you said you were 'trouble' the day we first kissed?"

I stop the swing's lazy movement and turn to my girl. "What I said had nothing to do with Father Maridale. I mean, I tried to respect his wishes."

I run my hand through my hair, take a breath, then cup sweet girl's chin so she'll look at me and see how serious I am about this. "I love you, Kay, but the trouble part I talked about is true. It's not that I *was* trouble; I *am* trouble, baby girl. I'll never really be right."

Her hand rests on my back, right about where feathers that will never stop falling lie hidden beneath the T-shirt I'm wearing.

"I am broken, remember?" I reach back and press her hand to the falling feathers, the broken wings. "I may be healing, but I will never be whole."

"You'd never hurt me," she whispers, her hand sliding up to where the ink angel is kneeling.

God, I hope not, I think. But to Kay, I just nod…and pray she's right.

We sit back and I resume rocking for a while longer. Kay tells me she plans to go to the cemetery, but not until evening. I half-expect her to ask me to join her, which I'd do in a heartbeat. But though she hesitates and chews her lip in what I guess is contemplation, the invitation never comes.

I suspect her reticence has to do with the secret she's been trying to share with me. I don't care what it is; it won't change my feelings for her. But she sure seems to believe it might. When she tried to tell me yesterday morning, and I sensed she literally wasn't able to, it just about broke my heart. But her secret has to do with what happened the night her sister died, and that kind of shit runs deep. Her mother turning her back on my girl sure didn't help matters.

Damn, I'd like to have a nice, long talk with that mother of hers, the coldhearted woman who abandoned my girl at her most vulnerable time. No wonder Kay can't find her words, she obviously fears I'll turn my back on her too. Never, *never*. I'll always be here for my sweet girl, no matter what the fuck has happened in her past.

Now that the subject of Sarah has come up, Kay looks down and out. It's such a beautiful day, though, and it'd be a waste to allow despondency to prevail.

I feel like we need to do something that will cheer Kay up, so I throw out, "Hey, would you want to go fishing today?"

My girl's eyes light up. "Yeah, that sounds like fun." She smiles slyly. "Besides, I believe we still have a bet, mister."

Oh, shit. Not the wager that would require me to sit in the front of the church between Missy and Kay if I don't catch more fish than my girl. That is so not happening.

I scramble. "Well, I think that bet is off, babe. You're already living on my property, and that's what I was going to ask for when I won, remember?"

My girl pokes me in the arm and laughs. "When, not if? Aren't you the confident one? You're that sure you'll win, eh?"

I nod, and she frowns. "Hey, there's a very good chance I might actually catch more fish than you, you know. And that, my friend, would result in a victory for me." She gives me a *take-that* expression. "I haven't gotten what I want yet, Chase."

"All right, all right," I concede. But the whole time I'm acting all nonchalant with Kay I am telling myself I damn well better win this stupid-ass bet.

A half an hour later we're down at the creek on my property. Kay's sitting on one of the banks, clad in the tank top and jean shorts she had on earlier. She's holding her pole, while I bait the hook.

"I knew you were going to freak out over the worms," I say, quirking an eyebrow as I glance up at her.

"It's not that I'm afraid of them, Chase. I just feel bad impaling them like that." She glances distastefully to the end of the line, where I've done exactly that to one of the slippery buggers.

I laugh. "Oh, sweet girl, pitying earthworms." I shake my head and kiss her cheek, before I sit back down and pick up my own pole.

"Do you think we'll catch anything?" she asks.

I shoot her a sidelong glance. "It usually takes more than a minute."

"Smart ass," she mumbles.

Another few seconds pass, and restless girl says, "I've always heard it's best to fish early in the morning. Isn't this kind of late? It's after two."

"That would have been ideal," I agree. "But we were too busy fu—uh, we were preoccupied this morning, remember?"

Kay blushes. "Yeah, we sure were."

Baby girl's cheeks are so red I have to turn my head to keep from laughing. What I wouldn't give to know what part of what we did this morning she's thinking about right now. Hopefully, all of it. I sure can't forget a single moment. In fact, I soon realize I'd better direct my thoughts elsewhere, as I am starting to sport a rod that has nothing to do with fishing. I shift, adjust myself, and concentrate on the scenery.

It's pretty down here by the creek. The banks are grassy and there are wildflowers up along the crests. The tall trees in the surrounding area provide a fair amount of shade where we're sitting, but the sun is still shining brightly through the canopy of leaves above us.

I suddenly remember that I slipped the sunglasses I bought for Kay yesterday—the ones like the junkie destroyed—into the pocket of my jeans before we left the house. When I see my girl shielding her eyes with her hand, I figure the time is right to give them to her.

I take the sunglasses from my pocket and hold them out to my girl. "Shades?" I lift an eyebrow.

Kay glances down at what I'm holding and her caramels widen. "Oh my God, Chase, you bought me new sunglasses." She takes her new faux-designer eyewear from my hand and holds them up. "They look exactly like the ones that jerk destroyed."

"Yeah, I remembered you saying the day we met that you bought the pair I fixed at the dollar store up by Agway. I was up there yesterday, getting some of the stuff for your surprise, so I figured I'd stop in and buy you a new pair."

My girl slips on her new shades and smiles over at me, looking quite cute and beautiful. "Thank you," she mouths.

I kiss her cheek, and whisper against her skin, "You're quite welcome."

"You're too sweet to me," she says when I lean back, like maybe she doesn't deserve this gesture. But she so very much does.

Over the next hour or so we catch a few fish. They're all bluegills though, so we throw them all back in. Overall, when we add up everything, we determine I caught one more fish than Kay, so I win the bet. *Thank-fucking-Jesus.*

Kay tells me to choose a new prize, since she already lives in my apartment. I say just a kiss will do. But one kiss leads to another, and then another, until we end up making out on the bank by the creek for the next thirty minutes. Not that I am complaining.

Later that evening, after Kay leaves for the church cemetery, I go out to the back porch, sit down on the swing that Kay and I were rocking in this morning, and call my brother.

Soon as he answers, Will thanks me for the money.

"What did you need it for?" I cautiously ask. I'm still worried he used it for something illegal.

And that worry is just about confirmed when my brother doesn't answer. "Will?"

"What?" he mumbles, sounding put out.

"Don't be fucking stupid," I warn.

He pauses, and then breathes out one long steady breath. "Everything is cool, okay? I am not being stupid."

I have no choice but to accept his answer at face value. I am too far away to do anything else. I change the subject to something positive, the artwork he e-mailed me. I tell him how fucking fantastic it is, and add that I think he has the talent to eventually get his comic book published.

Will tries to play it off, but I can tell he's pleased. I hear it in his voice when he gives me an enthusiastic, detailed summary of his apocalyptic-Vegas story line.

"I'm thinking about adding zombies," he says excitedly. "Zombies are big right now. What do you think, Chase?"

Some invisible string tugs at my heart. It moves me to hear my little brother say my name like that, like he used to, like he did when he looked up to me—once upon a time, a lifetime ago. Maybe there really is hope in believing I can fully rebuild this relationship with my brother.

What I really want right now is to tell Will how much I still love him, and how fucking sorry I am for ever having let him down. There are a hundred more still-unsaid things I wish I could blurt out, but it's too soon to start up with shit like that. I don't want my brother to freak and shut me out again, so I just take a deep breath and say, "I think zombies are a great idea, Will."

We talk a few more minutes, then my brother says he has to go, his ride is due to pick him up. "I don't want to keep her waiting," he tells me, "so I'll just talk to you—"

"Whoa, hold up," I cut in. "Her?" I can't help but slip into older-brother-teasing mode. Plus, I am curious. "And this girl drives? Are we dating an older woman, little bro? Have to say, kid, I am impressed."

Will laughs, and says all sheepishly, "She's only a year older, Chase. In fact, she just got her license a couple of weeks ago." He pauses, then adds excitedly, "Oh, yeah, and get this, her mom already bought her a car, a pretty sweet one too."

I don't really care about the car, but I do ask, "Does *she* have a name?"

"Yeah, her name is Cassie." Will is silent for a beat.

When he does speak again, it's in this softer tone, and I sense right away this Cassie-girl is important to my brother. "I like hanging out with her, Chase. She's...I don't know...I guess she's just different from most girls my age." He sighs. "Her life's not all that great, either. I mean, her mom has an important job and makes lots of money, but she's gone a lot for work. She got remarried a few months ago, so Cassie's got a stepdad now. He's home a lot, but he's a real piece of shit." Will's tone sounds angry, but then turns bereft when he adds, "Cassie lost her real dad a few years ago. Just like us, Chase."

There's a lump in my throat, hearing the pain in my brother's voice. He's growing up and needs a father, now more than ever. There's no one out there in Vegas to guide this kid. My mom is too wrapped up in her own shit—as usual. And Greg is okay and all, but Will is not his son. I know for a fact he hasn't made a single move to officially adopt my brother.

I think about the dream I had weeks ago, the one where my dad told me to take care of Will. But how can I take care of him when he's thousands of miles away? My life is here, and his is there. *Fuck.*

"Sounds like you're good for each other," I say, at last, to Will. "Maybe someday I'll get to meet this girl of yours. I'd really like that."

Will replies, "Yeah, I'd like that too. Cassie...she...I don't know, she reminds me of us. Except it's harder for her, I guess, being a girl and all. Mom had boyfriends but it's not like we ever had to deal with..." He trails off.

I sense my brother might be about to tell me something more, but just then I hear a horn beeping in the background on his end. He tells me Cassie is there and he has to go. I say good-bye and we disconnect.

While I wait for Kay to return, I push the swing back and forth with my foot. I think about how my life is changing, how so many things are coming together. I'm with Kay now, and we're so fucking in love it's crazy. Work at the church is going well, and I am finally making strides with my brother. We're slowly rebuilding something I so recklessly destroyed.

The swing creaks beneath me as it sways.

In some ways, it's almost like things are going *too* smoothly. This isn't the way my life generally progresses. I am not one of those lucky people whose dreams all come true and everything turns out fucking peachy.

But shit is good, I tell myself. *You can't deny that.*

It's true; shit is good, so fucking good. But damn if I can't shake the feeling that it's all about to hit the fan.

CHAPTER FOURTEEN

KAY

The week starts out great. Chase and I talk with Father Maridale early Monday morning in his office, though we give him the abridged version of what happened to me in my apartment parking lot Friday night. It's still enough detail to give context to why I'm now renting Chase's apartment.

To my surprise—and relief—Father takes the news rather well. Chase makes it obvious we're involved, he holds my hand reassuringly the whole time we talk. But instead of being angry, Father Maridale just smiles resignedly. "Just make each other happy," he tells us.

I always suspected the priest who leads our congregation is more hip and cool than he lets on, especially for a clergyman, and this absolutely proves it. "I expect you to be good to each other," he adds before we leave. "You've both known pain, but now you have a chance to see there can be joy in life as well."

I don't say anything, since we're halfway out the door (and need to get back to work), but if I get another chance I plan to tell Father that Chase Gartner is very good to me, too good perhaps. There's still this part of me that doesn't feel as if I deserve all the love Chase showers on me. Maybe I'll feel more deserving once he knows my dark secret. I keep trying to tell him, I do, but I physically can't. He has no idea how close I almost came to blurting it out yesterday when we first arrived at the creek to fish. But as I opened my mouth, ready to pour forth the truth, I literally could *not* do it. It was like the words were stuck, stuck in my throat, stuck in my past, anchoring me to silence.

Chase was turned away, messing with the lines, but I did get out one unintelligible word. When he turned back to me with one eyebrow raised, I couldn't say anything more. I couldn't tell him face-to-face like that why I blame myself for what happened to Sarah, so I waved it off and pretended I was clearing my throat.

I have to figure something out, though, some way to share what I have buried in the deep recesses of my soul. Keeping my secret is wearing me down, making me feel as if Chase's love could eventually slip away. This love we've created demands honesty, secrets will only hasten its demise.

Burdened with these thoughts, I find the workday tending to drag after our meeting with Father Maridale. Everyone else is bustling about, getting ready for the Fourth of July carnival to start while I'm stuck in the office. Chase is busy, outside on the grounds, helping the temporary workers who've been brought in to set up all the rides and stands.

But I am far from forgotten when it comes to my boy. Chase texts me randomly throughout the day, keeping me amused, and bringing a silly grin to my face every time I hear a new alert.

His first text reads: *Thinking about when you (literally) ran into me in the parking lot...*

Oh, what about it? I text back.

I should have grabbed you up in my arms that day, baby girl.

I reply, *You kind of did.*

Yeah, but I didn't take a chance and kiss you. And I so should have.

Those words make me sigh, and smile, and sigh again.

Ten minutes later...

Remember the day I fixed your ponytail? Put that tie-thing back in your hair?

Before I can even respond there's this: *I wanted to kiss you so fucking much, Kay. And when you hiked up your dress, shit, I wanted to go to you and hike it even higher.*

I blush, I love his words. I send a wink back to him.

Remember the first night you came over? Chase continues twenty minutes later.

Yes.

I should have kissed you then, girl.

You should have, boy.

I'll make up for it tonight, I promise. I'm not stopping until I've kissed you everywhere.

I fumble the phone in my hands, squirm in my chair. My boy is best when he's sexy and playful like this.

I have to bake tonight, you know, I remind him.

Oh, cookie dough, huh? You're giving me ideas...

And just then damn Missy rushes into the office and I hurriedly hide my phone.

"I'm just here for a minute," she says in a whirlwind, waving her hand. "No need to stop what you're doing. You're still making cookies for the sale, yeah?" I nod. "Good, I'll need them by tomorrow morning."

"No problem, I figured as much. I'm baking tonight."

"Perfect!" Missy smiles, turns, and is soon halfway to the door. "We'll talk later, Kay," she calls out over her shoulder. "Busy, busy, you know." And just as quickly as she came in, she is gone.

The fact that the only topic discussed was cookies lets me know Missy has not yet been enlightened to my change in living accommodations. Just as well, I am not in the mood for her disapproving looks and disparaging comments regarding Chase. He claims he's never slept with her, but there's something nagging me regarding this whole odd situation. Unfortunately, I don't have time to think about it for long, a bunch of business calls start to come in and it's back to work until five o'clock.

That evening, while I'm mixing and stirring in the kitchenette of my new apartment, Chase stops by to check on my progress. And to test out some freshly baked snickerdoodle cookies, of course. I remembered to invite him over via text before the end of the workday.

After my handsome boyfriend gives me a peck on my flour-streaked cheek, I tell him how much I love the oven he never got around to using. He watches as I transfer a tray of cookies from the oven to a cooling rack atop the breakfast bar. Chase sits down on one of the stools on the other side of the counter. He says he's glad someone is finally using all these never-before-used appliances and bakeware, and then he reaches for one of the still-hot cookies.

I playfully swat his hand away. "Not those, they're too hot to eat."

I hand him one of the cooled-down cookies from a different rack. "Here, try this one."

He bites into the cookie and immediately slows his chewing. "Mmm," he mumbles. "Damn, these are good." He steals another. "Like, exceptionally good."

"Thank you," I say, beaming with pride that my boy likes my baking.

While I open the oven and put in another batch, I ask Chase, "So, what's your favorite kind of cookie? I'll make them for you sometime."

Chase pilfers another snickerdoodle, holds it aloft, and ponders. "Well, I've always liked chocolate-chip, but I'm thinking these may be my new favorite." He finishes his newly christened "favorite" cookie in two bites.

I laugh. "I'm glad you like those, but I'll still make you some chocolate chip cookies sometime soon."

"You're too good to me, sweet girl," he tells me as he steals two more snickerdoodles.

"Well, you're even sweeter to me, so I guess we're even," I retort.

Before he can reply, and get us into a debate as to who is sweeter to whom, I stuff another cookie in his mouth.

We laugh and the fun continues. Chase stays late and helps me finish my baking project. Well, he helps some. What he mostly does is devour cookies, making me thankful I baked plenty extra. By the time we're finished it's really late. We're too exhausted to start anything physical, so we put the cookie dough-sexy times on hold. But Chase stays the night, holding me close, in an apartment filled with the aroma of freshly baked cookies.

To me, it smells like home.

The next night Chase and I are on our way to the carnival. My boy is driving, and I'm in the passenger seat. Tonight is the first night of festivities down at the church, and I suspect if it's going to be anything like last year's opening the grounds will be packed. A thought regarding the cookies I dropped off this morning passes through my mind. Missy told me to stop by the bake sale stand this evening so she can update me on the early sales of my snickerdoodles.

As Chase rounds a curve in the road, I glance over. "Do you mind if we stop by the bake sale stand at some point? I'd like to see how my cookies are selling."

"Okay," he answers slowly, frowning.

It's clear Chase is not too thrilled with the idea. But what would it matter to him? Something is off.

"Is there some reason why you don't want to stop by that particular stand?" I cautiously venture.

Chase places his hand on my jean-clad leg and gives me a sidelong glance. "No, it's not that, baby. I was just thinking about something else, something to do with work."

Hmm, sure, I think. But I let it slide, for now.

The carnival is hopping. The church grounds, bathed in bright and colorful lights, appear as they do no other time of the year, except for Christmas. Amusement rides spin and twirl, as the aromas of fried corn dogs and freshly-spun cotton candy permeate the thick, summer air. One of the many game stands lights up and bells go off as someone wins a huge stuffed toy.

Chase and I walk around, hand-in-hand, enjoying it all. We receive a few disapproving stares, but there are a couple of smiles as well. That's good enough for now. This town will just have to get used to the fact that its good girl is in love with its resident bad boy. I glance up at the gorgeous man by my side. Gunmetal blues, pouty full lips, a body he sure knows how to use. Jeez, could I get any luckier? I squeeze his hand.

"What?" he asks as he catches my gaze.

"Nothing, I just love you, that's all."

He leans down and kisses my cheek, murmurs sweet things in my ear. I melt as I always do. Chase Gartner has conquered me thoroughly. I'd just about die for this man.

When he straightens, he says, "Hey, did I ever tell you about the time my parents took me to a carnival like this. And my dad bought me a red balloon I was convinced was magical?"

I don't think I've heard this story, so I reply, "No, you never told me that one."

As we walk past the fishing pond game and a stand selling kettle corn, my boy tells me his story.

"I was probably about four or five. We still lived here, I remember that. And Will hadn't been born yet. Anyway, there was a stand selling balloons, kind of like that one up ahead." He points to a stand where big balloons of every color imaginable are affixed to the sides and the front. A few of the largest balloons flutter in the light breeze.

"Just like that stand, this one had tons of balloons, in lots of colors. But there was only one red one." Chase shakes his head and chuckles a little. "For some crazy reason, I was convinced the red one—since it was the only one, I guess— was special. I thought it was filled with magic, instead of just air, so, I begged my dad to buy it for me."

We slow by a spinning ride. Orange, pink, and yellow lights flash around us as I ask, "Did he get it for you?"

Chase nods, but it's a slow nod, like my boy is far away

now, back in time, lost in this memory. "Yeah, yeah, he did," he murmurs.

I bump his arm with my shoulder. "So...was it?"

"Was it what?"

"A balloon filled with magic," I tease.

We walk a little farther, past the stand selling balloons. Chase glances at the red ones, but we keep moving.

"I don't know," he finally says. "I never found out. I let it go and it drifted up into the sky."

I am about to tease him about losing his balloon, but then I notice the expression on his face. He looks sad and forlorn. "What? What's wrong, Chase?"

He shakes his head, raises my hand to his lips and places the softest of kisses on my fingers. "Nothing, sweet Kay, nothing is wrong. It's just that I remember my mom telling me to hold the string tightly, to not let it go for anything. She said if I let go, then my balloon would drift away. She was right obviously, that's exactly what happened."

"Is that why you let it go? Because of what she told you?" I ask, thinking maybe he was a kid just testing out the validity of what he'd been told.

But Chase shakes his head no.

I can't understand why this memory would bother Chase so much. I mean, little kids lose their balloons like that all the time. I recall losing a few of my own the same way.

But then Chase explains. "See, I did it on purpose, Kay. I *let* the string go. But not because of what my mother said. I just didn't want the red balloon, after all." He presses his lips together. "I guess I knew that balloon wasn't really filled with magic. I remember telling myself that if I let it go, then I'd never have to find out the truth. The illusion would remain. I could keep on pretending. That's why I let that damn red balloon go."

It's kind of a sad story, and Chase appears disheartened. I suddenly have an idea. I decide when I next go to the ladies room I'll buy Chase a new red balloon and surprise him with it. Maybe it can be my way to show my boy magic *does* exist. Not in the balloon, of course, but in his heart and mine. This love we carry for one another feels magical, that's for certain. And buying Chase a red balloon will be symbolic, something tangible to express my point.

After we share a corn dog, a funnel cake, and a soft drink, Chase and I finally make our way to the bake stand to check up on my cookies. Missy sees us coming and bristles a bit. She and Chase barely make eye contact. I look from one to the other questioningly, but neither says a word. *Whatever.*

While Chase pretends to be very interested in a pineapple upside-down cake that's for sale—a type of cake I know for a fact he dislikes—I ask Missy how the snickerdoodles have been selling.

"They're all gone, Kay. We sold every dozen."

She gives me a tight, but genuine smile, and I exclaim, "That's great!"

Chase smiles uneasily and asks me if I'm ready to go. I am, but after all the soda, I really have to run to the ladies' room first. Both look dismayed when I make this announcement. Nonetheless, I leave Chase with Missy, and hustle down to the facilities.

Good, maybe those two can finally work out whatever silly differences they obviously have with one another. It couldn't be anything all that important, right?

After I finish up in the ladies' room, I stop at the stand selling balloons and buy the biggest red one they have. On the way back, I take a path that runs behind the stands so Chase won't see the balloon I bought him until the last minute. I walk quickly, trying to keep the helium-filled balloon down by my side and out of sight. But, as I approach the bake sale stand, I slow considerably. Only because I hear Chase and Missy's hushed voices, and it sounds as if they're arguing.

I creep closer, hidden by the tarp covering the back of the bake sale stand. And that is when I hear Missy hiss, "You don't have to be so rude to me every time you see me, Chase. I mean, after all, it's not like we're strangers. You sure weren't pushing me away that night at the Anchor Inn when you were making me come...or when I was giving you head."

What?

"What?" I speak my thought out loud as I come out from behind the stand.

Missy stares at me like a deer caught in headlights. And Chase? Well, guilt is written all over my lying boy's face. He may not have fucked her, but it would have been nice to know he's obviously touched Missy Metzger...intimately. And I definitely would have appreciated being told Missy has her hands—and mouth apparently—on my man.

I clench the string wrapped around my fingers and the red balloon jerks to the left and to the right. Chase sees what I have. He knows the balloon is for him, he knows it's supposed to mean something. *So much for magic,* I despondently think.

Chase looks guiltier than ever as he closes his eyes and swears.

"Is it true?" I ask my so-busted boyfriend, even though I know the answer.

"It's true," he mutters, hanging his head in—I guess—shame.

I shake my head and frown. I just knew this was all too good to last, I can never hold on to anything special.

With that thought in mind, I turn away from the man who's the best friend I've ever had and, more importantly, the love of my life.

I don't look back to see his reaction as I release the red balloon into the black nighttime sky.

CHAPTER FIFTEEN
CHASE

I watch as the second red carnival-bought balloon in my life disappears into the night sky.

Fucking Missy and her big-fucking mouth. Speaking of which, she's yapping something right now, an apology.

"Little late for that," I say as I walk away and go after my girl.

Kay can't go far, I drove. Sure enough, when I approach I see her standing by my truck with her arms crossed. "Get away from me," she says when I reach her.

Sweet girl is too kind to pack her words with the kind of venom she's probably feeling right now, so her words come out more strained than threatening. I resist the urge to smile. Even angry my girl is adorable.

"Kay, it happened before I met you." I try to brush her hair from her shoulder, but she smacks my hand away. Harder than her usual playful smacks, the claws are definitely out.

"I don't care when it happened," she retorts angrily. "You should have told me. I've hung out with Missy, sat with her in church, all while having no clue. Dammit, Chase, I even went to the stupid Anchor Inn with her." Kay flails her hand. "And that's like the scene of the crime or something. Not knowing she's had her hands on you makes me look like a fool. I have a right to know that my friend blew my boyfriend."

When Kay puts it like that I can see her point. I should have told her a long time ago. And I planned to, I just never got around to following through. But, shit, we're always honest—and we've shared our sexual histories—so it was stupid of me to leave out what happened with Missy.

I apologize, since it's all I can do now.

My girl is still steaming. She's silent as she reluctantly gets in the truck. On the way back to the house, she makes me tell her exactly what happened that night at the Anchor Inn. I see her cringe and grip the seat like she'd probably grip Missy's neck if she were in the truck with us right now. "It meant nothing," I emphatically state.

Sweet girl softens up a tad, she sighs. "It's just…"

"What?" I ask. "Tell me what you're thinking."

Kay wipes some dust away from the dashboard. "It just bothers me, Chase, that she's been intimate with you. I know there are a lot of women in your past, but this was recent. And that kind of intimacy just feels like it belongs to us now, like it's something special, something that's just ours."

I put my hand on her knee, and surprisingly she lets me keep it there. "It is, baby girl, it is ours." I hesitate, gather my words, and try to explain. "What happened between me and Missy wasn't intimacy. We were just mindlessly fulfilling base needs." Kay winces and I hurriedly add, "What I'm saying is that it was meaningless. There's no comparison between the things you and I do and what happened with that girl. I love you, Kay, and the things I do to you—the things I do *with* you—every single one of them involves my heart. You own me, sweet girl. I told you that before, and it's true."

Kay mulls my words over and allows my hand to remain. I see this as a start.

She lets out a puff of air and shakes her head. "Is that it, then?" she asks. "No other women since you've been out of prison?"

"Just you, baby."

Kay huffs. "What about that night, at the Anchor Inn? Anything else I should know?"

I think about the coke and how I wanted to use that night. I need to share this with my girl too. She deserves to know all my bad, including the demons I still battle. So I tell her how very much I craved cocaine when I found out Missy had some in her purse. I admit I wanted a line...or two, and that I came dangerously close to asking Missy for some.

"But you didn't do it, so that's good, right?"

Baby girl appears so hopeful. She's always trying to find the bright side of a situation when it comes to me, no matter how fucked up that situation may be, yet another reason why I need to stay clean.

But my girl needs to know how close I came, so I am truthful. "No, I didn't use, that's true. But I wanted to, Kay. I wanted to...like, a lot."

"What stopped you, then?" she whispers.

I remove my hand from her leg and scrub it down my face. "I thought about how drugs overtook my life before. And the possibility of starting down that path again kept me straight. At least, it did that night." In an effort to put things in perspective for her, I add, "I can't promise I'll always be that strong, Kay. I intend to keep trying, but I may one day falter. You should know that, okay?"

Kay just nods and peers down at the hands she has clasped in her lap.

The rest of the ride is quiet and neither of us says much more. When we reach the farmhouse my girl tells me she's going to sleep up in her apartment…alone. I expected as much. It will take more time than the short ride from the church for Kay to forgive me for keeping her in the dark about Missy.

That's okay, I can be patient. I'll wait forever for my girl if that's what it takes for her to absolve me of my sin.

The next day I see very little of Kay. She leaves for work before I do, and when I text her, asking what time she wants to meet for lunch, she responds back to go ahead without her, she's eating in today.

It's pretty obvious my still-angry girl doesn't care to see me this afternoon. And who can blame her? I did something stupid that night, but worse, I kept it a secret. Not sharing it with Kay was a mistake I'm now paying for.

When it's time to leave, I catch up to Kay as she's settling into her car.

"Hey," I call out.

She turns her head away and snaps her seatbelt into place.

"Are we not talking now?" I ask, placing my hand on the top of the door so she can't close it and shut me out completely.

Kay avoids my gaze and stares at the steering wheel. "No, we're talking."

I had originally planned on doing something nice for Kay this upcoming weekend—setting up my grandmother's old record player out on the back porch and finding some classic ballad-type songs, so we could dance under the stars at night. But I'm thinking now that maybe I should move my plan up to tonight. The best thing for me and my girl is to get back to having fun. Even though it's looking like sweet girl won't be getting near me anytime soon. I still have to try.

"Why don't you come over tonight?" I throw out. "We can listen to old records out on the back porch. Maybe dance under the stars?"

Kay glances up and I raise an eyebrow. She sort of scoffs and tries to close her door, but my hand is still holding it open. "Chase…please." She sounds exasperated.

"Fine," I breathe out. I move my hand and take a step back.

Kay gives me no answer—not that I deserve one. She just slams the car door and drives away.

A few hours later, darkness has fallen and I am out on my back porch, alone, drinking a cold beer. I lie sprawled across the porch swing, one foot up and the other keeping the creaky swing rocking. Music plays from the old record player I did indeed drag out to the back porch. The hope is to lure Kay over from her apartment, and I am thinking this loud Led Zeppelin song just may do the trick.

Jimmy Page is jamming on his guitar as I glance over

at the apartment above the garage. Kay is definitely home, the lights inside burn brightly. I take a swig from the bottle. Mad-at-me girl surely hears this music. Any louder and it's sure to be heard all the way down at the church. Well, that may be an exaggeration, but still.

Damn, my hope that Kay would change her mind and join me is diminishing. I finish my beer, sigh, and slide the empty bottle under the swing. Sitting upright I begin to sort through the pile of old albums I brought out with the record player. I'm in the mood for something melodic, something that better fits how I am feeling.

At last I find what I want, a great Motown tune I remember hearing my grandmother play often. *Maybe this was her album, not Dad's,* I consider, album in hand. In any case, I slide vinyl from the cover and swap out Led Zeppelin for some Otis Redding.

The opening chords of "My Lover's Prayer" fill the air. I remain at the turntable, where I'm standing. I close my eyes and listen to the opening verse. As I do, I hear someone say my name. I spin around and discover Kay has made her way over, after all.

I can't suppress my smile, but I don't utter a word. I just go down the wooden steps and hold out my hand to the beautiful woman I love so much.

Kay slips her hand in mine and I tentatively draw her near. I try to assess her expression, but have no luck figuring much of anything out. My girl's face gives nothing away. "Am I forgiven?" I venture.

She bites her lip. "Yeah, you're forgiven." She touches her forehead to my chest.

My arms instinctively wrap around her, but I'm careful

to hold her like she's made of eggshells. Kay has come to me, willing to give me another chance. I sure don't want to fuck it up by overreacting.

Otis croons out the next verse, and I ask Kay if she'd like to dance. Sweet girl nods and places her hands at my shoulders. We begin to move slowly, just kind of easy swaying. My girl tenses at first, but by the middle of the song she's relaxed into me.

"I'm so sorry, baby," I whisper into her hair. "It kills me to see you hurting, to know I disappointed you. I should have come clean with you a long time ago."

It's all true, but I don't add that I just *knew* my ass would do something stupid like what I did. Hell, we're only a little bit into this new relationship—this change from friendship to love—and already my troubled past is causing us grief. My omission of fact was as bad as lying, I realize that now.

I start to say more—I'll fucking grovel if I have to—but Kay shushes me. "Let's not talk about it anymore," she says, leaning back just far enough so our eyes can meet. "You're forgiven, Chase. Just dance with me, okay?"

So, I do. I wrap my arms tightly around my girl, no more eggshell-careful hold. "I love you," I tell her, pressing our bodies close as the song continues.

We move and sway, move and sway. At one point, I spin her out, and on the return, I dip her down low. Kay giggles and tilts her head back. I lower my face to hers, my lips touching her mouth, carefully, cautiously, asking for permission.

My girl grabs my hair in her little grasp, pulls me as close as possible, and smashes her lips to mine.

Permission granted.

CHAPTER SIXTEEN

KAY

I forgive Chase for his lie, his omission of fact, whatever. It doesn't matter. Like he said, what happened with Missy occurred before I even met him. And I already know Chase is no saint. He's trouble, just like he warned that day by the lockers.

But as we dip and sway under the starry sky, slow dancing to old Motown music, I realize keeping my own terrible secret for much longer will have worse repercussions. It will undoubtedly do more damage to this relationship than one stupid, kept-from-me blow job.

So when Chase spins and dips me, and goes in for the kiss, I grab hold of his hair and smash my lips to his like he's holding the air I need to breathe. Sometimes, metaphorically speaking, I think he may be. Chase has brought me to life and given me reason. He sustains me, which is why the next words out of my mouth take every ounce of strength and courage I can muster.

The kiss tapers, and, as we right ourselves, I hurriedly say, "We have to talk."

The song ends and my concerned boy steps back, but his hands remain on my waist. It reminds me of the day I wrecked into him, the first time this man ever touched me, the beginning.

"I have to tell you what I haven't been able to, Chase. You deserve to know the truth of what happened the last night Sarah was alive. It's killing me to keep it from you, to keep it bottled up inside."

Chase starts to say something, but I put my hand up in the space between us. "I know," I rasp, "I *know* you said it doesn't matter, but it does." I take a ragged breath. "If anything, just look at the grief one small secret caused. And this secret, Chase, this secret I'm keeping is so much bigger—" A choked sob escapes me, interrupting my speech.

My boy draws me back into his strong arms and tries to soothe me. "Hey, hey, sweet girl, it's okay." I feel him kiss the top of my head. "There's no rush. If you really need to tell me, that's fine, but it doesn't have to be tonight."

I pull back. "Yes, it does. I have to get this out." I pause, and then whisper, "I just don't know if I physically can."

Chase presses his lips together and watches me for a beat. Then, he leads me up the porch steps and over to the swing. The music has long ended, but the turntable still spins, the needle playing nothing but static. Chase stops and shuts the record player off completely, and then sits down next to me on the swing.

I know I probably look like I'm close to losing it, and I really kind of am. My hands twist together in my lap, and I suck in a few uneven gasps of air. I sense Chase is about to tell me again that whatever horrible secret I am harboring, there is no obligation to share it right now, but I shake my head before he can begin speaking.

"Don't," I choke out. "Just let me do this."

I snatch up his hand and start stroking his fingers to

calm myself. Just this simple physical contact with Chase helps steady me.

"You need to know the truth, Chase, the real story." This gorgeous man, always so supportive, and infinitely patient, nods slowly and waits for me to begin.

I face Chase Gartner. The man who has a tattoo that reads: *As I stand before you, judge me not.* But on this night I am the one who plans to hold a life up—my life—for him to judge. I am the one who intends to spread my sins before him. And though he says he never would, there's no way he won't judge, or have an opinion leaning one way or the other. Will Chase see me as guilty of neglect? Or will he view what happened to my sister as truly just an accident? I steel myself to accept his response, be it good or bad.

And then I get started. Or, more accurately stated, I *try* to get started. But, like before, every time—*every* damn time I attempt to get my words out they catch in my throat. This secret lies deep, buried under years of shame, guilt, and grief. And I can't seem to find the tools I need to dig it out.

So, I start to cry.

"Why can't I tell you?" I sob angrily. My ire is not directed at Chase, but at myself and this inability to come clean.

"What is wrong with me?" I choke out before losing it completely.

Chase gathers me in his arms and rocks me while I weep softly, tears for Sarah, tears for all that's been lost, tears for all my weakness, tears for my irresponsibility. Finally, when I have nothing left, Chase loosens his hold and I sit back.

I place my hand on my chest and take a deep breath, while my attentive boy swipes wet streaks from my cheeks and smoothes back my hair.

I whisper forlornly, "I want to tell you, Chase. And I'm more than ready to tell you. But I don't know *how* to tell you."

Chase appears to consider this quandary we're in.

A beat passes, and then he gently says, "I have an idea, okay? It may not work. But then again, it just might."

"All right," I whisper, willing to try anything at this point.

My boy nods, smiles tightly, and kisses my cheek. He then twists on the swing—the chains creaking in protest—until his back is facing me. I stare at strong, wide shoulders, covered by a taut white tee.

Suddenly, it dawns on me what my boy is doing. Chase has found a solution. Sharing my secret may be less difficult if I don't have to face him directly. My mother's reaction all those years ago has obviously scarred me, but this, this may just work for me.

His cotton tee is worn and thin, so the darker inked portions of the tattoos lying beneath the material are not so hidden.

Hmm…

There may be one more thing we can do to almost guarantee this experiment is successful.

Slowly, I lift the hem at the back of Chase's shirt. He glances over his shoulder to see what I'm up to. My eyes meet his. "May I?" I ask, hem in hand.

Realization dawns in his blues, he knows me well enough that he quickly figures out what I'm trying to do—share my secret with the angel on his back. It seems appropriate. In fact, it feels right. So right that when Chase lifts and tugs his shirt over his head, the words I've been trying to say start to bubble to the surface.

My eyes stay fixed on the angel. The wings, the falling feathers remain in the periphery. But they don't go unnoticed. If Chase's wings are broken, then mine are shattered. Maybe that's why we work so well together, why we have from the very beginning. Some things are meant to be, and Chase and I have been destined from day one. We are two broken people who, when put together, become whole.

I reach out and tentatively touch the angel. A shiver runs down my boy's spine. Finding my voice, at last, I begin my tale, digging it out one detail at a time.

"The night Sarah died I was watching her. You've heard that, and that part is true. But, I wasn't sleeping when she went in the pool."

Chase is still as can be. He's allowing me to speak without interruption. His head stays bowed, his shoulders rising and falling with every breath.

My words are no longer bubbling at the surface, they're boiling over.

"I was upstairs when I heard Sarah screaming. I was in my bedroom...but I wasn't alone." My boy's breathing stutters, but I don't stop. "I was with Doug Wilson. We weren't having sex, but we were getting there. Not because I really wanted to, but because I feared saying no. He came over drunk that night, and even after I told him I was babysitting my sister and he should really go, he still forced his way in."

I don't detail how Doug pushed me aside in the doorway and told me laughingly to "get upstairs and spread 'em." If I share that tidbit with Chase, he will undoubtedly find Doug Wilson and fuck him up thoroughly. And though a part of me would relish seeing my ex brought to his knees, I have enough on my conscience these days. Like how I didn't stop Chase from hurting the junkie who hurt me. In fact, I encouraged it, counted on it. Chase's sin belongs to me. I have no doubt the junkie had to be hospitalized, and I condoned it all. But I shake these thoughts off, for now, and skip to the next part of the story.

"Remember how I told you Doug used to use my fear of upsetting my mother against me?" I pause long enough for Chase to nod once. "Well, that night was no exception. Doug threatened to break up with me and tell my mom I was to blame if I didn't just shut up and let him stay. That's why I was afraid to kick him out. Not that I really could have anyway. But still…"

I take a breath, and stare at the profile of the angel's bowed head. "Doug finished the can of beer he'd brought with him, then went into the kitchen and grabbed one of my dad's beers out of the fridge. Sarah was on the sofa watching television, and I remember her looking at me like she was wondering why I was letting this rude kid do these things. Her expression steeled my resolve, at least briefly, and I actually had the courage to ask Doug to leave. I told him I'd been watching a movie with Sarah and we wanted to get back to it." I pause, let out a harsh breath. This is still hard, but I go on, "I can hear Doug's response, still. He laughed and said, 'She can watch a movie without you, Kay, you're not that important.'"

Chase stiffens and I am imminently grateful I left out the part where Doug called me a "dumb slut" and said I was good for one thing only.

"Anyway, I went upstairs to use the bathroom—and really just to get away from that asshole for a minute. I was hoping maybe I'd think of a way to get him out of the house, but when I started back down the stairs, Doug was coming up."

I tell Chase how Doug blocked my way when I said we shouldn't leave Sarah unattended, and then I tried to get past him. "But Doug backed me up the stairs and into my bedroom. He said a few minutes alone wouldn't kill her." I swallow the lump rising in my throat. "God, he used those exact words, Chase."

I blink back tears and stare at the angel for the next few minutes. Chase doesn't move, he remains as still as a statue. I know he's waiting for me to continue—and I plan to—but a part of me wishes I could see my love's face right now so I could discern what he's thinking. We're getting to the hard part though, and I fear my words will fail me again if I take a chance and ask Chase to turn around. So, for now, I ask for nothing.

"I didn't stop him, Chase," I grind out, the angel blurring through my tears. "I was weak and afraid. I figured he was probably right. Sarah would be fine for a few minutes. I wracked my brain while Doug was pushing me down onto the bed. I was sure I'd locked all the doors, especially the one that led out to the patio...and the pool." I choke up. "But it must not have been locked, after all. I must have forgotten to slide the lock earlier."

At this point, everything rushes back, all the memories, all the feelings.

God, please help.

I break down completely, the floodgates opening. I sob, "My sister slid that door open, she went outside, she either got in or fell into the pool. She couldn't swim though. She couldn't swim, Chase. She couldn't swim. Oh, God"—I am back where I was four years ago—"God, please help, please, please help. Don't let her die, please, God, please."

I am wracked with grief as Chase turns to face me.

"It was my fault." I stare into Chase's eyes and see my pain reflected in gunmetal blue.

He shakes his head, but I continue, "My sister died because I couldn't find the strength to speak up to an asshole I shouldn't have even been dating."

More memories flood me, and I relive them now through my words.

"His hands, God, his hands, they were all over me, Chase, while my sister was outside drowning. And I knew nothing, nothing, not until I finally heard her screams."

My boy is trying to take me in his arms, trying to comfort me, but I'm pushing him away like he's Doug Wilson. "Kay, Kay," he says softly.

"I didn't want him touching me."

I slap at Chase, but he catches my hand. "I know, baby, I know. It's okay. He's not here, it's just me."

I finally still and let my boy hug me. "I'm a horrible person, Chase," I sob into his bare shoulder, "a horrible daughter, and a horrible sister."

"No you're not any of those things. What happened that night was just a terrible, terrible accident." He pauses. "In fact, if anyone carries any blame it's Doug Wilson. He should've never put you in that position."

Doug definitely played a role, but guilt still plagues me.

Chase asks, "What did that fucker do when he saw what had happened?"

I tell him the truth. "Doug ran away."

And that's exactly what happened. Doug Wilson took off.

After I heard Sarah's screams and jumped out of bed—thankfully, still fully clothed—I ran downstairs and out to the back. Doug was on my heels, but he stopped short when he saw me dragging my sister's lifeless body from the water. As I was administering CPR—to no avail—Doug turned and ran. To this day, no one—besides him and me, and my mother after I told her—knows he was there with me that night.

Oh, and now Chase Gartner knows the truth.

After I finish, and my story is laid out before the man I love, I say, "See, you're not the broken one, Chase. I am."

He trails a finger down my tear-soaked cheek. "That's not true, baby."

I catch his hand and squeeze it tightly. "Yes, it is true. I am shattered."

He takes a deep breath. "Then I guess we'll be broken together."

I look at him and shake my head in disbelief. "You don't hate me now? You don't want to run away and leave forever? I wouldn't blame you if you did."

Chase looks as pained as I feel right now. "God, of course not," he says. "I love you, Kay. Nothing changes that."

He takes my face in his hands and kisses my lips with fervor.

I can't believe this man's not turning away, like my mother did four years earlier when she heard the same story. My boy's love is so much truer though. His belief in me is so solid it makes me think maybe I am not to blame for everything that happened that night.

But, just in case, when our lips part, I lay my flayed heart out before me, and say three little words—to Chase, to Sarah, to God, to a mother who's forsaken me, "Please forgive me."

CHAPTER SEVENTEEN
CHASE

"There's nothing to forgive, sweet girl. You're not to blame for what happened."

I tell Kay this, again and again, but she continues to try and stop me. "No—"

I place one finger on her lips and cup her chin in my hand. "Shh…" I shake my head. "There is nothing you can say that will ever convince me you're responsible for what happened to Sarah."

"But I left her alone, Chase," Kay protests. "I didn't protect her."

"That wasn't your fault, baby. I told you, if anything, it's that asshole's fault. He took advantage of your fear of your mother and your fear of him. He forced his way into your house, he wouldn't leave, and he trapped you upstairs. How were you supposed to fight him?"

I get all those words out in what I hope is a soothing voice. But it's far from easy, since what I really feel like doing the entire time I'm speaking and comforting Kay is finding that dick, Doug Wilson, so I can lay him the fuck out. Fucking prick, putting my girl in a position like that—playing on her fears, on her insecurities, all the weaknesses that plagued her back then.

She's so much stronger now, and that's what I tell her. I

know it still tears her up that her mother disowned her after finding out the truth. But I tell Kay it's her mother's loss that she chooses to stay turned away. It's true. That heartless woman's firstborn is a beautiful, kind, and caring woman. Kay is the polar opposite of the heartless bitch who bore her twenty-three years ago. Her mother is only cheating herself by not speaking to the only daughter she has left. Of course, I keep these thoughts to myself, as the last thing I care to do is upset my girl any further.

As the night wears on, we remain on the back porch. My girl curls up and nestles under my arm, her head against my chest, while I keep the swing swaying. After a while, Kay asks me to play more music. I choose a song I've been listening to a lot lately, a song from one of my dad's albums that reminds me of my girl. It's a U2 song, aptly titled "The Sweetest Thing." I share my feelings about this song with Kay and she smiles for the first time since confessing her perceived sin.

That smile is so precious to me, because it's the first step of Kay forgiving herself, which is really all that matters.

The next night, the Fourth of July, we are once again out on the back porch, but things are much more lighthearted. I have Kay laughing and smiling, all due to my sorry attempt at making dinner an hour earlier.

"Okay, so I'll never be a chef on TV," I concede as I lean back against one of the posts.

We are outside getting ready to watch some Independence Day fireworks. Tonight is the last night of the carnival down at the church and their fireworks display is set for nine thirty. I check my cell, five more minutes. And then the black night will be lit up with more than just the blinking fireflies hovering around.

Kay plops down on the swing, a dish of vanilla ice cream in her hand. Yeah, dessert I had no problem with. It was easy, just scoop from the carton and you're done.

"Chase," my girl begins, laughing as she dips her spoon into the ice cream, "the cheese on a grilled cheese sandwich goes in the middle, not on the top."

"I was trying to make it fancy," I explain, defending my culinary faux pas.

This earns me more giggles, and I am so glad I messed up dinner after all. It's worth it to get my girl back to carefree. We've had enough heavy-heartedness the past two days.

A loud boom sounds off in the distance and the fireworks commence. And though they're not exactly close, the fireworks extend high above the tree tops, so we're given a pretty damn good show.

As the first spectacular sprays of color brighten the dark horizon, Kay sets her dish down and comes to stand next to me. I wrap an arm around her shoulder and she leans into me. A huge burst of pink and silver explodes high in the pitch-black sky. The colors sparkle and remain suspended in the air for a few seconds, before shimmering back toward the ground. The next explosion is even bigger—gold, purple, and green light up the sky. And then another firework goes up and bursts into a huge shower of red.

I "ooh" and "aah" like a damn eight-year-old as each pyrotechnic goes off, which elicits soft laughter from the girl under my arm. Without warning, Kay lifts to her tiptoes and kisses my cheek with her warm, soft lips.

When her lips remain, I turn my head so it's my mouth, not my cheek, she's kissing.

"I love you, mmm, so much," she murmurs, her words muffled somewhat by our mouths moving against one another.

I don't bother to say it back, showing is better in this case. So I back baby girl over to the swing until she has no choice but to sit down on it. I kneel before her on the wooden porch slats, and position my body between her knees.

"What are you doing, mischievous boy?" Kay asks, lounging back as I settle between her legs. "I know you're up to something."

"Always," I respond with a wink.

Kay is wearing a dress, one of those sexy, lacy ones I fucking love. So it's with joy that I drag the material up along her legs, slowly. Sweet girl lets out a little gasp, and I hoarsely say, "Watch the fireworks, baby."

Loud booms echo off in the distance, so I know the light show is still going on behind my back. Of course, I plan to do things to Kay that I guarantee will cause her some fireworks of her own. So it's really up to her which display she prefers to view.

When I glance up I see my sexy girl prefers to watch me at the moment. She's biting her lower lip and keeping her caramels on my hands as I slide her panties down her legs. I toss them behind my back. She watches as I kiss a path from the inside of her knee and up the length of her inner thigh. And she's fucking mesmerized when I pick up the dish of ice cream she set down earlier and spoon some onto my tongue. I close my mouth and arch an eyebrow at her as her eyes widen. *That's right, you're going to fucking love this, baby,* my wicked grin hopefully conveys.

I softly touch Kay's oh-so-ready core with my ice-cream-coated tongue, giving sweet girl a dose of very cold and very hot, delivered in one long, languorous lick. Her head lolls back. Baby, who's less shy about sex every time we're together, pushes her pink and swollen against me roughly. I slip my hot and cold tongue inside her and am rewarded with the sexiest moan I think I've ever heard.

And this is just the beginning, I am just getting started.

In fact, eating ice cream right off of Kay's pussy sounds like a delicious plan, so why delay? I'm sure she'll like it too—very sure, in fact—so I scoop up a big spoonful. The ice cream is melting, so I angle the spoon above her swollen sex and drizzle a little sweetness right onto my already-so-sweet girl's little clit. Baby girl gasps as vanilla drips down to where I plan to be very soon. I lap every drop up slowly, teasing, and savoring all the sugary sweetness combined with my sweet fucking girl. I cover her sticky pussy lips with my sticky lips, tasting and nibbling. And when every last bit of vanilla is gone, I circle her clit with my tongue until my girl comes undone for me.

When Kay rasps out she wants me inside her—like right fucking now—my cock is out of my pants in three seconds flat and I slide into heaven. The swing rocks unevenly as I thrust into my girl fast and rough. Kay shifts until she's practically lying down, and I shift with her, still on my knees. I hook my fingers under her right knee and hoist her leg up over my shoulder. This angle allows me to go so deep.

Shit.

My girl must like this new angle too, she's panting and moaning and asking for it harder still. That, I can do. I fuck so hard that the chains holding the swing up protest loudly. But when I slow to an almost stop, baby girl moves against me, keeping her little movements hard and rough. "More, more, more," she chants as she fucks my cock all on her own. "Please, Chase, more."

Fuck the swing. I give my girl what she wants. And though the fireworks down at the carnival are have long since finished, our own fireworks continue well into the night.

The next couple of weeks are amazing. At the risk of sounding completely whipped, I have to say being in love makes every day—every fucking hour—worth living.

Kay is happy and I am too. We take long walks on my property and talk about everything under the sun. More often than not, when we return either to my house or her apartment, we end up naked and loving one another for hours. We savor this happiness that we, two broken people, have somehow found. For the first time in a very long time I feel like life is good, very, very good.

Another bright spot is that my relationship with my brother is continuing to mend and improve. Will and I talk every few days, and we text even more. Little bro sends me more samples of his work and updates me on the progression of his comic book. More importantly, he shares his feelings, like how strongly he feels about his girlfriend, Cassie.

Just as I suspected early on, my little brother is really into this girl. He e-mails me a picture. His little girlfriend is cute—long and pale hair, ethereal features. She's very waif-like. But also, upon closer inspection, I note this girl appears kind of sad.

I recall my brother mentioning that Cassie's mother works all the time. He's since told me his girlfriend's absentee mom is an executive at some hot-shot company out in Vegas. Cassie has all the money she could want—including the new car Will mentioned before—but is it worth it? From Cassie's lost expression, it doesn't seem so.

I think about how Will also mentioned Cassie's stepdad. He's some younger guy her mom married not too long ago. My brother calls him "a piece of shit" and an "asshole," quite often, but he never elaborates much beyond these dispersions. It doesn't take a genius to suspect this guy is probably making moves on Cassie.

I've mentioned to Will that Cassie should talk to her mom and report any inappropriate behavior, but my brother always changes the subject. I don't think the dude's actually done anything yet, but it's probably only a matter of time. Will and Cassie both have trust issues with adults, so I'm sure that's where the hesitation comes in.

My brother's way of protecting Cassie is to be around her all the time. They certainly spend a lot of time together. It seems every time I speak with my brother he's either just returning from being with Cassie or he's waiting for her to pick him up so they can go somewhere. They also hang out a lot at Mom and Greg's house, sometimes I hear Cassie in the background when Will and I are talking.

But not today. No, today I have Will all to myself. But he's just surprised the shit out of me. He just told me he's staying over at Cassie's house tonight, like overnight.

"Mom's okay with that?" I ask.

"Well, not exactly," he admits. "I stay when Cassie's mom is out of town, but Mom has no idea her mom's not there." He hesitates. "Hey, you're not going to tell on us, are you?"

"No." I sigh. "I won't say anything. But make sure you're being careful."

Last thing I want is for my fifteen-year-old brother to knock-up his sixteen-year-old girlfriend.

"We're careful," Will says all huffy-like. "I'm not stupid, you know."

"Not saying you are," I reply.

We're both quiet for a few seconds, but then Will starts to share with me details of his sex life.

"Hey, hey, too much information," I protest.

I have no interest in hearing all the ways my little brother is giving it to his girlfriend.

"Okay, okay, I'll stop."

Will then softly adds, "It's not all about sex, though, when I stay over. I stay there mostly to protect Cassie when her mom's not there."

"What are you protecting her from?" I carefully ask.

"Her stepdad, Paul," my brother quietly responds. "When I'm there he never says anything to Cassie. He keeps his fucking sick mouth shut."

Concerned, I try to get more out of Will, but as always he clams up and changes the subject.

"Hey, bro, can you loan me some more money?" he abruptly asks, catching me off guard.

Fuck.

He asks for only fifty dollars, so I give in.

315

This all happens on a Monday.

Two days later, Wednesday, late afternoon, I am walking into my house after work and my cell buzzes.

I glance down to the phone in my hand. It's my mom calling. I press *answer* and say, "Hey, what's up?"

"Chase," Mom begins on an exhaled breath. "Sorry to bother you, honey, but I think we have a problem."

We? Okay. "And what would that be?" I cautiously venture.

Mom sighs. "Sweetie, have you been giving money to Will?"

There's no reason not to be honest, so I admit I have.

Another long sigh and a loud huff, I guess for good measure. She's obviously not pleased with my answer.

"Don't give him anymore, okay?" Mom doesn't give me a chance to respond, she simply adds, "Your brother used that money to buy drugs, Chase."

I swallow, hard. The last thing I'd ever purposely do is enable my little brother. But I guess I did exactly that by agreeing to his requests for cash without asking questions. I had a feeling, of course, but still. *Fuck.* I guess I was hoping for the best, hoping Will was on the up-and-up. Damn, I should have told the kid no. I don't want Will going down the same path I so unwisely followed.

"What did he buy?" I hesitantly ask.

"Weed," Mom says. "I went through his room earlier today when he was out and found his stash."

I am not thrilled to hear this, but I breathe a sigh of relief that she didn't find anything hardcore, like coke, meth, or motherfucking heroin. Mom, however, is far less calm than

I. She's going off like she just discovered a meth lab in Will's bedroom.

I try to put things in perspective for her. "He's fifteen, Mom. He's bound to experiment."

"Ha," she snaps, "look where experimenting got you."

She's got me there.

"Did you punish him, then?" I ask.

"You bet your ass I did. He's grounded from seeing any of his friends for the next week. And that includes that girl...his girlfriend...whatever."

This last is said dismissively and with disdain, like the idea of Will having a girlfriend is ridiculous. I imagine Abby rolling her eyes. She still thinks of my brother as a little tiny kid. That's part of the problem, even I can see that. From talking to Will these past few weeks it's become obvious part of his bad behavior, part of his acting out, is due to our mother. She treats my brother like a little boy, but yet she's severely lax on setting boundaries, if she even bothers at all. Like the sleeping over thing, she probably doesn't suspect for a minute that my brother and his girl are having sex. After all, she so willingly assumes that Cassie's-mother is home when those two are together. She's so out of touch. Maybe Mom has this attitude because Will used to be so clumsy and awkward. I don't know. But what I do know is her acting as if Will is still a small child is only bound to make things worse. And not acknowledging that he's dating a girl who is very important to him will definitely backfire on Abby.

I try to rectify this now, before it becomes a much bigger problem, as it inevitably will. "Mom," I begin carefully, "her name is Cassie."

"Who?" Mom sounds all clueless and distracted, but I know her avoidance game.

This woman exasperates me, but I somehow stay calm. "His girlfriend, Mom. Her name is Cassie. Jesus, don't you pay attention to anything?"

"Hey," my mother warns.

Okay, that last was maybe a little harsh, but come on.

"I don't need shit from you too, Chase," she continues. "Why don't *you* try dealing with Will for a while? You think it's so easy, don't you?"

I stay quiet and just let Mom vent. She's really angry at Will, but it's better if she takes it out on me. What she just said gives me an idea though. Maybe Will can visit me here in Ohio, get away from Vegas for a while. Not for the whole summer, Mom's not getting away with that shit, but a few days stay would be nice. Will's been saying he'd like to visit soon. He's even expressed interest in meeting Kay. I told him she liked his comic book drawings, and he said she sounded "cool."

I throw my suggestion out to my mother and she says, "I don't know, Chase. Wouldn't letting him go on vacation be more like a reward? The kid's supposed to be grounded."

"Aw, come on. Don't you really just want him away from his friends for a few days? If he's here in Ohio he won't be sneaking out to go be with them. Plus, I really want to see him. We've been getting along great lately."

Surprisingly, with no additional fuss, Mom agrees to let Will come to Ohio. I think her capitulation is partly because she's truly happy her boys are back on speaking terms, but I also know part of her hopes I'll talk to my brother about the weed. I plan to, I'll set him straight before he moves on to something harder, which—with our genetics—he inevitably will.

Mom asks me to hold on while she goes to get Will. In no time the kid is on the phone. He tries to play it cool, but I can tell he's excited to visit. While we talk about shit we can do when he gets here, Mom checks flights. She finds one from Vegas to Pittsburgh (the closest major airport) for this Friday.

"Book it," both Will and I say together as he puts me on speaker.

We hang up, and I am elated. Two more days and I will see my baby brother again. Kay will get to meet him too.

I put together a quick plan, one that will require me to leave work early on Friday to get to Pittsburgh in time to pick Will up. His flight comes in at seven, and I need time to drive to the airport and park. Unfortunately, if I leave early, Kay won't be able to come with me. But maybe it's better if I spend the ride back alone with my brother. It will give us time to discuss him scamming me for money, and then using what I gave him to buy drugs. Art supplies, yeah right, I knew that sounded suspect. But I am not going to worry about any of that bullshit until I have Will face-to-face.

I run my hands through my hair and scan the living room. There's so much I have to do, like get one of the upstairs bedrooms ready for my brother. But first things first, I want to tell my girl about my brother's impending visit. I can't wait to hear her reaction, so, without further ado, I head next door.

As I'm walking up the steps to the apartment above the garage, I think about how I thought things were good earlier. Well, shit just got a whole lot better.

My brother, my girl—the two most important people in my life—will be here with me, all three of us together, in just two more days.

Could life get any fucking better?

CHAPTER EIGHTEEN

KAY

I go into work a little later than usual on Friday morning. Truth be told, I am still catching up on much-needed extra rest. See, Chase came over Wednesday evening to tell me about his brother coming into town. My boy was so happy he couldn't quit hugging me, even while I was fixing dinner. All that hugging led to kissing, and kissing led to touching, and since it seems we can never get enough of one another, dinner went onto the back burner, literally. We didn't get to my homemade chili till hours later. And then yesterday evening I was over at Chase's. We never even got to dinner. We spent the entire evening in bed.

Love, it sure makes you silly...and kind of horny, I think as I settle in at my desk, yawning.

I suppress an out and out laugh, but my lips remain curved up in a ridiculous grin as Father Maridale walks in. When I see his serious expression though, my smile falters.

"What's wrong?" I ask.

"Kay, I don't know if anyone has told you yet, but Mrs. Wilson was in a fairly serious car accident yesterday evening."

"Oh, no! Doug's mother?" I am not sure I heard correctly, but Father nods in confirmation.

I may not like my ex-boyfriend all that much—in fact, I kind of despise him—but I wish no harm to his mother.

She may have been a bit meddling in the past, but she was always kind to me.

"That's terrible," I say. "Will she be all right? Is there anything we can do?"

"I don't know if she'll be okay," Father answers sadly, "but I know she could use our prayers."

"Of course."

The Wilsons aren't part of the Holy Trinity congregation—they belong to another parish—but that doesn't mean Doug's mother won't be in all of our prayers these next several days. My heart goes out to their family, and I feel bad for all of them, even Doug to a degree. But I still send up a selfish prayer that I don't run into my ex-boyfriend. Surely, he's in town, probably over at the hospital right now with his mother.

My stomach twists at the thought of coming face-to-face with Doug Wilson. He's a walking reminder of the poor choices I made the night Sarah died. Not to mention he's the entire reason why I even found myself in that position to begin with. Worst of all, I'll never forget that he left, he ran off as Sarah lay lifeless in my arms.

Father Maridale gets a call and leaves, which is just as well since my hands have begun shaking. I squeeze them together. There, that's better...for now.

It's no mystery why all of this is hitting me so hard. It's because of what day it is. Today is an anniversary of sorts, but not the happy kind. Quite the contrary—Sarah's horrible accident occurred four years ago today.

I think most people have forgotten the exact date, no one has said a word as of yet. But *I* will never forget—July nineteenth is burned in my brain, seared into my soul. I know

Chase would want to know the significance of today—and I should have told him—but I couldn't bring myself to burden him with the information that the day his brother is coming into town is the four-year anniversary of Sarah's death. So, while Chase is picking his brother up at the airport this evening, I'll be at the cemetery, spending time with Sarah. And my guy has no idea.

I had originally planned to ask Chase to come with me tonight, especially since he's the one who's been helping me come to terms with the fact that not everything that happened the night Sarah died was in my control. But when Chase came over the other night, so hyped up about his brother's impending visit, I couldn't ruin his happiness.

I try to work on a few things to get my mind off of today's significance—like getting started on organizing next month's activities calendar—but I can't concentrate at all. I can only think of Sarah.

My little sister would have turned ten this year, but she'll forever remain six. Sarah will forever be a child, a child who never was given a chance to grow up. She'll never someday find love like the kind I've found with Chase. Usually I can accept a sad fact such as this, but today it just makes me feel guilty.

I try to distract myself from these morbid ruminations with more work. I spend over an hour updating the bulletin, then keep busy finding other mundane tasks to occupy my time. But the guilt doesn't fade completely; it only recedes from the forefront of my mind.

When I hear someone come into the office, I glance up from my seat at the desk to find my blue-eyed boy. "Hey."

I check the time. "It's only eleven. Aren't you a little early for lunch?"

When I look into Chase's eyes, I know immediately that Father Maridale has told him about Doug's mother's accident. That means he is well aware that Doug is in town.

Chase walks over to my desk and kneels down next to my chair. "You okay?" he asks.

I nod, but my observant boy doesn't miss my hard swallow.

"Hey…" He pivots my chair so we're eye level. Cupping my chin, he rubs my cheek with his thumb. "Why don't you come with me to pick up Will? No one will care if you leave a little early today."

Clearly, Chase doesn't want me running into Doug while he's gone. But I have to stay put; I have to spend time with Sarah this evening. I wish I could just tell my guy why I need to stay, but he has an obligation too—picking up his brother—and I don't want him driving to the airport and worrying about me anymore than he already will be.

So I say, "I'll be fine, Chase. I'll stay here on the church grounds, and then go straight back to the apartment."

He frowns, and I snatch up his hand. I hold it close. "I know you're worried about me running into Doug, but I'm sure he's staying at the hospital. Pick up Will, okay? Everything will be fine." I squeeze his hand. "I'll be waiting for you and Will back at the house. I can't wait to meet him."

This brings a smile to my boy's face. I try to lighten things up from there by talking about all the things he and I can do with Will over the next few days. I don't know what fifteen year-old boys like, but I suggest we take his brother to see one of the summer's big action-adventure movies. It's based on a comic book, so that's sure to be a plus.

Chase agrees. "That's a great idea. My brother will love it."

Everything is good for now, back to normal. Well, as normal as things can be under the circumstances.

Chase and I go to lunch, and afterward, on the walk back, my boy teases me a little. He's trying to get me to smile bigger than he is at the moment. He's so happy today, anticipating seeing his brother. I wish I could share more fully in his enthusiasm, but my heart feels burdened. Even so, my boy gets me to smile a little here and there.

When we reach the church office there's nobody around. Chase pulls me to him and kisses me, far dirtier than he should on church property. Still, I love every second. I love it even more when my incorrigible boy whispers all the filthy things he's planning to do to me later tonight. "You're brother will be at the house," I remind him.

He runs his hand down my back, cups my ass, and moves me to where I can feel he's getting hard. "He won't be over in your apartment, baby," he whispers huskily into my ear.

Good point.

We kiss and grind shamelessly for the next several minutes, but then we hear a noise and stop. It turns out to be nothing, just the air conditioning coming on, but in the interest of "better safe than sorry," we separate, but not before promising one another this *will* continue later.

Chase leaves and I actually feel much better, definitely distracted. As usual, my boy has done a good job of making me forget the worries of the day. But, as time passes, one by one, the worries plaguing me earlier seep back into my consciousness.

How can I forget Doug Wilson is in town, or that his mother is in the hospital and in serious condition? But what brings a lump to my throat is the thought that it's almost time to go to the cemetery behind the church and visit with my dead little sister, the little girl who died four years ago today.

Work ends and I start my journey. I leave my purse behind in the rectory. I don't bring Peetie either. Today it's just me, for better or worse. The sun burns low in the sky as I walk past the iron gate and make my way to the back of the graveyard.

But when Sarah's grave comes into view, I falter. There's someone standing there—a woman—right in front of her marker.

I creep closer. This lady doesn't hear my approach. Her head is down, and her hair, the color of mine, shields her face.

Oh, my God.

I know this woman. I don't need to see her face. I'm not even close enough for her to hear a word I say, but my mouth opens of its own accord and one word tumbles forth, "Mom?"

I don't know how she hears me—maybe there's some unbreakable mother-daughter bond that is still there, alerting her to my presence—but my mother turns to me and our eyes meet, caramel-on-caramel. I release a breath I didn't realize I was holding and sway unsteadily on my feet.

My body is torn. Do I run to this woman or crumple to the ground. I kind of do both, I take a few steps in my mother's direction, and then pitch forward. I land on my bare knees, the skirt of my dress puddling around me as my fingers dig into the cool blades of grass.

My mother turns and comes to me, and for the first time in a very long time I see compassion in her eyes.

"Kay," she whispers when she reaches me. "I had a feeling I'd find you here tonight."

This woman... This woman, who has rejected me for four years, has apparently sought me out. But why? Why tonight? Why this anniversary and none of the others? Are four years of no communication sufficient penance in her eyes?

Tears blur my vision and I rock back on my heels. I look away. But my mother is not deterred—she kneels down right beside me. She says my name again and reaches for my hand. I don't want her to touch me, so I resist. But I ultimately let her wrap her cool fingers around my hand. She's always had this hold over me. I am powerless around her.

My mind wars with itself to take some sort of a stand, one way or the other. Part of me fears this woman, and that part urges me to twist my hand from hers and run away, fast as I can. But another part of me is drawn to this person who gave me life. And that part wants nothing more than for my mother to grab me up, hold me, and tell me I am forgiven.

I can't make up my mind; I don't know what to do. Hell, I can't even move. But I don't have to decide anything as my mother pulls me into her arms.

I resist a little, out of fear she'll end up re-breaking my

just-now-mending heart. But there's something in me—some bond forged by shared DNA, perhaps—that's stronger than reason or emotion. Deep in my heart I long for what we all desire, I want my mother to accept me, love me, for who I am. And that need for acceptance, that craving to feel loved, makes me relax into this woman whose arms I've not felt around me for almost half a decade.

She holds me and I am transported back in time. In her arms, I sob like a child, "Mom, Mom…Mommy."

I am no longer a woman of twenty-three—I'm a little girl who wants her mother. My cheek presses to her bosom, my body shakes. I am wracked with grief.

My mom grips me tighter, but I am inconsolable. "Kay, oh, honey, what have I done? God forgive me. I am so sorry. I've missed you every single day, I have. I denied it to myself for so long, and why?" She pauses, choking up. "I was wrong about so many things. I've spent years believing something I found out today isn't even true. Can you ever forgive me, Kay?"

I pull away and swipe and swipe at tears that keep coming and coming. I stare at my mother. I don't understand what she's talking about. Is she asking me to forgive her for disowning me? Does she seek absolution for not speaking to me for four years? Has she finally realized what Chase has been helping me to believe is true—that it doesn't matter I left Sarah alone? That if anyone carries a modicum of blame, then that person is Doug? And what did she find out today that changed her thinking? I am so confused.

My mother touches my cheek. Her eyes assess mine. She must see my uncertainty, as she takes a deep breath and begins her explanation.

She tells me she came into town early this morning, after she found out about Doug's mother's accident. I should have considered my mother might show up in Harmony Creek; she and Mrs. Wilson are still great friends, after all.

"Doug was at the hospital," she says, and I tense at the mention of his name. "Kay, he told me the truth. He told me what really happened that night."

I scoot back. "What are you talking about?" I ask, more confused than ever. "I told you the whole story after Sarah's funeral. You know everything."

My mother's face fills with guilt. "That's not what happened. Well, not exactly. There was a detail you were unaware of. We all were. That's the blank Doug filled in this morning."

My mouth is agape, I am unsettled and lost. I stare at my mother. I can't shake this feeling that my world is shifting on its axis. "What did he say happened?" I nervously ask.

What does Doug Wilson know that I don't? What has he been keeping a secret for all these years? Obviously it's something big if it's enough to have turned my hard-line mother around. I close my eyes and wait to hear what she has to say.

"Kay, Doug's broken up about his mother…I think that's why he told me. He wants to make things right. He said he can't bear the guilt of keeping his role in Sarah's death silent any longer."

His role? He already bears some responsibility, but is there more? I open my eyes and stare at where my knee is touching my mother's. Mine is bare, my mother's is clad in expensive linen.

"What did he tell you?" I prod.

She takes a breath. "Kay, Doug was the one who un-locked the patio door." *What?* "He said he went outside to put something in the recycle bin out near the pool." *His empty beer can.* "He said he forgot to relock the door when he went back inside."

Yeah, forgot because he was too busy hurrying to get to the stairs, to trap me there, to back me into my bedroom. *Fucking asshole.* He's kept this secret for all these years. If he'd only come clean right away, this rift between me and my mother might never have taken hold.

Doug confesses his secret now because his mother's been in an accident? Does he think he can bargain with God? He's so arrogant he probably does.

I am seething. All the rage I've kept bottled up for four years—rage at myself, rage at my mother for abandoning me, rage at God for taking Sarah—it all redirects to Doug Wilson. He better hope he doesn't run into me.

I swear and my mother frowns. "What?" I hiss, scooting farther away. "So, you think everything is okay now?"

She shakes her head. "No, no, I don't. I know it will take time for us to heal. I know I reacted too harshly—"

"Harshly?" I interrupt, not wanting to hear her excuses.

I yell, "Fucking Doug kept what he did a secret for four years." My mom winces but stays quiet. "He allowed me to believe it was my fault, he allowed *you* to believe it was my fault. I've thought for so long that I was the one who neglected to lock that door, and all this time…"

One desperate sob escapes me.

"Doug is a fucking bastard," I whisper.

I try to stand, but I can't. My strength has abandoned

me, I have no more fight. The truth should be setting me free, yet I feel no lighter.

I start to cry, and my mother closes the gap between us and enfolds me in her arms. "It's nobody's fault, Kay. It's taken me a long time to accept this, but Sarah's drowning was an accident."

I cry harder as I cling to the back of her blouse. "You hated me for four years, Mom. How could you do that? You missed my graduation. You missed my first day as a teacher. I'm good at what I do, but you wouldn't even know that—you know nothing of my life."

"I never hated you, Kay—"

"Liar," I weep. I try to pull away, but she's so much stronger.

My mother expects me to be angry with her, she tells me this. But she also says she's tired of holding on to her own anger, anger she's taken out on me for far too long. I ask her if she plans to excommunicate Doug Wilson like she did to me, but she just shrugs her shoulders. And it's then that I notice how much older my mother appears.

There's gray streaked through her hair and deep lines on her face. Maybe being apart from me has hurt her too. She may be stubborn and hard, but I am bound to her. I don't want to do the same thing to her that she did to me. I've tasted revenge, and it's not always sweet. The time we have on this planet is too short for playing games. Anything can happen, at any time. I think of how suddenly I lost Sarah, how suddenly Chase lost his dad. Death makes permanent decisions without our consent all the time, why hasten the inevitable?

Besides, I'm tired of not being on speaking terms with

my mother. Maybe she and I can start anew. Things will never be as they should—there's too much water under the bridge—but surely we can scrape together something to make up for all this wasted time.

So I stay where I am.

I sit with my mother for a while, right there on the evening-dew-coated grass. I talk with her in a way we haven't spoken in years. And she actually listens. I even tell her a little about Chase. My mom smiles and says he sounds like a special guy. She has no idea of what an understatement that is.

Eventually, my mom and I stand to stretch our legs. She gives me a look, a sad smile, and I know what she's thinking. She wants us to go over to Sarah's grave, together.

I nod, and we walk arm in arm to my sister's granite marker. My mother and I kneel in the shadow of the old oak and hold tightly to one another as we reminisce about a little girl we both loved and lost.

My mother does most of the talking, and that's fine with me. I listen as she shares some of her earliest memories of my sister—Sarah being born, her holding her new child for the first time, her handing Sarah to me so I could hold a baby sister for the first time.

"Remember that day at the hospital?" my mother asks, tears in her eyes.

How could I forget? I think of how tiny and pink my baby sister was. "I loved her already, then," I croak out.

Mom squeezes me near. "I did, too," she whispers as she kisses the top of my head. "I did, too."

I share one memory of my own—that autumn day in the apple orchard—but I keep the rest to myself. I also don't mention the journals I write in, nor do I share how I recite three precious memories to Sarah every week right here at this grave. These are pieces of my life I share with only one person, the man I love and trust—Chase.

I'll give my mother a chance, sure. I mean, I can't deny I still love her. But forgiving her completely for what she's done to me may take a little longer.

My mother grabs up my hand and our eyes meet. She smiles at me, in a way I used to see her smile only at Sarah. Maybe she really does love me. I squeeze her hand a little, and it seems we reach an unspoken understanding, to take things one day at a time.

We've got a long haul ahead, but this is a start, a new beginning.

My mother leaves the cemetery before I do. I stay at Sarah's grave, kneeling in the grass.

Ten minute pass, then fifteen. I think about leaving, heading home, but I can't seem to move quite yet. Now that I'm alone, I am overwhelmed with emotion.

Tears stream down my cheeks. Out of sorrow, out of relief—I don't know which. My guilt over Sarah's death began to diminish when Chase heard my admission and didn't turn away, but finding out it was Doug Wilson who unlocked that door—not that I had forgotten to lock it in the first place—has allowed the last remnants of guilt to lift and leave me forever. I feel freer than I ever felt before. However, I can't stop crying.

Losing my guilt doesn't make grief disappear. In some ways it heightens my sorrow, since sorrow is all I have left. I will always miss my Sarah—this is a fact—and nothing will ever lessen the ache that resides in the deepest recesses of my heart.

I lie down and place my cheek against the grass. It's cool to the touch and smells of life. I inhale deeply, and eventually the tears begin to slow.

Life…

I think about how I have been living lately, really living. Mostly due to one man, my blue-eyed boy, the one person in this world who teaches me more about life and living on a daily basis than anyone ever has in the past.

Chase. Finding him has made all this loss so much more bearable.

I sit up and brush myself off. It's almost dark. Chase should be on his way back with his brother by now. I long to hear his voice, and I want to tell him all that has happened this evening. Also, I can't wait to meet this brother he loves so dearly.

When I get to the car I call Chase's cell, but it goes directly to voicemail. I find it odd he's not answering, but I don't think too heavily on it. Even as I leave the church parking lot and turn right. I don't dwell on why my boy may have shut off his phone.

But something in the back of my mind tells me perhaps I should.

CHAPTER NINETEEN
CHASE

I am supposed to pick my brother up in the baggage claim area, but when I get there Will is nowhere to be found. It's after seven. I check the monitors, the flight from Vegas landed fifteen minutes ago. My brother should be here by now.

I watch a few bags go by on the carousel, then read a couple of the tags. Yep, definitely luggage from the Vegas-to-Pittsburgh flight.

Stepping back, I watch passengers from Will's flight retrieve their belongings. Soon, the bags and people are all gone, but still there's no sign of my brother.

What the fuck?

I call Will, but there's no answer. Next I dial Mom. She answers and when I tell her Will wasn't on the flight, she—of course—panics.

"What? I dropped him off at the airport, Chase. He had his bag, his boarding pass, he was ready to go." She sucks in a breath. "Oh my God, do you think something happened? Maybe he's been kidnapped. Oh, Chase." Mom's voice has progressed from worried to shrill, and now she's just flat-out crying.

I calm my mother as best as I can, I tell her Will probably

just missed his flight. But the truth is I'm worried too. *Shit, this fucking sucks.*

Just as I am about to panic myself, someone beeps through. I pull the phone away from my ear and check the screen. It's Will. *Thank God.*

Mom breathes out an audible sigh of relief when I inform her that her youngest son is alive and apparently well. Before I switch over to my brother's call she asks me to have Will call her as soon as he and I are done talking.

"Will do," I say in what I hope is a comforting tone.

Then, when I switch over to Will, I become all, "Where the fuck are you? The flight you were supposed to be on came in half an hour ago. Mom's about ready to have a heart attack, you know."

Will kind of groans, "Dude, I'm sorry, but something came up, my plans changed." He pauses, sighs. "Did you really have to call Mom, though?"

"Yes, Will, I really did," I snap back.

Truth be told, I am trying to keep my anger in check, but this kid is getting on my last fucking nerve.

"She is your mother," I continue, "and when you didn't show up what did you expect me to do? Just go home? We thought something happened to you. What the fuck went wrong anyway? Where are you?"

Will is quiet for a beat and then he says softly, "I'm still in Vegas. I'm with Cassie. Something happened at her house and she needed me."

I sense this probably has something to do with her pervert stepdad, but I don't press. My little brother's compassionate heart does serve to lessen my anger though.

"Will, isn't this something her mother should handle?" I say with care.

Will huffs, "She's never around, Chase. She works all the time. She left unexpectedly today for some work thing." Exasperation shades my brother's tone. "I couldn't leave Cassie alone all weekend, not with that dick. The things he says to her... Chase, you'd fucking kill him. At least I keep my temper under control."

I let that one pass, Will does have a point.

"Anyway, this time he really scared Cassie with the fucked up shit he was spewing. She had to lock herself in her room. She called me just as the flight was boarding and told me what was going on. I told you her stepdad leaves her alone when I'm there, so I really had no choice, bro. I took a cab from the airport to her house. I'm sorry, Chase, I..." Will trails off and sniffles.

He's been acting all tough, but I know my brother and I can tell he's crying a little now.

I pinch the bridge of my nose. "It's okay, Will, I get it. But you have to call Mom. She needs to know where you are and everything that happened."

Will promises to do so, but then throws me for a loop when he blurts out, "Hey, maybe I can still come out to Ohio. My ticket is one of those types you can change, so it's still good. Cassie could come too. She has lots of money in her savings. She can buy her own ticket and—"

"Whoa, whoa, whoa," I interrupt. "You can't bring your sixteen-year-old girlfriend with you. What the hell do you think her mother would say?"

Will is quiet, but then offers, "What if Cassie gets permission? Would you care, then?"

I'm thinking my brother will say anything to get me to say yes to Cassie coming to Ohio with him. I can't fully trust the kid—he's already duped me with the borrowed money—so I say as gently as I can, "I don't know about that, Will. You're welcome to still fly out, but I think Cassie needs to stay in Nevada."

"What about her stepdad?" Will asks frantically. "Am I just supposed to trust he'll leave her alone while I'm across the country?"

"Will," I begin, "your girlfriend really needs to talk to her mother about this guy."

This is met with silence. I switch the phone to my other ear. "So, are you coming to Ohio, or staying there?"

"This is so fucked up," Will spits. "You wouldn't leave *your* girl if she needed you. I know you wouldn't."

"That's different."

"The fuck," my brother explodes. "This is such bullshit. You're as much of a hypocrite as Mom."

The fist at my side clenches, and the hand holding the phone tightens. "That's not fucking true," I grind out.

Will throws back, "Whatever, dude. All I know is every fucking time I need someone they're never there...including you. This is so typical. You may as well just be back in prison. You're such a fucking ass."

My brother disconnects before I can respond. I know he's just frustrated, but his words still fuck with my mind. "Fuck this shit," I mumble as I turn off my phone and stomp out of the baggage claim area and out to my truck.

All I really want to do is see my girl and tell her what has happened. She'll make everything right, she settles me. But I'm too full of anger and venom to put this on sweet

Kay. She has her own shit to deal with—she's finally accepting that the night Sarah died was truly just an awful accident. She sure doesn't need my family drama shit piled on top of that.

I leave the airport and hit the highway. It's starting to get dark, but it doesn't matter. The ride back to Ohio becomes a blur. My frustration, my stress, my anxiety, they all escalate with every fucking mile I log. By the time I hit Harmony Creek all I want to do is stop these feelings, especially the one nagging at me, telling me I've once again fucked things up with my brother. Not that the little shit should have even put me in that position. *I may as well be back in prison…*what a dick-thing to say. But the thing eating at me the most is what Will said about me being like our mother. Fuck that. I don't treat my brother like a child, I don't let him get away with shit, and I sure as fuck don't disappoint him. *Shit.* Or do I?

It hits me that maybe Will isn't entirely off base. Maybe I am like Mom, in more ways than I care to admit. We've both battled addictions—gambling for her, drugs for me. And we're both too easy on Will. Am I doomed no matter what I do? Is my path set?

Well, if that's the case, then why bother? Why try so hard to be different?

I hit the gas, but I don't head home, to my house, to where Kay and forgiveness await. Nope, I don't deserve forgiveness tonight. In fact, all I crave is fucking escape. So I drive straight to where I know oblivion can always be found. I head to a place where I'll never be questioned for the mistakes I make, not by myself, or by others.

I drive to Kyle Tanner's house.

One thing about Kyle's place, in the past, there was a party every night. And it seems nothing has changed as I drive past the line of cars parked along the rutted side of the long gravel drive leading to the Tanner house of sin.

I find an empty spot up close to Kyle's ramshackle house and park. In front of me is a car with steamed-up windows, rocking to and fro. I get out of my truck and chuckle as I walk past. Music is blaring from the dilapidated structure as I close in. A few guys are out in the yard, drinking, getting high. It's just another night of sex, drugs, and rock 'n roll at the Tanner abode.

I get a few "hey man" nods as I step up to the propped-open door. The greetings aren't from anyone I know, but I nod back nonetheless before I step into the house. Inside, the air is thick and hot, reeking of dope and sweat. People are dancing to the raucous music, pressed together on the tiny living room floor.

It's steaming hot out tonight, but it's absolutely stifling in here. Some of the girls have stripped down to just bras and panties. This isn't the junkie crowd that hangs out in the parking lot at Kay's old apartment. No, these people are younger, some even underage. This is the youth of Harmony Creek, here to get wild and have a good time. For some this will be remembered as a blurred-out summer of rebellion, but for others this will mark their entry into a dead-end lifestyle. I know the outcome of the latter all too well. I've walked this path myself. But even the sick sense of déjà-vu that washes over me can't make me turn around and leave. Instead, I ask a blonde walking by where I can find Kyle.

This girl is skinny, young. She has spiky hair, and she's

wearing short shorts and a distressed tank top. Her dilated eyes take me in as she slurs, "He's in the kitchen, gorgeous."

I start to walk away but she grabs my arm. "Hey, don't go." She tries to pull me to her, but I don't budge. "Let's dance," she whines.

This girl is so fucking spun that I feel a little high just looking at her.

She starts to take off her tank top and when I see she has nothing on underneath I walk away. Girl-so-spun has nothing I desire. On my way to the kitchen someone hands me a full bottle of vodka, unopened. What the hell, I crack the seal and take a long pull. I take another drink, then another, and another. By the time I walk into the kitchen, half the bottle is gone and I'm officially buzzed.

Kyle is seated at the table, dirty jean-clad legs kicked out in front of him. He's smoking a blunt with another guy and a kind-of-pretty girl.

He laughs when he sees me. "Fucking Chase Gartner, I knew you'd come a-calling sooner or later."

"Whatever," I murmur before I take another long pull from the bottle in my hand.

"Welcome back, man," Kyle says as he nods to the kind-of-pretty girl.

She passes me the blunt, and I don't hesitate. I take a hit, hold, and then exhale slowly. And so it continues, we pass and smoke. It's been so fucking long that the weed hits me fast. I hand the blunt back to the girl and take another swig from the bottle.

I feel myself stumble.

Not literally, but I'm at the precipice in my mind, looking down, to where everything is black and empty, like I'm about to be.

The four of us sit around the table, talking about nothing, stupid shit that I forget a second later. I drink the rest of the vodka. Or maybe we shared it, like the blunt. I am not sure at the moment. All I know is that when I sit the empty bottle back on the table, Kyle stands up. He gestures for me to follow him. Without hesitation, I do.

Kyle and I go into the living room. It's as crowded and hot as earlier, maybe more so now. We push and elbow our way through the throng of dancing bodies. When I sway to the right I notice there are two people fucking on the couch. No one else pays them any heed. I watch for a minute, just for the fuck of it. Kyle waits for me, laughing at my side.

"You want a turn?" he asks me.

The girl riding the guy glances over her shoulder at us. She winks at me, then turns back. Shit, it's the spiky-haired blonde I talked to when I first came in. The guy whose dick she's riding would have been me four years ago, but it won't be me tonight. I tell Kyle as much and push him so he'll move. He does.

We continue through the crowd until we reach a narrow staircase in the corner. I follow Kyle up the steps. We turn right at the top and go into a cramped bathroom I've been in so many times before. And the same scene from back then plays out now.

Sitting on the edge of the tub, Kyle chops up a rock of coke he's taken from his pocket.

"This is new stuff, Gartner...pure, clean." On a handheld mirror, he cuts lines. "You're gonna love this shit, man."

I have no doubt I will. Kyle rolls up a twenty and hands

it to me, then places the mirror with the fat lines of coke on the countertop right the fuck in front of me.

I hold the rolled-up bill in my fingers and stare down at my old vice. The white powder beckons, spread out and waiting for me like my own personal whore. I lean down over a line and place the rolled-up bill to my nostril. I close my eyes—

—and just then someone knocks.

I open my eyes, lower the bill, and straighten.

"Fucking occupied," Kyle yells to whoever is knocking on the door.

The person leaves, but I don't resume what I was doing. It hits me hard and fast that I don't want to snort this line. I don't need this shit anymore. Stress, anger, and frustration have led me here, because old habits are that fucking easy to slide back into.

Shit, look at me. I am already drunk and high. But this is where it stops.

The hole in my heart that used to press me to use with abandon isn't so open and gaping anymore. It's not fixed, but it's healing. The fissures and cracks have been filling with love from my girl. And she's really all I need. It was a mistake to think she can't handle me, she's seen me more troubled than this. Case in point, the night she was accosted in the parking lot.

Fuck. I have to get out of here. I can't be here a minute more. I want to go home, home to Kay.

I drop the twenty on to the grimy floor and walk away. Kyle yells out something, but I put my hand up, like I'm saying, "Shut the fuck up and leave me alone." And, actually, that's exactly what I am saying.

Kyle doesn't follow, not that I expect him to. He fears me, as he should.

When I get to my truck, I drop the keys on the ground. When I bend to pick them up everything spins. I am entirely too fucked up to drive, it's obvious to me, even in the state I'm in.

I turn on my phone, but hesitate to call my girl. I don't want her anywhere near the debauchery down here. I figure it's a hike, but I can walk to the church. Kay can pick me up there. That'll give me time to calm down some too, maybe sober up a little. Right now I feel really high-strung, despite the booze and weed.

As I walk away from Kyle Tanner's house, even in my wrecked state, I realize something. Tonight I may have stumbled, but I got right the fuck back up. I stopped when it mattered. So maybe I have changed a little.

And that means there's hope for me, after all.

CHAPTER TWENTY
KAY

When I return to the farmhouse I'm surprised to find Chase and his brother have not yet returned from the airport. Full dark has fallen and more than enough time has passed to account for the return drive from Pittsburgh. I step out of my car and glance around. There's definitely no truck in the driveway. And the house is dark, closed up tight.

I lean back against my car door and try to reason out what might be causing Chase and his brother to be delayed. I checked the flight status earlier and I know Will's flight came in on time, so the only thing I can come up with is that Will was probably hungry and they stopped somewhere to grab a bite to eat.

But why is Chase's phone turned off?

I suddenly wish I had Will's number, because, I don't know, something feels off. And if I had Chase's brother's number I could find out what's going on. *Maybe.*

I decide to try Chase again.

In the darkness, with a background symphony of frogs singing down at the creek, I dig my cell from my purse and call Chase's cell once again. But like before when I was leaving the church, the call goes straight to voicemail, which means his phone is still turned off. Again, I can't imagine why Chase would purposely shut down his cell. Maybe his battery died.

I push off the car door and reluctantly go up to my apartment. Truth be told, I am not myself. I'm still reeling from the episode at the cemetery—seeing my mom and learning the truth. Doug unlocked the patio door. *Unbelievable.*

Four years wasted, four years spent believing something that wasn't true. I carried so much blame. I lost my mom's presence in my life. And why? All because Doug Wilson kept a secret of his own, one that could have changed so much. Has it come too late? Where will we all go from here?

I can't even consider. In fact, I try to block out the events of the evening for now. I need to behave as if nothing is wrong when Chase and his brother finally do arrive. Later, once Will is asleep, I'll share with Chase all that has happened and ask him for his opinions.

Up in my apartment, I flip on a lamp and toss my purse onto the sofa. I head back to the shower, unzipping my dress—dirtied and wrinkled from my time at the cemetery—along the way.

The hot water does a good job of reviving me. I actually start to feel more emotionally balanced by the time I'm dried off. With a renewed calm, I slip a blue eyelet lace dress—the one I know Chase loves—over my head. I don't bother with makeup or shoes; I just go back into the living room and plop down on the sofa.

The minutes tick by silently as I wait for my boy and his brother to come home. At some point, I glance over at the kitchenette.

Should I make some food? I wonder.

If I'm mistaken about their delay, and Chase and his

brother haven't stopped to eat, they may very well be hungry by the time they get here. But just as I stand, with the intention of making at least a couple of sandwiches, my cell phone buzzes.

I glance down, see Chase's name flash across the screen, and answer with haste.

"Chase, is everything all right?"

When my boy slurs my name as a response, I know immediately something is very, very wrong.

"Oh my God, what happened?" I ask, panicked. "Are you okay? Is everything all right with Will?"

"No," Chase begins, his voice drifting, like the phone's slipping out of his grip, "nothing is right, baby."

My heart races with fear. "Chase, please, you're scaring me. Tell me what's going on."

He exhales audibly. "Will wasn't on his flight, Kay. He, uh, changed his mind, he's staying in Vegas. Sometimes plans change, you know." He laughs. "And I'm sorry, baby. I wasn't planning on going there, but something came up with his girl, and Will didn't show. So I did it, I went there. And it was the wrong thing to do." Chase sounds messed up, he's barely making sense. And I know, I just *know*, it's not solely because his brother has blown him off.

"Where are you?" I ask carefully. "Do you need me—?"

"I always need you, baby girl," Chase kind of chuckle-slurs.

Now I know for sure he's been drinking, a lot. Or he's done something else. I pray it's not the "something else."

I breathe in deeply. "Chase, let me come get you. Just tell me where you are, okay?"

He lets out a long sigh. "I'm at the church, Kay, out on

the front steps." He pauses and for a moment stillness hangs in the air. "I walked here from Kyle's house," he adds at last.

I squeeze my eyes shut. Chase at Kyle's means only one thing, my boy has fallen. I don't judge though, I just tell Chase to wait for me there, and then I disconnect. I slip on some shoes, grab my purse, and leave to go pick up the pieces of the man who sounds as close to broken right now as I've felt all evening.

Ten minutes later, when my obviously fucked-up boy gets in the car, he's all over me, kissing and touching. He can't get close enough, it seems. "Touch me, baby," he says as he leans across the console and drapes himself all over me.

Chase is beautifully disheveled. His face is angelic, but his hair is devilishly tousled. And his eyes are bleary-blue, bloodshot. There's also no mistaken that Chase smells of alcohol and weed.

"What did you do?" I ask. I need to know just how far down he's fallen.

"Hmm?" he replies distractedly as he settles back into his seat.

I drive away from the dark, empty parking lot, silently thankful the carnival ended yesterday.

As we head to the house, it seems Chase can't decide what he wants to do. He leans back over the console and kisses down my neck. His hands are busy, one on the back of my seat, keeping my erratic boy somewhat upright, and one slipping under my dress. Chase caresses between my thighs and I swerve a little. Thankfully, this drive is going to be a short one. And good thing this stretch of the road is completely deserted this time of night.

My boy's fingers travel higher. But when he slips under the edge of my panties, I have to say something. It's either that or drive off the road.

"Stop," I murmur. "I can't concentrate when you do that."

Chase chuckles, smug that he has this effect on me. He's exceptionally cocky in this state, I note. I push his hand away. But my effort is half-hearted at best.

I know this is where I should be firm, resolute. Chase has tripped and fallen tonight, and I should refuse his advances. Wait until morning. But I've fallen too, just in a different way. So what does it matter? Both of us are messed up, in our own ways. Maybe that's why my body responds so strongly, urging me to encourage, not discourage. So I quit resisting. But when we reach Cold Springs Lane, Chase sits back of his own accord. He closes his eyes.

I turn into the driveway and cut the ignition. "I screwed up tonight," Chase says as he scrubs his hand down his gorgeous, but tortured face.

"Why?" I whisper. "Why didn't you just come home after you found out Will wasn't coming?"

He glances over at me and shakes his head. "I don't know, baby. I don't have a good reason. I felt overwhelmed, I guess."

I start to think he's not going to elaborate, but then he sighs and says, "I disappointed Will again. He still wanted to fly out to visit, but he wanted to bring his girl. I said no and he flipped. He said I'm like our mother. He said I may as well still be in prison."

"Oh, Chase." I place my hand on his forearm.

Chase pulls at his hair as he rakes his fingers through

the strands. "I just keep letting that kid down, Kay. I didn't tell you my mom told me Will used the money I gave him to buy weed. He lied to me. You were right to be worried."

I squeeze his forearm and his muscles flex of their own accord beneath my hold. "I'm sorry, Chase."

"It doesn't matter. When I left the airport I wanted to forget, forget everything. I wanted to feel numb, like I used to in the past. I felt lost, I guess. It was stupid, I know, but I couldn't stop. I drove to Kyle's."

"What happened there?" I whisper.

Chase admits he drank...a lot, hard liquor, vodka. Then, he tells me he got high. He smoked with Kyle and his friends. Not too much, but still. My once-addicted boy did something he hasn't done in years—and that in and of itself is significant. With Chase's history I know what potentially comes next—more drugs, harder drugs—coke, pills, God knows what...

With this in mind, I ask, "Was that it? Did you do anything else?"

"No, but..." Chase presses his lips together and looks over at me. "I almost... Uh, Kyle chopped up some lines and...and I was going to. Fuck, Kay."

My boy turns away and I lean as far as over the console as I can and wrap my arms around him. "It's okay," I whisper. "You didn't do it, though, right?"

"I almost did, baby. I was so fucking close, rolled bill in hand, bent over that shit."

I freeze. I remain perfectly still with my arms around my guy. *How did he stop?* I wonder.

"And then I thought about you, sweet girl," Chase whispers, as if he's answering my thoughts.

He relaxes into me. "I walked out, left Kyle in the bathroom with the coke he'd just cut up. He had said when we first went in that I'd like it...and I was sure I would. I wanted it in my body, that's for sure. I was ready to feel like I used to, wasted, uncaring. I can't lie to you about that, sweet, sweet girl."

I rub the back of his neck, play with his hair. "It's okay, Chase. You didn't do it, you stopped."

"Yeah, but I wanted to do it. I wanted to shut everything out, get lost. But then I realized I care too much. I care about Will, I care about my life. I don't want to fuck it up again."

Chase straightens and I lean back some, so that we're sitting and facing each other in the darkened car. "But mostly it was you who stopped me, Kay," Chase continues. "You give me strength, even when we're not together. You save me...you'll always save me, baby girl. Just knowing you love me like you do."

His gaze holds mine, and I can't help it, I have to touch him. Leaning forward, I cover his face in kisses. I kiss him and lick him, sloppy and wet, and he loves it. The skin under my lips tastes so good, so right...so Chase. My boy groans under my assault, and then he pushes me back into the driver's seat, coming right along with me, hands roaming my body, lips covering my neck, the whole way. "I need you, baby," he groans into my ear. "Let's go inside."

I need him just as much right now, though I don't tell him why. I'll wait until he's sober and not high to share with him the events of my own tumultuous night. Not to mention, I am sick to death of talking...and thinking. I long for an escape as well.

We end up in my apartment, since it's the closest to

where I've parked. Clothes are discarded hastily, a hodge-podge of fabrics left trailing from the living room to the bed-room. By the time we tumble together onto the bed, we are both naked, bare, in body and soul.

I've never experienced Chase fucked up like this, and it's definitely different. He's more aggressive than usual, which is saying a lot. He's rough and crude, with his mouth and his hands. But I like it, it makes me wet, it makes me want him in this coarse way. "I don't want it easy," I tell him.

He smirks, cocky, drunk, high. "Good, you're not getting it easy, baby. You're getting fucked hard, harder than all the other times when I went easy on you." My boy flips me over onto my stomach and hoarsely says, "Scoot up. Hold on to the headboard. You're gonna need to."

I grab at antique iron bars, and tremble with anticipation. I want him. I want him like this. He pushes me deep into the mattress with his weight. His skin burns heated against mine as he covers me with his body. I am breathless. His arousal jabs at my ass cheek, letting me know he's more than ready. And so am I. I try to shift to feel him where I want him, but I can barely move.

Chase doesn't let up. In fact, he does the opposite, gives me his full weight. He knows I love feeling him on me like this, so encompassing, so consuming.

Chase scoops up my hair and licks the nape of my neck. "Is that too much, baby? Am I crushing you?"

"No, I like it." I gasp. He chuckles and eases up slightly.

"Is your pussy wet for me?"

"Yes."

"Let's see. I want to feel." He reaches down between

our bodies and slides his fingers along my slick core. I am soaked, so turned on. Chase groans, "Fuck, Kay."

His fingers leave me and I feel him handling his length behind me. He nudges at my sex. "Spread your legs some more, sweet girl." His voice is husky and thick. "Open up for me."

He taps my ass with his cock, and I do as he asks. With no further warning, he sheaths himself inside me with one hard thrust. "Fuck, Chase, God," I yell out, gripping the headboard bars.

He slams in deeper and holds still, making me squirm, which serves to harden him even more. This is a lot of Chase. But I want it. My boy buries his face in my shoulder, and his teeth graze my skin, making me shiver.

"Tell me what you want, baby." He bites down hard. I whimper and he lets go. "Ask me for it," he demands.

His cock is stretching me to capacity, while his whole body crushes me. I feel invaded, taken, conquered, and I love every bit of it.

My boy bites down once more where my skin is still tender from his first bite. I cry out, "I want you to fuck me, Chase. Fuck me."

I rotate my hips beneath him, arching my ass up into his hips. He pulls out all the way—pauses—and reenters me on yet another long, hard thrust. "Yes," I hiss into the pillow.

My boy's mouth is at my ear, and he whispers, "Do you like my cock in your pussy, Kay?" He moves his hips, sliding in and out, in and out. *So good.* "Say it, baby. Tell me you love the way I fuck you. Be dirty with me."

I like this dirty Chase, this crude and irreverent man. I want to go where he's taking me. I need to be dragged down to where he is so we can build ourselves back up, together, stronger.

So I tell my boy the absolute truth, I share with him that I love everything he's doing and I want even more. When I say, "I like the way you fuck when you're messed up like this," my boy groans, and then he pounds into me harder still.

Chase asks to hear more, so I confess all the filthy things I've dreamed of him doing to me. He tells me a few ideas of his own. That makes me share even more. I think my ability to match my boy on dirty and filthy surprises him, but he's more than happy to do everything I ask.

He calls me the dirty names I ask him to, he puts his fingers in places no fingers have ever been, and he yanks my hair back when I scream for him to as he finger-fucks me from behind. But what sends me over the edge, what makes me scream in ecstasy, is when Chase does what he does best—fucking hard and dirty. He does this with finesse, though, moving me to where I suit him best. He positions me so I can take all of him when his thrusts become punishing and rough.

And that's what Chase does now—punishes me with his cock. We're both covered in sweat, me on my back, Chase on top, between my legs, pounding hard. It's *his* hands that now grip the antique iron headboard bars, giving him the leverage to fuck me into oblivion. Chase once told me he could never imagine me craving oblivion, but he was wrong. I crave it now, in this way. Chase owns me and he can annihilate me if that's what he wants. And I fear he might. But just when I think it may be too much, that this man may actually break me, Chase slows and stops. He pulls out and lowers his mouth to where his cock was just tearing me up.

I cry out his name.

He licks and kisses everywhere, his tongue probing where I throb, where I still feel the part of him that was just giving me so much pleasure and enough pain to render me incredibly sensitive to what he's doing. now. I come swiftly, hard, my walls clenching with a powerful release.

I catch my breath, finally relax.

Chase moves back up my spent body and thrusts into me once more. I'm still euphoric as I feel him pump a few times, lazily now. He stills and releases into me. Then, my dirty, gorgeous boy collapses onto me to catch his own breath.

I hold on to him tightly, my fingers twined in his sweat-dampened hair. He shifts so that his weight isn't too much, and though we're not actively having sex anymore, he's still inside. "Don't leave me," I whisper, arching to keep him where he is, even though I can tell he's only partially hard now.

He chuckles. "I think it's inevitable."

Just then he slips out and we both groan at the loss.

"Just give me a few minutes," my boy rasps in a tone full of promise.

I don't doubt him, and sure enough a few minutes later Chase is hard and back inside me—body, heart, and soul.

When we wake the next morning, things are subdued. Chase is hung over, and I'm back to thinking about my mother and all she told me yesterday evening.

My boy and I are wrapped up together in the covers, facing each other as I finally share with him all that happened the night before. When I get to the part about Doug leaving the patio door unlocked, Chase's expression darkens. His body tenses so much I fear he's about to dart from the bed and track down my ex, which wouldn't be too difficult since he's probably still at the hospital with his mother.

I caress my boy's arm and try to get him to relax. "Just forget it, Chase. I don't want to dwell on this. I don't want to waste any more time blaming and hating." I pause. "I've been thinking. Life's too short, and Sarah wouldn't want us taking our pain out on each other. My mother's done that long enough for all of us. I think we should let it go."

He calms and assures me he'll leave Doug alone. But something in his blues—which are darker than I've ever seen them before—tells me if those two ever run into each other... I can't even think about it, but I do spare a second to imagine the look on Doug's face when he sees Chase coming at him.

I smile, but only briefly, because Chase is saying, "You should have told me it was the anniversary of the day Sarah died. I would have worked something out with Will. We could have changed the ticket." A beat passes. "Not that it matters, since he didn't show up anyway. But still." Chase sighs, and adds, "I do feel bad, though, for not coming straight home."

I touch the rough stubble on his cheek. "Don't feel bad, Chase. You didn't know. And you're right, I should have told you. From here on out I'm telling you everything, no matter how big or small. And I want your opinions on all of it too."

My sweet guy is listening intently. He pushes hair that's fallen to my cheek back into place, and says, "Speaking of opinions, how do you feel about your mother? Are you going to give her a chance?"

I can't really read how Chase feels about last night's unexpected reunion, but I know for a fact he's not a big fan of my mother, seeing as how she hurt me so deeply, and for so long. So it's with caution that I ask, "What do *you* think I should do?"

"I think you should do what your heart tells you."

I sigh, roll to my back, and stare at the ceiling. "I can't just instantly forgive her for turning her back on me, but...I think I might want to try. Maybe over time we can reach an understanding."

Chase draws me back to him and kisses me on the cheek. "Then that's what you should do. You know I'm with you on whatever you decide. I'll stand behind any decision you make."

And this I know, I know Chase Gartner—*my* Chase Gartner—will always have my back.

Maybe I sensed this potential in him the day we met in the church parking lot, maybe I knew Chase was my destiny the minute his hands touched me, steadied me, kept me right. My boy was upfront with me from the start, calling me on my bullshit and asking me if I'd give him a chance, a *real* chance. And I did.

In doing so, I learned how to start taking chances of my own. And look at what I gained—I gained a best friend, a lover, and a future. Who knows where this love will take us. This love that has blossomed over lunches at a diner, this love that was nurtured by two broken people opening up to one another, sharing their fears, their hopes, their disappointments, and their dreams.

But this love isn't all serious moments. It's playfulness and fun too. This love is stolen hair ties and stolen lemon-lime sodas, hiked-up dresses, and first kisses by lockers. From mended cheap sunglasses, to mended priceless hearts, this love is healing. It's also daring to open up, finding the joy in laying souls bared. And forgiving, always forgiving. Whether it is forgiveness found dancing under the stars, or forgiveness found in confessing to inked angels, this love fosters forgiving.

The love I share with Chase is good and bad. It's real life, from sunset picnics on rooftops, from baguettes and brie, from making love under the Eiffel Tower…all the way to secrets kept to secrets revealed, to red balloons lost, magic found, tripping and falling, and picking each other back up. Because when Chase and I fall we will always be there to catch one another, like that day in the parking lot—the beginning.

This love is full circle. It will only end when last breaths are taken.

Chase and I are in this for the long haul. I've stood before him and he's stood before me. And this is what it's all come down to: Chase Gartner is my future, my forever. And I, I am his.

EPILOGUE:
LEAD IN TO *NEVER DOUBT ME*
(JUDGE ME NOT #2)

CHASE

On Sunday after church Kay and I walk back to the cemetery, together. We kneel at her sister's grave.

Sarah Stanton.

I hold the love of my life's hand as she recites three things about her little sister she will never forget. "One, you always had to have Hello Kitty Band-Aids on your cuts and scratches," Kay begins.

My girl takes a breath and glances at me. I take her hand, squeeze reassuringly.

She focuses back on the granite marker and continues, "Two, when we had our little tea parties you always wanted the tiniest cup, the one with the chip in the china." Kay sighs and murmurs, "I don't know why."

My girl waves her hand in front of her face to keep from crying.

"And three…" Her voice cracks. "You cried the first day of kindergarten. But when I promised to take you to your school and walk you to your classroom, you stopped."

A single tear trails down Kay's cheek. She goes to swipe it away, but I turn her to me and gently dab it dry. I hope my eyes convey to my beautiful girl how much I appreciate that she's sharing this—her most private ritual—with my undeserving ass.

In case she doesn't know, I tell her.

She responds, "I've wanted to share this with you for a while now, but I wanted to wait until after you knew everything. I'm glad you're here with me today."

"Always, baby. Not just today, always."

I want our future to be always, I truly do. I know in my heart that someday I will ask this woman to be my wife. I love her that fucking much. So much that I can't imagine a life without her. I am a part of Kay, and she is most definitely a part of me. We are dug into each other's souls, burrowed in to stay. When Kay feels pain, it hurts me. When she's happy, I am fucking joyful. And seeing my girl happy is my number one goal. If I can put a smile on her face at least once each day, make her life a little brighter, then I know I've done my best.

Since today is shaping up to be all about sharing and shit, when we get back to the house I decide to show Kay my sketchbooks from prison. I promised her she could someday see them and today feels right.

Not that I expect her to, but she doesn't judge as she turns the pages of each book. But she does slow at the sketch of the beaten prisoner in the cell, the drawing depicting the cellmate standing at the bars, indifferent to the suffering right behind him.

"You saw that?" she asks quietly. I just nod.

Next, my girl reaches the drawing of the heroin addict shooting up. She studies the angels and their pornographic poses. When she looks at me and raises an eyebrow, I just shrug one shoulder.

"Pervert," she mumbles. She's not judging, she's actually trying to lighten things up.

"Look who's talking," I volley back, playing along. "If you stare any longer you might burn a hole in the paper."

She swats my arm and we both laugh. But then my girl grows quiet. I ask her what's wrong and she says, "Nothing, it's just…"

My eyes meet hers questioningly, and she continues, "Well, it's just I have to still write down the three things I told Sarah today at the cemetery, and I was wondering if maybe you'd like to see the journals. That way you'll learn more about Sarah, what she was like."

I tell Kay I'd love to see the journals, so she goes next door to her apartment to retrieve them.

While I wait for her to return, my heart swells with happiness that sweet girl wants to share with me what she has left of her sister, but my heart also breaks a little at the same time. My girl should have so much more than these fragmented memories she's trying to hold on to. She should have her sister here with her, alive and well. I think I finally realize how very close Kay and Sarah were. In many ways, with such a big age difference, Sarah was like Kay's daughter. Maybe someday I can give my girl a child of her own. Not a replacement for the sister she lost, never that, but a new life that may lessen her sorrow, a new life that's part of her and me.

But all of that is for way down the road, not for today.

Kay returns and we sit on the living room couch. She opens the first journal and hands it to me.

I begin to read, and shit, do I learn a lot about little Sarah Stanton. In addition to what I heard Kay say earlier today at the cemetery, I discover Kay's little sister loved chocolate-chip ice cream, but hated any that was fruit flavored. Sarah loved cloudy days, but feared thunderstorms immensely. She was just learning how to ride a bike the summer she died. When Kay and Sarah's father gave the bike to a thrift store down the street the training wheels were still attached.

I turn the pages. Kay follows along, her eyes wet.

When Sarah was a toddler she played patty-cake with my girl almost every single day. Sarah knew there was no Santa Claus, but believed in the tooth fairy. And then I reach this section: Sarah loved the color purple, and she called my girl Kay-bear, never Kay. Sweet girl touches my hand and informs me these were the three things she told Sarah the day she met me in the church parking lot. I read the last entry from that day: Sarah couldn't sleep unless she was holding Peetie. The stuffed rabbit I saved from a junkie-filled parking lot the night I meted out justice for Kay. Now, it means even more that I retrieved that little bunny.

I set the journals down and I notice Kay crying softly. I hold her until the tears subside. Afterward she asks me to make love to her. I ask if she's sure that's what she really wants. To me, she looks sad at the moment, like maybe she might need some time alone as opposed to me all over her. But she tells me the opposite is true—when we're together, like that, it's an affirmation of life.

I never thought of sex that way, but I try my best to think of it like that today. When we get started, everything I do, I do slowly and gently. Careful and tender touches, soft caresses, and light kisses. When I finally bury myself deep inside the woman I love I move differently—*so-o-o slowly*—allowing us both to savor the connection.

And for the next hour, I make slow, sweet love to my girl.

The next night, Monday evening, Kay and I are watching a movie in my living room. My girl is all nestled into me, which I fucking love, and my arm is draped over her shoulders. The movie we're watching is a comedy and we find ourselves laughing at all the same parts.

Things are better and brighter today. Father Maridale relayed this morning that Mrs. Wilson will recover completely. She has a long road ahead, but she'll be fine. Mrs. Wilson's upgraded status means Doug-fucking-Wilson is back in Columbus where he belongs. Far away from me equates to very lucky for him. If I ever run into that motherfucker, he'll be sorry real fast for keeping his bigger-than-we-realized role in Sarah's death a secret for so long. I may have told Kay I'd let it go, but I don't think I really can.

I tense and my girl gives me a questioning look. I shrug it off and try to think of something else. But now that Columbus is on my mind, I can't help but be reminded of Kay's mother.

Mrs. Stanton is also back in Columbus. I'm sort of all over the place with that one. We shall see how it all plays out, this mother-daughter reconnection. That lady better not renege on my girl, I can tell you that. So far, though, things look good. Kay's mother is staying in contact. She called earlier this evening, in fact, and even put Kay's dad on the phone for a few.

My girl seemed so light and happy afterward, that's why we went with a comedy for tonight's movie. I'm glad

Kay's talking to her parents. She needs her family, just like I need mine, even if both our families are pretty much fucked up.

Speaking of which, just as the movie ends my cell phone rings. I check the screen and groan to Kay, "It's my mom. Maybe I should let it go to voicemail and call her back tomorrow."

"What if it's about Will, though?" Kay says, sitting up.

"Good point," I respond.

I haven't heard from my brother since Friday after he blew up over my refusal to allow Cassie to come with him to Ohio.

I answer my cell, and, as usual, my mother is in somewhat of a panic. I only half-listen initially, but when she catches her breath and slows down a little I quickly catch up.

Shit.

I sit up swiftly and glance over meaningfully at Kay. She places her hand supportively on my arm.

"What the hell are you saying?" I ask my mom. "What do you mean Will ran away?" Kay's little hand tightens and slides down to my wrist to cover my hand.

My mother fills me in on what's going on. Will was supposedly staying at Cassie's house this weekend. "So much for being grounded," I mutter.

Apparently, the day he skipped his flight and went to Cassie's he did call Mom like I told him to, but instead of demanding he come home, she gave him permission to stay the weekend.

"That was three days ago," I say, rolling my eyes. "Doesn't he have to check in with you or something?"

Mom ignores me and continues, explaining that Cassie's mom was on some weekend business retreat and just returned home today. Of course, this was all news to Mom since she assumed Cassie's mother was home all weekend. Anyway, Cassie's car was missing from the driveway, but her mother didn't think much of it at first. Then, she went into Cassie's room to gather laundry and noticed a bunch of her daughter's clothes were missing, as well as a suitcase.

"Cassie's mother said the room looked like nobody had been in there in days," my mom says.

Fuck. Where could my brother and Cassie have gone? Would they really run away? Maybe something worse happened with the stepdad that prompted them to leave?

"Has Will called you?" my mom asks, interrupting my thoughts.

"No," I respond.

Worry creeps up my spine.

My mom kind of sobs, and I ask, "What about the stepdad, Paul? Will said when I talked to him on Friday that the guy was home." I don't add that the stepdad had done something to upset Cassie and that's why Will blew off his flight. Why worry Mom further?

"Where was this Paul-guy all weekend?" I continue. "How could he not notice Will and Cassie weren't there?"

"I don't know, Chase," my mother says, sniffling, a little calmer now, but not much. "I guess he was in and out of the house a lot over the past couple of days. That's what Cassie's mother said, anyway. Paul didn't even notice they weren't there until this morning."

Sounds like a great guy, I think sarcastically as I roll my eyes.

Just as my mother is declaring she's going to call the police—which I agree is the right thing to do—the doorbell rings.

Kay and I look at each other, and I know she's thinking the same thing I am. "Fuck," I mumble.

Kay bites her lip. I think about how Will asked if Cassie could come with him to Ohio if he still were to visit me. Next, I calculate how long of a drive it is from Nevada to Ohio. Definitely enough time has passed for the two of them to make it here.

"He wouldn't," I mutter.

"What?" my mother on the phone and Kay who's at my side ask simultaneously.

The doorbell rings again. *Shit.* I ask my mom to hold on, but I keep the phone at my side. Kay stands up when I do and follows me to the door. When I open it, my brother is standing on the porch.

I raise the cell to my mouth. "He's here," I say somberly.

My eyes meet Will's fiery greens. I shake my head at my brother, like I'm saying *what-the-fuck*. And I kind of am saying exactly that.

I tell my mother I'll call her right back, but not to worry. Will's okay. I add that I'll get the details on Cassie's whereabouts as well. My mother protests, but I hit *end*. I need to take care of one thing at a time, and this takes precedence.

I lower the phone and my brother smiles at me. "Hey, bro," he says, all casual and smug-like. "Guess what? I made it to Ohio, after all."

He glances at Kay, who's at my side. My little shit brother smiles all charmingly and says, "Hi, I'm Will, Chase's brother."

Kay says hi back, all while squeezing my arm. My girl is holding me back, like I'm about to go off on my brother. I am a little, but mostly I'm just shocked.

It's then a young girl steps out of the shadows at the base of the porch steps. She stares down at the ground. Will catches her attention and motions for her to come up on the porch. When she reaches his side she places her hand on his arm, just like Kay's hand is on mine. It seems to strengthen my brother's resolve. I see it in his face.

My brother firmly states, "This is Cassie. And before you say anything, Chase, I am telling you now we're not going back to Vegas. We can either stay here with you...or we'll just leave and keep driving east."

"Did something happen?" Will knows what I mean. And apparently so does Cassie. When I glance at her, her eyes dart skittishly away.

My brother's girlfriend positions herself behind Will, he answers for her. "Nothing happened, but we decided to leave. It's better if Cassie's away from that place."

I almost ask Will if he's high. I mean, what the hell is he thinking? I know he wants to protect Cassie from her stepdad, but this has gone too far. They need to tell the girl's mother about this creep. I feel sure she'd kick him out in a heartbeat; she just doesn't know what's going on.

"Will—" I begin, but my brother interrupts.

"I'm serious, Chase. Can we stay with you, or not? It won't be forever, just until we figure things out."

"Figure things out?" I scoff. "What kinds of things? You're both in high school. Or are you just not going to go back in the fall?"

Will looks away but I reach out and gently coax him to

meet my gaze. He lets my hand stay on his shoulder. "Will, you're only fifteen," I softly remind him.

But my brother is resolute, his greens bore into me. "I'm serious, Chase. We aren't going back. What's it gonna be? Can we stay here or not? It's your house, it's your decision."

Three pairs of questioning eyes fall on me. My wayward brother, my love, and this runaway girl who I've just met all await my answer.

So I take a deep breath and tell all three what I've decided...

The story continues in

NEVER DOUBT ME,

the next novel in the Judge Me Not series.
Expected publication: Spring 2014

ACKNOWLEDGMENTS

As always, my gratitude and appreciation extend to all the readers, bloggers, and reviewers who read and support my novels. Some of you have been with me from the beginning, and some of you are new, but I thank all of you equally. Also, thank you to my copy editor, Gail, Damon at damonza.com for another stunning cover, and Benjamin at Awesome Book Layout for always awesome print and e-book formatting. A special thank you goes out to Julie at AToMR Tours for organizing a great cover reveal in August and for what promises to be a wonderful blog tour this October.

Last, but not least, a huge thank you to my family, my friends, and especially to Tom and the extended "E" family.

ABOUT THE AUTHOR

S.R. Grey is the author of the bestseller Harbour Falls, and Willow Point, the first and second books in A Harbour Falls Mystery series. She is also the author of I Stand Before You, the first novel in the Judge Me Not series. Ms. Grey resides in western Pennsylvania. She has a Bachelor of Science in Business Administration, as well as an MBA. She is currently working on Wickingham Way, the third novel in A Harbour Falls Mystery series, to be released in January 2014, as well as Never Doubt Me, the second novel of the Judge Me Not series, due out in the spring of 2014.

Other interests include reading, traveling, running, and cheering for her hometown sports teams.

BOOK CLUB / DISCUSSION QUESTIONS

Spoilers—do not proceed if you've not read *I Stand Before You*

1. Kay and Chase believe they are "destined" to be together. Do you believe in fate and/or destiny? Do you think some things in life are predetermined? What about in your own life?

2. There are many instances of "judgment" in *I Stand Before You*. Have you ever prejudged a person or situation when you only had limited information? When you received more information, did you change your opinion?

3. Kay's mother, Ruth, turns her back on her daughter, her only remaining child. When Kay sees her mother at the cemetery were you concerned it would end badly? Did you find Ruth Stanton believable? Should Kay trust her? Give her a chance?

4. Kay is burdened with guilt over the death of her little sister, Sarah. Do you understand why she feels this way? Did you place any blame on Kay? What about after her mother revealed Doug's secret?

5. Chase stays clean, up until the night his brother doesn't show up at the airport. Do you feel as if the culmination of events led Chase to Kyle's house? Were you surprised he went there? What did you think of his actions while at Kyle's?

6. Do you think Kay forgives Chase too easily for keeping his indiscretion with Missy a secret? Do you see how her keeping her own secret influenced her decision?

7. Chase is so anxious to rebuild his relationship with his brother, Will, that he trusts him implicitly, even when he senses he should not. Have you ever trusted someone you knew was probably lying to you? Why? How did it turn out?

8. How do Chase and Kay give each other strength? Give an example of how Chase positively influences Kay, and vice versa.

This is just as starting point for discussion. Please feel free to formulate your own questions.

10348633R00231

Made in the USA
San Bernardino, CA
12 April 2014